FAERY SIGHT

Faerie Legacy Series, Book 1

PATRICIA BOSSANO

WaterBearer Press

FAERY SIGHT

Faerie Legacy Series, Book 1

Published in the United States by WaterBearer Press
Escondido, CA 92030
www.WaterBearerPress.com

Because of the dynamic nature of the Internet, any Web addresses or links contained in this book may have changed since publication and may no longer be valid. The views expressed in this work are solely those of the author and do not necessarily reflect the views of the publisher, and the publisher hereby disclaims any responsibility for them.

Cover design and art by Tamra Gerard

Identifiers:
ISBN: 978-0-9994-346-6-6 (hc)
ISBN: 978-0-9994-346-7-3 (sc)
ISBN: 978-0-9994-346-8-0 (e)
Library of Congress Control Number: 2017914940
BISAC: Fiction, Young Adult Fiction: General / Fantasy / Magical Realism / Fairy Tales, Legends & Mythology / Coming of Age / General / Epic / Saga

This is a work of fiction. All of the characters, names, incidents, organizations, and dialogue in this novel are either the products of the author's imagination or are used fictitiously. Any resemblance to actual persons, living or dead, events, or locales is entirely coincidental.

Manufactured in the United States of America

WaterBearer Press Edition: October 2017

Al correo de las brujas y las brujitas.
May we live on and prosper.

Dearest Inaara Girls;

Always follow your heart ♡

Patricia

To my mother, Celeste.
From your loving daughter,
Xiomara
1856

PROLOGUE

A desolate March wind howled from the Cantabrian to the foothills of the impervious Pyrenees, heralding a fierce storm. Country folks penned their livestock and closed their doors and shutters against the weather; they lit up their hearths in preparation for a cold night. Boys scurried about, bringing in armfuls of firewood to store near their stoves, while inside their homes, girls stopped the chilly drafts by cramming rags in every crack and fissure attending their walls.

Farther up a ways, where the mountains were beautifully timbered but could not yet be called inhospitable, nestled in a verdant valley only a four-day journey from the coast, stood the citadel of Santillán, the seat of King Bautista and his beloved wife, Paloma. The stronghold covered about five square miles and had but one entrance, which was centered at the south-facing wall and was used by residents and visitors alike. From each corner of the massive rectangular fortification rose the mighty watchtowers that had served as defensive posts stocked with weapons in years past, but now contained a vast supply of tools and the township's grain silo. From the balustrades atop these towers hung the traditional ensigns of Santillán, designed by Bautista to communicate the state of things to approaching visitors, be it a lively fair, a farming exposition, a cavalcade, a livestock event, or whatever exhibition Bautista Santillán had decided to host—all for the prosperity of his people and his kingdom.

Upon entering the citadel, one found oneself in the middle of Santillán's bustling market street, stretching right and left along the entire length of the township and lined with colorful marquees boasting every craft and crop available. Across this main thoroughfare was the chapel square with its central fountain and gravel walks surrounding it, and behind the quaint chapel stood the royal hall with its many turrets and colorful triangular banners trembling in the breeze. The back of the royal hall overlooked Paloma's serene gardens, shielded from the liveliness of town by finely manicured laurel hedges. There were meandering walks shaded by clusters of junipers and globe willows. There were benches scattered about where Paloma often sat in the late spring afternoons to enjoy the fragrant racemes of wisteria she had lovingly planted or the restful trickling of ponds, where the koi fish drifted lazily beneath lily pads. Here, Paloma and Bautista took their early morning walks in the summer, making decisions and planning for the future while laughing together to the merry tune of a myriad of twittering birds bathing in the tall basins strewn about the trails.

Filling the remaining vacant space within the citadel were the dwellings of the hundreds of people who worked in Santillán and who made their living cultivating crops or raising livestock outside the walls.

But on this March afternoon, the very character of Santillán appeared to be missing; there were no banners gaily swaying in the breeze atop the turrets, the balustrades were devoid of cheery colors to draw the eye, and no bartering or bargaining could be heard along the market street; in fact, the marquees had been taken down, leaving the thoroughfare looking forlorn and at the mercy of the harsh winds. There were no children splashing in the fountains, and birds could not be heard within the dense bluish green branches of the junipers. The ivy clung shivering to the stone walls of the towers, and to complete the glum picture, the somber black ensigns hanging from the topmost balustrades lapped at the forbidding skies above, as if tempting the wrath of heaven to strike it all down rather than let its inhabitants dwell in the darkness that had enveloped Santillán in bitter depression since the death of Bautista two weeks prior.

From the terrace of the northeast tower, a man of about sixty, whose face was both kind and wise but in whose eyes blazed a fierceness that at once alerted his interviewers that he was someone to be reckoned with, appraised the dreary scene below then raised his gaze to the threatening weather coming from the west. "So it seems nature can *in fact* emulate the state of the human soul," he mused broodingly. This man's name was Clemente. "Indeed! The same agony and turmoil my queen suffers is what I can see in these turbulent clouds … I can smell it in this wretched wind!"

For a brief moment, his aging body sagged, as he took upon himself the pain he knew Paloma suffered. Indeed his own heart ached with the loss of Bautista, a man whom Clemente had considered more a son than a sovereign. How it grieved him that Bautista's life had been cut short. How it angered him that Paloma had been deprived of Bautista's love.

But Clemente was not the sort to give in to despair—especially when his strength was so dearly needed. He gathered his black cloak tightly around his body as he headed for the zigzagging staircase that would take him down to the grounds. Although paced by the dull ache plaguing his left arm, Clemente hurried down the steps. Groaning with frustration, he regarded the offending limb, cursing inwardly at the persistent pain he'd been ignoring for the past two days. His pace slackened as he bent his arm at the elbow and swung it irritably, making circles in the air, until the discomfort lessened somewhat. Then he resumed his purposeful descent, for he was on an errand for the queen.

Clemente, after Paloma's parents, had been first to hold the infant lady in his arms and had been enchanted by her from that day forth, seeing the promise of greatness in her even at that young age, clamoring over her first steps, bearing witness to her first words and duly writing them down for posterity. He had been her tutor and advisor, and over the years, he had become, after her husband, her truest, most loyal friend.

Clemente reached the bottom of the tower and headed toward the royal hall, noting that the koi in the pond had ventured so deep in their habitat that they could hardly be distinguished. "It will be a fierce storm!" he muttered into the wind that tousled his thick, gray hair. "The dismissal of Arantxa is sure to ease Paloma's mind." He reasoned upon entering the hall through the side service door, which was held open for him by a young servant girl who had seen him approach. "Is the seer in her chamber?" Clemente asked of the shivering girl who hurriedly closed the door behind him and did her best to straighten her windblown hair.

"Sir, she is." The girl curtsied.

Clemente brushed past, leaving her to fuss with the lace cap blown askew on her head.

Arantxa, the seer, lived in the service wing of the royal hall at the top of a turret doggedly shunned by the rest of the servants who had been forbidden to enter the chamber by Arantxa herself. In the aversion they felt toward her, the servants had taken Arantxa's command a step farther and never even ventured near the staircase, which accounted for its lamentable state of uncleanliness and disrepair. Clemente, however, took the dingy steps without hesitation, while outside, the churning black clouds snuffed out the waning light of the afternoon. The spiraling stairway darkened considerably, and Clemente swung his arm again, breathing deeply. Frigid gusts pushed through the fist-size portholes on the walls, rousing the dust on the crumbling stone steps, but he continued his deliberate climb, lost in his remembrances and oblivious to the cold and dust.

Months before, Arantxa had arrived in Santillán, her body broken, her face badly burned, and although considerably healed from the damage done by the fire, she still limped pathetically and bore open lesions, which in their gruesomeness, had excited a lively string of unpleasant rumors concerning her hasty departure from the neighboring kingdom of St. Michel, where she had resided before. Initially, Clemente had agreed with Bautista that Arantxa could be but a harmless fortuneteller and healer who only wanted to recover from her unfortunate circumstances and make a living away from St. Michel, where it was rumored that she had been tragically struck down. And, indeed, Clemente had tried to reassure Paloma of this, but the queen would have none of it. Try as she might, Paloma could not hide her distrust of Arantxa and believed her to be something much more shadowy than a meek soothsayer; after all, what exactly had Arantxa's unfortunate circumstances been? What if, as rumors went, her injuries had been self-inflicted or at least a consequence of her own actions? Even darker tales had reached Paloma, difficult though they were to believe, that Arantxa may have played some part in the death of King Edmond of St. Michel. But Paloma's concerns had been dismissed by Bautista and Clemente, blind as they were to the elusive truth veiled under Arantxa's piteous appearance and the heartrending avowal of her intent to spend the few *months* left to her in peace. In return for the roof over her head and the nourishment she would receive, Arantxa offered to see the future, always with the king's best interest in mind.

Perhaps Paloma's pregnancy had made her senses keener, perhaps premonitions simply could not be dispensed with, or maybe because after Bautista's death, the rumors about Arantxa had resurfaced with a life of their own among the people of Santillán and were now tinged with an ominous flavor; after all, had not the king of St. Michel died mysteriously? Hadn't Arantxa's injuries occurred immediately after his death? Whatever the case, after the harrowing riding accident that had killed Bautista, Clemente at last came around to Paloma's view of things. So, powerless to do what the queen wanted above everything else, which was to have Bautista alive and by her side again, Clemente longed to, in the very least, ease Paloma's suffering by whatever means he could.

Clemente stopped; an exasperated groan issued from him as he yet again swung his arm, while with his free hand, he exerted pressure on his shoulder and chest. He gazed upward at the timbers that made up the drafty inside of the turret and counted three more rounds of stairs before he reached Arantxa's door. Feeling the reassuring weight of the money bag in a fold of his cloak, Clemente climbed several more steps, anxious to rid Santillán of this woman for the sake of Paloma. He was prepared to compensate Arantxa for her services, plus give her a few months' pay to help her along. There was no question in his mind, however, that Arantxa would be dismissed that very evening, and furthermore, he would require her to leave at once. *What was she after …? Lurking outside Paloma's chamber?* The possible answer to that question had been bothering him the entire day, but all he could do was speculate. Arantxa's unconvincing response still rang in his ears. "The queen suffers cruelly," she had croaked. "I can help."

Resolved anew by this recollection, Clemente climbed on.

When Paloma had married the handsome king of Santillán, Clemente's heart had swelled with unspoken satisfaction and pride to see his beloved lady become a rightful queen; he knew he had contributed to her becoming the woman who reigned at the side of one such noble man as Bautista. Paloma's sense of justice and her earthiness were the qualities Clemente admired most in her, and as a diligent tutor, he had prepared young Paloma to be a wise and just ruler. He had dutifully nurtured her mind and soul, and he had done it well. Oh, happy day! A mere eight months before when Paloma, at the arm of her adoring husband, announced to their clamoring subjects that she and Bautista would soon be parents.

Clemente reached Arantxa's door at last. He bent forward, taking deep breaths while supporting himself with his hands on his knees. He wiped the drops of sweat from his brow, taking a moment to collect his thoughts. Having caught his breath and feeling sufficiently composed, he straightened up and stood in the darkened antechamber, poised to knock when Arantxa's muttering, coming from the other side of the dilapidated wooden door, reached his ears and made him lower his fist. He stepped back in confusion. Had she said Paloma's name? Yes! There was no mistaking it. Without hesitation, Clemente edged silently against the stone wall until his shoulder made contact with the graying door, straining to see through the gaps in the boards while his ears absorbed each and every horrifying utterance coming from within the chamber.

Excruciating moments passed like entire hours, during which he could not tear his eyes off that narrow gap extending the length of the old door. Paralyzed with shock and revolted to the point of no longer feeling the dull ache that had reached his fingers by then, he watched, horror stricken, as Paloma's worst fears crystallized before his eyes. Clemente witnessed magic of the darkest kind unfold in Arantxa's bleak chamber, where at the end of what seemed an interminable hour, the deformed, haggard soothsayer had effectively discarded the repellent appearance with which she had limped into Santillán months before and managed to replicate the fair Paloma's visage for herself.

Clemente's mind worked feverishly to piece it all together. Such complete physical transformation was not to be believed, yet his eyes did not lie. No matter how much his brain rejected it, here was absolute, irrefutable proof of Arantxa's treachery. He irritably wiped his watery eyes and angrily wedged himself further against the narrow gap, forcing his mind to accept what he was seeing, that he might act on it. *How did I not see it!*

Arantxa's transformation was not the only horror Clemente had beheld; there was more. Her belly was just as swollen as Paloma's. Arantxa was with child, and no one had known it. *How did she manage to conceal it all this time!*

Clemente reeled.

Then Arantxa prepared to leave her chamber. She carried with her a vial whose toxic contents he had seen her mix, and he knew it was meant for Paloma. The moment for Clemente to act was at hand, for he must not give Arantxa the opportunity to carry out her unspeakable scheme. He must kill her. But his knees were buckling beneath him. He could no longer feel his arm. His chest felt constrained, as if an anvil had been deposited on top of him, and at once, he knew what was going to happen. Clemente was going to die outside Arantxa's door. He would not be able to stop her. He would not be able to save Paloma. A wretched cry threatened to escape his throat, but the door swung open, stopping a mere inch before crushing him against the wall. Sweat broke out of every pore on his body, and blackness began to engulf his mind. He saw Arantxa pass to the stairway in a whirl of silky fabric, a stolen trophy, and Paloma's lustrous red mane spilled loose over her shoulders.

Clemente managed a few steps toward the stairwell after her, but a searing pain shot through his chest, causing him to collapse and fall down several steps. There his valet found him the next morning, still unconscious, with a broken leg and bruised ribs. Later that same day, the people residing in the royal hall would be told that Clemente had suffered heart failure.

Confined to his bed and choosing to remain mute, Clemente listened to every word uttered by the physician caring for him and by the servants who brought him his meals. He discovered that Arantxa had disappeared and that Paloma had turned a new leaf regarding the grievous loss of her husband; she no longer kept to her room. The fact that Paloma had not been to see him left Clemente in no doubt of Arantxa's success.

Clemente stared off into space, hour after hour and day after day, repeating to himself that he had failed, failed to save Paloma, failed to kill Arantxa, and failed to die. In time, however, he resolved that there must be a reason for his survival; and determined to discover it, he resolved to continue life under the impostor's rule.

After weeks of silence, Clemente miraculously regained the ability to speak, but he deliberately fueled the belief of those around him that his severe episode had damaged not only his body but his mind as well, so that he might continue his investigations without being suspected of treachery.

And so it was that for years to come, Clemente walked with a heavy limp. He pretended to barely remember who he was, all the while staunchly watching Arantxa and waiting for any sign or word of what might have become of the real Paloma and her child, anxious for any knowledge that might enable him to expose the deceiver.

Chapter I:

Glamorous Girlhood

The rolling hills and meadows attending Santillán and the neighboring kingdom to the west, St. Michel, were welcoming enough and granted easy passage to those seeking destinations to the west or to the south. But to the north, well beyond the verdant meadows, the jagged ridges of the Pyrenees plainly declared "no trespassing"

Those giant creations chiseled in stone, rising so violently from the fertile valleys near at hand, couldn't help but substantiate the impenetrability of those faraway peaks. The Pyrenees were, in fact, an inaccessible backdrop to the civilized world of Santillán and St. Michel—to be regarded with fear and awe and best left unexplored.

Albeit unimaginable, the indomitable granite peaks were actually a serrated stronghold jealously guarding a treasure—a hidden realm beyond our natural world. They cradled a magnificent pear-shaped basin that spread for miles under the sky, unbeknownst to those humans below who assumed nothing could possibly survive at such altitude or on such arid, rocky terrain.

But the outward granite edges of the cradle were superseded by an inward range of sloping hills, thickly timbered with the evergreens that acted as a protective lining of sorts. The western, narrower portion of this basin was occupied by a sparkling lake whose clear waters were rendered green by the white sands that made up its bed, and it was warm as a bath, owing to the springs that fed it from the blazing depths of the earth.

Playful slopes, beautifully wooded in varying species of conifer, framed the eastern shore of the lake, and within the cool shade of the forest, layer upon layer of pine needles blanketed the dark soil. A crisp, alpine scent permeated this cool heaven, where nothing but the song of the breeze through the thick foliage and the chirruping of birds could be heard.

Opposite the lake, on the eastern end of the basin, were dense marshes buzzing with insects unknown and sleepy-eyed reptiles that lounged in the sun or snaked through the thick grasses and reeds protruding from the shallow sloughs. The central territory within the realm was the arboretum, where skillfully tended species of trees and exotic plants thrived in spite of the elevation; there the earth itself could be heard breathing, and the murmur of the breeze through the trees carried with it the sounds of trickling water from the numerous springs and creeks that carried its nourishment. There the vegetation changed with every step, and the air was saturated with the fertile smell of dark soil. There swayed the wispy willows whose tendrils reached to the ground, the aspen leaves quivered happily under the dappling sunlight, and noble oaks rose on weathered trunks to spread their branches like veritable trees of life protecting all that lived below.

Yet beneath the emerald canopy of the trees, there was unexpected and intense color. Cool blue grass grew in mounds near the creek banks, and heavy white and purple racemes of wisteria bowed down to the water. Patches of hyacinth, with their green blades and dark pink blossoms, stood at attention, saturating the mild air with their sweet scent. Lush lilac shrubs, with their heavily perfumed panicles, trembled in the breeze, adding a dusting of petals to the ground around them. Cheery daisies atop their leafy stems bent with the breeze and leaned playfully toward the proud tulips, who ignored them, while the bashful violets carpeted every inch of earth left unadorned by the showier flora.

Such was summer in the Realm of Faery, where all of it—lake, arboretum, and marshes—existed safely within the virtually inaccessible rock cradle of the western Pyrenees.

On one such day in the arboretum, a creek skipped merrily over pebbles and tripped over an occasional fallen branch on its way to a makeshift dam. It spilled boisterously over the series of sun-bleached boulders arranged in the shape of a half moon and whirled into the large pond below, leaving it refreshed and renewed as it continued to wind its way deeper into the woods.

A small rock was tossed into that pond, and it hit the water with a gurgling *plunk*. The serene sound of rushing water was suddenly interrupted, and the chattering of birds stopped momentarily—the whole forest seemed to pause and listen—then a girlish voice was heard. The forest exhaled, and the chattering resumed. It was just Celeste.

Tall for an eleven year old, Celeste stood on tiptoes at the edge of the water, lifting her thick mane of light brown hair and deftly knotting it on top of her head. Checking her reflection in the water, she secured the knot with two straight, polished sticks and fanned the back of her sweaty neck with her hand. "So are you going to help me or not?" she asked, and judging by the bite in her tone, it wasn't the first time she had made that request. She ruffled the skirt of her sleeveless frock, tempting the breeze to cool her legs.

Bobbing midair, drowsily staring at the sun-bleached boulders over which the water spilled, was the faery, Nahia, whom Celeste had addressed. A fair-skinned female, about the size of Celeste's forearm, looked longingly at the cool water beneath her. She was decked in a long, gossamer chemise, and her blond ringlets, streaked with sea-green highlights, clung to her damp forehead and neck.

"Well?" Celeste insisted. "You have delayed enough!" she declared, lifting her frock over her knees and sitting at the edge of the pond. She put her legs in the water with a sigh of relief, for the summer heat was unbearable.

"I don't think we should do it," Nahia answered at last. Celeste tensed up crossly at this, and Nahia made haste to add, "What if something goes really—I mean *really*—wrong?"

The flecks of gold in Celeste's brown eyes blazed in frustration as she stood up again. "You can't renege now! You already promised!"

Nahia backed away instinctively even though Celeste would have to walk on water to be able to get at her, but just the same, the precaution was taken. "I know, I know," the faery stammered. "Just let me think a little …"

Seemingly at her wit's end over the faery's continued excuses and ploys to delay, Celeste blurted out in frustration, "Think? What do you mean *think*! You should know better than to think! You'll give yourself a nosebleed!"

"I'm going to ignore you said that!" Nahia bristled.

"What is it you have to *think* about, Nahia …? I already told you how simple it all is, and you said all was clear!" Celeste growled. "You always do this to me! And it makes me want to strangle you! At the last minute, you change your mind! I warn you, Nahia, keep your word or else!"

Celeste's nerves appeared to be on the edge of snapping like a twig, so Nahia bit her tongue rather than saying, "Or else what?" Instead, the faery managed a peevish, "Alright, fine! I'll get the potion … But you're certain your mother is already tired?"

"Yes, Nahia, yes, and once again, yes!" Celeste cried with no small effort to keep her temper in check. The heroic mission she proposed to undertake could not be pulled off without the faery's assistance, and to brawl with Nahia at this crucial moment would most definitely spoil her plan. So she drew a deep, calming breath like her mother had taught her and continued in measured tones. "I have been walking with her all morning; she even swam in the lake with me today! Just moments ago, I left her at home, and she said she would drink a pitcher of citrus water before taking a nap." The smug look that came over Celeste's face clearly said that there could be no arguing the promising nature of the circumstances described. But just in case, she added as earnestly as she could, "Nahia, I tell you she's ready. And we're wasting time!"

The faery appeared infuriatingly doubtful, pursing her lips and flaring her nostrils in mock concentration.

"Would you stop that?" Celeste glowered, pointing at the faery's face.

"Stop what?"

"That ... That thing! What you do with your nose!" Celeste spluttered, her self-control teetering.

Nahia tried her best to look confounded, which only added to Celeste's edginess.

"You puff up your nose! And you know I know what that means!"

"You mean *flare* ...?" Nahia corrected Celeste tersely, bobbing to and fro. "I *flare* my nostrils, if that's what you mean."

At this, Celeste lost all semblance of restraint, her suntanned cheeks flushed pink. "Flaring, puffing! What in the great big *woods* does it matter what you call it! What matters is that I know what you mean by it, you boasting little fiend!" Celeste fumed, pacing back and forth on the edge of the pond while Nahia hovered safely above the water, quite beyond the reach of more than just Celeste's words. "You know I can't do this by myself, and you want to rub my nose in it, don't you? Don't you! You miserable excuse for a faery!"

The faery bit her lip and only looked at Celeste through narrowed eyes, which did nothing to accommodate Celeste's sense of urgency. They stared stubbornly at each other, the human livid, the faery gloating.

Celeste and Nahia had been born on the same night and had been told by their mothers that, because of this seemingly ordinary coincidence, they were birth sisters. This designation, however, had been a double-edged sword, for even though there was no one who knew Celeste better, no one whom Celeste trusted more or felt closer to— besides her mother, Paloma, that is—they couldn't seem to avoid getting into competitive squabbles. Countless times, one or the other would take things too far and feel compelled to creep up later, offering an abandoned nest of robin eggs to help hatch or fancy glass beads to decorate a new dress, earnestly trying to make amends. It was so much worse, though, when the snipes and comments had the ring of truth as Nahia's did when she ranted about their respective ancestry, a subject that wore on Celeste's sense of self like no other. They were both the daughters of queens, as Celeste often reminded Nahia, which should have been enough to settle any argument between them, but Nahia would happily discredit Celeste's claims to royalty in a most provoking fashion, saying, "That is tittle-tattle, and no one can *really* prove otherwise. *I*, however, am a true princess, the faery princess born to Queen Oihana, ruler of the *real* world, not just some human fantasy world that more than likely doesn't even exist." These ravings of the faery would invariably end, much to Celeste's humiliation (and not a little rage), with a pompous "so you should address me with due respect."

Thus the *physical* portion of their arguments would begin, where ingenious traps were set that, more often than not, carried such consequences as undesirable hair texture and color or angry rashes in places that made it impossible for them to sit at ease for hours on end or, on occasion, even bellyaches that made them green with discomfort.

Theirs was a sibling relationship: at times sweet and fulfilling like no other but, once on the dark side, spiteful, petty, and rash. Celeste often found enough annoying legitimacy in Nahia's words to arouse her doubts. It was at these times that Celeste felt most keenly that she and Paloma inhabited the Realm of Faery as mere guests, and in it, Oihana was the only queen and Nahia the sole heiress. Paloma's kingdom was so far away, it may as well have existed only in her stories, as Nahia sometimes suggested. And, although she would never admit it to Nahia, Celeste knew the only thing keeping the notion of that human kingdom a reality was Paloma's word. Oh! That she could prove to Nahia, and to herself—once and for all—how real Paloma's world actually was.

So it was that at the age of eleven, with only minimal knowledge of how or why Paloma came to be in the realm, convinced that she knew best, Celeste had worked herself into a frenzied belief that neither Paloma nor Oihana had been able to hit on the solution to Celeste and her mother's estrangement from their human kingdom simply because the solution was laughably straightforward, and therefore it had escaped their notice. "What is our predicament?" Celeste's reasoning began. "We inhabit the Realm of Faery, owing to a spell cast upon my mother by an evil witch. What are our limitations? We are not to leave the Realm of Faery lest my mother be transformed into a hideous apparition. But ..." the golden flecks in her eyes would flicker gaily at this part, "have Mamma or Oihana tested our limitations? No," Celeste beamed inwardly. "But *I* will test them, and *I*, Celeste, will show them how foolish we've been to wait all these years without questioning."

Celeste's plan was quite simple. Paloma would be transported to the western boundary of the Realm of Faery; there she would wake from a heavy sleep—brought on by the sleeping potion prepared by Nahia—and upon waking, she would find herself unchanged. And there Celeste would be, feasting on the look of wonder and elation she would surely see on her mother's face when she found herself beyond the boundaries of the realm, yet unaffected by the fabled curse.

To enlist Nahia's assistance with the potion had been a key factor, and Celeste had managed to convince the faery by presenting her case in this way: "We couldn't have asked for a better opportunity to gain the court's praise and admiration; you must admit it. If we pull this off, no one will be able to question your ability as a potion maker, and they'll have to bow down to the range of my keen intellect for putting this scheme together, and I might add, a keen intellect makes up for glamour any time." Celeste ignored Nahia's frown at that last remark and breezily proceeded to the inevitable flattery she knew would be required to convince the faery. "Not only the potions part, Nahia. Imagine what your mother will say when she hears that you managed to keep human height for over three hours." This Celeste said with brows arching dramatically, almost to her hairline, for she knew her birth sister's vanity was a force to be reckoned with, and with cleverly stated prospects such as these, Celeste knew she had her before the faery had even conceded a vague smile.

The anticipation of exposing their gross oversight to her mother had become such a fixed notion in Celeste's mind that she already fancied herself the center of a glorious reception in Handi Park (the seat of the faery queen, Oihana, and her troop) to commemorate her accomplishment. She could feel the heat of all those admiring, luminous faery eyes fixed on her as she regaled them with the details of her astute plan. Oh, how glorious would Paloma's return to her fabled kingdom be. How admired they would be by the scores of subjects awaiting them there. And how Nahia would at last have to acknowledge that they were of equal rank.

And so, goaded by their youthful aspirations and individual visions of the glory soon to be showered upon them, Celeste pressed and Nahia—with mock indolence—gave in at last.

Giddy with anticipation, Celeste left the pond with Nahia gliding briskly at her side, switching sharply from one side of Celeste to the other and back again, clearly trying to act the part of a heroine pressed for time to save the world. Celeste smiled as she went, in spite of being mildly annoyed by Nahia's antics. She reflected that at least the faery's flying was silent. Should faeries have thick bumblebee wings, Celeste would have had to swat at her out of sheer irritation. But as things went, faeries—Nahia included—had no wings to flap or beat at all, so the exercise was mercifully quiet. Of course, it hadn't always been like that. Celeste could remember a time when a lot of groaning had *indeed* taken place; this was when Nahia was learning to fly, and it was evident that her exertions were excruciating, for it required complete focus and strength of mind to bid one's body to leave the ground and maintain it airborne. But Nahia had been a fast learner. In a week, she had managed to make long leaps, that is, rising from one point and landing at another over six feet away, with only two very minor sprains. In a month, Nahia had mastered the part about willfully remaining airborne, having sustained only one scrape when she crashed into a branch during her ascent. And by the second month, Nahia need only picture a destination in her mind, and her body would rise off the ground and take her to it.

At the end of the elderberry lane leading away from the pond, the girls parted ways. Celeste took a right turn to her home in the grotto, and Nahia darted left, back to Handi Park to fetch the potion she had mixed and kept hidden in preparation for this day.

"I'll race you!" Celeste called after the faery, taking the crooked, narrow path back to the grotto at a trot.

"I'll beat you there!" challenged Nahia.

Celeste pressed forward as quick as she could, certain that Nahia could not possibly get to Handi Park and back to the Grotto in the ten minutes it would take her to arrive at her home.

Of the few things Nahia could do that Celeste couldn't, flying was the one she truly envied. She would often watch Nahia when she thought the faery didn't notice and secretly marveled at the similarities she spotted between a faery in flight and a gleaming hummingbird; Nahia could be suspended in midair and directly zip up or down, right or left, sometimes so swiftly that it seemed she could truly disappear and reappear. Of course, Celeste knew that was not so. Neither Nahia nor any of the other faeries had the power to disappear at will. They could make a speedy retreat, or they could deny one the gift of faery sight, that is, deny permission to see what lies beyond the screen of the natural world. As a rule, the gift of faery sight was denied to the whole of humanity, for whom the Realm of Faery existed only in folk tales and superstitious minds. To Paloma and Celeste, however, the gift of faery sight had been granted upon their entrance into the realm through the keeper of the forest's consent. That being the case, a faery needing to escape a sticky situation involving either of the two humans, mostly Celeste, had no recourse but to be quick. And Nahia was quick.

Celeste bristled irritably when Nahia flitted into the grotto only instants after her.

The grotto was Paloma and Celeste's cozy, safe home, but it hadn't always been so. Over the years, Paloma had transformed it from a bare cave with dirt floors into the lush habitat Celeste now called home. The bare boulders that framed the entrance were no longer visible under the thickly flowering jasmine vines whose stems, if not trimmed regularly, had to be parted like draperies in order to enter. Inside, the dirt floors had been paved with ingenious designs using only the smoothest pebbles found at the lakeshore or on the creek beds—that had been a tedious project in Celeste's opinion, as she had been made to find and deliver the pebbles for the floor's mosaics. The dirt and rock walls were covered in Spanish moss, but in some places, Paloma had overlaid beads and pebbles to make colorful pictures for Celeste. Their furnishings couldn't help but be austere in nature; a large bedstead, for many years filled with only leaves, now sported a fine feather mattress and matching pillows; Celeste remembered vividly when they had finally gathered enough feathers for it, and she had had no idea one could sleep in such luxury. At the foot of the bed sat a trunk that held the linens they had woven themselves and some of their clothing; many of these remarkable creations were gifts from their faery host. A circular wooden table with three chairs set around it—for Paloma insisted on having a chair for Bautista, even if he would never be seated at it—occupied the center of the room near the hearth. There were four shelves cleverly fixed to the wall on either side of the fire, where they stored the few utensils they needed: spoons, bowls, plates, cups (all crafted in delicate glass within Handi Park), and some items of food such as dried herbs, fruits, and seeds.

"Celeste," Nahia whispered. "Look ..." she said importantly, her round, aquamarine eyes darting warily to the doorway, lest Paloma appear without warning. The faery briefly lifted her chemise, showing Celeste that the small vial containing the potion had been cleverly strapped to her thigh.

With an arch look, Celeste went in directly, refusing to spare even a single comment on Nahia's peculiar methods. Even before Celeste's eyes had completely adjusted to the cool darkness inside the grotto, she could tell Paloma wasn't there. She whirled back toward the door, pulling the polished sticks off her hair in a temper—the knot was disheveled anyhow. She hadn't counted on having to search for her mother. But Celeste had not taken three steps back into the warm sunshine before she ran right into Paloma who was, at that moment, returning home. Nahia, who had been following Celeste's every move, collided with the back of Celeste's head. The faery instantly recovered and hovered to one side as if she had meant to do just that.

"Going somewhere, ladies?" Paloma inquired cheerfully, looking from her daughter's startled eyes to Nahia's shifty expression.

"Um ... well ... we were just going to look for you, actually," Celeste stammered.

"And here I am. Let's go in then," Paloma said, parting the jasmine curtain and ushering them into the grotto. Nahia flitted in, tapping the shoots of the wind chime as she went so they let out their hollow music.

"We wanted to let you know that we were going to the pond, Mamma," Celeste lied, and then, most conspicuously, she blurted, "But before we go, did you already have a drink? Do you need a drink?" She didn't have to look at Nahia to know that the faery's eyes had probably rolled clear to the back of her head.

"No, my *dearling*, I have not." Paloma smiled innocently at her daughter's strange mannerisms.

Celeste, however, took Paloma's use of one of her baby words as a sign that her mother was in playful spirits, and she felt heartened. Celeste didn't waste any time.

"You said you wanted to nap after our swim, and instead you've been out and about. Where were you?"

"I would rather not say in front of Nahia, but I suppose there's no hiding it now," Paloma said with a hesitant grin as she pulled three medium-sized eggs from the pouch she had been carrying.

Nahia gasped.

"For dinner?" Celeste cried, eyeing the eggs hungrily.

"Certainly, my darling. And if you're going to the pond, go a little farther up the creek for me and see if you can catch a salmon."

"Ooooh, excellent!" Celeste cried, all the while thinking how perfectly suitable it was that they should have her favorite dinner on this night when they would celebrate Paloma being free of the curse at last. Then to Nahia, who floated between Celeste and Paloma with a mutinous frown and her fists on her hips, she said, "Oh, Nahia. When will you be finished with your egg prohibition?"

"Never," Nahia said breathlessly. "It's beyond me how anyone can eat liquid birds like they're nothing. It's barbaric."

Paloma carefully set the eggs inside a bowl on one of the shelves and interjected with a smile. "Let's remember, dear, that only a summer ago, you ate omelets and casseroles and meringue puffs quite ravenously until you realized what those favorite dishes of yours were actually made of."

"Yes, well, to think you could have kept quiet about it and let me enjoy those things," Nahia replied, addressing Celeste who, on a vengeful fit, had indeed been the one to reveal the horrible truth about the main ingredient in the faery's favorite dishes.

"You'll help me catch a salmon won't you, Nahia?" Celeste said, trying to return to the moment at hand. The sun no longer shone through the jasmine over the doorway; it was right above them, which meant that the afternoon was beginning and that they should make haste.

"Oh, alright," Nahia agreed.

"And in the meantime, you lay on the bed," Celeste said to Paloma with a meaningful look toward the faery. "Nahia and I will get you a cool drink. And would you like a peach before they go bad?"

9

Paloma declined the peach, and Nahia did not waste an instant. She darted to the shelf and leaned casually against one of the cups. By the time Celeste came around to fill it with cool water, the faery had already emptied the contents of the vial into it.

Celeste carried the cup to where her mother reclined on the bed and handed it to her. Paloma took it, saying, "Thank you, dear," and Celeste felt suddenly compelled to pick off a yellowing chunk of moss from the wall. For some reason, Celeste couldn't bring herself to watch her mother consume the laced beverage. She wondered if perhaps she was feeling guilty; after all, it was a very underhanded thing to do, and what if she was wrong. What if something dreadful happened? But that was absurd. Everything was going according to plan, and it would turn out just perfect. She could almost taste the salmon and hear her mother's surprised and pleased laughter.

Paloma's cup dropped to the floor, startling Celeste out of her self-satisfied thoughts. Paloma's head had wilted and lolled to one side, and the sight of her mother in such a state made Celeste's belly squirm uncomfortably. "That was *too* quick Nahia! Are you sure you mixed the right ingredients?"

By way of a response, Nahia looked genuinely appalled. "Of course I did," the faery said defensively.

Celeste bent tentatively over the still figure of her mother, her cheek close to Paloma's nose and mouth, trying to feel her breath. Satisfied that Paloma was breathing properly, Celeste recovered her eager spirit of adventure and darted out of the grotto. "I'll be right back," she called to the faery. Celeste went around the side of the hill to the bramble patch where she had concealed the litter she and Nahia had put together two weeks earlier. She returned presently and laid the cot alongside the bedstead. "Ready?"

"Yes," said the faery, and she closed her eyes in a great show of concentration.

Celeste waited, tapping her sandaled foot on the mosaic floor, and just when she began to despair that the faery may not be able to manage the shape-shift to human height, Nahia seemed to materialize before her, and they were suddenly eye to eye. "You did it!" Celeste shrieked and gave the faery a delighted squeeze. Nahia beamed, trying not to look too surprised at her own success.

With Celeste at her head and Nahia at her feet, they gently lowered Paloma onto the litter, which consisted of two somewhat narrow poles, each about six feet in length, joined together by tightly woven ivy stems. The cot, with Paloma in it, was ready to be glamorized by Nahia so as to make it weightless. But the hours Nahia had devoted to practicing this particular ability proved ineffective, and the bragging and taunting that the faery had subjected

Celeste to seemed to rebound on her most unpleasantly when Celeste, feeling thoroughly justified, abused the faery for her lack of dedication.

Conscious as she was of the time, though, Celeste bit back any additional remarks and instead lifted her end of the cot to determine whether or not they would be able to carry Paloma all the way to the far edge of the lake. To Celeste's surprise, Nahia had succeeded in dispersing most of the weight, and she eagerly motioned for the faery to pick up her end of it. This Nahia did, and the two girls walked out of the grotto with the sleeping Paloma resting between them on her ivy litter. The wooden chime rang hollowly as they passed.

Celeste set forth cheerful and encouraged. Nahia trudged behind her, looking a little faint.

The air felt stuffy under the canopy of trees, and both girls were sweating profusely by the time the vegetation began to change around them from the lovingly cared for arboretum to the predominantly coniferous landscape near the shore of Moon Dancer Lake. Both were breathing quite heavily, but it seemed to Celeste that Nahia wheezed and huffed a great deal more than herself, which concerned her that the faery might be weakening too soon; after all, Nahia was still green at shape-shifting. Celeste thought it better to distract her by lightening the mood with a little conversation. "We'll all have such a good laugh when this is over," Celeste declared heartily, and when Nahia only grunted, she persisted. "To think I was the only one who thought to do this. You know, to test the limits of the curse? But don't worry, I won't brag about it."

Nahia broke her silence and remarked airily, "You may have thought it up, but you couldn't have done it without me, and you know it!" At this, the faery accidentally dropped one of the poles, and Celeste couldn't help but drag the cot a few inches before coming to a stop.

"We may as well rest," Celeste panted, setting her end of the litter down and stretching her back with a moan of relief. "Why didn't we think to bring any water? And why are you looking so fretful?"

"I just feel a little dizzy is all," said Nahia, stretching her neck from side to side and shaking her arms

"Well, why don't you shrink down for a bit and get fully rested. I'm sure we have less than an hour to go."

"I better not. I have this strange feeling that if I shift back down, I won't have the energy to enlarge myself again."

Celeste looked alarmed at this. This could really wreck the plan. She couldn't possibly pull Paloma the rest of the way there all by herself. The way back would, of course, be nothing. Paloma would be so thrilled to have been set free of the curse that she would certainly relish the walk back.

Trying not to dwell on how disappointing it was that Nahia didn't yet know how to shift humans to faery size and how that would have made things so much easier, for if that were the case, she could have simply carried Paloma in her arms, Celeste marshaled her thoughts and said, "But you're doing so well, Nahia. Look, you've remained at human height for over an hour now, and what an excellent job you did in lightening Mamma's weight! We couldn't have gotten this far without that," Celeste exclaimed truthfully. "Just one more hour. What is that to such a faery as *you*?"

This put an impish grin on Nahia's flushed face. "You're right on that score," she said. Celeste's words had had the anticipated effect on her. "But as soon as we get to the lake, we're going in and cooling off."

They resumed their positions and lifted their sleeping cargo, which, much to their discomfort, seemed to be growing heavier.

The air had been thick with the scent of pines, a definite sign they were approaching Moon Dancer Lake, but it seemed to have been so for over an hour, and the girls had been silent for half of it. The heat and exhaustion inevitably made one or the other start to distrust what had been a perfectly simple plan all along, and the bickering would ensue.

"Well, I sure hope you're right. Do you know what my mother will do to me if something really bad happens?" Nahia grunted, purposely breeding uncertainty again.

"Calm yourself, will you. Nothing bad is going to happen." Celeste wiped the sweat from her forehead, making muddy smudges on her face. "Look at it this way, if nothing else, this is the longest you've been able to keep human size," Celeste said, again trying to flatter Nahia into speeding up her pace.

Nahia smirked, and her crystalline aquamarine eyes stood in striking contrast to her flushed face. "It takes a great deal of energy for a faery to call herself to human height, you know, and to maintain it for such a long period of time—under all this strain even." She couldn't help adding, but the flattering wasn't having the same effect as before, and Nahia quickly fell back to brooding over the heat and her aching arms. "Who would've thought your mother was so heavy."

"It's because she's asleep," Celeste groaned irritably, wishing she too had someone to urge her along with flattery. "If only you took the time to practice all your lessons, you would've been able to make her light as a feather, and I wouldn't have to listen to your bellyaching."

"You'll listen to *all* my bellyaching just like I listen to yours, or I'll leave you here to fend for yourself!"" Nahia countered angrily. "At least I *can* change my size—now *there's* something worth bragging about. Your brains are not all that impressive."

The uneven terrain and the constant winding between trees and shrubs demanded their full attention, so it was no wonder that in the midst of their spat, Celeste lost her footing, and one of the litter's poles fell hard over a rocky patch. "Watch it!" Celeste yelped, casting a guilty look at the sleeping Paloma. Gently setting down the other pole, Celeste eyed Nahia accusingly and couldn't help seeing that the situation was deteriorating. Nahia didn't want to help, or so it seemed to Celeste. Paloma's white gown had a thin layer of dust all over it, and this further upset Celeste, knowing how meticulous Paloma was with her appearance. "This is no good," she cried, dropping to the ground and shaking her head in defeat. "It's so hot! And it's taking so long!"

When the faery failed to respond, console, or encourage her, Celeste looked up at Nahia, and the sight of the "I told you so" clearly stamped on the faery's face made Celeste boiling mad. Refusing to give in to despondency, she climbed to her feet, and after brushing the dust off her skirt, Celeste set her jaw, determined to see things to their successful end and to hold Nahia to her word, no matter how much the faery wanted to back out. Having taken her position at the head of the cot, Celeste glowered loftily at Nahia. "Well?" she said expectantly.

When the faery again took her share of the burden, Celeste stole another worried glance at the sleeping figure of her mother before continuing, and she muttered loud enough for Nahia to hear, "We're getting there, because we're getting there, and Mamma won't mind the dust so much once she finds herself free of the curse."

Having traversed the arboretum and having snaked between evergreens, the girls finally emerged onto the white sands of Moon Dancer Lake. They began bordering it, already exhausted from the two-hour excursion. The sun was low on the horizon as they crept westward along the shore, where it was mercifully cooler due to their proximity to the water.

"Do you suppose the base of those hills will be far enough?" Nahia said, jutting her chin toward the hills rising up ahead of them.

Celeste smiled. "I would say so. And when we get there, we'll jump in the water and get cooled off until my m—"

A loud moan issued from Paloma, startling them both. They stopped and lowered the cot to the ground as if it were a nest of angry wasps. They gaped at her, holding their breath. Celeste could not believe her eyes. At first, she thought the sunlight was still too bright and that she was seeing spots, but the look of horror in Nahia's face told her they couldn't both be having the same hallucination. Paloma's supple, fair skin was shriveling with every passing second, her cheeks were hollowing, and something had begun to rattle alarmingly in her chest, and it didn't escape Celeste's attention either that Paloma seemed to labor for each raspy breath she took. The thick, red braid she and Nahia had tied with a ribbon and that rested over Paloma's breast began to discolor and retexture itself into a matted, grayish clump. Celeste's mouth went completely dry. She stood there shaking her head in disbelief, unable to utter even a syllable.

A stunted shriek escaped Celeste when, with a sudden jerk, Paloma's inert body lunged into a sitting position. Her mother's eyes were open wide yet eerily vacant, and as Celeste looked at her in terror, Paloma's emerald eyes began to glaze over with a sickly opacity that shook Celeste to her very core. A noise like an agonizing growl issued from Paloma, and Celeste gaped in shock as her mother began to convulse rhythmically. She realized Paloma was coughing, trying to dislodge something that seemed to have wedged itself in her throat. She was choking to death! Celeste's panic at this was such that she was jolted into action. A horrific fear had gripped her heart, but it had also pumped her full of strength. Before Nahia could stop gawking, Celeste had grabbed hold of both poles, swung the litter around in a single desperate motion and bolted back, dragging the litter behind her, to the safety of the outlined territory, to the safety of the pine forest.

When she could no longer hear the rattling in Paloma's chest, Celeste allowed herself to stop. She doubled over, her insides convulsing from the exertion. She spat several times, clearing the dust out of her dry mouth, and she wiped the tears that the heaving had forced out of her eyes. When her own breathing was somewhat normal again, she straightened out and realized in a panic that Paloma was now much too quiet. Celeste did not want to look. What if she had killed her? But she gritted her teeth and spun on her heels, determined to think on it no more and face the calamity at once. Trembling from head to foot, she looked at her mother's wilted body and felt that life had come back to her limbs when she detected the rhythmic rising and falling of Paloma's breast. Paloma's partially shriveled skin had a waxy sheen of perspiration, which Celeste dreaded would soon turn to mud owing to the layer of dust accumulated during the journey. But even as she continued to stare, Paloma's skin seemed to regain some of its previous elasticity, and her hair, although dull, showed encouraging signs of becoming red again.

Fifty feet away, Nahia looked on in shock. She hadn't moved. Celeste spotted her, and the swift eye contact seemed to awaken the faery from the fear-induced paralysis. "Get your ruffles over here now!" Celeste hollered furiously, and Nahia broke into a dead run toward them.

Paloma continued to breathe shallow, and so long as she did, Celeste continued to tremble. They dragged the litter the rest of the way to the edge of the forest, as if it was made of glass, and they set Paloma down under the shade of a thick pine. "Oh, Mamma! Please don't be dying. What have I done?" Celeste cried. "It's all your fault, you stupid faery!"

"Me? Me! I wasn't the one with the keen intellect, you, you … human!" Nahia screamed, instantly assuming the compact size most natural to her—much as she had avoided it for fear of not being able to resume human height later—and zigzagged angrily above Celeste.

"You should've stopped me. You could've! Aaah!" Celeste screamed in frustration, because even as she said the words, she knew how wrong it was to blame Nahia, but in her desperation, it seemed rational that the faery could have, if she had really wanted, imposed her objections with more finality. Her scheme had gone so wrong. "Will you stop buzzing around me like that?" Celeste lashed out irritably.

But Nahia kept darting back and forth within inches of Celeste's head, irate and babbling in her own anxiety.

"Right. As if I could stop you once you got something in your thick, human skull. If I remember correctly, I *did* try to stop you, and what did I get? I'll tell you what I got: a hefty measure of your temper, that's what I got! I'm the one who's tired of your …"

But Celeste only heard every other word the faery uttered. She needed to make that wrinkled skin go away. She needed to make sure her mother's eyes returned to their sparkling green. "It'll be fine. I know she's alright. It'll all go away," she chanted more to herself than to Nahia as she feverishly rubbed Paloma's limbs.

Three feet overhead, Nahia continued to rant about things Celeste was too distraught to pay attention to.

"Oh, please don't wake up yet, Mamma, please."

"If she does, I know you'll find a way to blame me. And you know what? I won't stand for it anymore. You love to cause trouble and have *me* blamed for it. And that's the—"

"Oh, do be silent already!" Celeste rose to her feet. "Could it be that you're so in love with your own voice that you don't care whom you're driving mad with your incessant prattle?"

"I … um … I—"

"Hurry up. We have to take her back." Celeste made to grab her poles again, but she was forced to stop.

Her jaw clenched in fear and embarrassment as she looked at the magnificent unicorn standing between her and the trail back to the grotto. Neither she nor Nahia had heard or seen him until he was upon them.

Nahia froze in midair, panic-stricken. "Celeste? Celeste! This is it. My mother is going to dispatch me into the light," Nahia hissed urgently into Celeste's ear, not daring to take her eyes off the unicorn. "But not before I *destroy* you. Do you understand me? You got me into this whole muddle!"

"Hush up, will you," she said out of the corner of her mouth.

15

The unicorn held Celeste under his condemning gaze, and the liquid black orbs that were his eyes seemed to crush her like an insect, making her feel ridiculously small in his obvious censure. She, like Nahia, had heard tales about this unicorn, and they knew he was none other than the keeper of the forest. It was because of him and his powerful magic that the Realm of Faery thrived at such high altitudes. It was he who drew the hot springs to the surface, making the winters bearable and the flora so varied. It was through him that she, a *human*, and her mother had survived their death sentence eleven years before. How had she not seen the folly of her plan? How could she have doubted, nay, failed to *recognize* the immense wisdom surrounding her in the shape of her mother, of Oihana, and at present, of this stark white creature who exuded intelligence and discernment and who seemed to shame her for her ignorant arrogance.

"I'm so sorry," Celeste squeaked. "I thought it was a good idea. I thought I was doing the right thing. I'm so sorry ..."

The unicorn ignored her and advanced toward the cot, his powerful movements fluidly evident beneath his pearlescent white coat. He sniffed Paloma as if assessing the damage done to her. He then turned to Celeste who promptly dissolved into apologies again, but a brisk, resonant neigh from him put an end to her babbling. He tossed his head dismissively, pointing them back to the arboretum, and they wasted no time. Nahia shifted into human size again, her earlier fears of not being able to accomplish it had been completely subdued by the unexpected appearance of the keeper of the forest, and with renewed strength, though in shameful defeat, they took up their cargo and wound back through the forest in astonished silence. Celeste's head was filled with the shame of having been wrong—and of having been caught at it by no less than the unicorn himself. In her dejected silence, she also tried to contend with the ghastly images of her mother's transformation boiling out of control in her mind. How could such decay have taken place so quickly? And, amazingly, how could it have stopped almost as swiftly? She had only to pull her mother a few feet in the opposite direction from the boundary.

Covered in sweat, arms numb and legs quaking, Celeste and Nahia entered the cool safety of the grotto at last. There was hardly any daylight left as they set the cot down alongside the bedstead, and Celeste lit the lamp nearest her.

"Do I look as bad as you?" Celeste asked dryly, looking Nahia up and down. The faery was covered in smudges and had enough dust up her calves to make it seem as though she wore boots.

"I don't think I collected as many twigs and pine needles in my hair as you," Nahia answered flatly.

16

"Well, let's get her cleaned up, and then we can go to the pond and jump in, clothes and all," Celeste proposed.

They worked speedily but delicately, pausing at every shift or sigh issuing from Paloma. All the while, they hoped she wouldn't wake up fully until they had finished cleaning her.

"You'd better be thankful that your potion worked," Celeste muttered, determined to spread her ill-humor as far as she could and possibly even some of the blame.

"I would say my potion is the only part of this plan that worked properly," Nahia countered evenly, handing Celeste the wet cloths they would use to wipe away the dirt clinging to Paloma's skin.

Celeste looked at the faery, hoping a rebuttal would come to mind, but when none did, she took the cloths and went straight to work on Paloma's dusty skin. She took the opportunity to carefully inspect her mother and ascertain how far she had come in returning to her original form. Celeste was relieved to find that a lot of what she thought were the lingering effects of the wicked brush with the boundaries were no more than caked dirt. She wiped Paloma's slender arms and hands, meticulously cleaning between every tapered finger. Again and again, she rinsed the cloth in clean water and lovingly wiped down her mother's calves, which her dress had not covered during the entire trek, taking added care with her feet.

"Are you about done?"

"With her face and neck, yes," Celeste replied distractedly.

Paloma shifted on the cot, causing them to freeze and stare at her yet again, but she merely let out a restful sigh and continued to slumber.

"We need to hurry," Celeste whispered, taking down the sheet on the bed and fluffing Paloma's pillow for her.

"You sure muddled things up this time." Nahia clucked her tongue sympathetically, the little crease between her eyebrows denoted her concentration on the maple leaf, twice the size of Celeste's hand, that the faery had imbued with glamour so that all the dust accumulated on Paloma's dress would cling to it instead.

Having heard no malice in Nahia's voice, Celeste trusted herself to say, "The plan was a very good one." Then, when Nahia looked at her in astonishment, Celeste added, "If only I had known it would end so badly."

"You *did* know! You're just stubborn," Nahia said offhandedly and resumed the dust collection.

Celeste opened her mouth to retort, but finding no valid argument once again, she kissed her mother's forehead instead and plucked one last dried-up leaf from Paloma's hair.

Nahia sat back to inspect her work on Paloma's dress. "He sure looked angry though, didn't he?" she said of the unicorn.

"I thought he might run me through," Celeste admitted in a whisper and couldn't repress a shudder. "If he had, I would've deserved it. I almost killed her, Nahia," she confessed bitterly.

Nahia gave Celeste a commiserating look, the kind she, like Celeste, saved for moments of extreme pain or defeat or shame. Celeste wiped her eyes briskly. "I know, I know," she sniffed.

Satisfied that all the dust was gone from Paloma's white dress, the faery sat back and leaned against the wall. All commiseration had gone from her voice when she said, "I think we can be sure that he'll tell our mothers what happened. And you'll just have to—do you hear me? *Have* to tell my mother that *you* made me do it."

Celeste felt a surge of exasperation. She grappled for a way to change what had happened or, in the very least, to vary the conclusion she kept arriving at, that all the blame rested with her. "Well," she muttered at the faery, "we can't be certain he'll tell. In the first place, how will he communicate it?"

"I don't know. But surely my mother has had conversations with him before, and they seem to understand each other just fine," Nahia said worriedly.

Paloma shifted on the cot again, and Celeste said, "Let's put her up on the bed and go get ourselves cleaned up."

With all the glamour now gone and Paloma's weight back to normal, it was a struggle for the girls to lift her up, but once they got her on the bed, Paloma obliged and groggily rolled over onto her pillow. Although the light of the lamp was too dim to clearly see her features, Celeste felt gratified by her mother's restful breathing and the once again soft feel of her arms and face. *Stupid me. Stupid, stupid me. To have endangered my own mother in such a stupid manner. Oh, but I do hope he doesn't spread the news of what I've done.*

"Let's just wait and see, Nahia," Celeste said soberly, still gazing at the sleeping figure of her mother. "But if it is all revealed, I promise you I *will* take responsibility."

Nahia, who had shifted to the compact size most comfortable to her as soon as Paloma had rolled over, looked abashed for a moment, as if she were sorry she had extracted such a promise from Celeste. In the darkened grotto, the faery's aquamarines gleamed like jewels as she stared at Celeste.

"What? Why are you just floating there?"

"Nothing. Just, um, it's just—can we bathe yet?" stammered Nahia, tucking her turquoise streaked curls behind her ears.

***

18

Refreshed by a long dip in the pond, Nahia returned to Handi Park, and Celeste returned home to find Paloma seated at the small table. In the lamplight, her mother looked puffy eyed from sleep but otherwise cheerful and not in the least suspicious.

"You couldn't catch any salmon?" Paloma yawned.

Celeste hadn't even thought about salmon. She shook her head guiltily. "The water was too warm, I suppose. There were none we could see."

"Yes," Paloma agreed. "It has been so hot these past few days. Well, it looks like it will be just eggs tonight." She smiled, and Celeste mirrored her tentatively.

Later that night, under the covers in their bed, Celeste snuggled close to her mother and kissed her. The unsettling shudders that had been sending that prickly heat from her stomach all the way to her head ever since her foiled attempts at glory were finally letting up. That she had been sweaty, dusty, exhausted, and frightened out of her wits just a few hours before seemed a far away nightmare now that she was clean and relaxed, lying next to her beautiful mother in their cozy bed. She was so grateful no permanent harm had come to Paloma.

"Tell me again about when you met me and when you met the faery court. Please?" Celeste begged.

Paloma laughed in the darkness and gathered her daughter to her bosom in a tight squeeze. "I have no excuse tonight, because I feel so incredibly rested! I can't believe I slept so late!"

Celeste squirmed uncomfortably and gave Paloma another quick guilty kiss.

Chapter 2:

A Personal History

The story had been told to Celeste on many a night and in much the same way every time, always with the same omissions, always with the same ending. She smugly thought that Nahia could never even dream of brewing a potion so effective in soothing or transporting Celeste as this story did. In Celeste's mind, it was a spell tenderly cast in the dark by Paloma's smiling voice and by the beatings of her mother's brave and resilient heart. Nestled in Paloma's arms, where Celeste felt most secure and strong, with an eager smile quivering on her lips, she listened as the tale thus began.

"The joy of seeing you on that first morning took away whatever fear and discomfort I may have had the night before. And, of course, of those discomforts, you need never find out." At this, Paloma would tickle Celeste until she giggled, and it never occurred to Celeste to inquire further on that point. "Someone was looking out for us that night, someone who chose to rescue me when he saw I had been left to die and guided and aided me through much peril to bring us to our new home. Indeed I decided that I must have died, for surely I had been reborn." This part would inevitably cause Paloma to pause and ponder, but only for a moment, and then the smile could be heard in her voice again. "I awoke with sunlight already streaming through the entryway, as there was no door then or sweet jasmine to block the way, and I found myself on a bed of leaves on the ground. We were inside a cave carved directly into a hillside, for I could smell the rich scent of soil and see the roots of shrubs and trees protruding from the ceiling of our new dwelling. On the ground next to me, someone had placed a delicate glass bowl filled with berries, which I ate, and a pitcher of water, which I drank—too exhausted to even consider their source or whether they might harm me, which they did not. Then I heard you stir, and I looked upon you in the light of day for the first time." This merited a reminiscent kiss on the forehead, which Celeste received with a smug grin. "You nursed contentedly and fell asleep on our bed of leaves, which, of course, by then I had dressed a little with pieces of my tattered nightdress. While you slept, I studied you, beginning my inspection from the top. I found that Her Highness, the princess, had a perfectly round head covered in soft, blond baby fuzz." Celeste smirked in the dark. "Your tiny eyebrows were perfect little arches, and your cheeks, Ah! *What's this?* I thought, putting my finger lightly on your cheek."

"My father's birthmark!" Celeste chimed in.

"Yes, your father's birthmark, and just like his, it was right under your right eye. But I had to look at it closely that first time, because I thought perhaps it could be a speck of dirt or even blood left over from the birth. But it was not. In fact, you were wondrously clean."

"And so were you."

"And so was I, although I knew that I had fallen asleep exhausted and covered in sweat and scrapes and dust. What possible explanation could there be for our current state of spotlessness?"

"Faeries!" Celeste blurted.

"Yes, well, but we're not quite there yet." Paloma smiled and stroked her daughter's hair. "We were alone; I was certain of that. Yet there could be no question that we had been tended to while we slept, and although I still had my night clothes on, the same ones in which I had stumbled miserably through the woods the night before, they themselves were clean! I realized that in addition to our cleanliness, the sweetest scent of citrus flowers, quite unexpected given our circumstances, clung to our skin. I sniffed my own wrist and confirmed that indeed I had been rubbed down with some sort of ointment. *How in the world did I not feel this?* I wondered. I lifted your tiny foot to my lips and planted a tickling kiss on its chubby little sole. It too smelled of citrus flowers." Paloma reached under the bed covers for Celeste's foot (she was already laughing in anticipation of this). When Paloma had managed to tickle Celeste's foot, which was much larger now, she went on, her voice full of laughter. "Of course, this woke you up, and you instantly put your tiny fist in your mouth and began sucking on it hungrily. As I watched you, I again noticed that little birthmark beneath your eye, which reminded me of your dear father, and I couldn't help exclaiming, 'You seem so far away, my darling husband ... so far gone.'" Celeste wriggled tensely under the covers, because she knew what was coming.

"And I was so startled to hear the croaky voice coming out of my throat. Instantly I realized that what I thought had been a nightmare was, in fact, reality. Afraid to speak again in that horrible voice, and much as I dreaded it, I began to understand and accept that I had indeed been cursed. I remember thinking then, *Surely we should be dead.*"

"But we were not," Celeste hurried her along, anxious for better parts to come.

"I think you've heard this story one too many times, young lady," Paloma protested.

Celeste simply snuggled closer to Paloma, grinning broadly in the dark. The wooden chime in the doorway sang its hollow song in harmony with the breeze.

"'Indeed we are not dead, and in time, this tiny little mark will aid in retrieving what is rightfully yours, my sweet princess,' I said, kissing those chubby little feet of yours peeking out from under my torn night dress. 'I shall call you Celeste,' I said, trying as best I could to ignore the voice coming out of me, along with the other distressing aspects of the curse such as the unsettling feel of my tongue against the vacant places in my gums. For not only had my voice changed, my whole appearance had been stolen from me. Yes," Paloma hurried along when Celeste made to interject again, "by a foul, ghastly witch! But I would *not* be injured beyond my body! So I said, 'We will figure something out, you and I,' and I swallowed all the bitter tears someone weaker than I might have shed."

Celeste relaxed her limbs.

"And so several days went by in similar fashion: I cared for you in the safety of our small cave, not daring to venture out lest the withered body fail me. And every morning I awoke to a pile of berries and nuts, sometimes even beautiful orange blossoms cleverly linked together to make a subtly perfumed necklace."

"That had to be Usoa," said Celeste, thinking of the long ropes of flowers Usoa, a venerable old faery teacher, would produce while Celeste practiced her weaving.

"I know it was," Paloma assured her. "But sometimes the offerings were more extravagant: there would be sweet, juicy plums; crisp, red apples; occasionally, a tender peach; and as always, plenty of cool water. But it was the nightly rubdowns with scented ointments that continued to baffle me the most. Try as I might, I could not stay awake to detect our stealthy caregiver, and I would wake up every morning giddy to discover that you and I had once again been sanitized without our knowledge. Soon after, I would simply wake up laughing, knowing I had been bathed before I had even opened my eyes, because I could smell the citrus oil under my nose.

"As the strength came back to my borrowed limbs, curiosity began to get the best of me. I knew someone watched over us night and day. I could sense a nurturing and caring presence, forever vigilant, and this made me feel immensely safe in our new world. I confess to you, I indulged in fantasies that it was the ghost of my Bautista, your father, that had brought us here and who now cared for us. It would be so like him, so willful even in spirit, to remain earthbound to protect his family." Celeste and Paloma sighed in unison.

"I rested and doted over you, and you were perfectly content with your surroundings, not lacking in any essentials, thanks to our invisible benefactor. Fully recovered and having grown accustomed to the achy, disfigured body I was forced to inhabit, the day came when at last I felt ready to venture out and evaluate our situation more accurately. So I bundled you up as best I could, and I stepped carefully out of our cave. Through the forest, I carried you, feeling the warm patches of sunshine reaching the ground through the thick branches of the many trees. You squinted in the bright sunlight, and a tiny vertical line formed between your perfectly arched eyebrows, and I found you even more beautiful under the canopy of trees.

"I breathed the clean air, finding a peaceful joy in the beauty around us. The sense of well-being and safety mystified me. Knowing that someone watched over us gave me a serene feeling of belonging, as if a warm welcome had been extended in unspoken words. With you safe in my arms, I walked deeper into the green freshness of the forest, pausing to notice even the smallest of God's creations while I made our way to a clearing from where the sound of water beckoned. Parting the wispy branches of an enormous willow, I found a secluded pond with its own little waterfall. The long tendrils of the willow reached all the way to the ground like curtains, and they swayed in the breeze, making a whispering sound like voices, and the voices said—"

Again unable to contain herself, Celeste quoted what her mother had heard on that morning long ago, and which had been repeated to her on countless restful evenings. "The keeper of the forest has seen your misery, and he is pleased by the courage you have shown." A mild tremor shook Celeste as she spoke the words, because just that afternoon, she had met the keeper of the forest for the first time and face to face under the most upsetting of circumstances. But in the dark, Paloma didn't notice her daughter's discomfort and continued placidly.

"So I whirled on the spot, holding fast to you and wondering if I had indeed heard the words or if I had just imagined them. My heart beat fast in my breast. With every glance, I expected to find an explanation for what I had heard. 'The keeper of the forest has entrusted you and your child to us,' the singsong voice continued, and to add to my distress, I suddenly felt ashamed that I might be seen. You see, in spite of all the evidence, I had not really believed that our secret benefactor could possibly be another person, someone who could communicate with words, and the idea that another human being might see me in such a state was positively mortifying. I held you closer to my heart and tried to hide as much of my loathsome self as I could, but then I heard that singsong voice again saying, 'Bathe in the water, and close your eyes while you do it. Show us your mind, and let us see you as you were before this injustice befell you.' I didn't know what to do. I felt certain my sanity dangled by a thread at that point, and it seemed outrageous for me to help it along by following instructions from the voices that, quite conceivably, might be only in my head. Yet the existence of ghosts and mysterious creatures in the forest could be no less believable than what had happened to me after the death of my Bautista. So I made a decision. I disregarded my concerns and gently placed you on the soft ground; then I boldly took off what was left of the ragged night dress and let it drop at my side. I kicked off the mules whose leather soles were so badly slashed and worn as to provide no protection and minimal comfort. I tiptoed into the water with nothing to cover my skeletal, shriveled body but a long tangle of matted graying hair.

"'You must see yourself as you were and believe the image in your mind to be as real as the water that touches you,' the trees seemed to whisper, and I gave in to the cool tingle of the water lapping at my legs. I turned my face toward the specks of blue sky beyond the dome of branches, closed my eyes, and submerged myself for a few moments, whirling slowly in the clean water. I became aware of a sort of rhythmic pulsation circling my midsection, which then spread up and down my entire body, filling me with an irresistible urge to laugh. I emerged filled with glee, indeed, laughing out loud and oblivious to the hollowness of the body the old witch had left me with. I splashed in the watery paradise, feeling the nagging aches that had plagued me begin to miraculously dissipate. I cast a curious glance toward you and rejoiced at the sight of you safe in your grassy nest, staring wide-eyed at the enormous mobile made up of swaying green branches.

"I closed my eyes again and invited visions of my lost self, of me before I had been cursed. I filled my hands with water and threw it up in the air above my head, letting it splash my cheeks as it came down. I stood there, feeling splendidly happy. That tickling sensation was still with me, you see, and when I opened my eyes, it was sheer delight just to see. But I could also feel an irresistible vigor coursing through me. I didn't have to look at myself to know what was happening; I could feel it. My body became saturated with energy, which my heart pumped through my veins, and within minutes, it was restored in its entirety. The crinkled skin had been washed away. My teeth felt strong and whole in my mouth. Imagine my elation when I heard the familiar sound of my own voice again, and although I couldn't tell you for sure, it seemed to have a new, silvery quality to it, just like my sight seemed sharper and brighter than it had been before. Oh, I felt I could fly if I wanted! But instead, I submerged myself in the water again, craving it and delighting in it. I broke the surface again and ran my fingers over my face, marveling that my skin felt supple and young again. I stared at my hands too, and aside from them being a little pruned, they were my own hands again. I then smoothed my hair and pulled it over my breast; it was my own red hair! Eager to share the excitement with someone, I raced over to you and was startled to spy a shimmering bundle at your side.

"You looked at me in perfect contentment, but nevertheless, I knelt beside you to make sure you were unharmed. Having confirmed this, I turned my attention to the new gift left for us and found it was clothing this time. I picked up one of the garments, and it was, without a doubt, the most exquisite thing I had ever beheld. The only word I could think of to describe it was iridescent. The gown, light as air, seemed to capture the light and refract it into every color of the rainbow, with a hazy luminous quality I couldn't explain.

"And there were tiny beads woven throughout the bodice and throughout the length of the full skirt, which was made up of countless ribbons. The fitted sleeves flared at the elbow, also in ribbons."

"Do you think I'm tall enough to wear it yet?" Celeste asked longingly.

"Not quite," said Paloma. "And no sulking, please."

"How is it you can see me sulking in the dark, but you didn't see whomever placed that dress there in plain daylight?"

"They were very quick, our new friends," Paloma laughed. "But it wasn't just my dress; there was a second gift. A white, very delicate piece of clothing with a rich silky feel to it, soft enough to put on an infant, and that was exactly who it was made for, an infant."

"Me!"

"You. The intricate detail on it baffled me, from the delicate lace on the neckline to the embroidered flowers on the skirt and its sequined hem. It made every royal christening gown ever made pale in comparison, and I could not stop fawning over it. I reflected on the fact that only twelve days before, I had felt my life coming to an end. I had been full of hate toward the witch who had transformed and exiled me, and I had despaired over the misfortunes that had changed my life. But on this new day, I found that laughter came easily once more, as it had during my childhood years, and although I continued to miss Bautista, I truly felt I mourned for him no longer. The sting of tears did not come at the thought of him, and I told myself, 'I now have a child, and a new home has been granted to us, with invisible but caring friends, and I have a purpose and a mission to accomplish for you, my darling Celeste, and for me.'

"So I decided it was best not to question or wonder about the origin or reason for the attentions bestowed upon us, and I accepted them, and although I knew I should go mad with curiosity, I would be respectful of their anonymity. 'Keeper of this forest,' I said, 'I thank you and your woodland spirits for the kindness you have shown me. I am forever indebted to you.'

"No sooner had I finished my little speech than I was struck with the acute notion that the gowns had a very special purpose, a preparation of sorts. Maybe these were the worthy garments we should wear to meet our silent benefactor. But who is our benefactor? Who provided these clothes? To whom have we been entrusted? I could do nothing but wonder.

"I continued to admire the intricate detail again and again, and it was the reproduction of a tulip, in miniscule beads, on the bodice of your dress that triggered the echo of an old idea. It was the memory of a tale told to me by Clemente, my faithful tutor, on one of those nights when, as a child, I had pleaded with him to ignore my strict bedtime and tell me a story instead. He had complied, and the story had begun as follows: There is a day in the middle of summer when one might have a hope to glimpse the royal court of the little people. Clemente's voice had been so earnest, and my young mind had been so eager that I fancied I could see the bewitching little creatures weaving their glorious gowns in magical groves carpeted in spring flowers. You see, Clemente had impressed all that and more upon me, and to seal my belief in it all, he had confided a warning as well: 'You mustn't repeat this, young lady, not to anyone, for the faery folk are very private.'

"Being eight years old, Clemente's stories had become fact to me. Yet much as I thought I had outgrown them, there I was, a full-grown woman, holding my daughter in my arms, and still I struggled to distinguish between childhood memories and reality. But when I looked at what I held in my hands, I could not deny that it was the very gown I had imagined as a little girl so very long ago.

"But I couldn't waste any more time on flights of fancy. I had been, after all, naked this entire time," Paloma said in a playful tone, and Celeste let out the expected giggle. "And I longed to wear the miraculous creation given me. I held the dress by the collar line and stepped into it, pulling it up to my waist; then I slid my arms into the sleeves and pulled them up to my shoulders. It was marvelously flexible, stretching and clinging to my shape like a second skin, except for the flaring ribbons on the sleeves and skirt. I laced the delicate cord at my breast and noticed the pair of delicate woven sandals that had fallen from the folds of the skirt. I slipped my feet into them, and they too were a perfect fit.

"I felt like a woman again, as if my skin were full of radiant sunshine, although I probably looked more like a very well-dressed wild creature, for my hair had started to dry, and I'm sure it was a gnarled red mess all over my shoulders and back. But I didn't care. It was the dress, with its ever-changing shades, that continued to bewilder me. I thought it alive with the color it absorbed from my skin or the red in my hair or the green of the trees. I also noticed that the dress was made up of single threads, thick and thin, braided together with impossible precision, almost as if by tiny, magical hands. And those threads, they were not the coarse types found in regular clothing or even the finer threads that had been purchased for my royal apparel. They were something altogether different, something I had imagined as a child, and again Clemente's factual voice seeped into my mind: 'Exquisite gowns, worn by faeries to welcome the summer solstice … Woven with threads of sunshine and moonbeams that faeries alone know how to catch…' So real had Clemente's voice been to me at that very moment that I looked around, expecting to see a sprite or a gnome at any moment. But I saw no one.

"I dressed you in your perfect little gown and held you at arm's length to admire you properly. You looked absolutely divine, and I knew we were ready—I didn't know for what, but we were ready. Then something unexpected happened," Paloma said, propping herself up on her elbow, and Celeste did the same, for this was the most exciting part of the story. "My heart began to beat faster, and I held you close as I looked around in disbelief. I blinked numerous times, but the vision would not go away. I was seeing what I had not seen before. They were perched on the trees and sitting on the soft grass—"

"Faeries!" said Celeste.

"Some peeked from behind boulders or tree trunks with their luminous eyes and hair to match, while others floated about, inspecting us in return—"

"Faeries!" Celeste called out again.

"I felt my knees wobbling, but I steadied myself lest I drop you, and I made a respectful bow to our general audience."

Celeste took great pleasure in quoting her mother, and she knew by heart every single expression uttered by Paloma during the long ago experience they were knee-deep in remembering at the moment. "I thank you, my lords and ladies," said Celeste most reverently.

"And once my eyes had fixed on the most regal creature in the whole assembly, I continued in these words—"

Celeste now sat up straight on the bed, and her eleven-year-old voice rang true and clear in the dark grotto. "'Your Majesty, I am but a humble guest in your forest, and I despair for not having anything to offer you in return for the magnificent gifts you have bestowed upon us.'"

"Then," filled in Paloma, "the regal creature with the amethyst eyes and lavender locks acknowledged me and nodded in return, saying—"

"'We will care for you and your child, as the keeper of the forest has commanded, but I must beg you to remember that the gift given you carries boundaries, and only here, in the Realm of Faery, will you retain your true form.'" Celeste finished her recitation, and had it not been for the darkness in the grotto, Paloma would have noticed an alarming change of color and expression in her daughter's countenance. How could Celeste have doubted the story she had known by heart since she had learned to speak?

"I was heartily shaken by this announcement. I confess that I believed this creature's magic had overcome the witch's spell entirely. But I went on listening, hoping my disappointment would not be so obvious as to offend anyone. When, as if reading my thoughts, the faery queen spoke again." Paloma paused, and Celeste started (she had almost missed her queue.)

"'You have been harmed by a powerful one, indeed, and what has been done, I cannot undo,'" Celeste quoted soberly, again disagreeably assaulted by the memory of her own stubbornness and officious behavior. "I am Oihana, sovereign of this troop," Celeste finished flatly, and Paloma picked up the thread again, oblivious to her daughter's discomfort.

"I bowed respectfully, and then this glorious creature and her troop retreated into the woods, gliding smoothly between the trees like colorful orbs made up of ribbons and porcelain limbs, leaving me alone to come to terms with the fact that, no matter how I looked at it, you and I were trapped in this forest. I started back to the grotto with you in my arms, deep in my troubled thoughts, when I felt an unequivocal presence, something watching us, and not the faeries who had just left us. At first I saw it out of the corner of my eye, and a low tremor swept through me, rooting me to the spot yet compelling me to turn, and when I did, I was face to face with a magnificent white horse.

"At that moment, the distinct sound of hooves rang in my memory, and I recognized it as the sound that had accompanied me through the terror and pain on that fateful night. Each time I had stumbled, or when the pain of labor had been such that I lost myself, I would come back to my senses, and the soothing sound of hooves on the moist earth would fill the air around me. How could I not have realized that before? I looked intently at the noble horse; he was white and beautiful, and I recognized him as the keeper of the forest, my ghost, my savior. He pawed the ground with his formidable legs, and when he tossed his proud head, I gasped at the sight of that fearsome, spiraling horn atop his forehead. The keeper of the forest. A unicorn."

Celeste sighed uneasily. After the day's experiences, the word "fearsome" conveyed a whole new range of meaning to her, but either owing to the exhausting traipsing in the heat or her youthful ability to forgive herself, the unsettling feeling inside her had been reduced to a mere handful of butterflies in her belly, which rather than fluttering about, seemed more concerned with finding a place to settle down for the night. Celeste dropped down onto her pillow and stretched lazily.

Paloma felt around in the darkness for Celeste's face, and having located it, she placed a kiss on her daughter's forehead. "Now, my dear, it is time to sleep," she said firmly.

"Good night, Mamma," Celeste yawned widely. "I love you."

"I love you more."

Chapter 3:

Glamorous Fifteen

That was the summer in which the weather changed, as is sometimes the will and whim of Mother Nature, marking the beginning of a drought that would last seven years. Of course, no one suspected anything was amiss until fall came and went, and they realized they hadn't seen the first snow yet. The faery court conferred on the issue, and after a strenuous week of stargazing, reading signs, and recording the activity of woodland creatures day and night, Nahia brought the news to Celeste that Oihana and the troop elders were in agreement: they were entering a drought. This got Celeste and Nahia to thinking, with a wealth of narcissistic superstition, about whether or not they had had a hand in it.

"He was so angry with us," said Celeste, speaking of the keeper of the forest and the recent encounter they had had.

"You mean with *you*," Nahia corrected her.

"Fine then. He was so angry with *me* that he must have decided to punish *me* and everyone else along with *me*."

"He *is* powerful enough to affect the weather, that's for sure," Nahia remarked sagely, which only validated Celeste's fears and reinforced her conviction.

They decided not to share this intelligence with anyone, for it would certainly lead to the question of *what* had brought on the keeper's wrath, and the answer to that question was something Celeste and Nahia had agreed never to reveal. The possibility that Celeste had been responsible for bringing the drought upon the realm became a fact in their eleven-year-old minds, and it remained so, even after the seven years had passed.

Certain of her guilt, Celeste experienced a great many involuntary shudders and suffered unexpected flushed cheeks when she heard anyone lamenting over the lack of rain or the abundance of dust. Indeed everyone seemed to be having a hard time keeping their homes clean, even underground in Handi Park. Celeste's guilt, however, was not of a crippling kind, and soon enough, she was only mildly concerned about the drought. By mid-January, they had had several light dustings of snow, and things appeared to be as normal as ever. Life in the realm continued at its easy pace, and Celeste found joy in wandering far and wide within the keeper's territory, always with Nahia coasting at her side. The girls considered it their job to scout every corner of their boundaries, and as a result, no one knew the realm better than they.

What the girls called the realm was a pear-shaped basin insulated from the towering granite ridges of the Pyrenees by a range of wooded hills. The basin tapered to the west, and there sparkled Moon Dancer Lake, with its sea-green water and white, sandy shores. To the east, where the basin was most rounded and the hills were not quite so steep, the marshes teemed with bugs, birds, and exotic plants. But the places Celeste and Nahia frequented most were within the arboretum, in the expanse between these two very defined regions, all within a couple of miles from the grotto Celeste called home. There was Paloma's pond, a mere twenty-minute walk from the grotto along the path lined with elderberry bushes. There was the underground miracle of miracles as Paloma referred to it, or Handi Park, as it was known by the two hundred faeries who called it home. To the north and west of Handi Park, there were caves to explore, animals to chase, tame, or play with, and always new springs to discover, some hot, some cold, some smelly, but all wondrously exciting and fun to plot, for Paloma had given them the assignment to chart the realm, and Celeste and Nahia had taken to the project like bees to flowers so that within a month, they had (with fair accuracy) sketched the realm on a large bed sheet and had labeled every location they had ferreted through thus far. The map hung on the back wall of the grotto, and over supper on Fridays, the girls would target their weekend destinations.

Any given day held varied experiences for Celeste and Nahia, some they enjoyed while others they merely endured. There were arithmetic lessons, reading and writing too, with Paloma by the pond. Once a week and during special events, there were viewings of the night sky with Oihana in the celestial observatory in Handi Park. There were hours to be spent sitting before the loom in the grotto with Paloma or in Usoa's workshop in Handi Park, surrounded with spools of freshly spun silk. During cool winter evenings, they could sweat to their heart's content in the steaming hot caldera, the deepest chamber in Handi Park, with its dark granite walls glowing like embers by the light of the firing ovens. There the girls watched the burly Arnaud, with his blazing orange eyes and his bare, coppery chest glistening in the heat, while he melted quartz and sand into glass. He taught them how to mold it and blow it into bubbles that would harden into the exquisite goblets and dishware to be used throughout Handi Park. Thus occupied, Celeste and Nahia's days had turned into weeks, the weeks had turned into months, and the months had turned into years hurriedly, when grim jobs awaited the girls, and slowly, when they were burdened with anticipation.

Four years into the drought, one such burden of anticipation struck Celeste and Nahia, causing time itself to come to a disobliging standstill, or so it seemed to them.

On the first day of January, Celeste awoke with a chill exactly at ten minutes past midnight (Paloma breathed heavily beside her), and she was about to pull the blankets up to her chin and roll over again when she realized that two small, very round aquamarine orbs were floating above her. The shock of such an apparition at such a time and the realization of who it was were instantaneous.

"We will be fifteen this year," Celeste and Nahia whispered in unison in the pitch-black grotto, and it struck them as so funny that they clamped their hands over their mouths to stifle the laughter that came right up to their throats, but all that did was force it out their noses with a loud snort.

"Girls," Paloma grumbled drowsily.

"You're a nut," Celeste whispered laughingly. "You came all the way here just to tell me that?"

"Of course! It only took me ten minutes. But anyway, I'll see you tomorrow."

"Good night then. And watch out for the—"

Nahia bashed into the wooden wind chime hanging from the center of the threshold among the jasmine vines.

"Wind chime," Celeste finished, her voice filled with suppressed laughter.

The hollow shoots colliding with one another made it seem like cyclonic winds were blowing furiously, and it sounded as if Nahia tangled herself more and more with every effort she made to get free. "You need to trim this jasmine," growled the faery, no longer bothering to whisper as she wrestled with the long tendrils that curled down like a curtain. This, of course, only knotted her up even more. "For the stars in heaven …"

Listening to Nahia and vividly picturing her predicament, Celeste tried as hard as she could to laugh quietly, but that only made the bedstead shake, which predictably added to her hilarity. It took Paloma lighting a candle and giving them a stern look for the girls to sober up somewhat. Nahia looked innocently at Paloma from the web of strings and jasmine stems in which she was caught, frozen in the act of fighting them. Paloma had to purse her lips and look away momentarily or else she would have started laughing as well. Celeste guffawed to her heart's content at the sight of the quartered faery.

Half an hour later, Paloma and Celeste had freed Nahia's arms and legs, and they had gleaned the bits of leaves and jasmine petals from her hair. They had also untangled the wind chime, and Paloma cautiously held it to one side while Nahia passed, successfully this time.

"Good night … *again*," the faery called back.

"You too," Celeste giggled as she watched the sea-green orb that was her birth sister disappear between the low-hanging branches of the trees crowding the way to Handi Park.

Back in the cozy bed, Celeste pulled the thick winter blankets right up to her chin and smirked in the dark, thinking about the reason Nahia had left her comfortable bed and come to the grotto at that ungodly hour in the first place. *This summer I'll attend my first solstice celebration*, she thought smugly, then she rolled over and slept another seven hours, dreaming of Moon Dancer Lake and a tall male faery unlike any other she had ever seen, who, just by looking at her, made her heart race.

Celeste awoke with a start. The wintry sunlight already streaked through the doorway, and she lifted her hand close to her eyes, certain she had touched the cheek of that male faery and been shocked at not finding it smooth. She ran her thumb over the tips of her fingers musingly.

Thus began the year its unhurried progression. The mild seasons only added to the nerve-wrecking sluggishness with which winter became spring, and when, at last, spring threatened to turn into summer, Celeste and Nahia thought up and immersed themselves in a fabulous new project to help them speed up the passage of the few weeks left before the solstice.

Since their arrival at the realm, Paloma had enjoyed the pond immensely, and her only complaint had been that it was so far from the grotto. Indeed on countless occasions, she had had to double back for forgotten bath sheets to dry herself with or a comb or even items of clothing.

The thought came to Nahia on one such day when Celeste sent her back to the grotto to fetch pins for her hair: "You're so much *faster* than I. And I'm already in the water," Celeste had pleaded.

Nahia had returned from the errand positively beaming and bursting with excitement over the idea that had entered her mind, but it was Celeste who had acted on it and whose tenacity had seen it through to completion.

They were to build an outdoor boudoir for Paloma.

"I can't believe we didn't think of this sooner!" they said to each other excitedly as they pored over drawings and fabric selections.

Amets and Sendoa (the only male faeries daring enough to involve themselves in a scheme cooked up by Celeste and Nahia) measured and cut the timber that would make up the sturdy wooden frame required. The freshly cut posts were polished and carefully hidden in a thicket close to the pond until the assembly phase began. Meanwhile, Celeste and Nahia worked feverishly on the covers for the structure. They needed six sheer panels: an enormous one for the top, three for the side walls, and two to make up the front. Not being as skillful in weaving, Nahia left that task to Celeste who calculated the size of the panels at about one-sixth of what they would be in the end. Celeste would then weave them, and Nahia, who had recently mastered enlarging objects, would glamorize them into the full size required. The sheers were then sealed with a resin solution Nahia concocted so that not only did they repel water, but they had a delicate, tinted sheen so that from the outside, one could only make out silhouettes. This, they thought, would make it soothingly private for Paloma. The canvas for the floor cover, being more of a slack, rough weave requiring no sealing, took less time to produce than the six sheers put together.

What an ordeal it had been to keep this thing a secret! Especially for Amets and Sendoa. They were required to retain full human height while they worked, because the wood and the precise grooves notched into them could not be glamorized to a larger size later without risking accuracy. At the end of two weeks, however, when all the pieces were complete, Celeste, Nahia, Amets, and Sendoa snuck out during the night while Paloma in the grotto and everyone in Handi Park slept. It took them several hours to assemble all the pieces together, tie the coverings in place, and arrange the many things Celeste and Nahia had, over the two days prior, transferred from the grotto and Handi Park to the hiding place in the thicket.

The measly three hours of sleep Celeste managed that night were no deterrent to her excitement. As soon as Paloma showed signs of waking, Celeste was up and pulling her out of bed. "You must come see, Mamma," Celeste pressed, leading Paloma out of the grotto and down the elderberry lane at a trot. Paloma arrived at the pond, one step behind Celeste, breathless and with a hesitant smile softening the slight frown.

Beside the enormous willow, with its pendulous branches, stood a high-peaked marquee. The two sheer panels that made up the entryway to the rectangular structure had been parted invitingly and were tied with ribbons to the frame posts on either side.

"Welcome to the hall of glamour," Celeste announced with an ecstatic grin.

"Oh, I knew you'd be here early," Nahia cried, blowing in from Handi Park just in time, as she did not want to miss the inaugural visit. The faery floated over to Paloma's available side, and the three of them entered the hall of glamour together, dropping their sandals outside.

"Oh, girls," was all Paloma seemed able to say—over and over.

They stepped into the soft grass covered with the dark green canvas Celeste had woven. The mild air inside the marquee smelled of flowers, and although Paloma recognized everything she saw, Celeste could tell it all looked new to her in this brand new place. Paloma spent the better part of an hour perusing through the various treasures Celeste and Nahia had brought in. Not only were most of their clothes and footwear already in there but also every primping gadget they could ever need—combs, brushes, hairpins, curling rods, anklets, bracelets—all neatly stored in shelves and baskets. It was endless. It seemed impossible that they had amassed so many things over the few years they had been there. There were sparkling jars full of balms, pomades, perfumes, oils, scenting and tinting extracts—courtesy of Nahia, which was why Paloma and Celeste made a quick mental note to use them cautiously, if at all, as they might be experimental drafts. But there were safer things as well, like dainty glass vials full of extracts from their favorite flowers emulsified in oil to massage onto their bodies after each bath.

"I'll keep your orange blossoms well supplied," Nahia promised.

"You are *too* kind, young lady, and please, thank your mother as well, for sparing them."

"What about my hyacinths?" Celeste protested.

"Those grow all over the place, just outside. You can get them yourself," Nahia replied in mock outrage. Orange blossoms were one thing; they came from Oihana's grove in Handi Park where optimal conditions could be manipulated for a nonnative plant. But hyacinths sprouted like weeds. Celeste was just being bossy.

Dizzy with pleasure, Paloma went from one niche to the next, examining every inch of the girls' surprising handiwork. There were bath sheets neatly folded and stacked on a shelf, there was a small settee on the canvas-covered floor where one could recline or sit while lacing their sandals, and she was delighted to find a basket full of crushed petals at the base of the wardrobe to permeate their clothes with their sweet scent. Sighing with pleasure, Paloma blew a kiss to Nahia. To Celeste, who stood grinning at the entryway where she had retreated to better take in her mother's reaction, Paloma smiled most significantly, tears glistening in her eyes. The hall of glamour was a complete success.

Although only for two weeks, the spontaneous boudoir project had taken Celeste and Nahia from the work they traditionally did this time of the year. Since the age of ten, Celeste and Nahia, along with the rest of the faery court, had toiled away in Handi Park for an entire month before the solstice celebration began, spinning silk and weaving patches or sections of costumes for the exalted moon dancers (but never a moon dancer's *full* costume, for so much superior glamour went into its crafting that only the moon dancers themselves saw to the finished product and were very guarded when it came to their techniques and designs, forever watchful of their originality). The moon dancers' performance was the crowning event of the solstice celebration; it was the embodiment of faery spirit expressed through dance, song, and flight. All legends circulating outside the realm were due wholly to a moon dancer's power to enchant and mesmerize; it was they who lured, who could possess a man's soul and hold him prisoner for love or for war, for vengeance or for whim. A moon dancer was second only to royalty.

For five years as minors, Celeste and Nahia had been relegated to threading glass beads in whatever color schemes and sizes were requested of them. They had sorted through pigments and made paint to decorate the tree trunks near the shore and made endless chains of daisies to be used as garlands over the branches. But this year, Celeste and Nahia had left their old tasks to the younglings under fifteen and concentrated on their own costumes, determined to exceed even the moon dancers in ingenuity.

"I caught Ederne coming out of Nere's rhythm and dance hall yesterday," Nahia said out of the corner of her mouth. She had one end of a string pressed between her lips while from the other end she tried to thread two dozen tiny beads for the bodice of her gown. "Nere said that Ederne has decided to become a moon dancer and is working quite *diligently* at it."

"And how is she going to make her costumes, I wonder," Celeste remarked archly as she continued to deftly spin the lilac silk for her dress into a tight spool. "That she can't even twist two threads together is beyond my comprehension. Bulk-made dresses just won't do for a moon dancer, you know."

The beautiful but reticent faery, Ederne, held a permanent grudge toward Nahia because of a fact that Nahia had no control over. Oihana's troop, like every faery troop, was matriarchal in nature. This meant that the title of queen could be passed only to a direct female descendent of the queen, in this case, Nahia. Ederne, being the daughter of Oihana's brother, could aspire to the title only if Oihana and Nahia were to vanish, leaving no female offspring to inherit the title. It had never occurred to Nahia to hold this advantage over her cousin's head, but Ederne, incapable of disregarding her lesser standing, never passed up an opportunity to belittle or injure the young princess.

Celeste also endured Ederne's affronts, simply because she was Nahia's friend and a *human*.

"I'm sure she'll find someone to terrorize into doing the weaving for her, but I doubt it will ever get that far. She's bound to disjoint herself before she becomes a moon dancer," Nahia scoffed and instantly choked. The convulsive coughing caused the string pressed between her lips to drop, and the already threaded beads spilled to the floor where they bounced and scattered with much rattling. "I think I swallowed a bead! A pretty green one too," Nahia cried croakily.

Just then, Ederne poked her head into old Usoa's loom workshop where the girls were working, and coiling a lock of her long red hair between her fingers, she warned Nahia in husky, languid tones, "*Next* time it might be something *bigger* than a bead. If I were you, I would certainly be more careful of what I say … and to *whom*," she added with a look of deep repugnance toward Celeste.

Flushed to the roots of her turquoise-streaked hair, Nahia soared above her seat, and with her hands balled into fists at her hips, she issued a wrathful warning of her own. "Do not threaten me, Ederne. It is you who should take care, and if I were you, I'd be more selective where you bathe and what you bathe *with*, because if I *ever* suspect you have had a hand in any collision or hit or even a near miss involving Celeste or me, you will find yourself enduring the effects of undiluted banewort on your raw flesh!" declared Nahia, swelling impressively before her challenger.

Ederne's irises flared a brilliant red before she stormed away with a brooding glare stamped on her face.

Celeste eyed Nahia suspiciously, but she was also very impressed. "Banewort? How have you managed *that* without poisoning yourself?"

"I dip my hands in a special blend of resin before I handle the stuff. It's like wearing clear gloves, nothing gets through them." The faery would have let the casual reply stand, but noting the concerned doubt on Celeste's face, she added a mitigating piece of information. "Ederne, you realize, is honing her gift for targeting energy quite effectively. You know that twice already I've seen her knock fairies over with just a flick of her wrists. Soon she will be launching unsuspecting victims with surges of well-practiced, deadly force … against trees and such."

Knowing this to be a likely possibility, Celeste nodded her understanding of the extenuating circumstances expressed and found Nahia completely justified in experimenting with the deadly nightshade family of herbs.

As the month of May came to a close, Celeste and Nahia's excitement was positively contagious. The first days of June crept by with last-minute visits to the caldera to make more beads and to Usoa's workshop where, with a spindle in hand, they tapped their fingers impatiently at the slumbering caterpillars, urging them to leave their cocoons so they could harvest the silk, stain it, and spin it into new spools to finish off a collar or a cuff.

Promptly during the second week of June, a formal invitation arrived by messenger at the grotto. It was a clear plaque with a bluish hue to it. The very thick oval-shaped glass, which fit perfectly on Celeste's palm, had a message gracefully written in coral-tinted filaments suspended inside it. Celeste looked at it from the top then from the bottom and from the sides, marveling at the three-dimensional quality of the letters before she read, "Celeste, daughter of Paloma, we welcome you to our summer solstice celebration, which is to take place on the first night of the full moon."

Paloma, who had been reading over her shoulder, said, "That's only ten days away."

Celeste turned to Paloma, grinning broadly and waving the stone in one hand while she did a little boasting jig, then shaking her head, she said, "I still can't believe you haven't been to one. To think you've had an invitation all this time, and you haven't gone."

"I've told you, my *dearling*, when I found out that the etiquette of the Realm did not admit humans or faeries under the age of fifteen to the solstice celebration, I made up my mind to wait until we could partake together."

"But why does one have to be fifteen to be able to go, Mamma?"

"I've told you that too. There is probably so much rampant glamour out there during that one night that it could likely stun little ones to unconsciousness. Even ones who have been inoculated."

Celeste joined in her mother's laughter and again danced around the table with the invitation plaque securely in her hand.

When at last the morning of the first full moon arrived, Celeste awoke feeling agitated, as if she had been trying to sleep the entire night and had failed miserably at it. Ignoring her own bleary eyes, she dashed out of the grotto and through the lush beech forest to the aspen grove. Within half an hour, sweaty, flushed, and with her wild mane stuck with twigs and bits of leaves, she arrived at the clearing where the ivy-covered mound stood. It was eerily quiet there, so much so that it made her squirm uncomfortably to have to wait by herself. She told herself that that was exactly what the enchantments placed there by Oihana were meant to do, to persuade intruders to leave at once, for this was the entryway to Handi Park. But it still made her shudder when it seemed to her that the trees were listening or when she thought she saw something dark and tattered slither out of sight through the tall blades of grass or when a raven alighted much too close to her, only to cock its head inquiringly at her and flat-out try to run her off by aggressively hopping toward her.

"I'm here," Nahia announced happily.

Celeste nearly jumped out of her skin. "Ah! *You.*"

Nahia laughed heartily. "You'd think by now you would be used to this place," the faery chortled. But when Celeste continued to glare at her, the mirth drained from the faery's face, and she said, "Are you ready then?"

"Yes," Celeste mumbled, fighting the smile that was already making the corners of her mouth twitch upward.

Nothing could reconcile Celeste to Nahia as quickly as being reduced to faery size. Celeste simply loved that swooping swirling sensation in her belly, that unrelenting tickle that drove her to the very brink of insanity, and just when she couldn't take another second of it—just like *that*—it would stop. Celeste was reduced to what Nahia called "a more natural size" of about ten inches. That Celeste needed to be this size to enter Handi Park was simply one of the many perks to her frequent visits. Over the past two years, Nahia had become so adept at reducing Celeste's height and dispersing her weight so efficiently that all Celeste need do was hold Nahia's hand and allow her buoyant body to be guided.

Nahia drew Celeste into the mound through the access shaft concealed under the bramble and ivy; the shaft always made Celeste think of a very deep bird's nest, for it was such a tangled mess of roots and twigs. The passageway led into the dome of the atrium of Handi Park, where entire root systems, like a leafless version of the tangled mess on the outside, curled over one another on the rounded ceiling. They alighted onto a suspended bridge extending the diameter of the dome, from the center of which one could truly appreciate the ten stories of exhibition stands notched on the earthen walls below. During the annual harvest fair, Celeste and Paloma would stand on the center of this suspended bridge to gape eagerly at the lively and colorful displays below before proceeding to the wide, coiling promenade connecting the stands. An entire day could be easily spent spiraling the ten stories to the bottom and back up again, ferreting through the treasures on display and listening to the tales told by exotic faeries who came from as far south as Africa. This was Oihana's trading center.

Through the center of the atrium, not bothering with the promenading decks and with Celeste in tow, Nahia swooped down the ten stories at breakneck speed. The faery hardly decelerated upon nearing the bottom, where a bubbling spring in its rectangular pool radiated a bluish light. All was a blur to Celeste, even the circular receiving hall on whose walls were notched the twenty-one doorways to Handi Park, each about two feet in height and all marked with a different-colored lantern fixed to the wall. These doorways led to such places as old Usoa's chamber of looms and weaving, the caldera, the celestial observatory, and the entire urban sprawl of faery dwellings. Nahia whizzed in through the doorway marked with the royal amethyst lantern (Oihana's), and off they sped to the faery princess's chamber, where all was done up in shades of blue and green, making Celeste's summer solstice gown, hanging on the front of Nahia's wardrobe, stand out as the only thing in sparkling lilac. They had given their nearly finished gowns to Usoa the night before so the old weaver could put the finishing touches on each of their costumes.

"Oh, Nahia! What a magnificent job Usoa has done," Celeste exclaimed, gingerly holding her gown and admiring the intricate designs old Usoa had managed with the strings of miniature beads Celeste had threaded for the bodice and the three-quarter sleeves. Celeste grinned broadly, holding the dress over herself and checking in the mirror as she fanned out the full skirt over her legs.

"She *is* wonderful," Nahia sighed in agreement, her round aquamarines misting over at the sight of her own costume. The bodice was a fresh shade of sea-green silk, but the skirt consisted of string over string of glass beads, all in blue and green and every hue in between. The beads clinked a great deal at the slightest movement.

The girls had agreed to ready themselves for the evening at the hall of glamour with Paloma. So they wrapped their creations in silk sacks to protect them, and off they went to meet Paloma at the grotto for an early lunch. Then they were to bathe leisurely in the pond and spend the rest of the afternoon primping. Paloma and Celeste would remain at full human height, and Nahia would retain the compact size more comfortable to her, which also allowed her to stand on the tabletop and get much closer to Paloma and Celeste's faces for a more meticulous job of beautifying them.

While the light of the setting sun still blazed in the western sky, Oihana, with her entourage of six guards donning black tunics and bearing torches that burned with distinctive lilac- and rose-colored flames (giving off their respective aromas) made her appearance at the hall of glamour, dressed in a deep purple shirtwaist dress with a plunging neckline and a narrow skirt that covered her sandaled feet. She wore a high-collared, long-sleeved, silver-spangled coat, and her lilac-streaked hair had been done up in a thick coil of braids at the base of her neck. Her porcelain face gleamed, and her eyes, already luminous in the increasing darkness, sparkled with pleasure at the sight of her daughter and the two humans she was so fond of.

Celeste was a vision in lilac. Her waist-length mane hung loose down her back, but it was held away from her face by a diadem, which Usoa had covered in glittering dust that would soon sparkle under the moonlight. Nahia's sea-green creation gave her a breezy, serene air. Her shoulder-length locks framed her face in soft finger waves, and every single turquoise streak had been misted with a dewy sheen. Her skirt clinked agreeably as she curtsied before her mother. Paloma had chosen a long, flowing gown in ruby satin. She wore her red hair in a loose twist fastened with a comb, and a glittering tangerine shawl trimmed with golden braids covered her delicate shoulders.

"Shall we?" Oihana beamed at them, and when they all nodded eagerly, Oihana and Nahia shrank the humans to the size they would maintain for the duration of the festivities. Arm in arm (Oihana with Paloma and Celeste with Nahia), they were escorted over the treetops of Oihana's well-tended arboretum to the shore of Moon Dancer Lake.

Oihana and Paloma chatted sedately during the ten minutes it took them to unhurriedly get there, while Celeste and Nahia fussed over their coiffures and told each other how much they thought the other sparkled.

"Oh, look! There's the shore already," Celeste shrieked pointing urgently at the resplendent white sands. "And look at all the lights!"

The sharp line where the pine forest ended and the sandy shore began had been lined with stationary lanterns, which, from the air, looked like a glowing half moon. On the sandy side of the lanterns, hundreds of colorful lights darted and ambled in different directions. These were the faery host who, as the dark of night settled in, sparkled with their inner light. Their whole bodies were enveloped in a hazy radiance that matched the color of their eyes and the streaks in their hair. Indeed Nahia and Oihana's aquamarine and amethyst auras were already shimmering vibrantly.

"I can't wait to get there," Celeste whispered to Nahia, giving the faery's arm a fervent squeeze.

On the sand and in the center of the arc of lanterns stood a gleaming white terrace with an ornate balustrade, which had been constructed special, as it would be the first time the queen would be joined by the princess and their two royal guests. Four amethyst torches (burning bright and sweet for the queen) marked the corners of the terrace, in the center of which were four open arm chairs facing the water, each with its own footrest. There were two tables laden with food and drink, and Oihana's parlor maid stood to the side, ready to serve them. The balustrade opened at the front to a short set of stairs that led down to the sand.

As the four of them (and their entourage) descended onto the terrace, Oihana waved at the dozens upon dozens of glowing faeries already assembled and waiting for them. Paloma smiled regally and waved to those she recognized in the large group below. Celeste and Nahia gaped speechless until they alighted (to resounding acclamations) on the pearly glass tiles of the terrace. Enthralled by the lights and the sweet sound of flutes and harps, the girls were scarcely able to hear Oihana's opening speech, and Nahia had to be nudged that she might curtsey in acknowledgement of the applause from the troop honoring her fifteenth birthday.

Celeste could do nothing but gawk. Leaning on the smooth balustrade, she looked at the faery troop, males and females, resplendent in their fineries, laughing and talking with one another. Some walked, some floated arm in arm, while others swayed to the melodies drifting in the breeze. The traces of twilight were long gone, and Celeste watched the hypnotic activity of the multitude of luminous eyes and bodies all around her: blue, yellow, orange, green, silver, purple.

Bom-Bom Bomm! The booming call of the drums startled Celeste so badly she couldn't get her heart to slow down. She hadn't even seen the drummers directly behind the terrace. Bom-Bom Bomm! Instantly all eyes turned to the east with raucous acclamations. Celeste saw that Nahia, Oihana, and Paloma had already turned in that direction, and she followed their example. Bom-Bom Bomm! The excitement crested as a sliver of the full moon became visible, inching up behind the distant, jagged cliffs. Bom-Bom Bomm! The moon rose, bright yellow at first, although it would soon become milky white and before long would bathe everything in its silvery light.

The very air Celeste breathed seemed electrified with their combined anticipation. Bom-Bom Bomm! The lunar disk had completely cleared the ridges to the whooping cheers from the faeries floating about the terrace or standing on the sand. The last beat of the drums hadn't finished resonating through the balmy air when lutes, harps, and flutes struck at once, filling the night with a cadence Celeste couldn't help but move to. The music grew louder, and Celeste and Nahia clung to the balustrade again, watching with a mixture of excitement and envy when a group of adolescent faeries, which included Ederne in a provoking, sheer garment, took off at high speed and raced each other over the lake amid the riotous squeals issuing from the lady faeries partaking in the game. Oihana and Paloma had taken their seats and were absorbed in conversation, drinking wine from dainty glasses and eating from the tray of confections set on a table between them by Oihana's parlor maid. Celeste and Nahia looked at their mothers and then at each other.

"Suddenly it seems like it will be a long night," Celeste remarked, gazing longingly at the faeries who, at the moment, were no more than dots of light on the faraway shore.

"I see what you mean. I too thought there would be a lot more to do," Nahia agreed dejectedly, casting a languid glance toward her mother, as if holding her responsible for their sudden boredom. When Oihana didn't acknowledge her, she turned back to Celeste. "But the moon dancers should be performing eventually, and we know Ederne won't be among them," Nahia tried to console herself and Celeste.

"So in the end what was it?" Celeste revived a little. "Was it the offbeat dancing or the off-key singing? No wait ... Don't tell me ... It was the costume making."

"Well, the official story is that *she, Ederne*, chose to give it up." Celeste let out a derisive snort that Nahia acknowledged with a meaningful nod. "But Nere hinted that she had to let Ederne go, because she kept copying everyone else's moves. The fool hadn't realized that as a moon dancer, she's supposed to channel nature through her, let it flow out of her in the shape of song and dance. I guess she thought it was a routine she could learn."

"So the good news is that we won't have to endure her bragging," Celeste sighed. "Although I do wonder how Ederne would express nature. What do you suppose her feelings would be for the things that surround her? What would that look like?"

"I don't know, but I daresay it would come out as violent convulsions and strident squawks."

Celeste smirked and made to continue the abuse on Ederne. "You're ri—"

"Would you care to race across the lake with me?" Amets said, popping in front of Celeste so unexpectedly that her startled reaction was to shove him away from her.

Sendoa, who had arrived instants behind Amets, laughed good naturedly and gave him another shove to make room for himself in front of the girls, Nahia in particular. "Would *you* care to race *these* two across the lake with *me*, Your Highness?" he said in mock gallantry to Nahia.

The girls looked at the grinning boys, Amets with his warm, amber glow and Sendoa glittering with the silvery light of his eyes, and couldn't suppress thrilled smiles themselves. They turned inquiringly toward their mothers, who had been watching them with sudden interest, and no sooner had Oihana and Paloma nodded their consent than Amets and Sendoa snatched the girls from the terrace with loud whooping cheers, which were readily echoed by Celeste and Nahia.

"Don't you *dare* drop me," Celeste warned Amets, and his laughter rang in the night joining the hilarity of all the adolescents engaged in racing over the lake. A few feet behind them, the countless beads decorating Nahia's skirt sounded like muffled chimes in the wind, and Celeste laughed, thinking that in the morning, the skirt was sure to look like it had missing teeth.

It was past three in the morning when, having been returned to human size, Celeste and Paloma returned to the grotto. Paloma smiled indulgently as Celeste rattled on about what she had seen and heard and done. "Nothing quite like a faery's eyes, how they light up! Why don't our eyes do that? And I never thought Itzal could play the lute like that. I can't believe how fast Amets can fly! He outdid Ederne and her partner and Sendoa and Nahia! You know Nahia must have been helping Sendoa! But Amets outclassed them all, even with me in tow! And, oh, Mamma, were not the moon dancers extraordinary?"

"I do believe you won't *recuperate* from this anytime soon," Paloma said laughingly while tucking the blankets around Celeste who continued to chatter about costumes and hairdos. "But *I* intend to have some sleep tonight, so would it be possible to continue the reliving of your raptures over breakfast?"

"Oh, alright." Sighed Celeste.

Paloma kissed her forehead, and Celeste wished her good night before rolling over onto her pillow, where she continued to stare wide-eyed in the dark, recalling every detail of the sights and experiences the night had afforded. Before she dropped off to sleep, Celeste had made up her mind that the evening's most significant experience had been the races over the lake. She closed her eyes and shuddered pleasurably, remembering the speed with which Amets had carried her across the lake and back; the feel of the wind on her face and through her hair, which became a tangled mess behind her as they sped this way and that; the strength of his arms when he heaved her up in the air in celebration of their victory and caught her again as if she were a feather. And Ederne's displeasure that Celeste, a *human*, had defeated her at a faery game. Celeste chuckled into her pillow, remembering Ederne's surly departure from the lake, and she drifted off to sleep with a smile on her face.

***

Celeste looked forward to and enjoyed two other such celebrations, and when the seventh summer of the drought came to the realm, it found Celeste grown into a statuesque beauty of eighteen, with a dark blond, waist-length mane and skin tanned by the sun. She had large, brown eyes with flecks of gold that could blaze with temper or emotion in turn. This, she considered an encouraging resemblance to the eyes of faery. Celeste still bore her father's mark beneath her right eye, and she exuded health and vigor, whereas Paloma was being decimated by the effects of an illness that had devastated her the previous winter.

Chapter 4:

A Son's Duty

For seven years, the sky above the western Pyrenees had been cloudless, depriving the valleys below of even the hope of precipitation. What little moisture they did receive blew in with the coastal breezes in the shape of light dustings of snow in the winter and scant showers in the spring. But these did nothing to slake the thirst of the land that had been parched for so long.

A fair distance below the lofty cliffs sat the Spartan fortress of St. Michel atop a hill, from where it dominated the once fertile valley surrounding it. St. Michel was divided from its neighbor, Santillán, by a river whose white waters had been a sight to behold in years past. Now the sun-bleached boulders littering the river bed baked in the sun with no hope of wetting more than their middles, for the water level was the lowest it had been in over four decades. The vast measure of land belonging to St. Michel ranged over several miles of sparkling oceanfront to splendid mountain peaks. It encompassed meadows that could still have been called lush only two years ago, distressingly shallow riverbanks, and groves that were verdant no longer.

Until her son, Etienne, came of age, the widowed queen Elise had governed St. Michel alone, with only the memory of her beloved husband, Edmond, to sustain her. To honor him and to augment their only son's birthright, Elise ruled with an eye on efficiency and a frugality that she not only preached to others, but also abided by within her household. Predictably, St. Michel had flourished over the years and now endured valiantly through the drought. Her subjects were proud to call her their queen.

The loss of his father had deeply affected Etienne, a boy who, until the very day of Edmond's death, had been known to have an easy humor and a smile always at the ready. Etienne had loved and admired his father with all the fervor a five year old could muster, so it was no wonder that in order to fill the void left in his heart, the young prince had gravitated toward a man Edmond had appreciated and respected in life. This man was Baldomero whose cinnamon skin and dark, deep-set eyes contrasted sharply with the mop of white hair crowning his venerable head. His eyebrows and thick whiskers, under which a kindly smile always lurked, matched the rest of his hair.

Where horses were concerned, Baldomero had been King Edmond's right-hand man. There was no one the king trusted more with the care of his prized animals than knowledgeable, old Baldomero, a true horse whisperer, not one inducted into a clan through the rituals of some clandestine order or taught by some self-proclaimed master, but a true descendant of the people of the horse, a Bedouin. From Baldomero, Etienne learned the ins and outs of stable work while building a strong body for himself. During the first years after Edmond's death, Etienne eagerly performed any menial task assigned to him by Baldomero, simply for the opportunity to brush down the horses or feed them grain from the palm of his hand. But by his tenth year, Etienne had tired of stable work and hungered for the more responsible and rewarding charge of working or assisting in the breaking of colts. So he told Baldomero to bring back the boy whose place Etienne had taken, but only to do the shoveling and cleaning of the stalls, because the horses were not be touched by anyone but Baldomero or himself. It was during the prince's tenth year that Baldomero, certain of Etienne's love for a certain black stallion, gave the horse to him to call his own. "Surely your father meant for it to be so," he told Etienne.

The black stallion, with the dashing forelock and socked legs, was now his, not his father's, not the kingdom's, it was Etienne's, and he named the intrepid animal Al-Qadir. Although the prince didn't say it, Baldomero had but to look at him to know that the gift of that horse had meant the world to the ten-year-old boy, and old Baldomero knew why.

Etienne also knew and felt it keenly, as he would never forget that morning long ago when he and his father had taken their routine walk to the stables before breakfast to see the horses. There they had found Baldomero in a right state of agitation, his face ashen in spite of his cinnamon skin.

"I had suspected it, sir, but now I'm afraid it is done," he had said, shifting nervously on the hay-strewn floor. "Your Arabian mare *is* pregnant, and I'm certain the foal has been sired by a feral stallion," Baldomero confessed in painful distress.

But Edmond had not been angry. Instead, he had patted Etienne's back and given him a knowing smile that said, "Watch this." The young prince reacted with a grin of his own. Then, to Baldomero, Edmond said probingly, "A feral stallion you say?"

Baldomero nodded mortified.

"Hmmm. I think I know exactly what stallion that is," remarked Edmond with a playful wink to Etienne, even though he continued to pace ominously, much to Baldomero's unease, "I have seen him come out of those faraway hills several times before," he said, pointing to the distant woods east of them. "He carries himself proudly, that one, and with a pleasing sort of determination. Very muscular. Well proportioned. He looked to be about ... fifteen hands, wouldn't you say?"

Baldomero nodded some more. "A fine specimen, sire, if only he were properly groomed."

"Yes ... very fine, and very civil, I might add, as he's been coming out of the hills repeatedly. It would appear that the stallion has been properly *courting* my mare. Wouldn't you agree?" Edmond had turned to his son with this question, and Etienne felt the pressure of his father's eyes bearing down on him. He hesitated momentarily, but the sort of twinkle he had seen in his father's gaze prompted him to nod eagerly.

Edmond clapped Etienne on the shoulder, sealing the verdict. Just like that, Etienne knew the prized mare had *not* been disgraced, and her life would not be endangered, as the foal she carried need not be sacrificed.

Baldomero had also detected the king's intrigued, rather than censuring, demeanor over the affair and became visibly more relaxed. "Of course you are right, sir," Baldomero put in, suddenly feeling encouraged. "Your Arabian mare is not an imprudent one. No Sir. She would not choose a horse that was less than worthy."

And so the unborn foal was saved, and Edmond promised Etienne great things would come from it.

Etienne remembered that morning with uncanny clarity, because only two days later, his father had died, banishing the ready smile from the boy's face and etching the somber expression on his features that would characterize him for years to come.

The colt was born some ten months afterward during a windy night, and Etienne attended his birth with mixed feelings. He felt sad that his father wasn't there to share in the eagerly awaited event, but he was also excited to at last confirm that the colt would be the embodiment of what Edmond had foreseen almost a year before. The colt was expelled from his mother's body, a slippery tangle of four socked legs and a gangly gray body that would soon become a glistening black coat, or so Baldomero predicted. Etienne looked into the foal's dark, round eyes and fell in love at once.

Within his first year, the colt's spirit and alertness, and the intelligence so evident in his liquid eyes, made it obvious that the father, like the Arabian mare, had had a lineage to be reckoned with.

"Most definitely. Great things can be expected from this one," Baldomero continued to remark.

To call Al-Qadir his own, even after four years of watching him and caring for him, had a considerable impact in Etienne's life. His burning anticipation to see the stallion every day made it possible for the prince to cope with the strains plaguing his young life: there was his beloved, though ever fretful, mother to soothe; there was his sometimes irrational nursemaid to contend with; and there were tiresome lectures to endure, delivered by obsequious tutors who commended him to the queen for his truly considerable academic achievement, though only aiming to obtain Elise's favor for themselves.

Years passed, and at the age of fifteen, Etienne's strict academic routine lifted, and the hours previously devoted to lessons and tutors could be spent on the more practical aspects of his upbringing. Elise began allowing him more freedom; she even encouraged him to tour the kingdom with a minimal entourage. This gave Etienne a deep familiarity with the land and the plight of his people, but it also strengthened his bond with Al-Qadir who, with his tail carried high and his engaging alertness and distinctive gait, carried Etienne on trails or feral landscapes alike, with a characteristic ease surely inherited from his sire.

Etienne arrived at his twentieth birthday, and Elise, with evident discomfort, announced to him that, many years back, an arrangement had been made for him to marry. The news that he was to marry Berezi of Santillán, daughter of Queen Paloma of Santillán, fell on him like a pail full of rocks over the head. Etienne's initial refusal had been so absolute that the wedding, which Queen Paloma of Santillán expected would take place right after Berezi's fifteenth birthday, had to be postponed for an entire year.

But Elise's anxious entreaties and explanations had ultimately overcome Etienne's oppositions, leaving him with a bitter taste of resignation that accentuated his already taciturn disposition and further hardened his chiseled features. Yet Etienne managed to postpone a second wedding date for another year on account of the prolonged drought and its uncertain consequences.

Alas, when the drought entered its seventh year and they were all still managing to survive, Queen Paloma of Santillán pressed for the wedding to take place, hinting that the continued delay would be a most injurious insult to her and to her daughter. The new, non-negotiable date was set for the end of June.

The month of May came to a close with a swiftness Etienne found deliberate and offensive. Time bore him inexorably toward a fate he had been loathing and trying to delay for well over two years and which now stood, like a tomb marker, a mere four weeks before him. At the topmost terrace of the immense rectangular fortress, Etienne, now a fine-looking, though reserved, young man of twenty-three, donning the rougher garb more becoming of a field hand than the heir apparent, gravely surveyed the parched fields stretching before him over to the distant hills now covered in desiccated trees and shrubs.

"Calling to the rain again?" said Elise in mildly relieved tones. "I have been looking for you."

Etienne smiled wearily, but his voice was kind when he responded. "You're always looking for me, Mother. I would think that by now you would be certain that *here* is where I reside, and you would cease having to search for me."

Elise winced at this reminder of their one ongoing quarrel, which revolved around one's privacy and the other's desire to know his whereabouts at every moment. "It cannot go on forever, my son," she said soothingly of the drought.

At this, Etienne turned to her, his blue eyes squinting in the merciless midday sun, his light hair tousled by the sweltering breeze. "No, it cannot last forever, but say it lasts this entire summer. The trees, the already meager crops, the vegetation in general will not survive another year like the last, and we'll lose a cycle, maybe even two. You know we can't outlive that. Our stores are vastly depleted and won't hold up for another twelve months," Etienne declared, instantly regretting the helpless anxiety he saw darkening his mother's countenance. With a despondent grunt, for there was nothing he could do to change the facts, he turned his attention again to the dispiriting sight beyond the terrace.

"Surely something will happen, my son. Surely a change is on the way."

"Something *needs* to happen, Mother, and soon," Etienne replied without turning to look at Elise, thinking angrily of the drought and of his upcoming nuptials.

Having nothing further to remark and with a despairing sigh, Elise patted her son's shoulder before leaving him to his grim ponderings.

As Etienne watched the distant face of the cliffs in the east, the hot breeze suddenly turned into a prickly, scorching wind. A number of flies resisted the strong currents on the dusty balustrade of the terrace, and Etienne suddenly became aware that throughout that morning, flies seemed to have been abundant indeed, a fact that surely heralded rain, or so Baldomero believed. *Could it be?* he wondered. He shaded his eyes with his hand and looked intently at the wispy tips of what appeared to be clouds swirling above the ridges. He glanced back to where his mother had been. Elise was gone. *Just as well*, he thought. *It might turn out to be nothing.*

The hot wind seemed to be sucking all the moisture out of his eyes, and he rubbed them irritably to continue watching the rapid changes taking place over the mountaintop. The gauzy wisps thickened in spite of the considerable wind that he knew flogged the mighty cliffs. There was no doubt in his mind now. A most-promising storm cloud was forming itself up there. A crooked flash of light stabbed a point somewhere behind the face of the cliffs, and the dim rumbling of thunder reached Etienne's ears quite a few moments later. It brought the traces of a smile to his face, softening his otherwise reserved looks. A second, then a third bolt of lightning notched the pewter mass of churning clouds, and Etienne's sharp eyes at once recognized the long-awaited heavy rain trying to pass itself off as a thick haze. *I knew it! We have been delivered!*

The clouds soon spread far and wide over the valleys, and the downpour did not stop for several days. The river swelled once again, and the inhabitants of St. Michel gladly dealt with the excess water and the mud.

During the first week of June, however, reports reached the fortress that a landslide west of the waterfall, near the border with Santillán, had done some damage, and Etienne proposed to assess it at once. A tour of the land was scheduled straight away, and Elise consented to it, because the circumstances justified it, but would not let him leave until she received Etienne's assurances of his timely return. She accosted him soon after their noon meal.

"I won't be dissuaded, Mother. I have an obligation to our people, and I need to surmise their needs that we might take steps to assist everyone as soon as can be."

"Yes, dear, I'm not arguing with you there, but just *when* do you plan to return? Your wedding is to take place on the thirtieth of this month."

With obvious distaste for the mention of the event and wishing he could just say 'I'll return when I'm good and ready, maybe never,' Etienne scowled, and responded curtly instead. "I plan to be back by the twenty-first. Will that do?"

Elise assented, and Etienne headed for the stables, looking riled. "At least one good thing will come of my marrying," he muttered to himself. "I'll have Santillán's abundant supply of tools at my disposal."

Etienne's long strides soon carried him past two curtseying maids, a housekeeper, an obeisant valet, and a stiff-looking butler who promptly opened one leaf of the massive front door for him. Etienne nodded his thanks and was out in the lower terrace where the air was clear and smelled of recent rain. He vaulted over the veranda, and in no time, he had reached the stables, where good-natured, old Baldomero was the only authority he did not resent.

CHAPTER 5:

A JOURNEY OF THE HEART

The smell of clean hay, the low nickering of contented horses in their stalls, and the shafts of sunlight coming through the stable windows in dusty streaks greeted and worked on Etienne with all the efficacy of a calming spell. But it was the muffled pawing coming from Al-Qadir's stall that actually made him relinquish a smile. He knew in his heart that Al-Qadir was just as pleased to see him.

Etienne's features softened directly, fully effecting a detachment from the world outside, simply by walking in.

From the loft above the stalls where he slept, Baldomero, who had watched Etienne arrive and had seen the transformation of his countenance, called out in his intuitive manner as he climbed down the ladder, "It's not just the horse, you know. I'm glad to see you too, boy."

Etienne tousled Al-Qadir's forelock and warmly stroked his powerful neck before turning to clap Baldomero on the back. "Good to see you as well, old friend."

"So you'll be off for the next five days, I hear," Baldomero said with a knowing smile.

"It appears that way," replied Etienne, trying not to grin too broadly.

"Al-Qadir is very well rested," Baldomero pointed out, patting the black, powerful neck of the animal. "How many riders will you take?"

"I don't want to be burdened with more than two: a guide and a horseman to tend to the animals and help set up camp."

"Very well, sir. We have two draft fillies for them that will do quite well, plus a couple, or maybe three, mules to haul provisions?"

"Light on the provisions, Baldomero. I don't want those mules loaded with trappings that would take hours to set-up every time."

"Ah," sighed Baldomero. "That you ate grain like the beasts; that would save a whole mule from this expedition."

"Are you saying I require an extra mule all to myself?"

Baldomero nodded, his thick whiskers twitching with a smile.

"I see what you're getting at. You're saying my tastes are too particular?"

Baldomero laughed heartily at this. "I remember a time not so long ago when a young man swore to never eat such staples as smoked mutton and dark bread after only *two* days out in the wilderness."

"I was only twelve years old then," Etienne protested.

Baldomero wagged his finger teasingly, and casting his deep-set eyes on Etienne, he said in an affectionate voice, "Anyone can see that you *have* grown, and a fine picture you make, sir. But have you *matured?*"

Etienne frowned at this and replied somewhat defensively, "I have outgrown many of my childhood's poor habits if that's what you mean. And I *have* learned to make do when necessary." His frown deepened fleetingly, seeming to mull something over, then with an evasive turn of his head, Etienne added hastily, "But just the same, no mutton, please."

At this, Baldomero guffawed heartily, and Etienne grudgingly joined in.

Before sunset that very day, the two riders were ready, and the three mules were, after all, fairly loaded with supplies, ready to embark on the tour. Baldomero stood by Al-Qadir, holding him by the bridle and waiting for Etienne to say his goodbyes to the queen who fretted because of the late hour and once again reminded him of his promise to return promptly on the twenty-first.

"We'll make good headway in the next three hours, and we'll set up camp before dark," Etienne reassured her, and as Al-Qadir pawed the ground impatiently, he bent down and kissed Elise's forehead respectfully before turning toward the horse. While her son's back was turned, Elise quickly dabbed at her eyes with a lace handkerchief.

Etienne mounted his horse and looked down at his mother who had followed him and now stood beside Baldomero, her eyes shone with tears.

"There is nothing to worry about, Mother."

"I know, dear, I know. It's just that you reminded me of your father just now, so handsome, such a striking figure," Elise said tearfully.

Indeed, except for the whiskers, as Etienne did not care for beards or mustaches, he looked a great deal like his father and very fine with a white linen shirt and leather coat over his broad shoulders and chest. He wore tall, fitted boots over his coarse riding breeches, and his father's sword in its scabbard hung at his left side. His hand caressed the bejeweled hilt affectionately, and understanding his mother's remark, he gave her a sympathetic smile. With one last salute to Baldomero, Etienne clucked at Al-Qadir, and he was off at a brisk trot, followed by his two men and their three mules.

On average, the small caravan covered some twenty miles each day. They slept out in the open or in whatever uncomplicated accommodations were granted them through the kindness of the people they visited. The extended drought and the recent downpour had left many areas flooded, had destroyed entire crops, and had killed livestock. Although he saw that, in general, people were managing, Etienne dutifully recorded the condition in which he found things at every location and took note of the damage he observed and the complaints of the residents of his kingdom. As the number of pages in his journal grew with the recorded needs of his people, Etienne was again visited by thoughts of the single benefit his marriage to Berezi of Santillán had been reduced to—more equipment and tools to help his people rebuild and recover.

The quiet deference of his men gave Etienne several hours each day in which to ponder the very real prospect of the traditional entrapment he currently faced. He thought reluctantly of his future bride, a woman he had only glimpsed on two occasions, because the custom of the times and distance itself hindered the possibility of courtship, and he recalled miserably how, at first, Berezi had seemed pleasant enough. She was certainly beautiful, yet she had triggered a feeling of unease in him. Something about her demeanor bothered him unaccountably.

When he thought of her, he invariably saw her as a pampered creature, overdressed and weighed down with pretentious jewelry. To compound his already ill impressions, there were also things he had overheard, such as his old nursemaid declaring to the housekeeper that Berezi did not care about anything or anyone except riches, and only herself above that. Even Elise seemed displeased with the prospect of having Berezi for a daughter-in-law.

There seemed to be no two ways about it; his bride-to-be had no positive traits he could cling to or be somewhat comforted by. Etienne feared his hands would be full with this woman for his queen. Yet he could not object to the match, as there were no other convenient choices, and he couldn't go against the royal tradition. After all, to join the two kingdoms *would* be a most gainful venture, as his mother had explained, to herself as well as him, on several occasions.

But Etienne did not have to look forward to it, and indeed, he most certainly did not.

Such were the bleak reflections occupying Etienne's thoughts during the first four nights of his tour, and he became even more dispirited when the twentieth of June dawned.

Etienne and his men had covered over one hundred miles in five days, breaking only for two mutton-free meals per day and an occasional bath in whatever newly replenished creek they happened upon. They had seen and accomplished a great deal in that short period of time, and so they started making their way east, back to St. Michel. The two men were eager to return, while Etienne despaired that nothing could possibly deliver him from the grim fate awaiting him.

By midafternoon they had reached their last destination, which was the foothills below the landslide caused by an earlier flood. Etienne surveyed the peak rising before them, golden and restful in the nearing twilight, with a formidable gash on its granite face from where a great deal of water seemed to have rushed through, dragging tree limbs, rocks, gravel, and all manner of debris in its torrent. And, although steep, a wide grade had been created by that flood, and the newly formed slope appeared to grant access (through the face of the peak) to the previously inaccessible cradle of the western Pyrenees. A burning curiosity arose in Etienne, prompting him to that open ridge. Squelching all consideration for any danger such a climb could pose, Etienne ordered his men to set up camp for the last time.

"Unsaddle Al-Qadir for me and brush him down," Etienne said to the horseman. "Feed him, and let him rest for half an hour, and then saddle him again."

The horseman nodded and hurried to carry out the orders given him while the guide looked at Etienne with an inquisitive, raised brow.

"The rounded sections, Al-Qadir will negotiate just fine," said Etienne, more to himself than to his guide, but then he suddenly turned to the man as if he had been addressing him all along and continued. "But the steeps, we should be able to switchback and summit in that manner, wouldn't you say?"

The man gave a start and stammered incredulously. "You propose to reach the top?"

"Yes. It should be no more than an hour's ride, two at best."

The guide eyed the almost vertical landslide and could do nothing but pronounce it unstable at once. "Not advisable at all, sir."

Etienne looked at his man, cocking his head to one side and looking for all the world as if he couldn't believe the guide meant to dissuade him. "In these past days, have you not noticed that Al-Qadir is part goat? Has he not conquered whatever terrain your horses have skirted?"

Taken aback by Etienne's remark and clearly unable to settle whether or not the prince was joking, the guide finally replied, "Sir, if you want to summit, the switchback is the adequate technique."

"Right then. Could you make sure my canteen is full?"

At the end of the prescribed half hour, the two men watched Etienne, who looked fed and refreshed and quite keen to depart, as he mounted Al-Qadir.

"You are *not* part goat," Etienne whispered apologetically to Al-Qadir, out of earshot of his men, and he patted the horse's powerful neck.

"You are sure, sir, that you don't want me to come along?" asked the guide.

"I'll be back in under five hours," Etienne replied and directly turned Al-Qadir toward the base of the landslide.

The two men looked at each other, alarmed that they were being instructed to stay behind and fearing that something might happen to the prince while he was out of their sight. How could they show their faces back in St. Michel? And yet, how could they argue with the prince? "At least there will be a full moon tonight," the horseman said resignedly to the guide as they watched Etienne disappear into the thick brush.

"At least the horse will be able to see where he's going, and he really *is* part goat, you know." Observed the guide sagely.

The two men ate and rolled out their blankets by the fire they had built and prepared to watch Etienne scale the steep grade for as long as the light permitted.

After countless switchbacks and proving the accuracy of his estimations, the end of the hour found Etienne and Al-Qadir entering the cradle of the western Pyrenees through a massive stone gateway. There they had to opt for a more cautious step, as the floor was a veritable quarry littered with broken rock of all shapes and sizes. But having conquered the remnants of this massive erosion, Etienne found himself staring at a range of slopes, heavily wooded in conifers, stretching to his left and to his right, insulating from the rocky ridges whatever was on the other side of them.

"Well, what do you think?" said he to Al-Qadir. The sun was sinking in the west, making the sky a crimson mass above the cliffs. Al-Qadir pulled on the bit in no particular direction, simply rearranging it in his mouth, but Etienne understood it as "That way!" So they traveled a quarter mile to their right and arrived at the mouth of a wide watercourse that looked to have meandered through the shallow canyons between the forested hills. There the watercourse pooled into a deep basin, some four hundred yards wide, where it churned as it filled. Its runoff fell to a similar basin quite a few feet below, and judging by the thunderous clamor of rushing water and the thick mist rising between the fractured walls of the ridge, Etienne and Al-Qadir were standing above the famed waterfall dividing Santillán from St. Michel.

The deep azure continued to creep across the sky over Etienne, and he considered out loud, "Do we turn back to camp, or do we go see what is on the other side of these hills?" Etienne took the horse's noncommittal shake of the head to mean he wasn't ready to return to camp.

The first star began its nightly twinkling when horse and rider started wending their way up the hills and around the vegetation. Al-Qadir walked cautiously, pricking his ears at the sound of Etienne's voice, responding to the slightest pressure of his legs against his barrel and the smallest tug of the reigns. The forest grew denser around them, and it made for a tortuous progress. For the better part of an hour, the air around them seemed filled with the sound of snapping twigs and poky needles. There was an occasional hoof slipping on a gravelly slant, and the creaking of the leather saddle and girth could be heard over Etienne's muttering whenever he was forced to grip, slash, and move branches out of their way, which was often. At last, the dense woods began to thin down, and as they continued their descent, they were rewarded with occasional glimpses of the sky, visibly lighter in the east, owing to the approaching moon, but in the valley Etienne assumed was before them, he distinguished nothing, only a vast darkness. Down Al-Qadir went into yet another gully, and Etienne guided him out of it at a slant. When they emerged, the conifers around them were still dense, but being of a shorter variety, it afforded them a view, and the sight sprawling before them was not to be believed.

While they scuffled with tree limbs and negotiated the irregular topography, the moon had risen, and suspended a mere foot over the horizon, it now bathed everything in its milky gleam. What Etienne thought had been a valley turned out to be an oval-shaped lake at least a mile in length, whose tranquil waters sparkled under the moonlight. He dismounted and found the bottom of the slope to be covered in grass or clover or something Al-Qadir was certainly eager to try, so Etienne removed the bridle and bit and left him there to graze at will while he ventured down to the water, taking in every detail of this unexpected moonlit find.

From his new vantage point, the ridges Etienne had for years regarded as formidable and impregnable appeared to be a massive paling, no doubt molded in lava by Vulcan himself for the sole purpose of preserving this bit of world in its current pristine isolation. Having reached the water and scooped some of it in his hands, Etienne found that it was curiously mild in temperature. He thought that the heat and drought of the past seven years were a reasonable enough explanation. He drank it, and although he would have preferred to gulp down icy water, this went down satisfyingly enough. "It is so quiet here," he said to himself. He ran his wet hands over his hair, and finding several pine needles sticking through it, he distractedly began to pull them out. When he could feel no more debris stuck in his hair, he washed his hands and face and retreated to the cool grass near Al-Qadir, where he stretched himself out to gaze at the dark sky now teeming with blinking stars.

Staring at the vault of heaven above him, Etienne lost track of the hour. His limbs had so welcomed the relaxation, and his mind had wandered so far that when Al-Qadir nuzzled his head, it startled him badly. "Whoa," he called out, springing to his feet and, in turn, startling the horse. Al-Qadir reared, and Etienne bounded toward him to stop the reins from flailing at his side. "Didn't mean to spook you," said Etienne, stroking the horse's neck. "Are you thinking it's time to head back?" Al-Qadir continued to whinny and paw at the ground. "You're fine, boy. It wasn't that bad. You scared *me* more."

Al-Qadir nudged Etienne on the chest, forcing him to turn. "What is—" but his words caught in his throat, because what he saw upon turning, made him stagger backward in disbelief at first and then in irritation. Only minutes before, he had been congratulating himself on finding this quiet haven and had already resolved to keep the knowledge of it to himself, but now an entire assembly of people had arrived, throwing their lanterns into the water and hanging them from trees, as if preparing for a celebration, making an intruder out of him.

"You wait here," he said to Al-Qadir, moodily knotting the reins onto a shrub so that Al-Qadir wouldn't step on them. "I'm going to find out who these people are and where they've come from," he said, trudging firmly toward them. Etienne had not gone twenty feet before he realized that something was immensely wrong. What he had thought were lanterns *on* the shoreline were actually *over* the water, and furthermore, they were moving, seemingly of their own volition, for there was neither barge nor skiff in sight. Etienne's determined steps faltered as the notion of another inconsistency took hold of him. Upon glimpsing the many lights, he had initially and hastily concluded that just as many people *must* be there. But there were none that he could now see. *No lanterns, no people?* He stood stock still, groping for an explanation, urging his mind to take the lantern theory to its most outrageous limits when right before him (another inconsistency, this one having to do with underestimated distance) the smooth surface of the water came to life suddenly and momentarily as dozens of glowing creatures and their reflections, who seemed to have challenged one another to a race over the water, sped past him toward the center of the lake, leaving nothing behind but their buoyant laughter ringing in the silence.

Shaken, Etienne crouched down to remain inconspicuous in the bright moonlight. The racing lights had reached the west end of the lake, and he didn't have time to even hazard a guess as to what they might be before they were speeding back his way. Etienne focused his eyes on one bright green light or lantern or whatever it was that seemed to be faster than the rest and therefore could afford to show off its aerial skills by pausing or slowing down as if to taunt the others. This the creature did barely four yards in front of Etienne, allowing him an eyeful. But what Etienne saw didn't much improve his spirits. The creature's eyes flashed green. In fact, its whole body seemed to be locked inside a greenish orb. Etienne let himself drop the rest of the way to the ground. Sitting there with his knees bent and the heels of his boots wedged securely into the ground, he tried to make sense of what he saw. He shook his head one more time. There was no denying it. He was certain he had seen a very muscular replica of a man no more than a foot tall. His broad chest and brawny arms were bare, and his long hair was untied and hanging down to his shoulder blades. He wore a pair of light-colored trousers that covered his legs down to his shins, and his feet were bare as well. Then a screaming light, enshrined in her own rose-colored orb, careened into the green one's arms, and they spun in the air twice before he launched her higher still with a whooping cheer. All the while, she laughed gleefully. Etienne saw two or three couples do similar tricks, but soon the racers quit their boisterous diversion and made their way into the trees east of where he sat bewildered. Their silvery laughter was already no more than a distant chime in Etienne's ears. The surface of the lake smoothed itself down and innocently reflected the moonlight, just the moonlight. All returned to normal, and for a brief moment, he doubted he had seen anything at all, but the hundreds of lights still on the shore said otherwise. Etienne had not much time to ponder, for soon another set of glowing creatures pirouetted above the water, ruffling its surface in a wild dance that made the air around them positively quiver. Unaware that he had ripped at the ground when he stood up, Etienne now released the clumps of grass and dirt from his fists. He absently wiped his hands on his breeches and looked back toward Al-Qadir, as if expecting some sign of acknowledgement from him, but the horse just nibbled on the dewy clover, undisturbed.

"Those are … They're the …" Etienne began in a whisper, but unable to think of a word or name for "those" or "they," he simply let out a frustrated groan, to which Al-Qadir responded with a raise of the head and a pricking of the ears. Etienne just stood there for a few seconds, his head turning from Al-Qadir to the lake and back to the horse. The whirling creatures doing their dance over the water, he realized, were of the female kind. Unlike the stalwart male he had observed before, the females appeared to be all suppleness and bright transparency. This awareness and the sensation that these creatures incited in him brought back a distant memory. With paralyzing swiftness, the years melted away until Etienne felt he was six years old again, and all he could see before him was the rotund face of his old nursemaid, coercing him to sleep with rough-edged stories of kidnapping and torture, which, as she had vividly explained, had everything to do with children who didn't fall asleep when they were supposed to. "They will come and steal you away," she had said, tucking the blankets around him so firmly that he couldn't move. "They'll turn you into a hobgoblin if you don't behave." She had been convinced that he could not sleep through until morning unless he was properly frightened. "The *faeries*," the nursemaid had said in his ear one long ago night. And the flame of the candle had flickered *just* at that moment! And six-year-old Etienne had flinched under his blankets.

"I'll be damned," he whispered, staring out into the water.

Al-Qadir, who had ambled silently toward him, snorted softly over Etienne's shoulder, although this time it didn't startle him. Instead, Etienne gathered in his hand the reins the horse had untangled from the shrub. "Are you seeing this?" he whispered to Al-Qadir, but the horse just shook his head.

On the surface of the lake, the prismatic gowns of the creatures seemed to catch the light of the moon and refract it into a spectrum of colors surpassing anything Etienne could have ever imagined. They rose higher in the air then diverged in a dizzying spiraling motion, circling wider and wider until they had completely disappeared into the brush, leaving the stage empty and Etienne speechless. He racked his brain for every detail of his nursemaid's bedtime tales. *Were they always about horrible faeries whose sole entertainment in life depended on torturing humans?* he thought impatiently.

"No. She did tell me once about something like this," Etienne whispered excitedly. At his side, Al-Qadir snorted his concern.

"Glamour is the name they give their magic, those faeries," the nursemaid had said importantly, her already large features had been eerily magnified by the flickering candle. "And they bewitch you with their singing, little master, and they lure you to the woods where, even if you scream for help, no one could hear you in a thousand years." Etienne had pulled his bed covers up to his chin. "And they make you watch their dancing, and even if you want to look away, you cannot, because their singing is like an invisible twine that pulls on your eyeballs to make you see what they want you to see. But once you look … Ooooh." Her face had screwed up into a hideous grimace that had struck terror in Etienne's heart more so than the words themselves. "You'll see them for what they really are, with their sharp little teeth and that leathery skin of theirs." At that point, he had pulled the covers right over his head. "I shudder to think, little master," she had said, and her overweight body had indeed been a-waggling.

Until this night, Etienne had had no occasion to recall or even think upon such bedtime delights as he had been subjected to as a child, and much as he opposed the gruesome imagery employed by his nursemaid, now that he was so vividly confronted by it, he longed to explain away the vast differences he was finding between what was transpiring right before him and what the good, old nurse had instilled in him. "Some story to tell a child, faeries pulling your eyes out of their sockets." Al-Qadir pawed the soft grass and snorted in sympathy. Etienne tousled the horse's forelock, and with the first hint of humor in his voice, he said, "I guess now I've done it." The traces of a smile were already softening his countenance. "I have looked, and my eyes have yet to be pulled from their sockets." No sooner had he said this than he felt compelled to blink rather hastily, for his eyes were watering from staring so hard, and although he would not admit it, for a fleeting instant, a part of him *did* wonder if eyeballs had to first dry up before they could be snatched out. "Nonsense."

When he realized that all had been quiet for nearly five minutes, he wondered if what he had already seen would be the extent of it, but he was wrong again. Etienne didn't have time to even think himself disappointed when four creatures, made solely of a diamond-like brilliance, emerged from the water. This shocked him, because up until then, all the creatures had been strictly above the water; some of them might have skimmed the surface with their toes like that fierce male had, but the majority of them seemed happy enough to dart this way and that without touching it. But not these four creatures, still diminutive but perfect in their rounded, supple nakedness with the moon glittering over their wet bodies. "I shudder to think," the old nurse had said in his ear.

Some fifty feet away from Etienne, the lively enthusiasm of flitting lights ambling between trees or from one spot to the next on the shore—in groups, in couples, or individually, as if greeting or visiting one another—suddenly came to a halt. They all turned their attention, as did Etienne, to the creatures hovering over the rippling water. They floated there for a few instants, during which a riveting melody filled the air and a warm breeze picked up, instantly drying their hair and clothes. "Close your eyes, little master. Oooooh! Don't look at their dancing, or you'll be lost forever!" Etienne realized that the wet clothes clinging to their lithe figures had tricked him into thinking they were, well, they had not been naked at all, had they? Feeling a bit sheepish but far from deterred, he swatted away the nurse's warning voice and inched closer to the shore. Al-Qadir stayed safely behind.

These creatures were like soft angels dancing on the lake with their flimsy gowns made of sparkling lace and their softly gleaming eyes. "Mustn't look," the nurse screeched inside his head, but nothing mattered except that the rhythm of the melody should never stop, for if it did, the soft angels would stop, and that would be an unbearable tragedy. "I shudder to think." The nurse's ranting in Etienne's head was growing steadily fainter.

"Can you believe this?" he said to Al-Qadir, wishing the horse would sit back like a person and discuss these matters with him. Never had he longed for conversation as he did on this night, and at the same time, he rejected the very thought of it. Etienne wanted someone to answer his questions and settle his doubts, but the thought of another human sharing in this wonder was unthinkable. He concluded that the only thing to do would be to see, feel, and reason himself through this alone, well, with the nursemaid's faint ramblings in his head for support.

Unable to keep his eyes from the lake, Etienne allowed his legs to carry him toward the glittering sight of those dancers. The eerie song continued. "Moon dancer faeries are the worst," the nurse persisted in his ear, but the unseen choir prevailed. "They're the ones that pull the twine," she said in a panic so faded that he hardly understood the words. Etienne walked straight into the lake, hazily aware that he was up to the tops of his boots in water, but he could not be persuaded to do a thing about it.

The moon dancers skimmed the surface of the lake, a living mass of ribbons, long silky hair, and vaporous fabrics. *With all those ruffles dragging everywhere, it's probably best they're dancing over the lake*, he thought, momentarily distracted by a most sensible, though random, observation. *Otherwise they'd be a tangled mess over the trees.* But the ravishing smiles on the perfect porcelain faces drew him back. Their slender arms swayed in harmony with the delicious melody soaring in the warm summer breeze. "I shudder to think." Etienne rubbed his watering eyes (he kept forgetting to blink), and in the midst of that ongoing saturation of the senses, he caught something out of the corner of his watering eye, something even more extraordinary that managed to capture his attention, making his heart stop then resume with a more forceful beat.

From where he stood in the water, he turned to see if Al-Qadir had noticed her too. "Look," he said, straining to keep his voice at a whisper while pointing east to the figure of a girl, a full-sized *human* girl—he thought she had to be as tall as he—who had come out from within the trees not fifty feet from where he stood.

Al-Qadir chewed on his grass and gave Etienne a look that said, "I'm certain you've seen a *girl* before."

Etienne's heart pounded in his chest so loud that he fancied it would soon draw everyone's attention toward him. Never had he been this anxious, and he couldn't remember ever feeling so disoriented. His mind scrambled to gather his thoughts into a coherent sentence or perhaps even a plan of action, but with increasing alarm, he noticed that he could not even put his thoughts into words. His mouth went dry. "I shudder to think." The thought of his dry mouth made him think of water, and when he thought of water, he realized that a fair portion of the lake was already sloshing inside his boots. This added to his confused state, and when the thought struck him that the nurse might have been right after all, that no matter how pleasant they were to look at or listen to, he had been preyed upon by these creatures, and now that he was thoroughly entranced, they were teasing him—no, they were *luring* him to his destruction—with the likeness of a human girl.

Etienne couldn't move. "I'm done for," he declared, casting his eyes in Al-Qadir's general direction but not really seeing him. It occurred to him that if the mere sight of this girl could paralyze him like this, he was likely to die where he stood should she actually look at him. Unsolicited images involving a gorgon and a useless sword snaked into his thoughts, and instead of putting a stop to such ideas, Etienne resignedly told himself that after this night, all bets had to be off. Reality had been entirely redefined for him. Etienne's eyes remained fixed on the girl, who up until then, had failed to notice him, perhaps because he hadn't moved. He wanted her to see him, he was certain of that, and it seemed a simple enough proposition, so he attempted to backtrack out of the water but found that his boots had sunk into the sandy bottom. He literally had to pull himself out by the boots. With a sinking feeling in his stomach, he pleaded inwardly, *Don't let her look at me just yet.* But the girl turned her head as if summoned, probably by the suctioning sound made by his feet. She looked straight at him while he fought valiantly to keep his balance and make his way out of the water.

He stood dripping on the white, sandy shore in constant dread that he might scare her away. *Should I go to her, or should I let her come to me? What if she doesn't come to me and turns away instead?* His eyes bore on her as these thoughts raced through his brain, and he took in every detail of her appearance as he advanced cautiously toward her. In contrast with all the flouncing, vaporous costumes he had seen thus far, this girl wore a narrow sleeveless dress over her tall figure; the white fabric seemed embroidered in sequins that caught the moonlight with every breath she took. She suddenly turned away as if someone had called her, and Etienne stopped breathing, not daring to take another step without her knowledge yet, at the same time, seriously considering bounding over to her and being nose to nose with her when she turned again. But the fear of possibly causing her to have a heart attack prevented him from sprinting, and he contented himself with an inward prayer: *Please don't go.* Only the side of her was visible to him, and Etienne noted that although the dress reached to her ankles, it had been slit on both sides to allow her more mobility, or so Etienne thought. He was careful not to let his eyes linger on the length of the firm leg visible to him. The milky rays of the moon gave her an intangible quality that kept Etienne in constant terror that she might disappear. At last, she turned back to him, casually tucking a lock of her long hair behind her ear, and he felt certain she was looking straight at him once more. *Glamour is the name of the magic they do, those faeries*, said the nurse in his ear, and Etienne muttered again, "I'm done for." Nevertheless, he stayed his hand, overcoming the desire to check if there were any threads pulling on his eyes.

The song throbbed on, sweet and elusive. And another disheartening thought occurred to him. *What if I'm hallucinating? I could very well be half dead at the base of the mountain having this outrageous fantasy.* And suddenly this seemed like a perfectly lucid explanation. It was indeed more plausible that he had been unable to summit, that the unstable terrain had caused a bad fall, and that he had sustained a serious head injury. He despaired at the very possibility and discarded it most irrationally. *She has to be real*, he told himself, but for good measure, he also pleaded with the forces that be: *Let her be real.* Her features were soft in the moonlight, her cheekbones high, her lips full, and her neck slender and smooth above her straight shoulders. *Please don't run from me.* Etienne continued his advance; these would be the most tortuous thirty feet he had ever walked. Her arms hung at her sides. She stood tall and unmoved by the commotion still taking place over the water. *She must be a faery in human disguise*, he thought, creeping ever closer. The girl was a perfect mask of wild beauty. Her long hair swimming in the gentle breeze, and her eyes, her eyes were hidden from him in the dark, but they didn't glow like the small creatures' did. *If only I could look into her eyes, then I would know. But I'll soon be near enough, and I'll be able to touch her. Heaven help me if I'm hallucinating.* He was so close he thought he could hear her breathing.

She simply watched him, unperturbed and unaware of the madness raging in his mind.

He shifted hesitantly in his soggy boots, not knowing what to say or do. The moon had already traveled to the center of the dome above them, and the thought of time slipped into his mind. He could tell by the moon's position that over five hours had elapsed, and his guide and horseman must be scared out of their wits over what they'll have to say to the queen tomorrow. And at that moment, all his realities tumbled one over the other. Alive and breathing in this place where five hours had gone by, and he had completely forgotten his kingdom, his mother, his duty to his people, and his bride to be. And he realized that by the light of this moon, all his weighty realities had been transformed; one of them in particular had transformed so deeply as to become utterly immaterial. With a smile that softened his whole face, he confessed to the woman before him, "Somehow, I knew I would be delivered."

By way of a response, she raised her eyebrows in two perfect arches.

CHAPTER 6:

NEW EYES

Celeste's eyes narrowed suspiciously as the creature started to come out of the water. The considerable shock she had experienced on initially seeing this apparition had diminished somewhat, but she still felt short of breath, and her heart still beat too fiercely for comfort. Her mind, however, had already begun accounting for this new discovery, and as she had only noticed him when he was already in the water, her conclusions were to be expected and were along the lines of, *Who knew there were merpeople in this lake?* and the even more exciting prospect of, *Nahia will be so cross to not have been the first to find out.* An impish, little smile lit up her face at the mere thought of that, and suddenly she didn't feel tense anymore. Celeste was now determined to find out all she could about this creature from the deep and quickly made up a plan. *First, I have to discover what the merman's attitude and intentions might be.* Celeste went on, not allowing for the contingency that said attitude and intentions might be bad. *Then, I need to find out if the creature will be able to survive out of the water. I hope it can speak the human tongue.* Assuming that he must, or that if he didn't, she would be able to convey to him her intentions, she leaped to the last, more gratifying step of her plan. *That done, I'll bring him before the faery court, where my discovery can be properly acknowledged. Won't Nahia be green with envy.*

Cautiously, the creature continued toward her, and she appreciated the lack of sudden movements on his part. Given all her questions, she was glad for the thirty feet between them, as it would allow her more time to study him. She wondered that he had been able to walk out of the water on legs. *I would have thought that, so long as merpeople were in the water, they wouldn't be able to sprout legs in place of their powerful fins. But then,* she reasoned, *he shouldn't be walking out of the water. He would have to be dragging himself out and lay on the sand until he dried off.*

Of course, said a mocking little voice in her head, which sounded a great deal like Nahia, *it could be that this is no creature from the deep at all. It could just be a human.*

During her eighteen years of life in the realm, Celeste had never laid eyes on a human other than her mother, so the possibility intrigued her powerfully, and although she would never admit it to Nahia, as Celeste was now quickly restructuring her plan, he was more than likely not a merperson. But if he was a human, he certainly appeared rougher than she had ever expected a human male to be. Celeste admitted that she had no reasonable point of reference; in the end, all she had to compare him against were male faeries if and when they chose to take on the full size of a human, but even then, they had never looked quite as *imperfectly* perfect as this man did. Now that he was a mere fifteen feet from her, Celeste detected a sort of roughness in him that she hadn't even conceived of before: the skin, the hair, the clothing—rough, thick, bulky. She had no choice but to conclude that the ethereal beauty of faeries, the kind she was accustomed to, had to be an entirely different realm than that of human beauty. For, make no mistake, although rough, thick, and bulky, the man standing a few feet from her was most certainly beautiful.

He stood almost a foot taller than Celeste, and he wore a thick sort of hide over his arms and torso, which Paloma would call an overcoat. He wore breeches, and his legs were dipped up to the knees in a pair of boots. *Why wouldn't he take them off to go in the water? I know I would.*

Under the glow of the moon, Celeste could tell he had light hair, and she liked that he wore it long, down to the tops of his broad shoulders. While imagining what his hair might look like in the sunlight, a nonsensical image of Nahia's blond curls streaked with her distinctive turquoise hues suddenly popped into Celeste's head. She almost laughed out loud wondering how long ago it had been since Nahia had plastered her head with daisy pollen, foolishly thinking she would be rid of her highlights for a spell, but the pollen had attached itself so firmly to every strand of Nahia's fine hair that she couldn't brush it out or smooth it down with combs. Nahia had washed and scrubbed in a frenzy, but to no avail. She had then resorted to a half-cooked potion, which had reacted poorly with the pollen and had promptly begun to dissolve her hair; whole clumps of it began falling to the ground with muffled thuds. In desperation, Nahia had pleaded for Celeste to hack off her matted tresses before the potion melted all of it down to the roots, and Celeste had obediently cropped the once luxurious locks until the infected hair was gone. The five months it took for Nahia to grow out her hair to a fair length was affectionately remembered by their mothers as the bonnet period.

Celeste smiled at her own remembrances, and she noted that the man seemed to be on the verge of responding with a grin of his own. She liked how that softened his features all over. His straight nose didn't seem quite so stern, and his strong jaw ceased to appear menacing. The moonlight shone on his face, and his eyes were fierce, yet in their expression, Celeste perceived a yearning that sent a delicious shiver up her spine. The mounting curiosity she felt was almost more than she could bear. Here was this human, the first male human she had ever beheld, and she couldn't have asked for a more striking representation. Then there was the question of how he came to be standing in front of her, and how he had managed to fix her attention on himself so effectively, for Celeste was beginning to wish all would disappear except for him and her. (At every moment, she feared Nahia would arrive and spoil everything.) *I wonder if I'm the first human he has ever seen*, she thought eagerly, but all at once, her eagerness turned to apprehension, and the question of *where* he had come from took precedence over everything else.

Celeste was forced to consider that, in all probability, he had come from a world filled with humans, a world like the one Paloma had talked to her about. But over years of not having evidence of it, Celeste had grown to think of that world as myth. But with this myth coming to life before her very eyes and in the shape of this one man, another disquieting realization took hold of her. She could not break out of the boundaries of the Realm of Faery, and in her reasoning, it had followed that people outside the realm could not enter into it. Yet here stood evidence to the contrary, and Celeste could not make out or determine if any, or all, of it posed a threat to her home. Alarming as these thoughts were, she was quickly drawn back to the sight of his muscular arms and powerful legs, noticeable even through his heavy clothes. While indulging in the admiration of his physical attributes and his strange attire, her attention was drawn to the sword that hung by his side, and her mind immediately constructed the qualities of a warrior around him. She imagined him in the sunlit splendor of day and could hardly resist the urge to walk over to him and touch him with her own hands, to find out if blood ran hot or cold in his veins, and convince herself of the reality of him once and for all.

A little voice, she thought it had to be her mother's, said in her ear that she should be cautious; after all, she didn't know what his intentions were. But a much louder voice, she recognized as her own, screamed out that she was through watching. Her legs tensed in preparation, but he seemed to have arrived at the same conclusion and started before she did.

Her heart exploded into rapid palpitations the instant he took those last few steps toward her, and she realized that she had forgotten to breathe. A wave of dizziness swept over her as she took in a lungful of air, but there was no time for concern. He drew ever nearer. Celeste stood there, trembling inside, yet inviting him with every thread of her being. And yet at this crucial moment, when she could have been finalizing the first words she would speak to him or conjecturing his greeting and her probable response, another daunting possibility occurred to her, and its merit was indeed dispiriting. *How did I not see this before*, she chastised herself. *Nahia has to be behind all this*, she thought, casting a resentful look toward the man already at arm's length.

Celeste had never fallen prey to faery glamour, because her entire life had been spent in the company of faeries, so she knew all their tricks, and if truth were told, to her, traditional glamour amounted to no more than a lot of bragging on Nahia's part, at least where humans were concerned. After all, how could Nahia know whether she had the power to send a human into a stupor when she'd never even seen a human. Celeste had always believed that the idea of a faery being able to hypnotize a human was a myth. So she reached a conclusion. *This is Nahia trying to demonstrate the truth of her bragging*, Celeste thought angrily. *Who did she persuade to do this?* Her mind sped over images of the possible perpetrators, but not one of the boys she thought of matched the face of this man. *A faery would be hard pressed to take on human size and alter his features with nothing but glamour. He must be a true human.* She settled it sensibly, and this quieted her doubts. But whether Nahia had a hand in it or not, on this night, for the first time, Celeste thought she really understood what her birth sister had tried to explain on countless occasions, with an unexpected twist, of course. *I'm a victim of human glamour*, Celeste thought comically, and again she smiled.

He stood right before Celeste, so close she could hear the water squishing inside his boots. The tension of the moment seemed to have a paralyzing effect on Celeste, but she couldn't bring herself to worry just yet. At that most intimate moment, however, she felt Nahia's familiar pinch on her earlobe, accompanied by lots of whispered words in rapid succession. *What a nuisance*, Celeste thought, wishing Nahia would just go away, but the faery persisted until her words began to penetrate the thick stupor Celeste had worked herself into, and images began to form in her mind.

"What are you saying?" Celeste whispered out of the side of her mouth, refusing to take her eyes off the man but already feeling an unsettling flutter in her belly.

"Paloma awoke, and she's in quite a state. She calls for you," Nahia whispered urgently.

Nahia's words slipped cold and sharp into Celeste's heart. Her eyes flickered from the man to Nahia and back again. *Nahia would never exaggerate such a fact.* Celeste could feel the air shifting where Nahia fluttered, and knowing that faeries often like to appear luminous at night, Celeste wondered why Nahia had refrained from that small pleasure this evening. *No, definitely not exaggerating. I knew I shouldn't have come,* Celeste thought guiltily. She eyed the man regretfully, knowing exactly what she needed to do.

"Somehow, I knew I would be delivered," he said.

Having no hope of this encounter ever repeating itself, Celeste knew she would forever remember the pleasing sound of his voice and forever wonder what he might have meant with such words as he spoke, but she had to go to her mother.

Celeste could feel Nahia's knees on her shoulder where the faery had perched herself. "Let's go," the faery urged again. When Celeste turned away from the man, Nahia flitted forward to lead the way. Celeste couldn't bring herself to look back. A third possibility had gripped her imagination, and once again, she despaired that it might be the truth. Could he have been a messenger from the underworld, come to tell Celeste that Paloma would soon be … Oh! She couldn't bear to even think it. *Why did I leave her side?*

The previous winter, although mild, had been most harsh on Paloma. She had succumbed to a severe case of pneumonia, and although she pulled valiantly through the most dangerous state, no amount of caring or medicinal tonics had been able to restore her strength. Celeste had hoped that the end of winter would revitalize her mother, but Paloma had remained fragile and withdrawn in spite of the increasing warmth of spring, and Celeste cursed the season for bringing life to everything around them except her mother. Soon came the heat of summer, and Celeste fretfully observed that Paloma's condition still failed to improve. Moreover, she had neglected to take part in the preparations for the summer solstice festivities, an event that had every year consumed their attention, talents, efforts, and imagination for at least two months prior and that culminated in this evening of dancing, singing, and feasting on succulent confections. Since her illness had taken hold, aside from her daily strolls with Celeste, Paloma had completely retreated into the realm of her thoughts. She seemed to dwell in a darkness Celeste could not understand and that Paloma refused to explain. She held tight to her troubles, ignoring her daughter's accusations that she was giving up on life.

Upon approaching the pond, Celeste recalled the easy conversations following the long daily walks with her mother. There were the boulders they had sat on. Under the great oak, Paloma had taught her to read and write in the dirt with twigs and on slates with limestone sticks. How carefree Paloma had been then, and how at peace she had been with the world in those days. But over the past six months, Paloma's spirit had undergone a severe transformation, for she had sensed the finality of her illness and had been overcome with the need to reverse the spell that held her captive. Often Celeste would see her anxiously wringing her fingers or burying her face in her hands in desperation. "Time is so short," she would say to Celeste upon being discovered. "Too short for what, Mamma?" Celeste would ask, and Paloma would respond cryptically. "To get you back."

Celeste felt that her mother's sound judgment would soon abandon her, that if indeed her days were numbered, she was going about it in completely the wrong way, for who would want to live out her last days in torment and uncertainty? But when Celeste called her on it, Paloma would have none of it, and mother and daughter would quarrel.

Celeste missed Paloma as she had been before, and she couldn't understand what had happened to her mother; why such an extreme change? Celeste's biggest frustration had to be that Paloma would not give her explanations that satisfied her doubts. If in eighteen years she and Oihana had not been able to come up with a way to revoke the curse, what chance could there possibly be to discover a way to counter it now? And why did Paloma consider it imperative to accomplish it before she ... Oh! Celeste couldn't even think of it.

Celeste followed Nahia blindly through the woods. They were now on the elderberry lane, closing in on her home, and Celeste recalled with ominous clarity Paloma's waxen complexion earlier that afternoon and the beads of sweat on her forehead. "I think we walked too far today," Celeste had told her. "No, no, my darling, I love our walks," Paloma had disagreed. "And I love our talks," she had added. Celeste had helped her onto the bed and fetched a cup of cool water for her. "But I need to rest now. And when I wake, I must talk to you, Celeste."

Surely the heat had been too much, but Paloma had been in the mood to see for herself some of the preparations for the solstice celebration, and Celeste, even though she knew how it weakened her to walk such a long distance, agreed to take her to the shore of Moon Dancer Lake. There they had sat side by side, listening to the banter of the faeries that were busy making swing seats out of wide fragments of bark and hanging them from tree branches with vines. All the while the faeries had argued about whether or not the bark had been properly cleaned of mites and what a tragedy it would be for the elders to suddenly find themselves covered in bugs halfway through, say, the moon dancers' performance. And should they lace the ivy vines with fragrant flowers? On and on it went, and Celeste and Paloma had enjoyed the early afternoon so much that Celeste forgot her mother was ill. For a couple of precious hours, Paloma had been herself again. But Celeste had had to almost carry Paloma on the way back, listening to the short breaths her mother was forced to take while she, Celeste, could fill her lungs to her heart's content.

"There is something you must know," Paloma had said before she drifted off to sleep. And Celeste had stood watching her and listening to her until, at last, the short breaths lengthened, signaling a heavy, restful slumber. Her brow finally relaxed, and her forehead felt cool to Celeste's touch.

A rustling of leaves coming from the direction of the doorway to the grotto announced Nahia's arrival. "Why don't you go look at some of the dancing," the faery had suggested. "I'll stay with Paloma."

"She didn't do very well today, Nahia. I don't think I should leave her."

"It hasn't been worse than other times, but she's sleeping now, and it's not a restless sleep at all."

"You are right."

"Besides, you don't want to miss the moon dancers this year."

"Oh, no," Celeste smiled tiredly. "It *is* Ederne's debut. We can't miss that."

"Well, I can. I've seen her rehearsing for weeks now. You know, through the hole in the wall of Nere's rhythm and dance hall."

Not even bothering to change the dress she had spent the entire, hot day in, Celeste had gone to see the dancing as Nahia suggested. That she had seen Ederne and had grudgingly admitted that the rehearsals had paid off, and that within minutes of Ederne's performance, she had forgotten all about it, because she had made contact with a human man, seemed events to have taken place so long ago as to make Celeste question their veracity.

Through the thick darkness of the trees above the lane, Nahia plowed on, and Celeste walked briskly in the faery's wake, her feet keeping time with her anxious thoughts and memories. Outside the grotto, Celeste paused, suddenly fearing what she might see upon entering that earth and stone haven Paloma had made into a home for her. But Celeste had never been one to delay.

She walked from the cool night air into the warmth of her home, and the first thing she saw was the unicorn. Celeste felt as if someone had dealt her a horrible blow to the chest, for the unicorn would not be there unless something grave had happened or was about to happen. She quickly turned to look at her mother, and the sight of Paloma—pale and limp against the white linen covering the feather mattress—made Celeste's heart sink even further. In utter misery, she knelt by the bed and rested her head gently on Paloma's hand.

"Forgive me, Mamma," Celeste sobbed.

Paloma raised a shaky hand to stroke her daughter's hair, and Celeste wept wretchedly.

CHAPTER 7:

CELESTE'S DESTINY REVEALED

The unicorn sat like a sphinx at the foot of Paloma's bedstead. The light of the hearth played on his pelt, making him look like an ivory statue rather than a living, breathing creature.

Celeste's weeping, which had filled the cheerless air of the grotto upon her entering, settled into irregular sobs aided by Paloma's tremulous hand stroking her hair.

"My darling, Celeste," Paloma began in raspy tones, for the advanced illness had altered the timbre of her voice. This change had not gone unnoticed by Celeste over the past few months, and even though it seemed to make Paloma self conscious, Celeste thought her mother's voice as melodious and as comforting as ever. She couldn't help loving the sound of it, even when she realized that taking note of it had distracted her from the moment. "Just like a faery," Celeste heard Paloma remark. "Always focusing on sensual things, no matter the circumstances." She also heard Nahia's casual declaration: "Your mother is worried you're turning out to be more faery than human."

The thought that Paloma might be right, that she, Celeste, had disappointed her, made her want to cry all over again. But instead, Celeste choked back her tears and crawled into bed, snuggling next to Paloma as she had done ever since she could remember. "I love you so much, Mamma," she said in a voice wet with tears.

Nahia, who had carefully avoided the wooden chime, hovered just inside the doorway, paralyzed. Apparently the unicorn had arrived while she was away fetching Celeste, and the sight of him now had stupefied her.

Paloma gave her daughter a frail squeeze that told Celeste of her mother's dwindling strength. Yet her words were firm and conveyed determination beyond Paloma's weakened state. "You must choose your own path, Celeste.

You must do what is right and fulfill your destiny. Because in doing so, you *will* find love and happiness."

Paloma had never spoken about choices before, and suddenly this night, she announced that not only did Celeste have a destiny to fulfill, but that she must also choose a path that would bring her happiness. Celeste could think of nothing to say to this opening statement, so she continued to lie still, listening to the soothing heartbeats within her mother's breast, trying to forget that they might soon stop.

As discreetly as she could, Nahia settled herself silently on one of the shelves near the hearth, disposed to listen.

During her more positive lessons, Paloma had repeatedly encouraged Celeste to be confident, independent, and courageous. And, true to form, Celeste had become all those things and was willful to boot. Through the years, mother and daughter had had their share of discord, Celeste always wanting to get her way, and Paloma attempting to moderate her daughter's will. Yet as the years wore on, particularly after Celeste's foiled attempt at breaking the curse that held Paloma captive and estranged from her rightful kingdom, their individual trajectories had succeeded in defining separate goals for them. Celeste's goal would be achieved within the Realm of Faery, as the weaver of wondrous costumes as yet unseen by faeries, while her mother's foremost objective continued to be to end their exile.

"There is something I must tell you," Paloma continued slowly.

Celeste cuddled closer, feeling her heart break as she breathed in the sweet aroma of citrus flowers so distinctly her mother's scent. *It's not possible that she's going to leave.*

"I have never told you exactly how we came to be here, Celeste," Paloma said. "I never saw the need to tell you about the sordid past that has tortured me for years. I was certain we would find a way to reverse the spell that holds me prisoner, and in that conviction, I spared you a truth I hoped you would never have to learn."

Celeste propped herself up on her elbow. "I always knew there had to be more to the story you told me, but it seemed to pain you to discuss it, so I never pressed."

Paloma shook her head. "It didn't pain me, my darling. Rather I wanted to avoid burdening you with every detail of what happened. I didn't want you entertaining ill feelings for the world beyond the Realm of Faery, for the time would come for us to return to our rightful place in the human world, and I didn't want you to reject it."

Celeste rested her head back on the pillow, lost in her thoughts. What she knew of the world beyond the Realm of Faery wasn't much, so she couldn't say she harbored any ill feelings for it, much less reject it. In fact, with a prickly, unsettling feeling, Celeste had to own that she hadn't really considered it at all. She couldn't tell exactly when it had happened, she just knew that for quite some time now, she had had no illusions or designs to live her life anywhere but where she was. So to hear her mother declare that she anticipated a time when they would return to the human world made Celeste squirm most uncomfortably.

"I thought I had all the time in the world to set things right, you see?"

"I know, Mamma," said Celeste, endeavoring to hide the thoughts she felt were a disloyalty to her mother.

"As it happens, all I have time for now is to lay before you everything I had hoped never to disclose."

Celeste felt Paloma's forehead one more time. Nahia's white willow infusion was doing its job of keeping Paloma's fever down, and this eased her mind somewhat.

"Santillán," Paloma began, "lies in the valley below us, east of another large dominion known as St. Michel. It was from St. Michel that a woman named, Arantxa, came to us."

"Arantxa … I never heard you say that name before, Mamma. Who was she?"

"A woman who pretended to be ill and weak and worthy of our pity, but who turned out to have a selfish, greedy intent," Paloma said somberly.

"Is she the one, Mamma? Is she the witch?" How could she have been so disinterested all these years, to not even wonder what the name of this woman was? Celeste shook her head, disapproving of her own indifference.

"Yes, my darling, that is her name," said Paloma. "And she was more cunning and determined than we ever thought her capable. Even after the nightmare of that fateful night, I still could not accept or even conceive of her slyness."

What Celeste knew of that power was that for eighteen years, neither Paloma nor Oihana had been able to devise a way of undoing what that woman had done. Even she, Celeste, had tried it, and seven years later, her cheeks still flushed with shame on remembering the unlucky day when she had questioned her mother's and Oihana's ability to the degree of risking Paloma's life at the boundaries of the unicorn's territory. Celeste briskly wiped the tears streaking her face and silently begged to be forgiven.

The unicorn appeared unmoved at his post at the foot of the bed. Sniffling, Celeste eased back into her listening position, pressed against her mother's body.

"I know that you have learned a great deal while trying to help me out of this predicament. But I also know that things have changed for you," Paloma said, looking intently at Celeste, which made her insides flip uneasily. "You've become so absorbed in the realm of the little people that I wonder if you can fathom a life beyond it." Paloma's eyes filled with tears as she said this, but she shook her head, as if refusing to waste time on what she considered a weakness. "And I don't know what shall become of you alone with the reality I must reveal to you."

"Mamma," Celeste started, but she stopped when Paloma raised a shaky, though quite commanding, finger.

"I must place this burden on you, because Arantxa must not be allowed to go unpunished. You must own who you truly are and take back your place in the world you came from."

Paloma became so agitated that it frightened Celeste. "Please, Mamma. Please."

"No, no." Paloma shook her head feebly. "You *will* have what is rightfully yours, Celeste. You will do this for me. You will do it for your father. And, above all, you will do this for yourself. Do you understand me?" Paloma gripped her daughter by the shoulders, her feverish eyes seeking out the signs of comprehension in Celeste's face, but all Celeste could feel was concern for her mother's trembling hands.

Paloma fell back onto her pillows, weakened and parched, and Celeste raced to the table to fill a cup with cool water for her.

"I cannot let the past die with me," Paloma said faintly, and after taking a drink from the cup Celeste brought to her, she added, "I would see you reign over Santillán. I would have you know and love your father through the warm memories of his loyal subjects and by you yourself bearing witness to his accomplishments. If there are any yet to be seen." Paloma's voice trailed pitifully. "It's been so long, you see. Who is to say what Arantxa has done."

Celeste stood by the bed, the empty cup in her hand and her brows knitted in mute confusion. *Reign over Santillán?*

"Please come lay next to me. I feel so cold."

Celeste did as she was asked and once again snuggled at her mother's side.

"I reproach myself that I didn't spend more time teaching you the ways of the world outside the realm. And the result is that the ways of faery are more deeply engrained in your nature than the ways of humankind. I know that to you, a life outside the realm is unimaginable, and I blame myself."

"Mamma, you have done nothing wrong. And you *have* taught me," Celeste protested

"To read and write, yes. And to make candles out of beeswax or to use a loom. It is all so pointless now," Paloma cried ruefully. "I should have been preparing you for what was to come. I should have had you understand what you will be up against. But I thought I had more time. I thought *I* would be the one facing Arantxa, not you."

The understanding that Paloma expected her to face Arantxa washed frostily over Celeste. Was she to accept this without protest? Yes, an evil had been done to Paloma, but this evil had placed her, Celeste, in a world she dearly loved, a world that fulfilled her expectations in every way she could imagine. Was she to seek out that evil voluntarily? Was she to leave the only home she knew to tangle with unwelcoming strangers? The guilty fluttering in her belly said no.

"Arantxa lived in St. Michel as a reputed healer," Paloma began. "There she brewed potions to cure stomachaches or earaches, prepared cataplasms to soothe inflamed joints, and made predictions for King Edmond and Queen Elise, much in the same manner she later did in Santillán. But the death of King Edmond brought Arantxa's commonplace existence to a grim end. The rumors reaching Santillán were crude and wicked, and I'm saddened to admit that because of their gross callousness, they were very hard to take seriously. You see, it was said that Arantxa had intended to kill Elise, convinced that the queen's death would seal the love between Edmond and herself, a love that existed solely in the murky chambers of Arantxa's brain, where the delusion had originated. But the poisoned water intended for Elise and left in her room had been drunk by Edmond after all."

Celeste gasped in spite of herself. How could Paloma desire her to count herself as one of those wretched beings, enslaved by their own feelings? But Paloma continued with the morbid tale, and Celeste could not stop listening. She felt an enormous truth, as big as the sky beyond the trees, hovered above her, and soon, all the branches would part and Celeste would at last see what had been there all along.

"Upon hearing that Edmond was dead; Arantxa of course refused to believe it and raced to Elise's chamber to see for herself. There she found the queen holding her five-year-old son, Etienne, both of them transfixed with shock, but quite alive.

"In Santillán, the word was that Arantxa had cursed the queen and her son before returning to the dark chamber she inhabited, where they said she took hold of an axe and swung it at every piece of furniture within. Then she tore at her bed covers, all the while shrieking venomously at the stale air in her room. She shredded the dusty curtains with her claw-like nails, and when all that destruction failed to ease her anger, Arantxa went for the numerous vials lining the crooked shelves on the walls, vials containing painstakingly gathered poisons and concentrates so dangerous and potent that when they mixed over the broken glass and cold stone, they reacted badly with one another and caused a fierce explosion. The angry chemical burns

Arantxa sustained refused to heal and would not stop oozing for weeks after. Disfigured, debilitated, and unable to endure the suspicion in everyone's eyes, Arantxa exiled herself to a cave in the outskirts of town, and there she remained until she had healed enough. Attempting a new start, Arantxa left St. Michel and came to Santillán, where what we knew of her was nothing but scandalous gossip. That Arantxa had reacted as vehemently as she did to the death of King Edmond only proved that she had harbored feelings for him, and though everyone suspected her of far more than that, no one could bring forth proof of her treachery."

Paloma paused to clear her throat and take more of the water Celeste readily put before her. Her fever had begun to climb again, and Celeste put another layer of blankets over her to ease the shivering. With increasing distress, Celeste noted her mother's bleary eyes and trembling hands. She poured more of Nahia's infusion onto the empty cup and gave it to Paloma who drank it slowly while Celeste wiped the sweat breaking from her brow. "Please rest, Mother," Celeste pleaded sincerely while kissing her forehead, although, if truth were told, her mind burned with curiosity for more details of the horrors beyond the Realm of Faery.

Paloma shook her head again. "I don't have much time, and this must all be said, my darling."

Celeste took her place back on the bed, remembering that her mother craved the warmth Celeste's body afforded her and feeling immensely gratified to be able to give her at least that small comfort.

"Do you remember when we used to snuggle here, you and I?" Paloma said wistfully. "We'd go on and on about beautiful faeries and evil witches."

Celeste looked at her mother's profile in the flickering light of the candles and hearth. There was the faintest smile on her parched lips, and to Celeste, Paloma looked more beautiful than ever. For a few precious moments, mother and daughter were transported back to happier times: dark, cozy nights in their home, giggling and cuddling with one another in their feather bedstead, dreaming and weaving their own happy tales about the future.

"But that was a lifetime ago," said Paloma. "And I have let us down."

"You haven't let us down! How could you have?" Celeste protested, unable to dislodge the notion that the immense loneliness to follow the death of Paloma was already creeping into their warm bed.

"Never mind, my darling, never mind. What matters now is that you learn all you can about this woman, that you might defeat her and retrieve what is rightfully yours."

Again Celeste squirmed at the mention of this. How could she deny her mother's dying wish, yet how could she agree to it?

"As I said before, what we knew of Arantxa was nothing but rumors. So my darling Bautista took her in, arguing that he could hardly turn her out on the street without sound proof of the actions she was suspected of. Your father was such a fair-minded individual," Paloma paused, losing herself in remembrances, but only for a moment. "A few months after her arrival, Arantxa made her first prediction. She claimed to have seen the future and assured us the child I carried would be a daughter, so she insisted to your father that we transact your betrothal to the orphan prince of St. Michel. Your father found this betrothal to be a good idea, and I admit, I too thought it appropriate," Paloma sighed dolefully. "For the first time since her arrival in Santillán, I considered that perhaps she *had* been a victim, that she *had* been hated and mistreated simply because of her disposition and demeanor."

"Did you say *betrothal*?" Celeste, who hadn't heard anything her mother said after that word, asked with a panicked look on her face.

Paloma gave her a knowing smile and tried to ease Celeste's mind. "Yes, my darling, you are betrothed to Prince Etienne, Elise's son, but let that be the least of your concerns for now." These words were accompanied by Paloma's shaky fingers smoothing Celeste's hair in a calming manner.

This didn't do very much to soothe Celeste's mind. Her heart beat faster, and her cheeks burn with confusion. *Betrothed? Betrothed! That means I have to marry the man.* Incapable of complaining out loud at such a time, Celeste could do nothing but indulge in rebellious thoughts. *I won't ever marry. Not anyone. And certainly not that prince, that human I've never even met.* But Paloma's voice soon called her back to the moment at hand.

"So your father agreed to Arantxa's astute suggestion, not wondering why she was so determined to unite both kingdoms, not bothering to question her motives. And as my pregnancy progressed with no complications, I became distracted with the plans for your arrival into the world, and I let my concerns about Arantxa take second place. Then, during the eighth month of my pregnancy, your father suffered that senseless horseback-riding accident, and his death devastated me. I was so much altered by grief that I failed to seek the truth at a time when our fate could still have been salvaged." Paloma paused again, closing her eyes as if wishing she didn't have to relive her woeful past.

Celeste too felt weakened and anxious, because she knew Paloma wasn't finished, and although she feared the disclosure of the events to come, Celeste could not stop listening, nor could she placate the nagging rejection circling in her mind and pressing to be let out. *I won't be made to marry. I just won't.* She poured more water into the cup and held it to Paloma's mouth, but she only wet her lips with it, and with Celeste's help, she arranged herself into a sitting position.

"I gave in to sorrow, and I lost sense and interest in my surroundings, giving Arantxa the perfect opportunity to carry out her plan. You see, on the night that marked the two weeks since the death of my Bautista, I was awakened with the sting of a harsh slap on my face, but before I could even react or realize what was happening, an acrid-tasting sort of paste was forced down my throat by someone who kept saying, 'This will help. This will help.' In my darkened chamber, and in the confusion of having been thus awakened, that my assailant was a female was all I knew, and although the voice sounded familiar in a very odd way, there was an artificial solicitude in that voice that I should have been able to recognize. But I did not.

"Next she produced a small vial, which I saw gleaming in the dying embers of my fire, and it contained something that looked like water. This she spilled into my mouth, and although I didn't want to drink it, my body just didn't obey me. I imagined the acrid paste still coating the inside of my mouth had something to do with that. The woman filled my mouth with the clear liquid, and then she clamped her hand over it so forcefully that I couldn't even shake my head. The liquid just slid down my throat, and then everything went black.

"When I regained consciousness, I found myself on the floor of a chaise, bound with ropes and being jostled as we sped through the night on an irregular trail. But my head ached so badly, and whatever the woman had given me made me so drowsy that I collapsed onto the floor again, even with all the jarring of wheels underneath me. When I opened my eyes next, I was sprawled on a muddy ravine, no longer tied, with nothing on but a nightgown and a pair of mules on my feet, and try as I might, I could not explain how or why I came to be where I was. It occurred to me then, that I might be having a most vivid nightmare, but the dusty smell of the rocks, water, and dirt on and around me told me otherwise. I looked at the stars peering curiously at me from their perches in the dark sky, knowing they had seen what happened but could not tell it to me. I wondered if they had seen my punisher pulling me up the face of the ravine, over protruding roots and branches. Had they seen her drag me over the rough landscape and leave me on this precarious outcrop, hoping I might roll over and plummet a mile down to my death? Through the terror welling inside me, I imagined all manner of terrifying creatures watching me from within the fissures in those rocks, with their glowing, malicious eyes, waiting to pounce on me as soon as I tried to move. So I stayed there, willing my heart to quiet down while gradually becoming aware of every ache and scrape on my body, feeling the wretched nightgown sticking to me, and wondering if I would be able to stand when I decided it was time.

"When at last I thought myself clear-headed enough to do so, I wobbled onto my exceedingly shaky legs, and trying to ignore the brittle quality that seemed to attend my limbs, I tried to take stock of my position. I stood on a very steep, rock-strewn ledge, and the deafening roar of a waterfall seemed to surround me completely, which only added to my disoriented state. Eerie stories flashed inside my mind, of that young princess of St. Michel who was said to have died there. Her body had been found downstream two days after her disappearance, you see, and some peasants said it had been her broken heart that led her to the waterfall, while others said her love of riding her steed in the dead of night had been the death of her. Still others believed the young girl had thrown herself into the water as a means of escaping an arranged marriage. Whatever the case, the fact remained that for over seventy years, the roaring waterfall had kept the memory of that young girl alive to the inhabitants of St. Michel and Santillán alike. And we all avoided the already hard-to-reach waterfall for fear of her ghostly, beckoning voice.

"On that dark night, though, I found out that the legends were true, and I trembled where I stood when, through the roar of the water, I heard her screaming for help. And knowing what had become of her, my mind produced the most gruesome images of her poor body, forever locked and broken in the water's brutal embrace. And God forgive, Celeste, for one despairing moment, I believed that that water could perhaps bring a welcome end to my own predicament."

Celeste sat up again, her own eyes filled with tears for the expression of guilt on her mother's face. "But you didn't do it, Mamma," was all Celeste managed to say through the knot that had formed in her throat. How much this must have tortured Paloma, Celeste could not imagine, but she understood that the dispelling of all her demons was something her mother needed to do, no matter how painful.

Paloma smiled soberly. "It was you who saved me, you know. Because at that very moment, I felt you stir in my womb, and I knew there could be no such cowardly escape for me, not while another life, an *innocent* life, depended on me. So you see," she sighed, "the only true alternative I had was to endure. But to do that, I first needed to find shelter, and I needed it right away, because my labor pains had begun, and I knew they would brook no delay. Although I still felt light headed, I knew I had to be north from home because of the waterfall. Yet something felt very wrong about that assumption, and I couldn't stop wondering why. I dug and clawed my way away from the sound of water through an opening in the rocks to the top of a ridge thirty feet above me, hoping that the way home would show itself from up there. The satin nightdress hung from me in tatters; it had rips and tears all over it as if I had been dragged over rocks and beaten by swinging branches, which, in my mind, accounted for the many aches and scrapes I had. But there was no time to worry about my ill-fitting clothes or the wretched mules on my feet that kept coming off. I prayed that I could find shelter, that someone would find me, or that I might please, please wake up. Oh, that I could make out what it was that felt so wrong.

"I could not climb more than a few steps without slipping on the gravel and rocks. But when at last I reached the top, all I saw were more mountains; these were heavily wooded with trees and shrubs, and I eagerly scanned the darkness, hoping to glimpse a path or a trail, but there was none, no shelter, no people to help me. Crestfallen, I slumped down to the ground at the base of an enormous boulder against which I rested my back. At that moment, I heard that woman's voice in my head again, 'Do not dare return,' she said. 'You are now an outcast.' The woman had uttered these warnings before leaving me to die. But why? And how did she manage it? There I sat, floundering inside my own mind, trying to decide between what was real and what was imagined, knowing a revelation lurked just outside my reach. The first contraction overtook me and brought me back to the pressing matter of finding shelter, and it was at that most hopeless of moments that I saw what I thought must be a ghost, which, of course, you know who that was."

Celeste nodded. "The keeper of the forest."

"I wondered if I was hallucinating and tried to quiet my thoughts. It was then that the muted roar of the waterfall, which had surrounded me earlier, confounding my senses, reached my ears coming from somewhere most definitely lower than where I stood. This brought on a few seconds of complete lucidity, and at last I hit upon the source of my confusion. You can imagine my shock when I realized that I had not been on either of the accessible locations to the waterfall, not on the east bank and not below it. 'Good Lord in heaven. I'm *above* the waterfall,' I cried, knowing that this fact defied all probabilities. But I scarce had time to question how I hadn't realized it right away or how my captor had managed to get me there or how long it had taken her to do it, because I realized there was an even more horrific element to incorporate into the hazy representation of my current state.

"The words I had cried out buzzed around my head like an angry wasp, demanding that I listen to it, and I felt instant horror when I realized that my voice was not my own. I screamed in agony, but when a croaky yelp came out of my throat, my hand flew to my mouth, and I thought I might go mad. I shut my eyes tight, but in the inky darkness behind my eyelids, all I could feel was my hand clamped over my mouth. But it was bony and rough. And my mouth! The lips felt leathery and thin, and the tongue lolling inside it went through the vacant spots in my gums where my teeth had perhaps rotted off! Then and there, I recognized Arantxa's voice coming out of me. The hand clamped over my mouth was Arantxa's. The body I was in was Arantxa's. Arantxa was my punisher and my captor. Again she laughed in my head. "It will help," she had said, and I thought I would go mad when I realized it had been *my* laughter coming out of her mouth. And when she told me I was an outcast, it was my voice that rang in the air even after she left me. I could certainly have screamed then, no matter what it sounded like, but the pain of another contraction in my womb obliterated those horrific realizations, and I clung to that boulder, gasping for air. When the contraction stopped, I collapsed, exhausted and despairing that I would die in this darkness, but a distinctive equine nicker, which at once startled and relieved me, said otherwise. I reached for the keeper's neck and stroked the long, coarse mane there, and he allowed it. When that second nicker came, I had a clear notion that he meant I should ride him, and this I did. He was the only help I perceived as available to me, and he carried me into the wooded hills, while again I wondered how I came to be above the waterfall and how much time had gone by.

"I could no longer hear the waterfall, and I didn't care to determine how far from it I had been carried. I was simply thankful I didn't have to walk anymore, and when not breathing heavily through a contraction, I was aware of the dense foliage we were moving through, so different than the bare rocks I had been abandoned on. Into a cave I was carried, and the keeper of the forest deposited me on a soft bed of leaves." Here Paloma stopped, exhausted. "The next part of the story, you already know by heart." She sighed, closing her eyes, rallying her strength.

Celeste gave a faint smile. Yes, the next part of the story she knew by heart, and what a wonderful story it was, nothing like its sinister, cruel beginning. The image of Paloma as she had been that night, shriveled, frail, and disfigured, haunted Celeste more than ever, because she had seen it with her own eyes. *What a fool I was to have done what I did all those years ago.*

When she looked at her mother again, it was with renewed admiration and understanding that she had survived such an ordeal.

Paloma remained silent, staring off to a point far beyond the darkened walls of their home. Then, as if arriving at a timely conclusion, she said, "You know, it wasn't until that night that I realized I knew the truth about Arantxa, but I had been so wrapped up in my self-pity, I didn't care, and I didn't do anything about it."

"Oh, Mamma. How can you say such a thing," Celeste wailed. "You couldn't have known. No one could," she protested.

Paloma put her fingers on her lips, pressing Celeste to be silent, and then her words poured out of her in one long thread. "They told me the horse that carried my Bautista to his death had been mysteriously startled by someone or something, causing it to rear and buck. But *that* could not have been enough to throw your father off. It was the fact that the leather girth had come apart, you see, because it had been deliberately worn down. So when the horse lost its footing, my Bautista lost his balance, and when his saddle gave way, he plunged down a ravine.

"It was Arantxa who wore down the harness. Only days before, the stable man had questioned her as to what she was doing with the king's riding gear, and she had fumbled with excuses, saying that she thought it was her horse's tack she had in her hand. And I was told of this incident, but I ignored it," Paloma said, unable to hold back her guilty tears. "Then Arantxa shamelessly claimed to have witnessed the incident from afar. She said she didn't realize who it was, and I believed her, Celeste, I believed her."

Celeste squeezed her mother's frail hand in desperation.

"Now I am certain that Arantxa was indeed *there* and not just watching from a distance, for her ultimate plan was to do away with Bautista and then dispose of me," she whispered, shutting her eyes tight to squeeze out the tears clouding her vision. Her lips pressed together in a desperate effort to not let her sobs escape her.

Unable to console her or ease her evident remorse, Celeste cuddled closer to Paloma, and they cried on the same pillow, their foreheads touching. Celeste felt a strange darkness invading her soul. Knowledge and revelation would not always be bright as she had once thought.

"Celeste." Paloma swallowed hard, trying to steady her voice. "The night Arantxa abandoned me here, I discovered something else. At first I thought it a hallucination, a horrific trick of the mind, after all, my head was so muddled, and there was no moon that night, but I am certain of what I saw, and based on that, I've come to realize the magnitude of her scheme. Not only had Arantxa used her powerful magic to take my body and leave me trapped in hers, but on that night, as I lay sprawled on that ravine, I saw her standing on the edge of the cliff, silhouetted against the white waterfall behind her, and she did the most unusual thing, Celeste. She placed her hands on her hips, and she arched her back, much like a pregnant woman would, no, *exactly* as a pregnant woman would, to relieve the strain of her belly."

Celeste looked at Paloma slack jawed.

"Her clothes were wet, as were mine, and when she arched her back, her figure was exposed under the clinging fabric. I saw that her womb was just as swollen as mine," Paloma said breathlessly, tightening her weak grip on Celeste's hand until she saw in her daughter's face that she understood the implications of what was just said.

Celeste in turn was appalled at the truth sprawled before her. To imagine the scale of Arantxa's cleverness! Knowing what she knew of faery glamour,

Celeste could almost accept the possibility of Arantxa being able to change her appearance, but to maintain the illusion over years? That was a more complex achievement, and as Paloma had already explained, it obviously involved witchcraft. Arantxa's artifice baffled Celeste, for she could now see the whole scheme with great clarity. With the grisly narrative fresh in her thoughts, Celeste felt her entire existence become unhinged. The various events described by her mother made room for themselves in her mind, making connections she had never made before. *My father is dead, my father whom I never even met, and whom I'll never have the opportunity to meet, because he was murdered.* Everything around her seemed to undergo a peculiar change. Suddenly the walls of the grotto that had always protected her seemed to close in on her, smothering her. She tried to shake off the notion that the wonder and enchantment she had always taken for granted and that awaited her just outside her door was no more than a veil, cunningly designed to blind her from what lay beyond the unicorn's boundaries. The realm had forever been her home, and to Celeste, nothing could have been more real than that. Yet on this night, she felt the reality of that other world—Paloma's world—as something palpable, something that lived and breathed as surely as she did. The world Paloma had been cast out from, and the myriad details related to it, invaded Celeste with such strength, and impressed themselves in her heart and mind with such force, that her view of things had been irrevocably changed.

Conclusions followed thought with great rapidity in Celeste's brain while Paloma looked on, until at last she saw what she had hoped to see, that Celeste understood. Celeste believed. Celeste was enraged.

"Arantxa killed your father. She planned to take over Santillán by becoming me. And she *will* take over St. Michel, because she knew an heiress was on the way—her spawn! That is why she arranged for the betrothal. She will stop at nothing to get her revenge on Queen Elise. If she couldn't have the king, she shall have the kingdom. In her greed and lunacy, she seeks to appropriate what was his. And this means Queen Elise and the young prince are in grave danger. Unless…"

"Unless the true heiress of Santillán should return."

Paloma nodded approval at the hard look in her daughter's eyes.

"And armed with the truth about Arantxa's past and my identity, it is I who can stop her," Celeste said. A mechanical quality steeled her voice as if someone or something outside her was dictating the conclusive words coming from her mouth. She absently brought her hand to her cheek and placed her finger over the small birthmark beneath her right eye, a mark so like her father's, and the only thing belonging to Bautista that she had.

"Yes, my darling Celeste," said Paloma with a painful smile of relief. "But you won't be alone in that world. If he still lives, Clemente, my old tutor, will protect you, and most importantly, he'll believe in you. Remember that."

"I promise you, Mother, that I will uncover this truth so that your pain won't have been in vain," Celeste said. "But I can't, I won't promise that I will live that life, that I will marry." Hot tears spilled over Celeste's cheeks. Her inability to surrender her future to her mother, even as Paloma lay dying, tormented Celeste acutely. She looked guiltily at Paloma through the kaleidoscope of her own tears, and she couldn't help marveling at how beautiful she appeared. Her eyes still held a dim flash of green. Her cheeks were hollow. Her once lustrous red hair hung dull and wet with perspiration against her delicate shoulders. Her lips were blistered from the thirst and fever. But none of that mattered to Celeste. *Hopeless faery weakness for beauty*, she scolded herself. *She's dying, and I should ... I ...* But Celeste was tired of battling with herself. She was who she was, even if she didn't fully understand what that meant yet. And at that very moment, all she could and wanted to say was, "I think you're beautiful, Mamma." She sobbed. "Inside and out, you are beautiful to me, and I love you."

CHAPTER 8:

THE ENDING AND THE NEW

BEGINNING

A full day had gone by since the unicorn came to stay with Paloma, and faeries of every rank came to the grotto to pay homage to the human queen. Paloma mustered a dry smile through parched lips for them or a short remark to acknowledge their presence, and although Celeste could tell Paloma felt honored by their deference, she still restricted the length of their visits, worried that Paloma would drain herself entirely. By evening, Nahia's white willow infusion had stopped working, and Celeste was left with nothing but blankets for when the chills shook Paloma head to foot and cold compresses for when the fever burned her skin.

Paloma's fever yielded late during the second night, giving Celeste a respite from the angst-ridden pattern of chills and spiking temperatures. She curled at her mother's side with a basin full of cold water on the floor near the bed and a cloth floating in it, ready to be wrung and placed on Paloma's forehead. Through grainy, tired eyes, Celeste watched her mother breathe while Amets tended to the fire that warmed them (for the summer eves had turned cool after the rains). The flickering flames lit the grotto's wall cheerily, and Celeste was thankful for it, even though her poor spirits remained unchanged. Nahia floated about, hanging bunches of orange blossoms throughout the room. They were Paloma's favorite, and Nahia had been busy all afternoon gathering them from Oihana's gardens in Handi Park and tying them with green silk ribbons above and around the bed for Paloma to enjoy. The sweet smell of the flowers permeated the grotto, and Celeste smiled drowsily while Nahia looked around with a satisfied grin on her face. Celeste drifted off into a dreamless sort of unconsciousness, listening to the soft noises made by the two faeries.

Near dawn, the unicorn pricked his ears and suddenly turned his head, causing Nahia, who had also dozed off, to raise her head sleepily from the stack of blankets Celeste had left on top of the trunk. The faery watched anxiously as the unicorn stood from his post at the foot of the bed and went to put his soft nose to Paloma's forehead. Her crystalline aquamarines filled with tears at once, and a sharp, vertical line formed between her brows as she looked on. The unicorn began to nudge Celeste awake. Nahia stole a quick glance toward Amets and wasn't surprised to find he had already assumed human height and was standing stoically by the hearth, waiting to be of use to Celeste. His arms were folded over his brawny chest, and the brooding expression in his amber eyes told Nahia he too knew it was over.

Celeste blinked sleepily in the dimly lit chamber, feeling the warm breath of the unicorn on her face. She smiled, but only for a few instants, for she then realized what it meant. Her heart racing, Celeste turned to look at Paloma and fretfully cupped her mother's face in both her hands, attempting to wake her with her touch and almost lifting her off the pillow in doing so, but it was in vain. A sort of revulsion mixed with indescribable fear rose to the top of her throat at the lifeless feel of her mother's flesh, and she gently, though hurriedly, let her mother's head rest on the pillow again. The cold lingered on Celeste's fingers where she had touched Paloma, and she gazed at her mother in terror, feeling that death would claim her life too if she tried to touch her mother again. Instantly rebelling against that thought, she grasped Paloma's hands and rubbed them desperately. She pressed them to her own cheeks and to her chest, certain she could make the warmth of life return to her mother's body. Celeste kissed Paloma's lips, willing her to open her eyes and smile once again. The flickering flames in the hearth played tricks on her then. Had her mother's breast swelled into that old rhythm again? No. Crazed, Celeste rubbed the inert hands and the pallid arms frantically. She kissed the smooth forehead, the wan cheeks. Nothing. Celeste could rouse nothing; she could kindle nothing. She had never known that the life within a person responded to the touch of another living being with its warmth until it plainly and most hideously did not.

Celeste's fingers folded into fists, and she began to tremble uncontrollably. Tears spilled from her eyes in a torrent spurred on by her irrepressible grief. "How will I live through this? I cannot. I just cannot!" she wailed at Nahia who was now hovering over Celeste, clearly wanting to comfort her but not knowing how.

"Oh, Celeste. Celeste," Nahia spurted. "Don't cry like this, *please*! I mean, it's fine to cry, you *should* cry, but I just can't bear to see you like this. I don't know what to do. Tell me what to do," she said, darting over Celeste's head in a dizzying pattern.

"How can I tell you what do to when I don't even know what *I* should do?" Celeste hung her head and sobbed miserably. "I'm not ready for her to be gone. How will I go on without her? How can I go on alone?"

The faery slowed her zigzagging and alighted on the bed. She inched as close as she could to the figure of her friend bent over her mother's body and tenderly smoothed back Celeste's hair that she might see her face. "People will drift in and out of our lives, Celeste," Nahia whispered fondly. "But you know, no matter how painful a departure is, no one is ever *really* left alone. You, least of all. I'm here with you."

Amets, who had been edging closer to Celeste, came around to one side of the bed, where he paused hesitantly when he saw her raise her head. He nodded his solidarity with Nahia's statement.

Celeste looked from Nahia to Amets, and although her frame still shook with sobs, Nahia's words had quieted her considerably. She wiped her tear-stained face and blinked away the copious tears that made the flecks of gold in her eyes blaze yellow against the redness brought on by her crying.

The unicorn nudged Celeste once more, and when she looked at him, the knowing expression in his liquid black eyes flooded her with thoughts, disconnected phrases she imagined would make sense to no one unless their circumstances were dire. She stroked the coarse mane distractedly, wondering if Paloma had experienced the same influx of stirring yet commanding suggestions from the keeper of the forest while he carried her to safety on that long ago night. *This is not the end. Your strength will not fail you. This must be faced, and you are prepared. You will endure.*

Celeste rose to her feet, as if waking from a stupor, and she opened the lid of the trunk that still held some of the clothes that hadn't been transferred to the hall of glamour. She picked out a gown for her mother, the very gown she had worn after bathing in the pond for the first time, the first gift Paloma had received from the faery court. Still on the bed, Nahia nodded in silent approval of Celeste's choice.

"I will bring the news to Oihana," murmured Amets. He departed straight away, following the unicorn and leaving the girls to attend to Paloma.

Celeste began the woeful task of dressing her mother for her final journey. Nahia quickly positioned herself above Paloma's head to fix her hair as she had done countless times before. She brushed the thick red tresses until they were lustrous once more and then laced them with sweet blossoms from the jasmine vines. This done, the faery excused herself, communicating to Celeste that she meant to gather the wild flowers Paloma would hold in her hands. Celeste gave a distant nod.

To Celeste, Paloma appeared serene in the sleep of death. The traces of pain were gone from her face. *A sleeping angel*, she thought, arranging her mother's hands over her belly and lacing her fingers. Celeste bowed her head over Paloma's body, and there Nahia found her when she returned with plump white and purple racemes of wisteria.

Oihana arrived within the hour, dressed in a stormy shade of pewter. "All is ready," said the queen of faeries. Her regal amethyst eyes mirrored so much of Celeste's own feelings that she couldn't help feeling Oihana was the closest thing to a mother left to her. Unexpected came the vivid recollection of an overheard discussion between Oihana and the moody, reticent faery, Ederne, who, on that particular occasion, had demanded of Oihana that Celeste and her mother be returned to the human world. "Here is a human," Oihana had said of Paloma, "who has the air of a queen and the grace of a faery, a most compelling combination of character and beauty, which renders her irresistible and powerful." Celeste's heart had swelled with pride for her mother's sake, but Ederne had countered angrily, "To others of *her* kind, perhaps. But what is that to *us*? It is certainly nothing to *me*, and you should be ashamed to have allowed your court to turn into a band of fawning twits over a lowly human!" Oihana's categorical response and the flat tone in which it was delivered had made Celeste giggle in her hiding place. "As you say, it is *my* court and *your* thoughts and opinions about me or it will be solicited if *ever* needed. Know this, Ederne, Paloma, a mortal, has my respect and admiration. There are many a faery who strive for that sort of notice but will never achieve it. You will do well to remember that."

The memory brought a faint smile to Celeste's lips, which Oihana returned. "You are your mother's daughter," said the faery queen as if the same remembrance had touched her mind, and she let her porcelain hand rest on Celeste's tear-stained cheek for a few instants before leaving the grotto to oversee whatever last minute preparations were taking place at the burial site.

In the meantime, Amets returned with a litter he and Sendoa had fashioned the day before. It was nothing like the one Celeste and Nahia had put together all those years ago; this one was sturdy and elegant. Its poles were made out of bright pine, straight and smooth, and Amets and Sendoa had gone so far as to wax and polish them before stretching the vines between them.

"Oh, Amets, this is perfect," Celeste praised him most sincerely.

"Sendoa helped," Amets replied, not wanting to take all the credit. "He will be by later to ... well ..." he trailed off, shuffling his feet uncomfortably.

"To carry my mother to her final resting place," Celeste finished for him, surmising that Amets must be truly upset by the death of Paloma, maybe even for Celeste's sake. "Thank you," she stammered, suddenly flustered by the thoughts going through her own mind and quickly hiding her confusion by remarking on the litter again. "This is *really* beautiful."

"You're welcome," he faltered, looking as if he might want to say more, but a darting look toward Nahia dissuaded him. He managed a sad grin and walked out again.

Celeste and Nahia (who had assumed human height the better to help) took over the litter and cushioned it with feathers stuffed in silk cases, which they then draped with a long, white coverlet before carefully placing Paloma's body on it. They arranged Paloma's locks of red hair like a halo around her face and made sure there were plenty of colorful, perfumed blossoms to make it seem as if she floated in them. There were jasmine petals in her hair, and wisteria racemes held in her hands. There were dark violet petals strewn over her iridescent gown, and spikes of red, white, and pink hyacinths filled every vacant space on the litter.

Upon seeing her mother peacefully asleep on the fragrant and beautifully adorned litter, Celeste's eyes misted over. "I *do* thank the stars for your fastidious approach to detail." To which Nahia responded by swallowing hard and averting her eyes.

As dusk approached, the unicorn and Amets returned to the grotto. Amets fitted the keeper of the forest with a leather harness, that he might guide the weightless litter when the time came. And while Celeste freshened up and changed her clothes inside, with Nahia's help, he reverently fastened the litter to the harness. Amets then twined the leather straps with coils of ivy and morning glory whose blossoms were to remain open as Oihana had commanded. Nahia came out and waited for Amets to finish his work. As he made one last meticulous knot to secure the vines, he glanced at her, and they exchanged a doleful sort of helpless look that, had Celeste seen it, would have assured her of just how much her birth sister and Amets shared in her grief. Having resumed their natural compact height, the two faeries weaved through the trees toward Handi Park to dress for the ceremony.

The unicorn watched them until he could see them no longer, then he stood immovable with the precious cargo in his care, waiting for Celeste.

Dressed in a simple gown of uncolored spider silk, with her hair brushed away from her face, Celeste stood in the middle of the grotto where Nahia had left her. She let Paloma's words of praise, over her skill in weaving the very gown she wore now, wash over her in sweet warm waves as her eyes fell lovingly on her mother's handiwork, from the intricate patterns on the pebbled floor to the living walls covered in Spanish moss and mosaics. Their bedstead was neatly made, their table was clean, and their three chairs were tucked in, just as Paloma would have it. Surely tears should be wetting her entire front, but her eyes were dry. Her home still smelled of Paloma, and she promised herself it would always be so. Celeste closed her eyes. Feeling a serene air take hold of her and knowing she could delay no longer, she walked out into the cool afternoon.

Upon seeing her, the unicorn started down the elderberry lane.

Dimly aware of the familiar surroundings, Celeste walked behind her mother's body and succumbed to thoughts of the people and places in Paloma's past: Arantxa, Bautista, Clemente, and Santillán, her kingdom. She did not notice the golden blaze of twilight beyond the treetops, nor the fireflies ducking lazily between branches. The short walk from the grotto to the grave had become an inward journey into the deepest regions of Celeste's soul from whence came the understanding that she had become homeless and singular in her human nature in the course of just one day. Celeste realized that Paloma, not the realm, had been home to her. This new idea pelted her with the effect of a spiritual scourging as she walked behind the litter containing the body of her mother, but her eyes betrayed nothing of those grim reflections. She paused, because the unicorn paused.

They had reached the clearing at the end of the elderberry lane, already crowded with the faery host in attendance. There was the pond, and to her right was the mighty oak. Celeste found that the faeries had already dug a grave at the foot of it. The unicorn stood still while Amets and Sendoa released the stretcher from the harness; this done, the keeper of the forest retreated to the water's edge.

Upon seeing the freshly dug grave, Celeste only vaguely wondered if, when all was said and done, she would cry until she shriveled up into a brittle fall leaf. A little voice in her head said, "No, you won't." Her eyes darted from one luminous faery to another until her eyes met Nahia's aquamarines, wondering if the faery had slipped her a calming tonic of some sort. *No. She doesn't look guilty.* Celeste looked around to the unicorn, and when their eyes met, she knew at once that the prevailing serenity that held her together, giving her strength and purpose in spite of her loneliness, was his doing.

Paloma lay tranquil beside Celeste, regal in the simplicity of her burial arrangements.

The crimson twilight sky glowed beyond the darkened dome of trees. The soft singing of the faeries surrounding the grave, whether perched on the branches of trees or seated on the boulders damming the pond, broke the thread of her thoughts and transported her to delicious memories of her childhood. It was a song they had often sung for Paloma when she had allowed them to decorate her and play with her long, red hair. Celeste had the clearest vision of her mother sitting on a flat boulder by that very pond, wearing a flimsy white coverlet, as had Celeste. They had sat across from each other, laughing and singing, while Nahia and all the aspiring glamour trendsetters had hovered about them, pinning their hair and letting it loose again, coloring their lips with crushed berries or glittering their bodies with dew. Their lashes were made full, and their eyelids were made to sparkle. They would paint beauty marks on them, only to change their minds and briskly rub them off. Breezily, they would move on to enhance yet another feature, and Paloma would allow this to go on for hours, her clear laughter filling the air, overwhelming Celeste with contentment.

But what will I do without you now, wondered Celeste, feeling a painful knot at the top of her throat, yet the tears would not come.

The faery court continued their melodic singing as the body of Paloma was placed beside the grave by four human-sized male faeries, two of them being Amets and Sendoa. Six females reverently flanked them, their arms filled with more fragrant flowers. It was an eerie sight for Celeste to see so many faeries in human size, for during her eighteen years in the arboretum, she had never witnessed a simultaneous shape-shift of this magnitude; at best, she had seen one or two of them do it, usually at her coaxing or at Nahia's threats, as they are much more comfortable in their compact size.

There stood Amets and Sendoa, side by side at the head of the stretcher, their brows creased with effort and concentration lest they drop the noble queen. She had believed that handsome Amets might have had a soft spot for her years ago, but it hadn't been soft enough to consent to her kissing him. As she recalled the silly logic of that particular circumstance, a small smile fought its way through the solemnity of the moment and faintly played at the corners of her mouth. It seemed so long ago, and like most other circumstances, it had sprung from Nahia's bragging, which inevitably aroused Celeste's competitive nature. "Don't pretend to be wise enough to give *me* advice," Nahia had said. (Celeste couldn't even remember what advice she had been trying to give her.) "To give advice, one must have experience, and what experience could *you* possibly have? *You* haven't even been kissed."

Nahia's silky insinuation had antagonized Celeste to the roots of her hair, and that very afternoon, Celeste had cornered Amets and demanded he take on human form. That done, she had boldly moved toward him and attempted to press her lips against his, not bothering to ask if he would allow it, which was why she had been so shocked and infuriated when, in a panic, Amets had pushed her away.

"What are you doing?" she cried in disbelief.

"What are *you* doing?" he retorted, his amber eyes wide with suspicion.

"I want to kiss you," she told him, exasperated and unable to understand why he, of all faeries, would reject her. After all, he had often shown a marked preference for her.

"I can't kiss *you*," he said, roughly removing her hands from his shoulders, which further provoked her. "Don't you know that a faery's first kiss must be with one of their own kind, or the faery will be cursed for eternity to a life without love?"

Celeste could almost feel the swell of meanness that had overwhelmed her then. Rejection was something she was not accustomed to. That, coupled with the fact that the only faery she would ever kiss would be a faery that had already been kissed by someone else, completely leveled her.

"You mean you haven't kissed anyone yet?" she had sneered, deliberately seeking to humiliate him. Amets had only looked away, and when Celeste tried to pull him toward her again, he had shifted to faery size and darted away, leaving her there, rejected, unkissed, and stewing over how she would ever face Nahia after such a disappointment.

Those were simpler days, she thought, looking at Nahia who was perched on a branch of the mighty oak, from where she watched transfixed as the boys prepared to lower Paloma into the ground. Nahia wore a crinkle above her nose where her delicate brows seemed to knit into a frown of sorts, clearly mirroring Celeste's own mournful state.

The singing of the faeries ended, and a profound silence followed. Celeste turned her gaze from Nahia to the peaceful face of her mother one last time, for Oihana, who had been seated on that part of the oak where the thick trunk made its first split, was already floating down to cover Paloma's face with a thin veil. At once, Amets and Sendoa, along with the two other male faeries who had positioned themselves at the foot of the litter, picked up the corners of the white coverlet and coiled it onto their brawny forearms to lift Paloma as if in a sling. Then they lowered her into the grave by simultaneously releasing the corners of the coverlet, one coil at a time, until Paloma's body rested at the bottom. This done, the boys began covering Paloma's body with the dark, fragrant soil that sat in mounds by the grave. *She'll enjoy the perfume of this pure land in her eternal sleep*, thought Celeste, finding comfort in those things her mother had appreciated.

The female faeries now approached the grave with their flowers, and Nahia glided down from her tree branch to help them lace the soil with petals as the boys continued to fill the grave.

It was done.

The unicorn positioned himself at the foot of the grave like a sphinx guarding a treasure. They all knew he would remain there for a full day before disappearing again into the mountains.

The auras of the faery host glowed dim on this night, Celeste noted. They began to disperse, casting sympathetic glances toward her and murmuring quietly as they made their way through the trees. Soon the clearing was empty except for Nahia, who had perched herself back on her tree branch, apparently determined to stand vigil with Celeste and the unicorn.

Celeste scanned the darkening woods forlornly, listening to the silence, broken only by the sound of water spilling into the pond, and wondering again how she would ever manage without Paloma. It caught her completely off guard to see a pair of eyes—human eyes—looking at her from behind a maple tree across the way, expressing such heartfelt compassion as to instantly produce another painful knot in her throat. Recognizing him, she felt herself flush with surprise and confusion, and as surely as there had been no thoughts of him before that instant, now there was nothing but the image of him in her mind. The man from the lake had appeared like an answer to a silent plea, a plea she hadn't even realized she had formulated. Yet upon seeing him, she knew he was the one being whose presence completely assured her that she was not alone after all.

Celeste felt irresistibly drawn to his side.

A concerned nicker issued from the unicorn, but Celeste was beyond reach, already walking toward the man, knowing he was no longer just the man from the lake, for in the few steps it would take Celeste to get to him, he would become a link to the human nature she thought would be lost without Paloma. Somewhere behind her, she heard Nahia grappling for twigs, trying to prevent the fall, but the twigs snapped, and soon came the muffled thud announcing that Nahia had hit the ground. Celeste paid no attention, and she didn't pause out of concern; it wasn't the first time Nahia had gone limp with shock, and shocked she must have been that a human was in the clearing. Fortunately for Nahia, she hadn't been too high up on that tree.

Chapter 9: Checking In

Etienne had seen creatures he believed, as did everyone else, to be no more than myth or old bedtime tales, and in his mind and soul, he had undergone several levels of emotion as that first night had progressed. Enraptured at the sight of all the faeries assembled, and astonished as he was at beholding such numbers of them, he had been positively thunderstruck at the arrival of her, the only creature who was no myth. But she had left him standing there in his soggy boots, his mind filled with questions, his heart exploding with longing, and he had had no choice but to return to his camp when, after two hours of waiting, she did not return.

His guide and horseman were overjoyed to see him safe and sound, and they explained away his irritability as lack of sleep. After all, it had been close to sunup when the prince and Al-Qadir finally came traipsing into camp, demanding they pack up immediately and not be all day about it.

For the duration of the ride back to St. Michel, Etienne did nothing but plot his return to the lake. He thought moodily of the objections his mother would surely express and that he would have to deflect, because there were no two ways about it, he needed to see that girl again. If what it took to find her were hours, or even days of uninterrupted surveillance, he was determined to do it.

It was close to noon when he arrived at St. Michel, and Etienne headed straight for the stables where Baldomero greeted him.

"You look troubled, sir. Rough tour?"

"Not at all, old man," Etienne replied, dismounting and directly preparing to remove the bridle and girth to take the saddle off Al-Qadir.

Baldomero raised an inquiring brow at him. "Then what appears to be the problem, sir?"

Something told Etienne that not even old Baldomero would believe him if he were to tell the truth, so he said, "My mother will be upset that I'll be leaving again this afternoon, and I'm not looking forward to giving her this news."

"I see," replied Baldomero. "And where will you be departing to so soon?"

Unable to tell an outright lie to the old man, Etienne avoided the smiling, deep-set eyes and chose to say as little as he could. "There is a situation requiring further scrutiny, and I must investigate it myself."

Baldomero cocked his head of white hair to one side, and under the white whiskers, there lurked a suspicious smile. "Hmmm. And you won't tell me what it is that you *must* see to yourself?"

"Will you take care that Al-Qadir is ready within the hour?"

"Very well. Have it your way," Baldomero sighed, taking the hint good naturedly.

Etienne tousled Al-Qadir's forelock before leaving the stable. He hurried across the lawn, which was already showing signs of reviving, thanks to the recent rain, and he climbed the three steps to the lower terrace where he found the massive front door open wide. A bit disconcerted, he entered the cavernous foyer of his home and closed the doors behind him. He heard a female voice coming from his mother's parlor, so he headed there straight away, determined to break the news of his immediate departure and have the conflict break out and be done with at once. In his distraction, however, he almost collided with the stiff butler who seemed to appear out of nowhere, balancing an aperitif tray. "Good morning, sir. I shall fetch another glass directly," the butler offered politely, making to return to the kitchens for a third glass, while the tray appeared to float beside him, owing to the deftness of the experienced hand beneath it. It was obvious his mother had a visitor.

"Don't bother," replied Etienne, and the butler swiveled again toward the parlor while, with his free hand, he opened the door for Etienne.

Within the elegantly furnished room sat Elise, looking vexed with her visitor who had apparently not drawn a breath from the time Etienne passed through the front doors until he entered the parlor, maybe even longer. To his most unpleasant surprise, and before Elise had a chance to even offer her son a greeting, the woman sitting opposite her stood up and addressed him with counterfeit liveliness while the butler placed the tray on the small table between their seats. It was Paloma, the queen of Santillán—his future mother-in-law.

"Ah, young Etienne! What a pleasure indeed, and I feared I would not have the joy of seeing you today," she offered her hand languidly, and Etienne kissed and released it almost simultaneously while casting an inquiring look toward Elise. "But with the wedding already upon us, I thought it imperative to pay this visit. Ah, that we do most of our communication by post is beyond my comprehension," she declared, touching her forehead with the back of her hand, feigning bewilderment.

Etienne bowed and nodded in turn at the frivolous remarks, wondering when he might be able to interject or if he should even bother. He managed an uncertain, "Your Majesty, it's—"

"So dedicated you are to journey all those days on horseback. And sleeping out of doors and eating food out of a saddlebag."

Etienne fell to nodding again or shaking his head whenever the visitor drew breath. His irritation was on the rise.

"I'm so glad you're back, my son. I tho—" Elise began, but her attempt was fruitless.

The visitor continued her silvery chatter right over her host's remarks and not caring a thing about it. "Your mother has told me of your honorable determination to resolve the circumstances of your tenants," this she said with a twitch of disgust flaring her nostrils. "But now that you are back, it is time to focus on the *happy* event soon to unite us all," she said, wagging a knowing finger at him and eyeing Etienne up and down as she spoke, with obvious disapproval of his dusty peasant garb but choosing to let it go for the time being. "So I am come to invite you to a rehearsal of the special occasion. We want this rehearsal to take place on the twenty-sixth so that all will be fresh in your minds for the day of, and it will give our seamstresses and tailors ample time to make any adjustments necessary to the wedding clothes you'll wear—and your dress as well," she added, alluding to Elise.

"I beg your pardon?" Elise cut in, clearly affronted by what she heard.

"Oh," she laughed arrogantly at Elise's look of incredulity. "It is the bride's day, is it not? And my Berezi has such impeccable taste, you see. She'll have no one clash with the colors she has chosen for this special day, so we thought it easiest to just furnish the clothing that would most enhance her ensemble," she said airily, looking down her nose at Elise and then at Etienne's coarse garments once again.

"So you'll be dressing *all* the guests?" Etienne asked with evident disgust.

"Nonsense, boy! Only those who will be in the chapel. What humorous things you say."

"I *am* sorry, but we won't be able to attend your rehearsal," Etienne interrupted, all patience and past caring that, on hearing his refusal, the smiling countenance of the queen of Santillán rearranged itself into a mask of severity in less time than a sincere smile would have been able to dispel itself. "You see, I will be leaving for San Sebastián this very afternoon, *Madame*, and as you know, it is a four-day journey, one, I am afraid, that cannot be avoided."

Elise could not hide her shock upon hearing this news, but she dared not question Etienne in front of her guest, and she wasn't remotely eager to satisfy this new whim of her future daughter-in-law, so she said, with a coolness of temper Etienne had rarely heard before, "Surely you will grant that my son and I *know* how to conduct ourselves in formal occasions, which, of course, would render a rehearsal completely irrelevant, but I pray you will ease Berezi's concerns on that count. Regarding your gracious offer to provide our garments, it will not be necessary, as we have already been fitted and, indeed, our attire for the day of is pressed and ready to be worn."

The queen of Santillán looked sharply from Elise to Etienne, and to the latter she said, making sure he felt the full measure of her displeasure, "First, young man, I'll thank you to address me as *Your Majesty*. After all, a queen deserves no lesser title."

Etienne made an almost imperceptible bow of acknowledgment, never once allowing his eyes to quit her, lest she consider it an apology on his part for having consciously called her *Madame*. The woman's wounded vanity was, Etienne thought, a forthright revelation of her character, and he did not think it a cheery portent.

"And second," she went on, adopting a simpering tone this time, "I ask you, is it prudent to make such a long journey when so few days are left before the wedding?"

Etienne knew his mother most likely agreed with this, but he also noticed with some degree of satisfaction that Elise was not about to side with their visitor and oppose his intentions, so he expressed his justifications, knowing neither woman would be able to argue.

"It *is* customary that the bridegroom have a gift for his bride, is it not?" Etienne began, congratulating himself for his quick thinking. What he was about to say would earn him several days by the lake. "I have something very special due to arrive in town by the day after tomorrow. You must understand, I can't trust anyone to collect it but myself."

The mask of severity twisted itself into a jovial expression as swiftly as to make it obvious it had been a change of tactic rather than a change of emotion. "My dear, *dear* boy," she cooed, immediately snatching a glass from the tray and raising it in a toast, but as neither Elise nor Etienne followed her lead, she took a quick drink and proceeded. "Berezi will be so impatient to see what your wedding gift to her will be. Surely it is coming from Paris," she said with a hopeful wink, which Etienne did not satisfy. But she soon recovered and started again. "Of course I completely understand that you cannot attend the reh—"

"I must excuse myself," Etienne cut her short. As far as he was concerned, she had already taken up too much of his time, and he was not about to remain a moment longer enduring the woman's incessant nattering while the day spent itself. "Be so good as to convey my regards to Berezi." He bowed curtly in one direction and meaningfully toward his mother before leaving the parlor.

An hour elapsed in which Etienne bathed and dressed in clean clothes then prepared a saddlebag with basic provisions. He proceeded to the stables, and there Elise found him on the verge of riding out. Her countenance was duly riled, but he was resolved to depart in spite of whatever objection she could contrive.

Baldomero took the reins from him.

"You are truly going to San Sebastián?" Elise asked, clearly doubting he had had the initiative to order a gift for his bride.

"I am," he replied shortly, in obvious discomfort about lying to his mother, but also because it occurred to him that he would have to indeed produce some manner of gift for Berezi now that he had committed to one. *Why do I deceive myself! There will be no wedding*, he promised himself. Etienne shook his head, emboldened by this new certainty. He took the reins back from Baldomero, catching the suspicion in the old man's eyes. Surely by now the guide and the horseman had told of his impulsive decision to climb to the ridge, and surely they had filled him in on the fact that the prince hadn't returned until dawn.

Elise walked over to him and kissed his cheek. "Hurry back, my son. And please be careful."

Etienne mounted Al-Qadir. "I will, Mother, and don't distress yourself on my account." Elise gave a small, worried smile and backed away from the tall horse.

Taking the queen's distance as his cue, Baldomero leaned in to whisper, "I'll know where to look for you if you delay," said he and the expression in his deep-set eyes clearly added, "I know you'll be nowhere near San Sebastián."

Etienne spurred Al-Qadir onward, sparing a shrewd glance for Baldomero.

Thanks to the early afternoon light, and being that they were already familiar with the terrain, horse and rider managed the climb to the ridge in less time than the first trip. They arrived at the lake within five hours, and Etienne guided Al-Qadir east along the sandy, white shore. He set up a small camp at the edge of the trees near the water, where there was plenty of grass for Al-Qadir to eat. There he intended to wait until nightfall to see if the celebrations would resume. Until then, however, he explored the forest nearby, specifically in the direction he had seen girl disappear—to no avail, as it turned out. The woods appeared to be deserted. The lake too was devoid of signs of life, and again he was plagued by thoughts that he might have imagined the entire thing.

A restless night followed. Etienne started at every noise he heard, believing it to be a signal of her return or at least the return of the faeries, which would put an end to his annoying doubts. Inevitably, though, it would turn out to be the wind or a bird or a squirrel, and twice he glared at Al-Qadir who had stomped his foot while still asleep.

Morning found him bleary eyed and tense, with the distinct impression he had been trying to sleep all night and had failed at it. Feeling suddenly cold, he wrapped himself in the blanket he had packed and waited moodily for the slow-rising sun to warm him, all the while scanning his surroundings for any signs of life.

After a breakfast of stale bread and water from his canteen, he resolved to once again enter the woods in search of her. He left Al-Qadir peaceably munching on the thick grass.

Fruitless hours passed as he traipsed in circles through the woods. His fear of not finding even a trace of her grew with every step. He had been following a creek for the better part of an hour, and as afternoon approached, he thought it best to return to the lake to check on Al-Qadir and to be present in case the creatures should flock back to the scene of his first encounter with them.

Such were Etienne's resolutions when he happened upon a pond and was forced to pause and study this find, for it seemed to him there were signs of the place being frequented by the very creatures he was searching for, perhaps even his lady. The lush trees made it a secluded place where one could bathe in complete privacy, and the flowering landscape appeared to be tended to in contrast to the wild vegetation he had been trampling over for hours. The creek had been dammed at one end of the pond, and he walked over the boulders to cross to the other side, where he found a structure like a marquee of sorts erected beside an enormous willow. The panels made of a sheer fabric ballooned in the soft breeze, inviting him to go in. He waved one of them aside and entered. He found a collection of articles within that reminded him of things his mother kept in her chamber, the sort of things women use to groom and attire themselves. A wave of relief spread through him. *Not crazy after all.* A flowery scent permeated the air in there, and he took a deep breath of it, fancying he had detected that very fragrance clinging to her skin. Abruptly developing scruples over the fact he was trespassing, Etienne reluctantly left the marquee but decided to wait by the pond in case someone came to make use of it or of the things inside it.

Indeed, in a matter of minutes the activity began, and he crept stealthily behind the knobby trunk of an old maple tree to observe. His vantage point afforded him a view of the pond at his left and a narrow lane to his right. Fascinated, he watched as a dozen creatures bustled about, some in the compact size he had observed two nights before, but two others, males, after drawing lines on the ground at the foot of an enormous oak opposite where he had concealed himself, suddenly materialized at a height equal to his own and got to work on the lines they had made. In no time at all, Etienne realized what was happening: they were digging a grave. With great trepidation, he watched their progress, alarmed that the grave they were digging was large enough for someone roughly his own size, certainly not someone the size of these creatures who, as a rule, appeared to be no more than a foot tall. Terror clutched his heart that it might be his lady who would be buried there, that she might have died in the space of two days seemed a cataclysmic likelihood that he endeavored to put out of his mind. While he struggled thus, the grave was dug, and two mounds of dark soil stood neatly on either side of it. If not his lady, who would be buried there? This was the question nagging him at the moment, and it took all of Etienne's self-control not to jump out of his hiding place and demand an answer of the creatures before him.

Soon the surrounding trees began filling with lights as more and more faeries arrived, surely to attend the burial. Etienne estimated about two hundred of them were crowding the branches of the mighty oak and the edge of the pond. Again there were some who had assumed human height, this time males and females, and their job was apparently to flank the empty grave.

Suddenly, all eyes, including Etienne's, turned toward a magnificent white unicorn approaching from the narrow trail lined with shrubs. As astounding as this sight was to him, he was even more thrilled to see who followed the beast. Etienne's breath caught in his chest—she was there. His lady was not lying on the stretcher but walking behind it. Such was his relief at finding her alive that Etienne had eyes only for her. Nevertheless, he did spare a brief glance toward the person on the litter, but all he could discern was that the figure belonged to a human female, that she was covered head to foot in flowers, and that, because she was the only other human in the clearing, it followed that her death must signify a great loss to his lady. Etienne so wanted to hold her in his arms and console her, but that would have to wait; her aloofness and perhaps the etiquette of this strange court prevented it. As the minutes wore on, it tormented him that, although only a few yards away, the beautiful girl was quite beyond his reach.

Etienne waited and he watched. He employed his time in memorizing every detail of her countenance: the way her legs carried her, the subtle turn of her head, the graceful movement of her hands when she acknowledged the sympathetic glances and consoling embraces offered her, how the breeze played with her light brown hair, and how her skin made him think of honey bathed in sunshine. At times, he thought he had heard her voice, but her lips hadn't moved. The minutes ticked by, and he watched and waited.

As undecided twilight grew into earnest night, the faeries assembled began to glow in their colorful orbs, dressing the scene in a soft haze. When the body had been lowered and covered in its final resting place, when the faeries had dispersed through the trees, taking their light with them, and when she stood alone beside the imposing figure of the unicorn, Etienne felt his moment had finally come. The mass of faeries had left, all save one—and he remembered that one from the momentous first night at the lake, she was the one who had taken his lady away with her whispers. Etienne was resolved to not let that happen again, so he eyed the faery warily, that is, whenever he could take his eyes off the girl, the girl who looked so fragile. Yet she overpowered him to the point of complete submission. *If only I could make you look at me*, he thought. And instantly, she did. When her eyes fell upon him, the thrill of the liquid amber within them rushed through him like a galloping steed. His heart hammered in his chest, paralyzing him. Not only was she looking at him, but she was coming to him.

Out of the corner of his eye, he saw the faery, in her turquoise orb, fall from the tree, but his fleeting concern for the creature was short-lived as his attention would not be diverted from his lady. She cut the distance between them with her majestic strides until she was so close to him that he could smell her scent of rain and wind, of hyacinth and mystery. She was almost as tall as he, and she appeared free and untamed, not weak or frivolous as was his opinion of Berezi. *No, not this girl.* Overwhelmed by her presence but determined to engage her longer than a few minutes this time, he cleared his throat and opened conversation thus:

"This must be a great loss to you," Etienne heard himself say, hoping she hadn't noticed that his voice had faltered. He cleared his throat again.

"It was my mother we buried here today," she explained, and her voice sounded like a chorus of angels in his ears, or faeries. Two fat tears rolled down her flushed cheeks, and he longed to wipe them away with his kisses. She had been so strong up until then.

"She was very sick through the winter, you know, and she didn't quite recover like we had hoped she would," she said, lifting her hand to his face.

He allowed her, but he winced when he remembered that it had been two days since he had last shaved.

"It's so rough," she remarked absently, running her thumb over the fingers that had just grazed his cheek.

"I'm sorry. I have been away. I ..." he began excusing himself, cursing the hurried mode of his departure, which had prevented him from taking care of the basic grooming requirements.

"No, no. I like it," she assured him. "I knew it would be. I mean, I had a dream a long time ago that I ... never mind."

He in turn reached for her, hoping desperately that she wouldn't stop him and marveling at how in *his* world, a deep bow would have been the appropriate accompaniment to a verbal salutation, never such intimate contact as this. She did not stop him, and he cupped her face in his hands, wiping the tears away with his thumbs and resisting the desire to kiss her.

Meanwhile, the faery sat up on the soft grass where she had fallen and looked dizzily around. When she saw Celeste and the man almost hugging, she let herself drop again, rolling her eyes. "And she says *I'm* such a faery," she muttered. Of course, now she felt compelled to stand guard, not over the grave, but over Celeste. Nahia clambered up to her feet and brushed off whatever leaves or dirt clung to her skirt before soaring up to a tree branch from where she was sure to see it all. She hissed her indignation at not being able to hear what they were saying and looked away cowardly when the man's eyes caught her glance after her loud hiss.

"My name is Celeste," she said in no apparent hurry that he should let go of her.

"A most unusual name," he remarked, eyeing a long lock of her hair that played over her cheek. He tucked it lovingly behind her ear and offered her his arm that they might take a stroll.

"I was born in these woods, you know. And my mother was all I had," she confided, taking his arm.

Off they strolled.

"And what am I, day old fruit?" Nahia grumbled resentfully as she left the tree and prepared to follow as close as she dared. She chomped angrily on a thick square of tree bark she had ripped from a pine along the way. This she did as a way of battling anxiety and nervousness, and it was a most effective habit in that she always succeeded in transferring her anxiety and nervousness to the person listening to her annoying chewing noises, except this time, Celeste was not listening. Nahia voluntarily quieted down, not only because she knew she was not within earshot of the couple, but because she remembered Celeste's last tantrum over this little habit of hers. "I'll be damned if you're going to wipe sap on me again, you *human*," she griped bitterly, tossing the remains of bark.

"Yes. She was born here, and on the same day I was born even," said Nahia, though no one heard her. "And I am her best friend—her *only* friend," she added sulkily through the straggling bits of bark in her mouth. Experiencing the first mild symptoms of an upset stomach, Nahia deliberately fell behind while the man guided Celeste further into the woods toward the lake.

He listened to her talk about her mother and the things they had done together, and the more she talked, the clearer it became that through the accounting of her mother's life, she was soothing her own pain. Etienne lent himself to her without questions. He took in her childhood experiences as she told them to him, cherishing every word coming out of her mouth.

They had walked for the better part of two hours—the happiest two hours Etienne could remember—and the light of the moon through the branches was the only illumination they had. Her arm rested lightly over his, her voice painted pictures for him of all the things he had wondered about two nights before, and the occasional squeeze she gave his arm when the trail was too narrow or when she checked her footing delighted him more than words could express. He found himself hoping the trail would quit altogether so that he would have an excuse to just carry her in his arms.

She suddenly stopped. "We're at the lake," she cried in surprise, looking through the last row of pines before the shore.

"It's the only destination I know around here. Should we return?" he offered apologetically.

Celeste let go of his arm, but taking his hand instead, she pulled him the rest of the way to the beach. "This is where we first met," she said, lacing her fingers through his.

Etienne grinned broadly at this, and when Celeste questioned him about it, he replied earnestly, "Where I come from, you see, ladies are quite vigilant of their personal space. They would never consider such contact on first acquaintance," he explained, then lifting her hand to his lips, he placed a chaste kiss upon it.

"Is that so," Celeste remarked nonplussed. "My mother *did* want me to learn the ways of the world. I suppose this is what she meant," she said, attempting to withdraw her hand.

But Etienne would not release it. "No, I would not have you otherwise. Not for the world. I adore your freshness, the wild splendor that radiates from you, the—" he caught himself, evidently afraid that he had revealed too much of his feelings, but the timid smile on her lips let him know that his expressions had been received with pleasure. She squeezed his hand with a smug smile that made him want to scoop her up in his arms and kiss her. But he resisted again.

They stood in silence at the same place where they had first met. "You know," he said, his lips grazing her hand though he'd raised his eyes to her face. "I think I dreamt of you too."

Etienne couldn't tell if she had trembled or if it had been him, but something in the way her eyes lingered over him told him that her feelings most assuredly mirrored his.

"I must return to my mother's side," she said.

Etienne's heart sank at this news, but he was not about to intrude or dissuade her on what he knew was her obligation. He only nodded.

"But tomorrow, I want to hear everything. I want to know all there is to know about you."

"I'll be here waiting for you," he smiled buoyantly, and to his great surprise, she brought his hands to her lips in return and placed a kiss on each one.

"I'll be back tomorrow morning—first light," she promised, already sprinting into the woods without giving him a chance to formally wish her a good night.

"I'll be right here," he assured her again, and when she turned to wave to him one last time, he bowed gallantly toward her.

Etienne bounded along the shore to where he had left Al-Qadir to himself the entire day, and when he spotted the horse, he sneaked up behind him, swung from a tree branch, and landed square on his back, startling the poor horse into a full gallop. Gripping two fistfuls of mane, Etienne laughed as they thundered along the sandy shore and into the water. Al-Qadir's powerful legs splashed boisterously after the long day of lonely rest. The ridiculous plans of a wedding rehearsal, and Berezi herself, were furthest from his mind.

I love my life! I love Celeste! were Etienne's thoughts as he dozed off later that evening with a smile on his face that just would not go away.

CHAPTER 10:

SHIFTING ALLIANCES

Nahia had been floating aimlessly about, trying to get rid of the stomachache the tree bark had given her. At last she happened upon a patch of fragrant mayweed, with its distinctive white petals jutting around the plump yellow centers. Feeling fortunate, she avidly ripped a fistful of the narrow leaves and directly began chewing it up, upset enough to risk that it might not have the same soothing effect as when they were steeped. At the end of fifteen minutes, however, Nahia retched and heaved in pain, and the stubborn cramping did not subside until she had expelled every last bit of it.

Sweaty and weakened, Nahia leaned limply on a crooked branch of the willow outside the hall of glamour, breathing shallowly while intermittently spitting out the straggling bits of leaves and petals. It made her insides churn even more to remember how Celeste had been so absorbed with that man. She couldn't understand what the big fuss was about. "He's pleasant enough to look at, I suppose, but you can only look at someone for so long," she said to herself. (Like all faeries, Nahia enjoyed the sound of her own voice and often spoke her thoughts out loud, just for the pleasure of hearing herself talk.) Certain she had enough time, the faery walked rather than floated over the boulders damming the pond to get back to the graveside and wait for Celeste. "What can they be talking about for so long? I can't believe he actually has the patience to listen to her. *No* one has. Not for *two* hours straight anyway," she said, tossing around her turquoise-streaked curls. The colorful lanterns lining the edges of the clearing bathed everything in a soft, sort of purplish haze. "Amets probably did this. He's been very thoughtful to her these past two days." She skirted the motionless figure of the unicorn, who was still at the foot of Paloma's grave, and floated up to the first crook on the trunk of the mighty oak. There she nestled herself like a hen preparing to sit over her eggs. She brushed her skirt and preened her curls. "Not that Celeste will appreciate it," she said alluding to Amets. "Now that she has found that *man*. But I must give her that; he did seem quite taken with her."

"You really think so?" Celeste sang, gliding dreamily from the darkened forest into the purplish haze enveloping the clearing whose centerpiece was her mother's grave.

Nahia glared down at her, a brooding expression fixed on her face, special for the occasion. "Sickening," the faery remarked archly. "I haven't seen you so lovesick since you first noticed Amets in that way, and that was three years ago! For days you chased him, remember? Begging him to take on human form that you might *drool* all over him. You were a fool then, and you're being a fool now."

"I was just a little girl then. This is entirely different," Celeste replied defensively.

Nahia shrugged with an outwardly dismissive roll of her eyes that perfectly masked the fact that her own part in the affair hadn't been as dignified as she would have liked. (Thank goodness for the scant lighting.) The mere thought of that day made her flush with embarrassment. Amid the raucous heckling of three other male faeries (incited by Sendoa), Nahia and Celeste had cornered Amets, who had stood at human height between them, good naturedly at first. But he soon began to look worried when Nahia couldn't keep herself from flickering between faery and human size, owing to the anger working through her, which repeatedly broke her concentration. "I *am* his kind, and you have no business interfering! You seriously propose to deprive him of love for all eternity just to satisfy your silly whim?" Nahia had exclaimed in livid tones, and Celeste, ignoring the faery and tugging Amets toward herself, reminded him of the offer she had made to him. "I told you, you can kiss any faery *except* her," cried Celeste with an accusing finger pointed at Nahia. "And then you could fulfill your lifelong wish to kiss *me*."

"Ah, so *that* was your great plan, was it?" Nahia had cried out in a fury. "Anyone *except* me? Is that so? Well did you know," the faery had said, in turn pulling Amets toward herself, "that he always intended for his first kiss to come from my lips?" Celeste had started to respond, but Amets, in astonished disgust, shook himself free of their grasp and proclaimed, "I would sooner seek the company of snakes than be snared by maniacal, self-serving fiends such as yourselves." This, of course, had left them both in stunned silence, momentarily anyhow. They had watched him stomp away, closely followed by the other bantering faeries. "See what you did," Nahia had hissed. Quick as a flash, Celeste had turned to the faery with her hands balled into fists at her hips. "No, but I saw what *you* did. Are *you* sorry?"

In time, Celeste and Nahia had found it fit to bestow forgiveness upon Amets for his outburst. After all, he had to have been immensely confounded by the blinding flattery of being the object of their combined affections, dangerous though they were.

Nahia waved away those memories like so many annoying gnats and began listening in earnest to the things Celeste was saying, for her language was very animated: something about Paloma's expectations of *Celeste*, how *Celeste* felt unequal to the mission given her, but how what *Celeste* had been experiencing on this night had begun to work a change within her, *Celeste*, the miraculous effect that man had had on *Celeste*, and *Celeste's* excitement over their next encounter. Celeste. Celeste. *Celeste*. Nahia rolled her eyes, ignoring Celeste's agitation on purpose. "You know what I'm hearing?" Nahia feigned a yawn. "I'm hearing you, you, you, and you."

"You're such a … a pixie!" Celeste glowered.

Nahia's cheeks flushed pink, and her aquamarines flickered angrily. "Someone with more imagination could have come up with a different name to offend me, but not you! You're stuck on the same name you used to call me when we were five!"

"Pixie, pixie, *pixie!*" cried Celeste, most maturely.

The unicorn, who had been silent thus far, stood up in blatant disapproval of their squabble, and both Celeste and Nahia, having forgotten he was even there, froze where they were.

Nahia quickly motioned for Celeste to follow her away from the graveside, which Celeste did, feeling that mortifying sting of censure conveyed in the gaze of the keeper of the forest. She *would* sit by her mother tonight, but she needed to set Nahia straight first.

Once on the elderberry lane, headed toward the grotto, Nahia flitted over Celeste's shoulder, whispering urgently. "I'm not a pixie! And I tell you this, I'm not going to hang around here all night listening to your sappy stories about some … some hairy, brutish, brute!" she spurted into Celeste's ear and flitted breathlessly to Celeste's other side.

"He is no brute!" Celeste defended him. "You understand nothing of what has happened. And, as my friend, you should be interested in what I have to tell you instead of just being jealous, because I know that's what is wrong with you. That's all it ever is. You're jealous that I have found someone and you have not."

Nahia made no reply to this. Her mouth just hung open for a few seconds, and Celeste, who normally would have taken advantage of Nahia's silence to speak her mind without hindrance, looked suddenly weary. "Let's just let it go," she sighed. "I don't want to have this argument with you, not tonight anyway."

The girls had reached the grotto, one gliding, the other on foot. Celeste walked in first to the total darkness her home was in at this time of night.

Easily finding her way to the table, she groped for a candle and lit it with a smoldering coal from the hearth. Nahia floated in shortly after and watched Celeste sit on one of the three chairs around the small table before settling on the first shelf beside the fireplace. With Celeste watching her, Nahia fastidiously arranged herself, taking as long as she could; she tucked her curls behind her ears, fluffed her sleeves importantly, and brushed invisible dust and bits of leaves off the top of her skirt.

When she felt certain that Celeste was thoroughly annoyed, she began her speech in silky tones. "First let us get one thing straight. I am *not* jealous, rest assured of *that.*" Celeste let out a disparaging snort, which Nahia felt compelled to take issue with. "Jealousy would imply that we are vying for the same object, and on that score, I can tell you there is no competition whatsoever, number one, because I can take him from you whenever I should wish it, and number two, because I find him neither attractive nor amusing. So you can clearly see there is no ground for competition. Therefore there could be no jealousy."

Celeste gave her a complacent smirk. "Well, if this is true, all I can say is that I'm glad we won't be having another episode like the one we had over Amets."

"The Amets episode was what it was mostly because of *your* behavior," Nahia retorted, resuming the primping of her sleeves, convinced they were not quite poufed enough.

Celeste shook her head. "How do I get you to understand what is happening. How? Will you *please* stop fussing with those ruffles? There's no improving them unless you remove them altogether. Haven't you been told you look stupid in ruffles?"

Nahia hesitated. She could tell her demeanor was beginning to take its toll on Celeste, and this gratified her, because as much as she loved Celeste, at the moment, she felt an uncontrollable urge to antagonize her. She felt Celeste's behavior was reprehensible, but there was also a little bit of fear mixed in the censure directed at her friend, fear that Celeste was headed somewhere Nahia could not follow.

"You know, for a faery, you have no sense of grace. And just so you're aware, everyone thinks you look like a partially blown dandelion with that ridiculous frill you choose to wear," Celeste declared.

Thrusting her chin up in the air, the faery lovingly stroked her filmy skirt to taunt Celeste even more and retorted in a most condescending tone. "I wouldn't expect you to understand this. After all, *you* are not a faery," she explained as if to a child. "We are ethereal, vaporous beings, and I merely express my inner self through the tasteful garments I select to best compliment my nature."

Celeste let out another mocking snort. "*Express* your inner self? I knew it. You *have* been jealous of Ederne, admit it! And now you're thinking you too have the makings of a moon dancer."

"I refuse to even comment on that," Nahia shook her head dismissively. "You envy my natural ability. That is why you attack me so," said the faery with the air of someone tried beyond the limits of patience, but who had no choice other than doing their saintly duty. "No matter. I know it's your insecurity speaking, and that's the burden I accepted when I took you under my wing."

"What wings? You have no wings, *pixie*," Celeste sniggered. "You arrogant little bug. You're nothing but a large firefly with no more than a few tricks up your ruffled sleeve, and you haven't even taken the time to sharpen those," Celeste accused.

Nahia fell silent, remembering the all too familiar lectures from her mother. Nahia hated practicing glamour, and that had always been a source of disappointment to Queen Oihana who, much like Paloma, wished her daughter would show more interest in the inherent values and purposes set for her as a princess. Nahia's hands balled into fists at her sides, and she glared spitefully at Celeste as she uttered in measured tones, "You can say all you want, but hear this, though perhaps not in fashion as is your belief, I *do* have enough sense at least to not trample my mother's grave on my way to the arms of a lover who can do nothing more than take me away from all my mother ever wanted of me."

Celeste's slack jaw and the fact that her eyes immediately welled with tears told Nahia that her words had struck at Celeste's heart. The familiar flecks of gold sparked angrily, and the faery showed enough sense, indeed, as to stay beyond arm's length from Celeste.

"How dare you say such horrible things to me," Celeste hissed, having recovered enough to make a response.

Nahia flitted nervously then alighted on the highest shelf, experiencing that prickly though, by now, very familiar sense of regret for what had come out of her mouth. The harm was done, however, and she had to own, if only to herself, that she had meant it. *She has no business spending so much time with some … some stranger … some man,* she told herself.

"You've made up your own conclusions, and you haven't even bothered to consider what I think, what I feel, what I'm going through," Celeste cried, and when Nahia didn't respond, Celeste threw her arms up in the air and walked across to the bedstead, letting herself drop onto it.

Nahia watched her birth sister face down on the bed, her shoulders shaking with quiet sobs, and suddenly she couldn't tell anymore if she, Nahia, had misunderstood or if Celeste had indeed betrayed her mother as she had accused her of doing.

"It is not as you say at all. You don't understand what has happened to me," Celeste whimpered piteously.

"Yes, well, then let's talk," Nahia said, adopting a somewhat penitent tone.

Celeste sat up and wiped her eyes and nose on the hem of her dress.

"Urgh! Don't do that! That is such a beautiful dress, and you're covering it in snot."

"I'm sorry," Celeste sniffed.

"You look and act like a five year old, blubbering all over the place."

"Fine. Here. I'll use a handkerchief. Are you happy?" Celeste sniffed again, pulling Paloma's handkerchief from under the pillow to finish dabbing her eyes.

"Yes." Nahia descended to the lower shelf again. For the life of her, she couldn't understand why it was sometimes so difficult to communicate with Celeste. Here was a creature she considered her best friend, yet for all the nurturing exchanges they were capable of, there seemed to be an equal amount of pettiness that inevitably derailed them into nasty arguments. On the shelf, Nahia shrank a little, feeling sorrier for her blunt outburst. Celeste looked small and frail sitting on the bed, and her head hung in confusion as she twisted the handkerchief in her hands. "I'm listening," said Nahia, hoping her repentant tone would convey that she meant to hear her out and understand.

Heartened, Celeste cleared her throat. "When I saw him today," she began tentatively, "I felt something I had never felt before. It was as if I recognized him, only not as someone that I had met before, but as someone who is *like* me. Nahia, I feel like anything is possible so long as he is with me, because he knows me, he knows who I am. He sees the human in me."

The pleading look in Celeste's eyes unnerved Nahia. The faery shook her head. "You talk of him as if he has erased your entire past. All I see is that your mother died today, and no sooner is she buried than you've run off—"

"Oh, stop it! It's not like that at all. You're supposed to be my friend. You're supposed to understand what I'm going through."

"So I don't understand and he does. Is that it?"

"Yes," Celeste said timidly.

"And he knows you, inside and out, does he?"

"Yes."

"Then why can't you look at me when you say that?" Nahia wondered, leaving the shelf and floating across to the bedstead. "If he knows you as you say he does, is he aware that you have a father to avenge, that you are to be married, and that you have a kingdom to recover?" Nahia counted off these truths in her fingers and watched Celeste squirm with every blow.

"You're right. He doesn't know any of that."

Nahia sat on the bedpost nearest Celeste. "Here is what I think. I think that the two of you are besotted, and take note that I say *besotted*, not in love, but you cannot be blinded by your infatuation, Celeste, and you shouldn't waste your time indulging his and pretending to be his faery godmother. You'd have to be faery to begin with," she added and instantly cowered at Celeste's swift and vehement response.

"I know that! Doesn't anybody think I know that? I'm not pretending to be a faery. I know who I am, and as you said, Nahia, he is *a human* and so am I. That's what I've been trying to tell you! He and I have made a connection that can only compare to what I had with my own mother, and the only reason that connection has happened is because he is *human*! Do you understand? With my mother's death, I was left alone in this world, in *your* world, and he has come to me to let me know that I'm not the only one of my kind, that there is someone else, that there is *him*."

"Fine, fine. I understand that we faeries are not good enough for you."

"Oh, I give up!" Celeste sprung up from the bed and began pacing to vent her frustration.

"Just answer me this," Nahia pursued. "What are you going to do about the promise you made to your mother? Are you going to forget about that? Because if you do, you won't know how to live with yourself."

Celeste bit her lip, and had Nahia been able to see in her mind, she would have seen what Celeste imagined could happen: she and the man from the lake living happily in the mountains after he renounced his mortal world to come be with her, away from greedy, murdering humans and their arranged marriages. But Nahia saw nothing of those happy prospects, where the only foreseen hindrance would be gaining Oihana's approval and her permission that he might enter the realm as a permanent resident. All Nahia saw were Celeste's nervous glances toward her.

"When the spell he has you under wears off, and believe me it *will* wear off, it might be too late. You do realize that," Nahia pressed on, and Celeste shook her head.

"What spell? What are you talking about?"

"All this time, I've watched you try your best to help Paloma reverse the curse that held her prisoner," Nahia persisted, even though Celeste continued to shake her head. "How many hours have you spent with Usoa in Handi Park, trying to learn all you could about weaving and glamour, just so you could one day be the heroine in your mother's eyes. And now you're going to throw all that away because you made a *connection*?"

111

"I'm not trying to escape my promise. I will do as I promised my mother, and as far as the man is concerned, he has given me support and consolation on a level that you have not been able to give." Nahia made to protest, but Celeste raised a halting finger and went on. "Tonight's argument has been proof of that. He understands me where you tend to muddle things, and I cannot let him go, because he anchors me to a world I need to learn about, my mother's world. But mostly, I can't let him go because—"

"Watch it! Watch what you're going to say, because once you say it, you can't take it back," Nahia warned.

"I love him." The words tumbled out of Celeste's mouth, apparently before she could stop them.

Nahia's lips parted as if she would speak but could not. She leaped to her feet, balancing on the bedpost. Her hands had gone instantly to her hips, while her eyes searched Celeste for any sign that she might have said such a thing simply to antagonize her. But Celeste appeared so agitated and defeated at the same time, as if she couldn't believe it herself, that Nahia ended up just staring at her with her mouth open. *It must be true,* thought the faery.

Not knowing what else to say or how to react to her own confession, Celeste broke her gaze with the faery with a small shake of the head and walked out into the night, meaning to return to the graveside. Nahia stayed behind, teetering on the bedpost, still speechless.

***

I won't break my promise, but I won't be made to marry someone I don't love, Celeste thought as the tears began to flow. Longing for the unicorn's soothing influence over her to ease her confusion, her steps hastened down the darkened lane she knew so well. Above her, the summer stars sparkled brightly in the azure sky, and she knew they were the same stars he, the man from the lake, was gazing at. *Now that there is him,* she thought, *I could not possibly marry another.* She laughed quietly through her tears, reflecting on what Nahia had said about the spell wearing off. *Oh, how I do love you, Nahia.* For although Celeste had taken Nahia's observation in the more subtle sense—that the spell of initial love soon evolves into a temperate relationship as Paloma had told her—she felt certain that Nahia had meant it more literally, and the implications of that were quite comical. Nahia had surely figured that the man was plagued by a body odor or a physical abnormality of some sort and that he had cleverly disguised it with a spell, but that in a matter of weeks, or perhaps only days, the spell would wear out, and the offending flaw would become obvious to Celeste, thus dissipating her current *besotted* state, leaving

Celeste with no choice but to see the man for what he truly was: a smelly, hairy, deformed abomination.

"Oh, Nahia," Celeste grinned, but a nagging little flutter, surely with ruffled sleeves, prompted her to go through a quick recollection of the hours passed in his company, just to make sure no offensive odors or cloaked deformities had escaped her attention. When she satisfied her doubts that he had smelled quite clean to her and that, as far as she could tell, he was more or less physically perfect, Celeste stopped. Hugging herself contentedly, she closed her eyes and felt the gentle kiss of the summer breeze on her cheeks. Suddenly her outlook had been improved through Nahia's accidental humor.

There doesn't need to be a choice. I can keep my promise to Mamma and be with him as well, she thought happily. "If I uncover the truth about the murder of my father and my mother's exile, Arantxa will have to pay for the evil she has done, and I will insure the safety of that other queen and her son. They'll be so grateful that they'll gladly release me from the betrothal, and I'll be free to come back here and finish my days in his company and that of the only family I have known, Nahia and Oihana. *Him* ... Why didn't I ask his name?" she muttered. "That'll be the first thing I find out tomorrow."

Celeste hadn't quite reached the clearing when she made up her mind to race back to the grotto, not wanting to delay sharing this comforting resolution with Nahia. The faery had moved to the table where she stood staring at the flame of the candle. When Celeste walked in, Nahia eyed her with discontent. "Well? Any input from the stars?" she asked tartly.

Celeste beamed. "As a matter of fact, yes," said she, deliberately ignoring the faery's tone in the certainty that once she heard her reasons, Nahia would have no choice but to approve.

"I'm waiting," Nahia said, morosely picking at the wax dripping down the length of the candle.

"It's simple. I will see him tomorrow and the next day and next week too. It will be an intensive, dispelling effort, if you want to call it that," Celeste explained. "At the end of which I'll know if he has me under a spell or if we are really in love. And—this is the best part—he will be able to help me, you see, because he lives among other humans. Maybe he's even heard of my mother's kingdom or some of the people she told me about," Celeste went on excitedly, marveling at how well things were falling into place. "So what do you think?"

"I don't know."

"Oh, fine. Be a sprout about it." Celeste crossed her arms over her chest and turned away from Nahia in frustration. Why did her birth sister always have to fight her?

"I'm not being a *sprout* about it, I'm just—"

"What?"

"Worried. Yes, worried, if you must know! I don't think you're knowledgeable enough or experienced enough to take this on … this promise you made to Paloma. You know, in a whole other *world*?"

"What exactly are you saying?"

Nahia squirmed uncomfortably and wrung her fingers. "Well, it's just that … well, I … I just think you might need some help is all, the kind I could give."

Celeste eyed the faery disconcertedly, not daring to believe the surprising notion that had struck her on examining the faery's behavior. Clearly Nahia was struggling with something Celeste hadn't suspected until then. Could it be that all of Nahia's objections had risen from her fear of being left behind by Celeste? *Of course! If I'm to fulfill my mother's dying wish, I must leave the realm. And now there is this man whom she is most certain will take me away to his world. That makes, in her view of things, two very definite possibilities that I would leave her.* Tears smarted in Celeste's eyes, and her voice broke a little when she asserted most sincerely, "I have no designs to ever leave this place, Nahia. This is my home. You and Oihana are the only family left to me, you must know."

Nahia, who had been eyeing Celeste keenly, turned her eyes to the dripping wax again, trying to hide the satisfied smile that had replaced the fretful expression, but Celeste had seen it, and it was confirmed then and there: Nahia didn't want to lose Celeste, not to the fulfillment of Paloma's wish, not to the man Celeste would see again tomorrow, not to *anyone*. "You are my birth sister, Nahia, and no one can take your place in my heart, you know that, don't you?"

The faery graced Celeste with an incandescent smile, which Celeste returned with equal warmth.

"Oh, Nahia. I just know you'll love—*like*—him."

Nahia's eyebrow arched meaningfully. "If you *love* him, I suppose I won't be able to help *liking* him a little," the faery conceded.

"So does this mean I can trust you? Because if you are going to help me, I can't be distracted with worry over what you might be up to. Can I be certain you won't try to glamorize him—or me—behind my back?" Celeste said, feeling suddenly playful.

"Oh, please. As if I would waste my talent on less-than-worthy targets."

Celeste pursed her lips expectantly.

"Alright, fine. I give you my word."

"Excellent. The word of a faery," Celeste laughed.

"*I* am Princess Nahia, daughter of Oihana, queen of all faeries. My word is—"

"Alright, alright. But give me at least a couple of days *alone* with him before you begin blundering about."

"I don't blunder. I float or glide. I—"

"Oh, hush up. Two days, promise me."

"Fine."

"And, by the way, you're windblown at best. Please. Floating and gliding my foot," Celeste chortled.

"And you're impossible at best."

"And you're a sore loser who always has to have the last word."

"And you—"

"Ah ah *ah*," Celeste cut in, snuffing out the candle and leaving the grotto in darkness.

Nahia crashed against the wind chime as she glided out behind Celeste. The hollow sound of the wooden shoots colliding with one another followed Celeste away with the sweet memories it triggered in her mind, and she felt warm and happy as she walked into the cool night, laughing at the string of curses Nahia let out while getting untangled from the jasmine vines and wind chime.

"Two days," Celeste called to the blundering faery.

"Whatever," Nahia said, untangled and already on her way to Handi Park.

Celeste went back to the graveside, and she kept vigil the rest of the night beside the unicorn.

CHAPTER II:

A TRUE BETROTHAL

An early morning mist hovered low to the ground in the clearing. The creek spilled soothingly into the pond whose temperate water steamed copiously in the cool air, and the first lark sang out eagerly in the still bluish light before daybreak.

Celeste had fallen asleep on a blanket alongside Paloma's grave, and she rolled over under the thin coverlet when the lark twittered happily again. The chill over her flesh told her she was outside, and remembering why she found herself out of doors this morning brought on the moment of waking faster than Nahia could have turned up her nose at the thought of not sleeping on her own goose-down bed. Celeste could hear the unicorn quietly nibbling on the cool grass near Paloma's grave. Reluctantly, she resolved to open her eyes. This would be her first day without Paloma, this would be her first day as the only human among faeries, and she began to despair. But a steadfast baritone inside her head said, *I'll be right here*, and her heart skipped happily, suddenly remembering the discoveries of the night before, that she was not alone, that her feelings were returned with equal intensity, and that, "I promised to be there at first light," she cried in frustration.

The keeper of the forest stared after her reproachfully as she darted to the pond, shedding items of clothing as she went. "This behavior, young lady, is not befitting a princess," Celeste could hear Paloma calling after her. "This is part of Oihana's prized arboretum, and I'm certain she would not appreciate your littering it like this."

"Alright, alright," she said to the voice in her head and raced back to collect sandals and dress. She dropped them in a heap by the row of boulders damming the pond, and she jumped into the mild water, dousing away all traces of sleep.

Snatching the things she had left on one side of the pond and holding them over her head to keep them dry, she came out on the other side, shivering and covered in gooseflesh. Her teeth chattered in the cool morning air, and Celeste hurried into the privacy and warmth of the hall of glamour. Upon taking her first breath under the filmy canopy, the heartwarming memories encased within entered Celeste's mind, balmy and fragrant, prompting her to reminisce. But time was short. She briskly separated and moved the various things on the tabletop until she found her hyacinth balsam jar; it was empty. *Dratted faery*, she thought, remembering Nahia would not fill her jar, only Paloma's. So she tipped out a few drops of her mother's scented oil onto her hands and quickly rubbed herself down with it before slipping into her favorite dress. She took a deep breath of the sweet scent of citrus blossoms, remarkably her mother's scent. "Oh, how I miss you, Mamma," she said, bowing her head and supporting herself with her hands on the tabletop. She allowed herself a few moments' quiet reflection.

The dress she had chosen was the same sun-touched color of her skin. Celeste smiled, remembering how Paloma had had to double back and *really* look at her, because at first glance, it appeared Celeste was naked. "This won't do," Paloma had said, aghast. And that was how the braided patterns in light and dark shades of brown came to stripe the bodice. The dress was sleeveless and fitted over Celeste's shape. The full length of the skirt came down below her calves, and her feet peeked below the hem, wrapped in a pair of delicate sandals laced with sequined ribbons round her ankles.

The first rays of the sun poked horizontally through the trees, considerably brightening the inside of the hall of glamour. "I'm late!" Celeste jumped up and ran out of the marquee toward the lake. Her hair was loose and still damp, but she didn't care. "I'll be back later, Mamma," she called, casting a guilty look toward the blanket and coverlet she had left crumpled at the foot of the mighty oak, giving her mother's grave a disheveled look. *That won't do.* "Aaaah!" Celeste raced back to the side of the grave and hastily picked up her mess. She balanced her way across the boulders, avoiding the water, and tossed the blanket and coverlet into the marquee. She gingerly crossed the boulders again, and this time, she raced over the trail without looking back.

The mist over the pond dissipated and so had Celeste's footsteps. Only the lark and the sound of water spilling over the boulders disrupted the silence in the clearing she left behind.

In little less than half an hour, and with a painful stitch on her side, she arrived at the edge of the forest and saw *him* standing on the sandy shore of Moon Dancer Lake, its surface already sparkling in the early morning sunlight. He was casting pebbles into the sea-green water, oblivious to her approach. *So completely out of touch with his surroundings. I would have heard him coming from a mile away,* she flattered herself. Celeste smoothed down her dress and made sure no dry leaves or other debris were clinging to it. *Why didn't I bring a ribbon. My hair is probably as big as a beehive by now,* she thought anxiously, but as she walked onto the sand, her own shadow stretching before her told her it wasn't too bad. Still, she twisted the bulk of her tangled mane into a makeshift braid and draped it over her shoulder so that it rested over her chest. Celeste was almost upon him when he turned, startled. "You're here," he said, and there was such relief in his expression that Celeste felt an instant knot in her throat, for she realized her absence had caused him an entire night of anguish.

Celeste reached for his hand just as she had done the night before, unaware that the root of his fascination rested on how she seemed to do and say exactly what he secretly longed for. His dark blue eyes roved longingly over her face then settled for an instant on the small mark beneath her right eye. Celeste thought she saw a flicker of something like recognition in his gaze, but that couldn't be. *Maybe he doesn't like it,* she fretted.

"You are even more beautiful in the morning," he told her, and his roving blue eyes confirmed it. He squeezed her hands warmly. "And how are you today?"

"I'm late," she replied apologetically.

In mock deliberation, he examined the rays of sunlight still peeking from behind the trees before he remarked, "It is still first light, as far as I can tell."

She smiled gratefully and inched closer to him, still nervous about her tangled hair. "I've been thinking about you," she said tentatively. "About who you are and how lucky it is that you came to me when you did."

He nodded agreeably. "And who have you decided I am?"

"You are the answer to a need I hadn't realized I had," Celeste confessed. "And you are the bridge into a world I need to explore for my mother's sake."

He opened his mouth to remark or maybe even to protest, but she didn't give him the opportunity to question her meaning. She was prepared to bare her heart to him, and she dearly hoped that after hearing her out, he would be willing to help her. But there was a risk also, one that had dawned on her at the sight of that smile of his, that smile that made her feel elated to have caused it and wretched in its absence. Celeste *dearly* hoped the confession of her circumstances wouldn't trigger a change of heart in him and cause him to bolt, taking his smile with him.

But Celeste had never been one to delay, so in spite of the risk, she decided to bring the conversation round to Paloma at once.

"Can you smell my skin?" she said, leaning closer toward him.

His face changed colors a couple of times, so perplexed by her question was he, that he couldn't even breathe her in as she had invited him to do. "Orange blossoms," he said nevertheless, because he had indeed noticed it when she greeted him. "And yesterday it was hyacinth," he added.

Celeste smiled. "Orange blossoms were always my mother's favorite, and to smell like her—even a little thing like that—makes me feel that I'm keeping her memory alive."

He was nodding before she had finished her sentence, seemingly compelled to give her an admission of his own in return. "I used to wear my father's boots." He confided. "Although I can't say I had the good fortune of knowing him very well. You see, he died when I was very young."

Celeste's eyes filled with tears of both sympathy and confusion. I really don't know anything about him, she thought, suddenly feeling guilty for having had the joy of knowing her mother for eighteen whole years while he had lost his father early on.

"All I remember of him is that we both loved horses and that he allowed me to help (as much as a five year old could) with the breaking of some of his finer animals, but little as that was, it was more than enough for me to admire and love him and make me want to follow in his footsteps. So after he died, I figured a good starting point would be to walk in his boots," he laughed. "Imagine what his boots looked like on me. He was a rather tall man, you see."

Celeste smiled through her tears and embraced him tightly. "And now you've grown into your own boots," she whispered close to his ear.

"To follow in his footsteps," he said, circling her waist tentatively. "But come. There is someone I want you to meet."

Celeste looked surprised at this and wasn't sure that she approved of him bringing another guest into the realm, but she allowed him to guide her back toward the edge of the forest.

"Oh, he's beautiful," said she, delighted and relieved at the sight of the black horse tethered to a tall mountain pine.

"This is Al-Qadir," he said, tousling the horse's forelock and then hurriedly combing it with his fingers, as if he had suddenly realized the animal would appear to more advantage if his forelock were smoothed down.

Celeste watched him out of the corner of her eye and found it endearing that he should want his horse to make a good first impression. She smiled furtively. Al-Qadir nickered contentedly while Celeste stroked his mane and rubbed his powerful neck. "Such noble stature. Such magnificent eyes," she remarked appreciatively.

"My father had great expectations of him, before the foal was even born," he said reminiscently. "And in point of fact, I don't think any other horse would have been able to reach this place, so I suppose this means Al-Qadir has fulfilled my father's expectations. He has certainly exceeded mine."

This remark, of course, opened the door for Celeste to ask what he meant, and Etienne obliged with a brisk retelling of the hardships attending his expedition into the realm.

When the tale had been told and he patted his horse proudly, Celeste placed a tender kiss above Al-Qadir's nose and declared, "I'm forever in your debt."

He watched her keenly, his expression a mixture of jealousy for the kiss Al-Qadir received and complete satisfaction that Celeste should appreciate his horse so sincerely.

Tousling Al-Qadir's forelock, as she had seen him do, Celeste turned to face him and tried again to bare her heart (if she got sidetracked again, she would give up on baring it; she would just hurl it at him). "On the night my mother died," she said, giving Al-Qadir one last pat and turning to fully face the man. "I felt for the first time as if I didn't belong here. I suppose you can't really imagine that, but this is the only home I have known. With my mother's death, however, I suddenly felt like a stranger in a strange land, as if everyone I knew had changed. At first, I didn't quite know why that was, but then I realized that the faeries had not changed at all—*I* had. And it wasn't so much a change as an understanding that my whole life, much as I had denied it, I had believed myself to be a faery, or at least *part* faery. But in losing her, my mother, I discovered just how much of me resembled her and that it was a lot more than the part of me I fancied resembled a faery. Do you understand?" The man nodded, and she continued. "You see, Mamma left me feeling so alone and so out of place," Celeste said, caressing his tanned face with her long fingers. "But then you came along, and just through your being here, you gave me back that sense of belonging, which I thought had gone with my mother to the grave. All of that you did, and I don't even know your name yet," she said, remembering that was the first thing she was supposed to have asked upon meeting him.

"Ah, yes," he nodded again. "So I would say it is high time we meet formally." His eyes twinkled as he backed away a couple of steps with feigned solemnity. He then bowed deeply, and with a most dashing smile, he announced, "My name is Etienne, and I am beyond delighted to meet you, mademoiselle."

Celeste, who had been smiling expectantly, shrank back in alarm. *This has to be a coincidence*, she thought, fumbling for words while in her mind, fragments of the tale told by Paloma flashed randomly before her. She seized on a playful notion, the same notion that had struck her while Paloma agonized in her bed and which she had dismissed (to conceive of such silly thoughts at *such* a moment). *The kingdom of E,* Celeste had thought, *in the kingdom of E, father, mother, and son; all their names started with an E!*

"The kingdom of E ..." she echoed her own thoughts, unaware that she was swaying back and forth and staring past Etienne in total absorption.

Grabbing her by the arm to steady her, all playfulness gone, he begged of her, "Are you alright?"

Celeste shook her head jerkily. "No, I'm not. But before I completely lose my mind, please let me ask you something," Celeste said, focusing all her hopes on his lips and the answer that would soon come out of them.

"Very well," he consented anxiously.

"Where do you live, and what is your mother's name?" she asked directly.

He hesitated, clearly taken aback. "I beg your pardon?"

"Etienne. You say your name is Etienne, and I need to know where you live and what your mother's name is." She almost demanded this, a hint of panic in her voice.

Etienne smiled nervously, but under the tenacity of her stare, he rattled off the answer she sought.

"I live in the kingdom of St. Michel, in the valley just below these cliffs," he said, motioning toward the ridges he had christened as Vulcan's Palings and eyeing Celeste nervously when her eyes grew wide and her hand flew to her mouth. "My mother is Elise, queen of St. Michel, and I am the sole heir to my father's throne; his name was Edmond." Etienne finished, unable to disguise his concern, for Celeste stood before him shaking her head and not saying a word.

Celeste wrung her fingers as she turned away perplexed. She walked onto the sand, away from the shade of the trees, seeking the heat of the sun, for she suddenly felt cold. Etienne, who had seen the turn of her countenance (from flushed to ashen to flushed again), followed her, determined to have this reaction thoroughly explained.

"What is it? What does this all mean to you?" he asked, coming around to stand in front of her.

"If you are Prince Etienne of St. Michel," she returned, "then are you not engaged to a certain heiress of Santillán?" she accused, her first instinct being jealousy, never mind that *she* was the true heiress in question.

"Well, it's an old tradition. How in the world," he stammered. "I'm supposed to marry Berezi, the daughter of the queen of Santillán, on the thirtieth of this month. But you must hear me out," he pleaded, clearly panicking at the thought she might refuse him.

A bitter confusion took hold of Celeste. *This is madness. How can this be?* Everything her mother told her on her deathbed washed over her in prickly waves, forcing her to admit she hadn't truly grasped it then. Oh, she knew it had all been true for her mother, but she, Celeste, had refused to see it as her own reality also. *Is it ever a raw reality at this moment! What am I supposed to do now?* She felt foolish and childish. The plans she had cooked up the night before now mocked her cruelly, that she had expected to bring Arantxa to justice as simply as one would prune an over-grown tree, that she could spend the rest of her days with him, here in the realm. *What a fool.*

Etienne was all but shaking her and demanding an explanation. When she at last looked in his blue eyes, she saw worry and confusion in them, and again she felt that pang of regret at having caused him anxiety. She stroked his blond hair with a look of consternation in her eyes. Sighing wearily, she motioned for him to sit under the shade of the nearest pine.

"It's an old tradition, Celeste," he insisted earnestly. "I don't love her, I don't even know her, and I'm certain she has no feelings for me." Refusing to take the spot Celeste had designated for him just yet, he paced. "I am prepared … I am *prepared* to abandon my kingdom, my mother, my birthright, to leave everything behind if necessary." At this he stopped pacing and turned to face her. His deep blue eyes bore into her brown ones, and he declared, "If you will accept the offer of my hand."

Celeste smiled resignedly. She had wanted nothing more than to hear him say those words, and she could hug and kiss him for having said them, but that would have to wait. Instead she asked, "Now, will you sit down?"

Etienne shook his head, dissatisfied and clearly torn between demanding an immediate answer to the avowal of his intentions and doing what she asked of him at the moment. In the end, Etienne took his seat next to her, but he stared off into the blue-green water sparkling in the sunshine, unable to look Celeste in the eye lest he see rejection there. He had been so certain that she felt the same as he, but her reluctance to answer to the offer of his hand made him shy away with doubt. Could it be that Celeste dared not interfere with his betrothal? How in the world did she find out about Berezi?

Celeste wanted nothing more than to accept the offer of his hand, but she could not do that until he knew the truth. Wishing she could steady her racing heart, she lunged into it, determined to expose the entire history before him and have his answer, be it a renewal of his offer or a polite retreat from the circumstances. "What if I were to tell you that if you are betrothed to the daughter of the queen of Santillán, then *you* are promised to *me*, and *I* am promised to *you*."

"What?"

Celeste rallied her spirits for his sake. Etienne looked thoroughly stunned. She managed to calm her palpitations, although the thought of retelling every detail of Paloma's revelation made her feel as if she were at the base of an

insurmountable ridge, knowing her life depended
the top. It was the sight of Al-Qadir, who nibb
from them, that gave her the inspiration and co
moment, for he had accomplished just such a fe
realm.

"My mother's name was Paloma, you
murdered, his name was Bautista of Santillán

"How ... what ... I mean, why ... no, ho
with himself. He took a deep breath and
elaborate on this. How is it possible? How
of Santillán? And why do you say he was

Celeste didn't leave out a single detail,
as the narrative unfolded.

When she finished, and once Etien
able to confirm some of the details as t
mother, especially regarding Arantxa, w
current information. That Arantxa ar
slept forever underground revolted C
revenge such as she had never burne
rumination, noting that his gaze ha
his brow had furrowed repeatedly di
she whispered his name, "Etienne
about it. After all, just the night
marry that man whom she had ne
the name Etienne with that abl
undo her promises, and thank
was no stranger; he was Etier
him. *I love Etienne!* she procl
again. In contrast with her vehement
for his mother's life, the words that came out of her mouth were soothing,
sympathetic, "I know your mother will be fine. We will make sure of that,"
she said warmly.

He didn't reply right away.

"What are you thinking about?" she pressed on.

Etienne seemed to have come to a decision or to have reached a conclusion,
for he stood and helped Celeste to her feet as well. "That you are right,"
he answered. "That we *will* make sure everything turns out right." Then, all
traces of that distant gaze and worried frown were dispelled with his smile.
Directly, he wrapped his arms around her, breathing in the smell of her hair as
he whispered close to her ear, "I *have* been delivered. You are my true bride."

Celeste pulled away from his tight embrace, a knowing smile stamped on her face. "So *I* am the deliverer?" she asked, remembering his cryptic words from the first night they met. "Somehow I knew I would be delivered," he had said, and now she knew what he had meant.

He pulled her back to him and assented, "Yes, you are my deliverer."

"Oh, how unromantic," said she. An affected sigh full of laughter escaped her as she melted into his brawny embrace. "Fulfill your destiny, and in doing so, you will find love and happiness," she said, peeking at Al-Qadir over Etienne's shoulder; the horse looked back at her with endearing alertness. "That is what my mother said as she lay dying, and that is exactly what I'm going to do," she assured him.

"And you will not be alone. I will be there with you, because just like your father, mine died by Arantxa's hand," he reminded her, and in the same breath, he added, "Clemente still lives, and I will reach him on your behalf. I will get from him whatever information he can give."

"A more loyal friend I don't think my mother ever had," Celeste said wistfully. And then eagerly, for deep in her heart she felt that to have Clemente in her life would be like recovering a bit of her parents' lives for herself, she said, "When you see Clemente, please tell him I long to meet him and talk with him."

Etienne looked up at the sky. The sun was reaching its zenith. "If I leave now, I could be in Santillán tomorrow before dark."

Celeste winced. The situation was so fraught with complexities that she felt at every moment there was something new to understand and face. Now it was physical distance and time. "You're proposing to ride an entire day and a half nonstop?" she exclaimed aghast.

The softening smile had gone from Etienne's face, making his features appear stern when he replied, "It is imperative to see Clemente, I believe."

Celeste bit her lip, feeling a mixture of reluctance that Etienne should leave, and a keen interest to hear what Clemente might have to say. "You would leave at this moment?"

"But I would be back in no more than three day's time," he promised.

"Then I suppose it is best you go, for I too must discuss this with the faery court," she sighed. "You know, over these eighteen years, my mother and the queen of the faeries have failed to reverse Arantxa's spell. How will I ever manage to unmask her with only a few days to work on it before your wedding?"

"Don't you say that to me—*my* wedding—I am marrying no one but Celeste of Santillán," he said in mock ferocity, which she returned with a smug smile. Then, with a more hopeful tone, he added, "Clemente is bound to have helpful information for us."

Celeste smiled with increasing optimism. "Then meet me here in three days, but be careful getting down those cliffs—and be wary of Arantxa," she reminded him, already making haste to leave herself, but Etienne caught her by the wrist and pulled her back into his arms.

Realizing he meant to kiss her, Celeste quickly blocked his lips from hers with her fingers. "Wait," she exclaimed, and prompted by a sudden, illogical doubt, she added breathlessly, "Have you ever kissed anyone before?"

With an amused smile, he kissed the tips of her fingers and replied, "Well, my mother's forehead, I suppose."

"Because this will be my first kiss," she clarified, flushing beautifully. "And I'm not sure if … well, if *we* kiss … You see, a faery's first kiss has to be from someone of their own kind, that is, another faery. Otherwise, they are sentenced to a life without love, and faeries live a long, long time so you can imagine. Well, what I mean to say is, if you and I kiss, I don't know if … like faeries … humans—"

Etienne cupped her blushing face in his strong hands. "I thought you said you were *not* a faery," he said huskily.

"Um, no … I mean, yes, I did say that. What I mean is I—"

His face was so close to hers she could count his eyelashes, but her eyes kept dropping to his lips; they were so close to her own. Surely he could feel her breath on his face as she felt his.

"So if you're not a faery, and as you know, *I* am no faery," he said. They were forehead to forehead now, and Etienne closed his eyes. "*I* believe we should be safe," he whispered.

Celeste closed her eyes also, and she felt his lips close over hers, which sent an electrifying shiver down to her feet and all the way up to the roots of her hair.

Chapter 12:

The Witness

It was a little past midday on the twenty-third of June when Etienne and Celeste parted ways at the lake. She headed back into the woods, still twittering from the effects of that first kiss but expecting to reach Handi Park within the hour.

When he could no longer see her, Etienne mounted eager Al-Qadir. They rounded the lake going west toward the gap in Vulcan's Palings, where they would begin their descent, in turn expecting to arrive in Santillán by the next evening if they rode hard.

When sleep came upon him on the trail, Etienne dismounted and walked beside Al-Qadir for a while, determined not to rest until they had ridden at least ten hours. After crossing the bridge where the river was at its narrowest, Etienne allowed himself and Al-Qadir a two hour break on a soft mound of grass away from the road. He slept soundly and awoke to see the waning moon, whose position in the starlit sky told him it was two o'clock in the morning or thereabouts. Al-Qadir had had enough rest and showed his eagerness to continue by pawing the ground and shaking his powerful neck. They found the road again and continued on their way, now in Santillán territory.

The sun had barely set on the twenty-fourth when Etienne at last distinguished the citadel. For an entire day and a half, he had been consumed with thoughts of revenge, of what he might say to this woman who had planned and succeeded in bringing about the death of his father and the father of his beloved Celeste. Yet now, as he beheld the stronghold, he reproved himself for not having spent any time thinking up an excuse to tell Arantxa, for she expected him to be in San Sebastián retrieving a gift for Berezi. Etienne had intended to boldly enter the grand hall, unexpected, and demand to see Clemente. But that would not do. He needed time to think of something to say to Arantxa, and considering the lateness of the hour, he thought it best to sleep outside the stronghold so that in the morning, after making himself look as presentable as could be expected of someone who'd been riding over cliffs and across rivers and woods, he would make his visit.

So it was that Etienne entered the citadel on the twenty-fifth of June and made his way to the royal hall. He tied Al-Qadir to a post behind the chapel and promptly at nine in the morning, he entered the wide vestibule of the royal hall through its main door, which had been thrown wide open to allow the comings and goings of several servants who presently rushed by him with empty porcelain vases and armfuls of ribbons tied into globular bows, all of them in a provoking blaze of tangerine color. He dreaded they might be a testament of Berezi's famed *impeccable* taste. In deep consternation, he watched the servants scurry into the chapel at the end of the gravel walk. He shook his head irritably and turned his attention to the fact that no one had questioned his presence in the foyer and that, momentarily, there was no one there to announce him. But soon he heard a discontented female voice coming from somewhere up a staircase to his left. Etienne stood up straighter, close to the open front door.

"Mamma! I *must* have that red topaz, and you still have four days to make it so," cried a strident voice from an upper floor.

Etienne stood stock still by the door, realizing that this was Berezi and that soon Arantxa would respond. *That explains the color of those ribbons*, he thought grimly of the red topaz that would surely be enhanced by the tawdry bows.

Arantxa's cold address to Berezi took Etienne by surprise. He had imagined Arantxa would spoil and cater to her precious daughter, but instead she sounded harsh and annoyed. "I told you, I will not purchase or send to Madrid for a stone we have never seen, no matter how much the seller has assured you of its quality. Besides, your future husband has—"

"Aaaah! Who cares about that man! You have seen how he dresses, have you not? Can you conceive of him choosing something for me that I might consent to put on my person?" she brayed heartlessly. "What are the chances he is purchasing a red topaz in San Sebastián," Berezi snorted derisively.

"You have rubies, and you have opals. What is wrong with them?"

Etienne could tell Arantxa had started down the stairs. Suddenly he didn't know what to do, to be found eavesdropping? At that moment, however, one of the ribbon-bearing servants came back in empty-handed. Etienne clapped the young boy on the shoulder and said to him confidentially, "My boy, please be so kind as to alert Ara—, pardon me, Queen Paloma, of my presence."

The boy looked at him fleetingly confused. "Whom should I say?"

"Of course, tell *madame*, Etienne of St. Michel wishes a quick word with her."

"Mamma, don't be ridiculous! Everyone will be here on Sunday, and you expect me to show the same tired rocks they have all seen before? That is absolutely out of the question! The shame! The degradation!"

Arantxa had reached the bottom of the steps. There she stopped and looked up at Berezi, listening in disgust to her daughter's almost hysterical cries.

Etienne and the boy looked at each other. "Perhaps in just a moment," recommended the boy in a whisper, and Etienne slid out the door dragging the boy with him.

"That you were married already and someone else had to put up with your bleating," Arantxa seethed. "I'll not hear another word about it, do you understand me? You will wear whatever you choose from your existing, and might I add, *plentiful* stock of gems, and so help me, you will marry that man, as you call him, and—"

Etienne shoved the boy back into the foyer so as to formally interrupt the heartwarming exchange between mother and daughter.

"What are you doing there, boy?" Arantxa spat on seeing the boy stumble into the vestibule.

"Begging your pardon," he stammered, quickly removing his wool flat cap and twisting it nervously in his hands. "It's just … I just … You have … He told me—"

"Spit it out, you imbecile!"

The boy's distress at having roused the queen's temper appeared to cause him physical pain. Grimacing and on the verge of bolting, he hazarded one more attempt at responding. "You have … a visitor."

Etienne, who had been listening in utter reproof of Arantxa's treatment of the boy, stepped into the threshold relieving him from further scrutiny.

The boy ducked out of sight directly, leaving Arantxa and Etienne staring each other down. Again he noted the startling quickness with which Arantxa rearranged the repulsed expression on her face into a condescending smile.

She promenaded airily toward Etienne, her hand extended for him to kiss. A door slammed loudly upstairs. Apparently, on seeing her mother walk away, Berezi thought it fruitless to persist.

"Let us sit in the library," she directed without a trace of concern that her guest might have overheard the recent exchange with Berezi.

They entered a sunlit room lined with shelves filled with leather-bound tomes. Across from the door stood a smoldering hearth between two enormous glass panels that afforded a view of the lawn and laurel hedge beyond. Arantxa proceeded to and sat very composed on a red velvet chair in front of the hearth, motioning for Etienne to occupy the chair opposite her. Having recovered somewhat, Etienne relaxed enough to be struck by the resemblance

Celeste had to the woman before him; the perfectly arched brows and even Arantxa's counterfeit smirk, on which he thought he saw an elusive shadow of Celeste's beguiling smile, transported him. The sight of the dead queen in the forest, still palpable in his memory, made Etienne reproach himself once again for not having been more observant. *To think I was there looking at the real Paloma, dead and being buried.* But he couldn't think on it any longer, for Arantxa curtly interrupted his reverie.

"Pleased as I am to see you, you *must* explain how it is you are not in San Sebastián," she said, eyeing him with smooth superiority.

Her countenance denoted no suspicion, but Etienne could not afford to let his guard down. He needed to deliver his lie with sufficient credibility if he hoped to see Clemente without arousing her misgivings. *Just six days ago, I lived the life of a normal prince—not a happy prince, but a normal one. And look at me today! I have become a spy for an exiled princess and propose to battle for my life, and hers, aided by a troop of faeries.* But that mildly amusing thought was soon overcome by the unbearable knowledge of Arantxa's true identity and that she was responsible for the death of his father as well as Celeste's. *I shouldn't have come here today. I should have waited one more day*, he thought, suddenly fearing he would not be able to master himself. Beads of sweat had sprung on his forehead, and he hoped Arantxa hadn't noticed. Trying to steady himself, Etienne clutched the armrests of his chair so forcefully that his knuckles turned white. *I will not ruin everything by being rash.* He blinked tightly to clear his mind. *Celeste, if you knew how much I want to kill this woman right now with my own hands.* Etienne had bolted from the forest to the royal hall in Santillán, aiming to gather information to help Celeste come up with a plan, and here he was chastising himself for not having foreseen his own reaction upon coming face to face with Arantxa. He positively loathed her, and the only thing that saved her from having her neck wrung directly were the traces of Celeste's features in Arantxa's stolen looks.

"Forgive me. It wasn't my intention to impose on your hospitality this way," he began, his voice hoarse, as his mouth had gone completely dry. "You see, the merchant I was dealing with in San Sebastián had taken the initiative to deliver my purchase himself, thus I stumbled upon him but halfway to the city. I have been back at St. Michel as of last night, and my morning ride today has brought me here," *to rip your heart out for depriving me of my father*, "on an errand for my mother," *who would gouge your eyes out herself if she knew who you truly are.* Etienne cleared his throat continuously. He felt himself losing the battle against his murderous thoughts.

"Oh?" smiled Arantxa, still with no suspicion anywhere on her face. "And everything is in order with your *purchase*, I presume."

"Indeed, *Madame*," he said, and Arantxa's reaction to the word "madame" was as immediate as Etienne's reparation, for he could not chance her displeasure. "Pardon me, Your *Majesty*. Yes, everything is in order, and although it did not come from Paris, rather it came from Madrid, I do hope Berezi will be pleased." He added the part about Madrid as an afterthought, and with a wicked pleasure, he saw the voracious flicker that lit up Arantxa's eyes.

"And have you come to *deliver* this purchase?" Arantxa asked slyly, no doubt hoping Etienne would produce the very topaz Berezi had been braying about.

"I'm sorry to disappoint, but as I said before, I'm here on an errand for my mother, and I didn't think it wise to carry Berezi's gift on my person during such a long journey. Much too precious, you see."

"Ah, very sensible of you," Arantxa said flatly. The impassive look on her face promptly conveyed to Etienne that he should get to the business at hand. "Yes, well, for a few months now, my mother has been quite distressed over the health of the old man, Clemente," he explained.

"Oh?" Arantxa's smile twitched just a bit, but still not suspiciously, only annoyed.

"She had met him a few times in the past," *while the real Paloma was still alive, you demon,* "and through gossiping tongues, I'm afraid she has found out that he is rather ill, and she wanted me to pay him a visit and announce that she would like to see him this Sunday after the celebrations before his condition—well, how shall we put it—before it further deteriorates."

"He has been quite ill, indeed," Arantxa remarked, her face a picture of concern. "We fear he won't be with us much longer," she said, shaking her head and clucking her tongue pitifully.

"That is what my mother feared, so if it pleases Your Majesty, I would like to see Clemente to let him know myself that he is in my mother's prayers. It can't help but comfort him, I think."

"I don't see why not," Arantxa nodded guardedly, which gave Etienne a moment of concern. "I'll have you shown to his cottage." She reached for the small brass bell on the table next to her and rang it rather forcefully.

Several moments passed in uncomfortable silence between them until, at last, a young maid appeared at the door. "Summon the valet and tell him he is to show the prince to Clemente's cottage," she said harshly to the maid who shifted nervously on the spot while nodding to Arantxa and Etienne in turn. "Well?" Arantxa snapped, and the girl ducked out of site at once, forgetting to curtsey. Several equally uncomfortable moments passed without the arrival of the valet, and Etienne thought it best to make conversation.

"Only four days to the wedding," he said hesitantly.

This appeared to put her in good spirits, and she promptly replied, "Indeed. We have been under a great deal of strain here, and I must confess that if I hadn't taken the reins of this event myself, it could all very well have crumbled into a peasant festival." She laughed a mirthless laugh that repulsed Etienne to the pit of his stomach. "But as things go, I can assure that you and your mother will be quite *affected* with the outcome."

Etienne could not suppress a hair-raising shudder following this ominous expression. *Could she be insinuating something, does she suspect me, or is she merely making conversation?* The valet arrived, and Etienne sprang up from his chair. He bowed stiffly and nodded his thanks on his way out, trying to stifle a grunt of relief, for he could not endure the sight of her a moment longer.

From her red velvet chair, Arantxa watched him leave the room. Her eyes narrowed with suspicion.

Clemente's dwelling was not within the walls of the royal hall, rather it was a separate building adjacent to the west tower and surrounded by a pretty sort of wilderness the old man delighted in caring for. The outer walls of the cottage were gray, owing to the aged timbers that made up its single-story structure. It had an equally graying thatched roof, but the two window frames and one door visible behind a hedgerow were painted a deep green, which gave the cottage an air of being well cared for. The smoke billowing from the chimney said welcome, and the well-tended garden in front of the cottage spoke of the inhabitant's appreciation of nature. Etienne dismissed the valet and walked the rest of the way alone. The door was open, but Etienne stood politely at the threshold and rapped the frame with his knuckles. "Hello?"

"Come in then," a gruff voice called from within.

Etienne stepped in and found a neat sitting room to his right, furnished with three armchairs set around a small table in front of a crackling fire and divided from the kitchen area by a working surface strewn with a cup and plates left over from breakfast. To Etienne's left stood an austere wooden table whose only ornament at the moment was a clay bowl stocked with apples and peaches. There were four chairs properly tucked in on all four sides of the table, and a quilt-covered bed was separated from the dining room by an accordion-like wooden screen.

Clemente himself sat on the armchair closest to the fire, surely because the air was driest there and the warmth soothed his arthritic condition in the early morning. The old man looked pale and fragile. A thick blanket warmed his legs, and his face was like crinkled parchment. The shrewdness in Clemente's eyes, however, gave Etienne a moment of doubt over his previous observations concerning his health, and his doubts were confirmed when the old man—appearing to recognize his visitor—nodded him toward the chair opposite him.

"How is Elise?" he asked brusquely, his voice surprisingly strong.

Etienne was taken aback. The sharp contrast between the old man's feeble appearance, his soundness of mind denoted by the immediate recognition of someone he had not seen in several years, and the forceful voice coming out of him was not quite what Etienne had expected. But there were important things to be discussed, and if Clemente's body, like his voice and mind, was stronger than it appeared, so much the better.

"She is fine, sir," Etienne replied, taking the chair furthest from the fire rather than the one offered him, for the day outside was warming up quite nicely, and he felt it would soon be stifling in there.

"And what brings you here today?" Clemente asked sharply.

"Let's say that I'm trying to help someone uncover a truth," he answered, seeing no cause to delay.

"And who might that be?"

"Her name is Celeste, this *one* I'm trying to help," Etienne replied, duly noting the change of expression in the old man's face. "Someone you might know?"

"No," Clemente said soberly, "just a coincidence. An unusual name, you know."

"It is."

"It was my mother's name," Clemente added then cleared his throat, clearly at a loss over having volunteered that piece of information.

"Hmm ... I understand now."

"What is it you understand, young man?"

"That because of you, being the dear tutor that you were to Paloma, she would have chosen to name her daughter Celeste. To honor you."

Clemente's eyes opened wide, the color rose to his face, and his chin trembled irately. "Hold your tongue, young man. What do you think you're playing at, saying such things!"

Etienne at once reproved himself for his tactless response. The last thing he wanted to do was kill the old man of a heart attack. But in the time it took Etienne to mentally tap himself on the head, Clemente had collected himself, and his eyes now appeared to dissect Etienne with a stern gaze.

After a few uncomfortable moments for Etienne, the old man seemed to have made up his mind. He eased back onto his chair and said, more to himself than to Etienne, "I will listen to what you have to say." Then he added gruffly, "No need to look at me that way. I'm not dying. Not yet anyway."

Etienne shook off the look of concern he'd had on his face and apologized. "I'm sorry, sir. You gave me a scare."

"But be kind to me, young man." Clemente tried to smile. "And please take your time. Nowadays I seem to understand better when things are told to me slowly."

"Then I will do just that." Etienne smiled in return, deciding that he liked Clemente indeed, for in his eyes, he could already see the wisdom and kindness Paloma had told Celeste about. Etienne tried to imagine what kind of speedy conjectures were formulating in the old tutor's sharp mind at the mere mention of Paloma and a daughter named Celeste, and he decided not to keep him in suspense.

Clemente prompted him with a nod.

"On the first night of the full moon, I arrived at a place I never thought could exist. High above the ridges north of us …" Thus Etienne began the tale of Paloma and Celeste, and over the course of an hour, he had retold everything from what he had witnessed at Moon Dancer Lake all the way to Celeste's last words two days before, including Paloma's description of her arrival into the realm and her conjectures as to how it came about.

When he finished, Etienne looked away, allowing Clemente a private moment to wipe his tears and compose himself. He wanted to comfort him somehow, but a sense of Clemente's dignity prevented it. So instead, Etienne waited in quiet regard for the old man's grief.

"I have failed her, young man," Clemente said at last. "I have done nothing but fail Paloma since that night eighteen years ago." He wiped the copious tears with the back of his trembling hand. "And for the past eighteen years, I've been limping about as a decrepit old man with no recollection of his past, or so everyone believes, a broken man who has been *feebly* attempting to uncover a way to expose Arantxa. Oh, that I wouldn't have suffered that stroke, I would have had the strength to vanquish Arantxa that very night."

"You must tell me all you know, Clemente. Any details are bound to help Celeste. Surely you see that."

"I see it, young man, and I know I have a piece of information that is, given Celeste's location, bound to light the way."

CHAPTER 13:

TRUTH REVEALED

For almost two decades, Clemente had kept this to himself, and now that at last he had someone to discuss it with, he intended to go over every one of the wretched facts that had been branded onto his brain all those years ago. Even though it was much too late for Paloma, Clemente's old hopes of exposing Arantxa resurfaced with renewed vigor, because now there was Celeste.

As the tale began to unfold, Clemente fixed his eyes on a point in time quite beyond Etienne. The old man slipped out of the present and into that night eighteen years before, or so it seemed to Etienne who, in spite of his concern for Clemente's well-being, listened with selfish interest.

"I meant to dismiss Arantxa that night, you see. And I went to her chamber to do just that. But instead of barging in as I had intended, I paused at her door when I heard her utter Paloma's name. My curiosity was roused, and I thought that in listening a while, I might increase the evidence against her, add to the reasons I had to do what I was about to do.

"I didn't knock, which, in retrospect, perhaps I should have. Instead, I edged my way to the door, and I looked through a crack that ran the length of the dilapidated wooden planks. The light of three tallow candles sullied the room with a dismal sort of fog, and I realized, with no mild discomfort, that Arantxa scuffled about inside in complete confidence that no one would *ever* venture to her door. I tried not to even breathe too loud, determined as I was to build an infallible case against her.

"Covered in her usual black woolen robe, Arantxa limped sullenly toward a boar-hide-covered trunk in the darkest corner of the chamber. She lifted its heavy lid by the yellowing tusk handle and retrieved a delicate gown from it, which I immediately recognized as Paloma's. With great alarm, I realized that Arantxa must have stolen it just that morning, for I had caught her coming out of Paloma's room, where she had no business being. I tallied her offenses in my mind: she was feared by the staff, she was distrusted by Paloma and myself, and now I knew she was also a thief. Arantxa draped the gown over the open trunk and admired it while removing her prickly cloak. She cast a scornful eye toward the open trunk, where I noted nothing of interest except for an empty, though heavily locked, cage that rested askew over a pile of crumpled rags and blankets. Arantxa slipped into Paloma's gown, her leathery lips peeling into a ghastly sneer as she groped the silky fabric that hung from her as if from a scarecrow, and she held up its skirts to the light of the smoldering hearth, the better to see it. 'You know,' she said to the empty cage, but was forced to stop and clear her rattling throat, which triggered a coughing fit, and only after managing to spit something scabby onto the stone floor, which a gaunt rat hurried over to sniff and nibble on, did she continue. I was revolted beyond anything I had ever experienced—that she lived in such conditions. But Arantxa kept on in her croaky voice, and I strained to catch every word. 'I chose this gown for its color, you see. It looks just like thick, melted chocolate. Paloma *did* look glorious in it.'

I could tell she said this most grudgingly, and I shut my eyes tight whilst I massaged my aching shoulder. *What is she about?* I wondered, cocking my head to one side then the other, willing the ache to subside so that I might focus my attention. I knew exactly which gown that was, and the memory of it was acutely clear in my mind. Paloma had worn it at one of the many balls given by the king. Oh, Paloma had been a vision in it with her red hair, green eyes, and milky skin. How she had been admired. How Bautista's eyes had blazed with pride that evening.

'"How I envied her,' Arantxa hissed, as if plucking my thoughts from the air. She ran her crooked fingers over the silky fabric, and I hated her for sullying it with her touch. 'But never again. I am through being the meek *fortuneteller*, keeping to dark corners and being called upon solely for the amusement of those who think themselves so much better than the rest.' Her throat rattled again, and she angrily hacked out the offending scab. The rat hastened to retrieve it, and I averted my eyes cowardly until I felt those particular dealings had been dispensed with.

'"Are you even listening to me?' Arantxa spat, and I nearly jumped out of my skin, thinking she had somehow realized I was there, but she had not. She was again speaking to the empty cage, from which there was no answer forthcoming. I saw her hobble over to a wooden crate, which, judging by the black sack draped over it, played the part of a table. On it there were several small items I could not hope to distinguish, but Arantxa clawed delicately, almost fondly over them until she found the one she wanted. When she held it up, I could tell it was a dark, smooth oval with a perfect hole right through the middle of it, and I shuddered in spite of myself. *It cannot be*, I thought.

My mind worked furiously to account for it in some other way than what I feared it was, but at that moment, Arantxa took the object and brought it up to her eye, dashing all my hopes that it might be something else. *Good God,* I thought. It was a self-bored stone, you see, and she was looking through it at the empty cage in the trunk, which immediately made me understand that the cage must not be empty at all."

When Etienne continued to look puzzled by this, Clemente obliged with a brisk explanation. "There are only two ways a human can see a faery, you see." He lifted his hand with the index and middle fingers held up.

"You mean, Arantxa had a faery in that cage?" Etienne gasped.

Clemente nodded but wiggled the two fingers he was still holding up, pressing to continue with less or preferably no interruptions. "One, the human must be granted faery sight by a *faery.* Or two, the human may look through the eye of a self-bored stone that he might see the realm. But a self-bored stone, young man, is something the earth might produce once in twenty lifetimes, if that."

"But then, how did I manage to see the faeries?"

"As you said, the tops of those ridges were inaccessible prior to the heavy rains. I suspect the flood and the landslide you described caused a natural breach of sorts into the realm. Therein might lie the answer to your enjoying the gift of faery sight," Clemente replied. "Of course, that is only my opinion. I can only speculate."

Etienne's mind quickly took this new information and filled in the remaining holes in his understanding of the events that had transpired. He nodded, and Clemente picked up the story where he had left off.

"'In a matter of minutes, it will matter no more,' Arantxa croaked cryptically and then, hunching over the cage, as if to get a better look through the self-bored stone, she cooed, 'Ah, there you are.' The effect of her harsh and mirthless utterance, I tell you, was a ghastly one.

"I could not get my mind around what I was seeing and hearing. *Why is she wearing that dress? What won't matter anymore? And in God's name, how could she have managed to trap a faery?* Folk tales swam in my mind in a jumbled mess. At once, I believed it all, yet with my next breath, I discredited my own senses, hoping to find a more realistic explanation. But there were none to be had.

"'You stay right there,' Arantxa said to the faery in the cage. 'It won't be long now, and you'll pass into the light. I promise,' she cooed as if meaning to soothe the doomed creature, but a death sentence is a death sentence, regardless of how it is announced. She returned the self-bored stone to its place on the makeshift table. 'Won't you be relieved?' She again addressed the faery, who made no answer, surely because the darkness and the entrapment were taking their toll on the wretched creature. You see, faeries require light and freedom to survive. But even if she *had* made an answer, I would not have been able to hear it—deaf and blind as I was to her kind.

"In the meantime, Arantxa walked over to a perch by the window where she retrieved a vial. 'It has cooled down quite nicely,' she said croakily, holding it carefully between her thumb and index fingers. She tipped it unceremoniously into her mouth and made a grimace after swallowing its contents in one gulp. Arantxa's eyes clamped shut, and she convulsed suddenly, as if her stomach muscles had contracted violently, trying to expel whatever alien substance she had just ingested. I watched her teeter precariously on her feet, as if her insides might not accept the liquid. I saw sweat break out over her contorted face, giving her countenance an eerie, waxen sheen. She then set the vial down with trembling hands and tried to steady herself, grasping the windowsill, taking slow, rattling breaths. 'It's happening. It is *happening*,' she wheezed, and I hoped with all my heart she might have poisoned herself.

"But it was not so. The chamber was closed off, yet it seemed a sudden gust of wind swept around Arantxa's bony frame, and a musty scent, ensnared with the smoke of the hearth, reached my nostrils, even through the narrow gap. The chocolate gown swelled breezily as did her stringy graying hair, now loose over her shoulders and face. Arantxa was a frightful apparition in the flickering light of the candles, yet as moments went by, I realized in complete horror that the concoction was molding and reshaping her from the inside out. Arantxa's flesh and frame began to fill out beneath the loose fabric of the gown. Her greasy hair took on the luster and wave of Paloma's rich, red mane. Her height increased, her skin healed from old lesions and the effects of age itself, and the scars on her face were smoothed over. The leathery lips became supple and full. White teeth in two straight rows broke through her rotted gums, which were themselves taking on a pink, healthy shade.

"'Indeed. Powerful and beautiful!' Arantxa cackled. But even as she laughed her ugly laugh, the timber of it changed as it reached my ears. And it was the elegant and joyful laughter of my queen. Arantxa's voice had become the serene and cultivated voice of Paloma.

"'Triumph!' Arantxa exclaimed, whirling ecstatically, the gown flaring delicately as her now-dainty bare feet were revealed beneath it.

"I felt myself falling into a dark abyss. It took all my strength to keep myself upright and rational. *How has this been done?* I kept asking of myself until, in the madness of it all, I began to think it a hallucination. I groaned at the renewed pain now numbing my arm all the way down to my elbow.

"'Must see myself,' Arantxa moaned in frustration as she scrambled about the musty room, apparently looking for a reflective surface that would reassure her of the transformation. There were none.

"Through the narrow gap from where I continued to witness this nightmarish scene, I saw Arantxa hold her now youthful hands at eye level, and she appeared as thrilled by the look of them as I was terrified. She ran her fingers over the smooth and youthful new skin on her arms and neck, and she beamed at the feel of her new hair, grabbing clumps of it, as if daring to believe in her luxurious new self. 'I'll just have to wait to have a good look later in *my* new chamber, the *queen's* chamber!'

"Floundering in the madness that threatened my sanity, I consoled myself that in those emerald eyes, from which Paloma's kind nature decisively shone through, there now lurked the unmistakable darkness of a being without a soul, a darkness I knew would be detected by all and would, in the end, uncover this horrible masquerade.

"I fancied I heard a piteous whimper coming from the general direction of the cage, but before I could dismiss it as my own nerves, Arantxa glared resentfully toward the trunk, confirming yet again that, indeed, a living creature was trapped within. 'Is the light of these candles too much for you?' she cooed mockingly at the cage, and I shuddered again, pitying the ill-treated creature. 'Just as well,' Arantxa said dismissively. 'I only kept you alive in case the one thread didn't work, but as you can see,' Arantxa extended her arms and made a meaningful bow. And then, with a cruel finality in her voice, she added, 'When I open this trunk next, I expect to find you dead.'

"Arantxa reached into the trunk and, with obvious disregard that the cage with the faery in it might topple over, she fumbled for something at the bottom of it, a dagger, as it turned out. Arantxa slammed the lid closed, leaving the faery in fatal darkness.

"I watched her make a small puncture wound on the tip of her thumb. 'Santillán will blossom under my command, and I shall reign as I please. I shall conquer, and I will triumph,' she said through gritted teeth as she squeezed the droplets of blood into a second vial. She counted thirteen drops and then suckled the gash on her thumb before inspecting the vial. Arantxa resumed her admonitions. 'This child within me shall make the required alliance, and I will have the power of two kingdoms at my command. I shall rule and, indeed, I shall conquer.'

"I thought my senses were failing me, that my reason had deserted me. Arantxa was with child? How did I not see it before? Oh, it was obvious now, not only the protruding belly under the fabric, but that she intended to supplant Paloma. The case against Arantxa was infallible indeed. It was all too horrific and appallingly true. But how had such a transformation been achieved?

"I knew I would not be merely dismissing Arantxa. I meant to kill her. And within moments, it seemed, the time came for me to do it, because she was preparing to leave, and because as soon as she opened her door, she would find that I had seen all and that I understood all.

"But I failed, young man. I failed miserably, and instead, I watched her walk past me, knowing where she was headed, knowing what would befall Paloma … *knowing*. And this body of mine refusing to …" Clemente averted his eyes, reliving the frustration he had experienced that night.

"You cannot blame yourself, old man. You had a stroke, for heaven sake," Etienne objected vehemently, noting the old man's tortured voice and demeanor, but Clemente wanted none of his pity, convinced as he seemed to be that he should have managed to delay the devastating breakdown of his body.

"It took quite a while for me to recover from the shame and guilt I felt, but in the end, I decided the best I could do would be to dedicate my life to research," he declared gruffly. "I studied various forms of witchcraft and spell casting. I was determined to find a way to undo what Arantxa had done," he said with a gleam in his eyes that colored his whole face with a fearsome strength. "I spied on her every chance I had, anxious for any clues as to Paloma's whereabouts, but to no avail. Yet I refused to believe Paloma could be dead, even though I could find no possible reason for Arantxa to have let her live once the transformation had been achieved. It took me several months to piece together the bit of intelligence that gave me some degree of hope. Now, mind you, this was all found in books or deduced from the sometimes inarticulate accounts of peasants, yet I gathered that it took a full day and a full night for a faery thread to be fully assimilated into the object being glamorized. You see, my boy, this meant that Arantxa had to have kept Paloma alive for at least one, maybe two days."

Clemente shook his head, returning from his absorption.

"All my hopes turned to the possibility that Arantxa may have abandoned Paloma to her fate somewhere far away and that Paloma may have managed to survive. Alas, I had not the slightest clue as to where to begin my search." He sighed. "In time, Arantxa tired of my presence in the royal hall, and she banished me to this cottage. But still, when not dogging her steps, I continued to pore over books and study any rumors or stories I could find about the little people, for I knew the answer to Arantxa's success had to be found within the faery realm. But every book I consulted became a dead end, and every new idea became fruitless. And then one day, I saw that I had become old, and even my limping had become harder to manage. My obsession with the fruitless research had aged me to the crippled state you see me in now, and it poked fun at me for not accepting that Paloma and her unborn child had, more than likely, been dead and rotting on the ground for well over a decade."

Clemente patted the tops of his legs apologetically and looked up at Etienne with a cheerless grin on his crinkled face.

Etienne smiled compassionately. "Don't despair, old man. Too much justice is hinging on the success of this venture, and we're not going to fail now that we have found the truth."

This seemed to raise Clemente's spirits. His eyes smiled before the rest of his weathered face followed suit. "Surely I will live to see her, *Celeste*, come triumphant to Santillán and reclaim her ancestral home," Clemente said, reaching for Etienne's hand and grasping it tightly.

He warmly clapped Clemente's shoulder and declared his assurances. "You will, old man. You will," Etienne said, noting for the first time a somewhat discolored portrait hanging on the wall behind Clemente.

"What is it, son?"

"The man in that painting, is he Bautista?"

"Why, yes. That is Bautista. I painted that portrait of him and Paloma soon after they married," Clemente explained, taking a short moment to admire his own work. "Although small, that portrait used to hang in the library you know," Clemente remarked importantly, but then he clucked his tongue mournfully. "Arantxa took it down years ago, you see. She told the servants that Berezi had no need for sad thoughts of a father she would never meet. But one of Arantxa's chambermaids brought it to me and warned me that even though her instructions had been to burn it, she thought I ought to have it since I had painted it. I accepted it, of course, pretending to be completely ignorant of the handsome couple staring at me from the canvas, and I thanked her for her kind gift."

Etienne nodded absently. "He had a mark, the king, underneath his right eye? Or is that a … just a fleck of paint?"

"Most assuredly he had a birthmark," Clemente declared, making a great effort to turn more fully and reach the portrait with a shaky finger. "Right … there," he said, pointing at the oblong, *café au lait* spot beneath the king's right eye. Then with a reminiscent chuckle he added, "Paloma used to say that it enhanced Bautista's masculinity, for it looked like the healing remains of a recent scuffle."

Etienne agreed with Paloma. He remembered his own concern on first seeing Celeste up close and in the daylight. He thought that perhaps a branch had scratched her dangerously close to the eye. "Our princess, Celeste," he said, "has the same mark under her right eye in the exact same spot as her father's."

"Of course she would," laughed Clemente, clearly longing to see her already, but sobering quickly, he said, "You must tell Celeste what I've told you, about the thread in the potion. Perhaps therein lies the answer, and Oihana may be able to help."

"Oihana?" Etienne said blankly.

"My dear boy, has she not told you? Have you not heard the tales?"

"Well, um, yes … I mean not everything, not all of them."

Clemente laughed good-naturedly. "When you see Celeste again, ask her."

Etienne stood to take his leave. "Right then. If I start now, God willing, I will see her by nightfall tomorrow. I should leave you and take advantage of the light to make my return."

"My dear boy, I can help you get there in a *fourth* of the time."

Etienne eyed Clemente suspiciously. "You learned magic through your research, have you?" he said, taking his seat again and looking humorously skeptic.

Clemente laughed amiably. "No, no, my boy. This has nothing to do with magic, but it has *everything* to do with brawn and nerve. Have you ever heard of Wizard's Pass?" he asked significantly.

Etienne nodded and heaved a resigned yes, the exhalation immediately following said he was ready to have yet another myth dispelled.

"Although I haven't crossed it myself," Clemente said eagerly, again alluding to his legs under the blanket. "I *have* seen it."

Etienne leaned forward on his chair and gaped at Clemente with an expectant crease between his brows.

"About four hours north of here is the waterfall," began the old man confidentially, but he interrupted himself with an afterthought, "Have you a stout horse?"

"Yes. I've been to the waterfall, and my horse, Al-Qadir, is part goat. He can climb over anything," Etienne assured him, intrigued.

"Fine, fine. When you reach the plateau where you can't go farther in any direction, the waterfall will be at your left, and although the sight of it might be dissuading, you *must* scale down to the ledge, which is sometimes hard to see because of the thick spray. Only from that ledge can you even hope to glimpse the passage behind the rough curtain of water."

Etienne's eyes opened wide with wonder.

"I venture to say the passageway will be wide enough for you and your horse to enter."

Etienne continued to gape at Clemente. Surely there had to be more to it, but when the old man didn't say any more, Etienne quickly took stock of his options: twenty some hours on the traditional route versus presumably four to five hours across Wizard's Pass. There could be no question in his mind. Etienne clapped the old man's shoulder again. "Thank you, Clemente."

"Before you go, boy, promise me you'll take care of Celeste, that no harm will come to her," he said, grasping Etienne's arm with a remarkably strong hold.

"On my honor, Clemente, I will protect her with my life," Etienne declared. His heart pounded in his chest as he said the words, realizing he meant to give up his life for Celeste if need be. And though he had thought he was well aware of his love for her, the spoken promise had given him a keener insight into his own heart and who it belonged to.

"And one more thing," said Clemente, releasing Etienne's arm.

"Yes?"

"Come see me again, and tell me about the faery court," he said with a hopeful grin on his crinkled face.

"I'll do better than that. I'll bring you an emissary," Etienne laughed, thinking of that curly headed faery in her turquoise orb, the one who constantly buzzed around Celeste and whom Celeste called her birth sister.

Etienne made his way back to the stable where the valet had told him his horse would be ready and waiting for him.

CHAPTER 14:

AN AUDIENCE WITH A TRUE

QUEEN

Etienne rode hard due north, and within the hour, he thought it a sound idea to lead Al-Qadir off the trail. They snaked their way up the thickly forested hills until a faint rumor of rushing water reached their ears, and they could climb no farther. He then spurred Al-Qadir westward. The air grew humid, the ground became slippery, and through the breaks in the foliage overhead, the tip of an enormous cloud of mist could be glimpsed.

The steep terrain gradually leveled off as they advanced; trees no longer seemed as tall, and the undergrowth was not quite so dense, which eased their progress a great deal. The rumble of the waterfall was constantly with them now and growing nearer with every step. At last, having emerged from a shallow gulch, Etienne and Al-Qadir found themselves gazing, thunderstruck, at what appeared to be the edge of the earth. For beyond a row of drenched shrubs, valiantly resisting the swirling gusts, nothing but dense mist could be detected, and nothing could be heard above the clamor of the water. Etienne dismounted and guided Al-Qadir the rest of the way to the rim. "Well, what do you think?" said he, disconcerted by the sight.

Al-Qadir shook his head anxiously.

Etienne leaned over, straining to see what lay below, and felt a little anxious himself over the wet drafts that seemed to push back as if denying him. "Perhaps this is not the right location." he muttered, but a swooping gust thinned the spray just then, and for a fraction of a second, he saw the ledge Clemente had spoken of, some fifteen feet down. It seemed nearly impossible that that precarious foothold was actually the path Clemente intended them to take. Fortunately, the drop did not appear entirely vertical, and for Al-

Qadir's sake, Etienne thought, the idea of stepping into an incline, no matter how steep, had to be better than leaping into a misty void.

Etienne mounted and coaxed Al-Qadir through the row of shrubs to the most suitable starting point he could find, but no sooner had the horse put his full weight on his forward leg than the muddy ground yielded, and they slid the entire way down. The descent was so swift that Al-Qadir, on his haunches, had no opportunity to even react, which probably slowed and saved them both from flying straight off the stone ledge where they landed. When life returned to Etienne's limbs, for he had believed they were dead, he climbed off the horse and clamped both arms gratefully round his powerful neck. Al-Qadir appeared not to have realized how close to death they had been.

It was squally and loud where they stood, and they were both soaked to the bone. But having marshaled his riled thoughts and somewhat settling his quaking limbs, Etienne guided his horse toward the waterfall itself, trusting blindly in Clemente's word that at the end of this narrow, muddy path, he would see the passage that would take them across the curtain of water.

Etienne turned to the dripping Al-Qadir and said, as encouragingly as he could, "If we get through this, my friend, it will have saved you twenty-four whole hours of hard riding, and I will see Celeste an entire day sooner," he added with ill-repressed excitement.

As the wall of white water drew ever closer, and it seemed an impossibility to get nearer without being washed off by the torrent, Etienne saw that a natural depression on the earth wall would indeed shield them from that particular fate, so they ventured on to where the side of the mountain folded over them like an umbrella. Before he knew it, they had entered a half tunnel of sorts, sealed on one side with solid granite and open on the other to the waterfall. They were, in fact, walking across behind it.

The roar of the falls, which had been so loud before they entered the passageway, was positively deafening now that they were in it. Twice, one of Al-Qadir's hooves slipped, causing Etienne to ponder the tragedy it would be to lose this animal, yet twice they recovered and plodded on.

The quarter mile crossing took them the better part of an hour, and when they reached the other side, they found themselves on another muddy ledge, which Al-Qadir was only too keen to get away from. He didn't wait for Etienne to mount; instead he pulled him directly over the steep ridge, somehow securing his footing on the protruding roots and rocks staggered over the incline. Having reached drier ground, Al-Qadir shook his mane and body like a dog, and Etienne fell to his knees then sprawled himself over the gravelly terrain, exhausted. He was a mere hour away from Celeste now, and that in itself was miraculous and had been well worth the risk. "Thank you,

Clemente," he declared, staring up at the already evident signs of dusk in the sky and congratulating himself on his decision. Had he taken the other way, he would still be far from crossing into St. Michel territory.

Eager to get to Celeste, Etienne pulled a mostly dry shirt and breeches out of the leather saddlebag and changed into them. He would hang the coat and the rest of his wet things to dry after he found Celeste.

Horse and rider were off again, and having reached the gap in Vulcan's Palings and crossed the rolling hills beyond, Etienne let Al-Qadir skirt the lake at a spirited gallop until they reached the eastern shore where they were forced to slow down in order to enter the woods. Etienne knew Celeste was not expecting him until the next day, so he decided to go directly to Paloma's pond, certain she would visit her mother's grave before retiring for the night.

Beside the grave and strewn around the pond were dozens of colorful lanterns that illuminated the trees and the water with a soothing glow. There Etienne spied Celeste sitting on a large boulder at the edge of the water. Her arms were wrapped around her legs, and her chin rested on her knees while she stared at the sparkling surface of the pond in the peaceful light. He dismounted, absently stroking Al-Qadir's forelock and experiencing a strange sort of relief upon seeing her there, because he had, again, half expected Celeste to be a dream. In fact, now that he thought about it, from the moment he had first seen her, he had lived in constant dread of her slipping through his fingers, as if he were in love with water or wind rather than a human being. He stood in silence, holding Al-Qadir's reins and watching her watch the water. Her long mane draped down over her shoulders and back, shielding her from the cool night air. But when Al-Qadir shook his head, causing his bit and bridle to clink, Celeste lifted her chin and slowly turned her head toward him. Etienne dropped the reins, trusting Al-Qadir would not wander off, and went to Celeste. The searing fire in her golden brown eyes communicated a thousand levels of feeling. He had meant to gallantly assist her to her feet, but she had risen to her full height before he even reached her and embraced him tightly.

"It's so good to see you," he whispered into her hair, bewildered at how with one casual movement, such as simply rising to greet him, she could reassure him so completely that she was his as he was hers.

"How in the world did you manage? I wasn't expecting your return until tomorrow night," Celeste said with a confused frown.

"And I have disrupted your plans with another suitor?" he asked teasingly.

Celeste looked at him, even more confused, but she swiftly caught the humor in his voice and elbowed him lightly on the ribs. Thrusting her chin up in the air, she turned away in mock indignation. He had to place himself in front of her at least three different times, for she insisted on avoiding his face until, at last, she gave in and laughed at his persistence.

"It was all Clemente's doing," he explained. "He told me about Wizard's Pass and I must confess to you, in the past few days I have been acquainted with my surroundings in such a way as to make me feel like a visitor in a foreign land rather than the native I thought I was."

As they returned hand in hand to Al-Qadir, he told her the tale of the perilous crossing. Etienne continued his narrative while deftly removing the tack to allow the horse a well-deserved rest, free of a saddle. He also emptied his saddlebag and draped his wet clothes over a rounded shrub.

"That must be how Arantxa got my mother across," Celeste murmured. "For all the things she conjectured correctly about that night, how she got to the other side of the waterfall was the only thing that continued to baffle her to her dying day. She could not explain it."

"So now we know Arantxa is also acquainted with Wizard's Pass," Etienne said soberly. "But we also know she believed then, and still does, that your mother did not survive beyond that night."

Leaning against the mighty oak at the head of Paloma's grave, with Celeste snuggled close to him, Etienne recounted all that had passed between him and Clemente, and he conveyed to her the warmth with which the old man anticipated their meeting.

"We have to tell Oihana about the thread," Celeste said, sitting up straighter. "If there is anything to be done about it, she would know."

"Oh, yes. I am to ask you who Oihana is."

"You must be joking," Celeste blurted, but stopped herself from rolling her eyes, realizing that Etienne had asked in earnest.

"I'm afraid not. The faery tales I was told don't quite live up to what I've seen as of late," he said in all honesty. "Clemente also said you would want to mention the thread to Oihana."

"Clemente knows of Oihana?" Celeste exclaimed, clearly impressed by the broad range of knowledge displayed by her mother's tutor.

"Apparently he has read a great deal and interviewed a great many people on the subject," Etienne explained, discomfited over his own ignorance on the subject.

Celeste gave him an indulgent smile and proceeded to educate him by quoting Nahia. "Oihana is the queen of all faeries, and I mean *all* faeries, not just this troop, but all of them all over the world."

Etienne gave her an illuminated nod and an "Ah, of course."

"As such, she is wise beyond reckoning, and that is why we must go to Handi Park, the seat of her kingdom," Celeste declared, and finding no cause to waste another instant, she snatched the nearest lantern and grabbed Etienne by the arm.

Etienne managed to seize a lantern also, and off they went to where the woods grew denser and where the silence became gradually oppressing. But Celeste's steps were firm, and Etienne was certain she knew exactly what she was doing, so he allowed himself to be guided, fully aware that he had no choice or control or even an inkling of what was to come.

They had been trampling in the wilderness for what seemed like half an hour, at the end of which they arrived at a clearing surrounded by tall aspens. In its center, a rounded formation rose some ten feet above ground, and Etienne estimated it to be about twenty feet in diameter. To him, the place Celeste called Handi Park was no more than ordinary, and although he didn't say it, the thought of giant rabbits inhabiting this burrow-like formation *did* enter his mind.

"What do we do now?" he whispered.

"Shhh … We wait."

Etienne could feel things slithering over his boots, and the tiny hairs on the nape of his neck stood up, almost painfully, with a sinewy chill that seemed to go right down the back of his shirt. He shifted uncomfortably, but he didn't dare express the unsettling feelings assailing him. *I'm no coward*, he thought, raising the lantern and hoping to shed more light on his surroundings. He thought he saw something black and rather large flapping mutely from one branch to another, but he couldn't be sure. The lantern in his hand seemed to be more of a hindrance than help.

"It's eerie, isn't it?" Celeste whispered.

"What is?" he asked as casually as his nerves allowed.

"The sensations that come over you."

Etienne shone the light right over Celeste's face. "What kind of sensations?"

"Do you not feel them? Like someone or *something* is watching you?"

Etienne looked at her through narrowed eyes. Indeed, Celeste seemed to be trying to make herself as unobtrusive as possible, almost as if she were trying not to disturb whatever horror lay dormant at their feet or poised to attack behind the trees around them. He noticed that she moved very slowly, and always her eyes moved before she actually turned her head. She peered suspiciously at the murky darkness between the trees, then at the brambly mass in the center of the clearing, which of course unnerved him even more.

Still in a frightened whisper, she said, "Sometimes, you can actually feel them scurrying past you. Other times, especially when it's dark like tonight, you can see them (her body tensed visibly and her eyes narrowed to slits then popped open, as wide as saucers)—*over there*," she cried shrilly, pointing frantically to the gnarled silhouette of a dead brush oak.

Etienne hardly knew what he was doing. With one sweeping motion, he had forced Celeste behind him, he had rid himself of the lantern, and he had pulled his father's sword out of its scabbard. "Where!" he demanded of her, all the while wielding the blade defensively, into the empty darkness before them.

It seemed everything around them held its breath. Nothing moved, nothing made a noise until, "Um," said Celeste faintly. "I'm *so* sorry," she whispered.

This gave Etienne a moment's pause. He lowered the sword and turned to face her. "I beg your pardon?"

Celeste picked up the lantern he had discarded and handed it back to him contritely. "I meant to scare you, you see. Nahia has done it to me so many times. This wretched entrance can be so spine-chilling with all the enchantments Oihana has put on it that I thought surely you would be as unnerved as I always get. But you were so brave. You were prepared to defend me even," she squeaked pitifully.

"I see," he said pensively, returning his father's sword to its sheath. "Well, I *was* scared, but not nearly scared enough to let any harm come to you." He assured her gallantly.

"And I ask you, where is the fun in that?" she replied, shoving him lightly to show her disappointment over her thwarted attempt.

He put his arm around her waist and gathered her to him playfully, congratulating himself that he hadn't shouted when she screamed, for he certainly almost had. "So Oihana puts enchantments on this place to discourage any humans who may have breached the realm somehow?"

Celeste's detailed explanation of her experiences with Oihana's enchantments brought them closer to the brambly mound, where she readily pointed out the shaft from which a dim sort of light tunneled to the surface. "Clever," Etienne said, still not grasping that beneath him—sprawled over an entire square mile—were the dwellings of a troop comprised of some two hundred faeries.

"Beneath this thick ivy and prickly shrubbery," Celeste explained, making an inclusive wave over the rounded exterior protruding before them, "there are hundreds of ingeniously interlaced passages to guide us far and wide into Handi Park. Wait until you see it all from the *inside*," she added with a fiendish flash in her eyes.

Etienne had no time to consider Celeste's words (or her significant smile), and he couldn't have identified what came over him, for the attack came so unexpectedly. Although he was certain it had something to do with the faery with the turquoise-streaked curls, for he had caught a brief glimpse of her before he was struck. He was overcome with a most unsettling sensation at around his middle section and particularly at the mouth of his stomach. He felt irresistibly compelled to bellow it out, but when he tried, he found he had no air in his lungs to expel. The bizarre sensation engulfed his brain and his entire body at breakneck speed, and when his scrambling mind found no logical explanation for what was happening, he naturally began to panic. Unable to do a thing about it, even when he thought he was being squeezed into himself, as if through the narrowest of passages, Etienne felt himself on the verge of becoming mentally unhinged and prepared to roar out his last remonstration, even if he couldn't produce a sound. *I will not die quietly or without a fight*, his thoughts were a reckless growl in his head. Then, just as suddenly as it had begun, the attack stopped.

Celeste smiled down at him, and a flicker of understanding lit up his mind. He had not been folded inside out or been suctioned into a rodent's burrow, he had been compressed *into* himself. His skin, his bones, even his clothing, all of him had spiraled inwardly as if through his own navel. Hence the bewildering sensation he had kept trying to prevent by clutching his midsection. And now that it all had stopped, besides feeling unsteady, Etienne had to contend with the fact that he was a one foot version of his former self.

Celeste, now a giantess to him, looked down on him kindly as he endeavored to rearrange his riled countenance and keep his dignity intact in the process. Fortunately, his attacker soon pounced on Celeste, inflicting upon her the same fate he had suffered. Fascinated, Etienne confirmed that, indeed, it had been the faery with the turquoise streaks that was responsible. He watched her do it to Celeste, further understanding from his vantage point what had just happened to him.

In a matter of seconds, Celeste stood proportionately beside him.

"Ready?" she said sweetly, hooking her arm to his.

"Hmmm ... Yes," he replied somewhat shakily, although his manner was well on its way to being composed.

The entrance to Handi Park now appeared to him more majestic, yet in a sense, also quite foreboding, especially its height of ten feet, given his own current size. The faery, however, was nowhere to be seen. She had artfully shrunk them and then conveniently disappeared, leaving Celeste to lead Etienne into the shaft at the base of the mound. Once inside, Celeste guided him through the burrow-like formation that ended on one end of a bridge connecting both sides of the enormous cylinder they were in. From here, Etienne realized they were at the topmost part of an enormous atrium.

His nostrils were at once filled with the earthy smell of rich soil. He saw ten stories of chambers notched into the living walls below them, while above them, he could see entire root systems curling one over the other on the ceiling of the dome.

"This is Oihana's trading center," Celeste announced, pointing toward the spiraling ramps connecting all the chambers notched in rows down the length of the walls. The bottom of the atrium looked to Etienne to be about thirty feet below.

"You should see this place during the harvest festivals," Celeste said wistfully. "As evening has settled, we won't be seeing any faeries, for they go into their homes at this time. But during a festival, the walkways you see here are so crowded that you can't take two steps without bumping into someone."

All Etienne could do was nod.

After twenty minutes of winding down passages along boarded-up kiosks, they at last reached the bottom. They walked over to the spring they had been seeing at every degree of their descent, bubbling in its rectangular pool; the bluish radiance emanating from it bathed everything in a tranquil haze. Etienne gazed up at the ramps that had brought them down to this floor, and he shook his head in disbelief. He sat at the edge of the pool and inspected the circular hall they had arrived at. He counted twenty-one doorways notched into the walls around them. They were about two feet in height, and all were marked with different colored lanterns.

"We need to wait here," Celeste said in a confidential tone.

"Hmmm," was all Etienne could say, still staring wide-eyed at his surroundings.

In no time, a very old male faery appeared, dressed in loose black trousers and a black tunic. The sandals on his feet had a closure strap across the instep, and in his right hand, he held a spear with a lantern where the spearhead should have been.

"I am Celeste, and I seek audience with Queen Oihana," Celeste said rolling her eyes at the drowsy-looking sentinel who bowed unexcitedly and went back where he came from. Then to Etienne, in an even more confidential whisper, she added, "I know Oihana requires it of them, but it's downright annoying. I have to go through this every time I'm looking for Nahia even. They make me stand out here and formally seek audience with her. If you consider that she is usually the one who shrinks me down to size so that I can come in in the first place, it is flat-out offensive that she would fly down to her rooms just so I have to have her formally summoned, wouldn't you say?"

Etienne smiled blankly, then, realizing a remark was expected of him, he said even more distractedly, "She is a princess, is she not?"

Celeste's raised brow wrenched him out of his reverie as if scalded.

"You are not taking sides with her," Celeste bristled, crossing her arms in sudden disapproval.

"I um ... I mean, it's the same with you, is it not?" he spurted, grappling for words as quickly as he could. "Does she not seek an audience with you when she wants to see you? You are also a princess."

Celeste yielded with a smirk on her face, clearly pleased at a thought that hadn't occurred to her before.

"I'll have to try that on her," she chuckled.

Oihana and Nahia appeared momentarily, and the first thing Etienne noted on their approach was their eyes, for in the shadowy hall, their eyes seemed to glow, resembling luminous gemstones on their porcelain faces: amethyst for the queen and aquamarine for her daughter. He was captivated at once. Oihana wore a white shirtwaist dress with a scoop neck and long skirt. Besides the lustrous auburn locks with the lilac streaks framing her face, a delicate golden cord was the only adornment on her person, and she wore that around the base of her neck. Despite the simplicity of her attire, Oihana's demeanor spoke most eloquently of her nobility.

Etienne's eyes drifted reluctantly from Oihana to Nahia and were soon entranced by the cobalt blue, ankle-length sheath the faery princess wore. Over it, a silky fitted bodice, covered in what looked like dozens of curly chiffon scales, quivered hypnotically with every move she made (like her bouncy curls). Her feet were bare on the pebble-encrusted floor.

Etienne at once bowed reverently, mortified that he hadn't thought to do it sooner.

Giving Etienne an acknowledging nod, Oihana held out her hand to let him see what looked like a pewter snuff box on her palm. "If you will permit me," Oihana said serenely, and the sound of her voice sent his heart into wild palpitations and his thoughts into a frenzied scramble.

"Before we proceed to the tablinum, we must take care of this." She approached him directly and unclasped the solid little lid. Inside it, Etienne saw what looked like clear, glittering jelly. Oihana lightly dabbed her forefinger in the glutinous stuff and raised it to his face and paused, as if expecting his consent.

Distressed by the nearness of her and not daring to question what she meant to do, Etienne nodded inanely and shook involuntarily at Oihana's touch. She had merely wiped the glittering jelly on his eyelids. He felt a cool tingle there until the jelly dried, and then he was left to feel the subtle pull of it on the tender skin every time he blinked. Besides that, there were no other extravagant symptoms.

Oihana watched him blink several times with an amused look on her porcelain face. She closed the lid of the pewter snuff box and clasped it once again before explaining to him, "This will keep you focused. You see, there are certain *effects* we want to avoid your falling prey to," she said calmly, although her eyes flickered near imperceptibly toward Nahia. "These effects I speak of could conceivably confound or distract you to the point of incoherence, and from what Celeste has told me, we cannot afford either."

"You have just been made impervious to faery glamour," Celeste whispered over his shoulder, and Etienne stifled another jolt at the sound of her voice. He realized that at least ten minutes had elapsed in which his will had completely left him. He had forgotten where he was and that Celeste was with him. He had seen nothing but the two faeries before him, and he had heard nothing but Oihana's voice, and it rattled him to realize it had all been done while he still supposed himself in control of his senses.

"I am *so* sorry," he whispered to Celeste.

"No, no," Celeste whispered with a tolerant smile. "You did wonderfully. From what I've been told, humans have to receive this treatment before they even see a faery, otherwise they won't be able to break from the spell and could remain outside their minds and in the realm for years and years."

"But … you. What about you?"

Celeste shook her head dismissively. "My mother and I were placed under Oihana's care. She saw to it long ago that we should not spend our lives in a fog at the sight of them."

Although not completely satisfied, Etienne decided now was not the time to quiz her further. It would come eventually.

"Now, right this way, if you please." Oihana extended her arm toward a passage directly before them, marked with a sea-green lantern.

Etienne gallantly allowed Nahia to lead the way. She gave him a pouty, arched look before she proceeded, her gleaming eyes clearly saying she pitied him for the short-lived appreciation of her person. After her, Celeste followed, giving Nahia a playful push, for she had seen her birth sister basking in his adoration, even if it was glamour induced. To Oihana, Etienne offered his arm, which she took with a regal nod.

The passageway turned out to be an uncanny deception, for no sooner had they taken three steps through it that Etienne found himself in an airy circular chamber, or rather, the tablinum, as Oihana called it, appeared to be an actual outdoor location; a beach. To his right, a half circle wall was covered in a miraculously detailed painting depicting, of all things, the Bahía de la Concha. Etienne gasped at the enormity of the room and the astonishing accuracy of the rendition of the famed bay of San Sebastián. Monte Urgull rose to his left and Monte Igueldo to his right, and in between these two unmistakable landmarks; terraced among the slopes facing the water, was the city of San Sebastián, less populated than Etienne knew it to be, for surely the likeness had been taken several years before, but still, it was most readily identifiable. The sky had been painted to look like a cloudless summer day, and the lighting in the room gave the illusion of it being perpetually midday. Against the horizon, and this was no painting, breaking the breeze and the shallow waves before they struck the shore, was the rounded mass of the island of Santa Clara, rising from the water with its distinctive brambly appearance. Etienne fancied it would take quite a few strokes to reach it and he shook his head in disbelief.

Yet where the painting ended and the room began, Etienne could not be sure, for the shell-shaped beach, complete with white sand and sea-green sparkling water, stretched from the pebbled walkway where he stood, across the vast tablinum, and into such natural horizons as to make him believe he was indeed out of doors rather than underground. Etienne stepped onto the sand and proceeded to the water, keen to touch it and make sure it was not an illusion. He was not disappointed. The effect was absolute: lush green hillsides, blue skies, a pristine shoreline, and a crystalline pool embodying the Cantabrian Sea. They were in San Sebastián.

"Excellent," Etienne remarked, resuming his position beside Celeste but craning to see more and discovering new details of the magnificent tablinum with every eyeful.

"Thank you," said Oihana, motioning for them to take a seat on the pebbled promenade lining the sand where several concave cushioned chairs were strewn among lush citrus trees, which Etienne imagined grew thanks to the mild atmosphere within. "You see, as a rule, we don't live near to or frequent the coast, for there is less seclusion and safety there. However, we are not beneath thoroughly appreciating it, as you can see."

Etienne nodded; he seemed to be doing a lot of it in Handi Park. They arranged themselves so that Celeste and Etienne were opposite Oihana and Nahia. Etienne caught Nahia averting her eyes when Celeste reached for his hand, and he tried not to smile. It would take some getting used to their incessant *scrutiny* of one another, but he gave Celeste's hand a squeeze nevertheless, feeling vastly contented. "Excellent," he murmured again, relishing the company as much as the surroundings.

"Shall we begin?" said Oihana in her distinctive, self-possessed tone. "We are eager to hear your report."

Etienne cleared his throat and focused his attention on Oihana. Having the queen of the faery realm in front of him was an experience he could never have conceived of, and he found himself looking forward to hearing her speak at length, but Oihana wanted to hear him first. So Etienne obliged directly.

"Clemente, Paloma's old tutor, witnessed firsthand how Arantxa contrived to effect the transformation, and he would have been able to stop her had he not suffered a most debilitating stroke that prevented him from quite possibly killing Arantxa on the spot."

Etienne went on to scrupulously tell Clemente's story. Celeste and Oihana listened attentively. Nahia, however, found it difficult to sit still, and she arranged and rearranged herself on the cushioned chair, or she blew on the many curly chiffon scales, apparently enthralled by their delicate shivering, so that Etienne soon found himself hurrying through his narrative to keep from testing her short supply of interest. He directed the bulk of his monologue to Oihana, whose immense patience poured out of her in the most delightful receptiveness.

Etienne promptly arrived at the portion of the tale involving the faery's weaving thread, and a flash of eagerness surfaced in Oihana's porcelain face.

Chapter 15:

Hanging by a Thread

Celeste noticed the subtle change in Oihana's expression and felt instantly infused with hope. She squeezed Etienne's hand eagerly, and he appeared to catch her meaning that good news was forthcoming.

"Something *can* be done," Oihana said calmly, acknowledging Celeste's nervous smile.

On hearing her mother speak, Nahia sat up straighter and hurriedly adjusted her bodice straps over her shoulders, making a show of attentiveness. When her eyes met Celeste's, however, the arch, dispassionate gaze clearly said, "You haven't been paying attention, so don't expect everything to be repeated to you." Nahia thrust her chin out and turned her attention pointedly to Oihana with a dismissive wag of her head toward Celeste.

"A faery thread starts out as nothing more than spider silk or cotton or whatever fiber the faery chooses for her craft," Oihana explained. "But once the faery begins working on it, her inner light will travel into that thread, saturating it with glamour and endowing it with faery power. Glamour is no more than the impression of a faery's intention, designs, or purpose upon the object she is crafting, be it a weave or a glass sculpture or a gold medallion. There are many legends involving such articles crafted by faeries. Humans go to great lengths to attain or even steal one in the foolish belief that any faery craft will serve as protection against one's enemies or deflect ill fates, but the truth is, such articles will only do what they were meant to do, what the faery intended for them, and that hardly ever coincides with what a human might wish of it."

"Like a faery goblet that will, should you drink from it, only make you thirst more," Etienne interrupted, and once he began, it seemed he couldn't stop. "Your thirst will be such that, in desperation, you'll attempt to drink up a whole river, and although you're taking water in by the mouthfuls, your throat still feels parched. In desperation you start to believe that, perhaps, if you *breathe in* the water, your thirst will be quenched, and that's when—" Etienne stopped abruptly and shrank in his chair under the astonished gaze of his listeners.

Celeste watched him with a horrified look on her face, Oihana seemed mildly amused by his reference, and Nahia positively hung on his every word. "When what? You drown?" she asked breathlessly.

Etienne nodded to the faery princess, but he felt compelled to explain himself to the other two. "I had a nursemaid," he cleared his throat ruefully, "who told me faery stories when I was little to scare me into obedience. But I have since decided that her control tactics were … um … questionable. But please, do go on."

Celeste patted his arm soothingly, but Nahia reclined back on her chair, watching him with newfound interest.

Oihana nodded. "There are no two ways about it. A shimmering faery thread is a precious article indeed, and its production is quite dangerous to the faery herself. You see, it takes so much out of her, she is literally transferring her will into her craft, and that is not an easy task. The faery will be so weakened by it that she will be vulnerable to the point of visibility."

Here, Etienne had to interrupt again, seemingly determined to have more of his questions answered. "Clemente told me that I have been able to see you because I was able to breach the realm."

"Yes … You *are* able to see us through the magic of the keeper of this forest. Once you entered the realm, faery sight was granted to you, or rather, within the realm, we are as visible to you as all creatures in nature are," Oihana clarified.

"So when I leave, when I descend to the valley?"

"I could be gliding alongside you, and you wouldn't know I was there," Nahia said with a suggestive smirk that Celeste promptly squelched with yet another, more pronounced arched brow.

Etienne shrugged almost imperceptibly. But Celeste saw his disappointment, and she understood him; had it not been for that landslide, he never would have arrived at Moon Dancer Lake. He never would have entered the realm, and he never would have seen what could only be seen there. She readily identified with Etienne's thinking. It had been indeed a narrow window of opportunity, and she shuddered involuntarily at the thought of how easily it could have been missed.

Etienne shook his head and was on to his next question before Celeste could bring her own musings to a close. "And what about the glamour? How did I manage to see you during that first night at the lake without having had the … you know … the …" Etienne gestured with his fingers over his eyes, and Oihana responded at once.

"Ah, yes. It's one thing to see us at a distance and quite another when we are face to face as we are tonight. On the night of the full moon, you were at a fair distance from the nearest faery, I presume, and that would have been in your favor. Although, from what Celeste has told me, you were knee-deep in water when she diverted your attention."

Nahia chuckled, making her many chiffon scales shiver gaily.

Visibly regretting having brought it up, Etienne sat back and let out a resigned exhalation. "I'll learn. And in time, I'll adapt," he said.

Celeste again patted his arm sympathetically, and in turn, he gave her hand a warm squeeze and confessed in a whisper, "I can't remember a week so fraught with discoveries in my entire *life*."

"Here in the realm, we are safe to weave out of doors if we please, but traditionally, I require all faeries to weave in the safety of our dwellings or in Usoa's workshop. That way we can assist one another and rely on an environment free of distractions, which inevitably shortens the time it takes to complete the work.

"A completed piece will have whatever power the faery imbued it with and it must be used as such, for accidents might happen if employed for a purpose other than what it was created for."

Celeste elbowed Etienne subtly, thrusting her chin briskly toward Nahia that he might look at her. The faery had lapsed into inattention again. Her nostrils flared, then she pressed her lips into a thin line trying to stifle a yawn. Etienne quickly returned his gaze toward Oihana, sobering his face to mask the amusement Nahia's struggles caused him. Celeste, on the other hand, had reverted to a perfect picture of attentiveness, seemingly without trying.

"The energy within the thread at the time of weaving is quite potent," Oihana continued. "It will shimmer sometimes for up to three days. You see, each thread has the raw power that a faery will shape into the defined purpose of the completed creation. I'm sure you can appreciate the risks involved while there are loose threads. A single fiber can be used by a thief to achieve just about any magical result desired. The old man, Clemente, was right. That *was* the ingredient that made the transformation possible. You see, *intention* is the sole focus of the weaver, but *power* is the sole intent of the thief. I blame myself that the possibility did not occur to me."

"Don't say such things, Oihana," Celeste protested at once. "The education you give and the precautions you take with your troop make it impossible for anyone to risk such a thing, and you cannot possibly be expected to know the whereabouts of other faeries."

"Thank you, my dear," said Oihana sincerely enough, although she seemed to be leaving some of her thoughts unspoken. But then, as if waking from a reverie, she briskly added, "Yes, so retrieving the thread is the only way to undo the damage."

"And how do we get the thread back?" Celeste asked.

Taking a break from her shivering chiffon scales, Nahia sniffed casually. "Wouldn't the faery who produced the thread be the one who has to retrieve it?" Then, feeling encouraged by her mother's subtle nod, Nahia sat up straighter and added importantly, "But we're probably talking about a traveling faery. She would be virtually impossible to locate. She might even be dead by now."

Celeste looked from Nahia to Oihana and back again. "Is she right?" Nahia bristled at this.

"Nahia's assumption is correct in that it was a traveling faery, and we *must* find her, although you needn't despair over our prospects on that account."

"Why do we need to find her? I thought we needed to find the thread?" Celeste asked perplexed.

"No, we already know where the thread is. It resides in Arantxa. Now we only need to *retrieve* it. But to retrieve the thread, we need the faery who fashioned it," said Nahia.

"So at the core of our predicament stands an unknown faery, a faery who is long gone, in fact, last seen some eighteen years ago?" cried Celeste.

"If you lay it out that way, it sure sounds like an impossibility. It sounds like defeat," Nahia interjected.

"That is unthinkable," Celeste exclaimed.

"Pardon me, Your Majesty," Etienne said tentatively. "I thought I heard you say we shouldn't fret over finding this traveling faery."

Oihana nodded. "Indeed. I suspect the faery we seek is readily identifiable."

Celeste and Nahia exchanged quick glances. Neither knew what Oihana could be referring to. When Etienne gave Celeste an inquiring look, all she could do was shrug and whisper, "Can't help you. I'm at a loss too."

The black-clad, spear-carrying old faery ambled in, attracting all eyes onto himself.

Noting Etienne's puzzled expression, Celeste whispered promptly in his ear, "That is Oihana's footman. She can summon other faeries with her mind, you see."

"Ah," said Etienne.

Oihana turned her amethyst eyes on the gray-haired, gray-bearded faery and said, "Bakar, please be so kind as to bring Ederne to me."

Celeste and Nahia let out a very audible gasp, and when they immediately exchanged glances, their expressions said, "I should have known!"

Bakar bowed stiffly and disappeared through the passage to carry out his orders.

CHAPTER 16:

EDERNE'S FLIGHT

At the sound of that name, *Ederne*, Celeste felt a prickly heat explode in her stomach and travel up to her neck and face. Nahia had a similar reaction. Her cheeks turned blotchy, and she didn't look nearly as comfortable as before on her chair.

"I should've known," Celeste muttered.

"Known what?" Etienne said blankly.

Noting Oihana's mild look of discomfort at the thought that she, Celeste, might start a heated diatribe on Ederne, Celeste replied in a whisper, "I'll tell you later, when we're done here."

Bakar, the footman, came through the passage again and said, "Ederne is here, Your Majesty." He bowed and backed away, and once Bakar and the mild scraping of his sandaled steps had disappeared, they were left staring expectantly at the passage, but Ederne appeared to be taking her time.

"She can be so predictable." murmured Nahia, provoked by what she clearly thought was an attention-getting delay.

Celeste rolled her eyes but chuckled guiltily when Nahia said tartly, "Yes, Ederne. Four pairs of eyes are fixed on the entryway, just *waiting* for you to make your entrance."

Oihana lightly placed a hand on Nahia's arm to show her disapproval, and Nahia shrank in her chair just a little.

Ederne swayed in, looking sulky. Her sinuous body veiled in a flimsy burgundy tunic that didn't do much to hide the fact that she was naked underneath, her red hair appeared to whirl with an unseen draft, and her blazing eyes, full of venom, fell languidly on Nahia before she made a sort of extended blink, evidently in place of the curtsey owed to Oihana. "You sent for me?" she said in her throaty, languorous voice, although her eyes fell insolently upon Etienne who had courteously stood up when she entered the tablinum.

Over the years, Celeste had not been able to contrive a reason to like Ederne. In addition, because of the innumerable pranks Ederne had subjected Nahia and Celeste to, the sight of this particular faery usually predisposed Celeste to anger. Of course, Ederne was no ordinary faery. She was Nahia's cousin, which accounted for her resentment over the legacy of power falling solely upon the daughter of the queen—a direct bloodline—while the daughter of the queen's brother, in this case, Ederne, would only enjoy the glitter of lesser nobility.

With a dreamy sort of litheness, Ederne tilted her head to one side. Her eyes roamed over Etienne with impudent satisfaction over his acknowledgment of her, and her pursed lips parted only to address him with, "Thank you, but do be seated." Then, swaying her hips sensuously, she walked toward an empty chair and proceeded to place it beside Etienne. Celeste flushed to the roots of her hair and grasped Etienne's hand firmly.

Although pleased that he took his seat, ignoring Ederne's covetous glances and the display of her charms, Celeste found herself increasingly affronted by the faery's deliberate behavior. Coupled with that was the newly discovered possibility of Ederne having had a hand in her mother's fate, her *own* fate for that matter. Celeste felt herself flush crimson again while Ederne played with a long lock of her tresses. Her flickering red irises were fixed on Etienne. When Celeste managed to catch Ederne's eye, she delivered a most threatening glare, which Ederne airily dismissed. If Oihana hadn't begun speaking, Celeste's mounting annoyance would have caused her to attack, even if just verbally. But for the moment, she had successfully restrained herself.

"Ederne," Oihana said gravely. "Eighteen years ago, after your father passed into the light, we took you back from your self-imposed exile." The corners of Ederne's mouth coiled into a self-satisfied smirk, which only fueled Celeste's exasperation. "You knew the law before you left the shelter of the court, yet you disobeyed," Oihana went on frostily.

"What is it you seek to accuse me of, Your Majesty?" Ederne inquired languidly.

Celeste thought everyone could hear the beating of her heart as it thundered irately in her chest and ears, but she dared not interrupt Oihana.

"Only that you lied to me upon your return," Oihana said in an icily calm voice that made Nahia instinctively squirm on her chair.

"I have never lied to you, Your M—"

"To withhold information is also a lie, is it not?" Oihana raised her voice by a chilling octave. "You were weaving out in the open."

"Oihana, I—"

"Furthermore," Oihana went on, unyielding, "you allowed yourself to be discovered by a human, *and* you allowed that human to steal from you."

"My life was on the line," Ederne said throatily. "Surely even you would agree that my life is more valuable than a *measly* thread."

"To be sure, Ederne, I agree," Oihana said unfeelingly. "Nevertheless, I do not tolerate lies."

Ederne's smile washed off her face like dirt from the surface of rock, leaving nothing but a hard expression on the striking features. "I did not think it of consequence," she said callously.

At this, Celeste lost her ill-guarded composure. "Not of consequence? You may not have known it then, but do you realize that my mother is dead because of that?"

"I believe that *is* the human condition. All of your kind dies sooner or later, do they not? What does it matter how it comes about in the end? Besides, your mother is nothing to me," Ederne seethed, and rounding on the queen, she added, "In fact, her mother should be nothing to *you*, Oihana."

Several things happened simultaneously. Celeste leaped out of her chair and charged across, avoiding Etienne's feet and bellowing curses at Ederne as she went. Also enraged, Nahia had sprung up and shot a well aimed, though undefined blast of energy meant for her cousin, which, most unfortunately, hit Celeste between the shoulder blades, for Celeste had already pounced on Ederne. Excelling at potions more so than directing energy, Nahia caused Celeste to slide limply off Ederne and fall to the pebbled ground with her jaw clenched tight, narrowly escaping the spray of noxious red vapors emitted by Ederne as a defense. Unfortunately, Etienne, who had lunged after Celeste, caught Ederne's onslaught, which set him to flopping on the ground like a fish out of water, gasping for air.

Nahia quickly recovered from her mistake and directed her energy again, successfully this time. "You will hold your tongue in my mother's presence *and* in mine," she snarled at Ederne.

Ederne's hand went to her own mouth and unavoidably pinched her tongue between her thumb and index finger. She stamped her foot, screaming in a rage, but was unable to articulate her anger for the tight grip she had on her own tongue.

Oihana alone remained seated, observing the sudden bedlam with no more than an arched brow to denote whatever unfathomable thoughts crossed her mind. When the outburst settled, Oihana and Nahia exchanged glances, one stern, the other incensed.

Celeste writhed on the floor. The whites of her eyes showed while she grunted and breathed furiously through her nose, attempting to move or at least speak. Etienne seemed to be the one in most danger. His flopping had slowed down considerably, and the rising and falling of his chest revealed to them that he was breathing too shallow for safety. His lips had begun turning a worrisome shade of blue.

"As you were," Oihana directed.

At once, Celeste stopped her thrashing and scrambled on her knees over to Etienne who remained curled on the floor and quite still for a few seconds before he drew in the deepest breath he could manage. He let it out in obvious relief.

"Oh, you're fine, you're fine," Celeste cried shrilly, trying to gather him into her arms but managing only to hold his head on her lap.

"Let me do this a couple more times," he said, taking another deep breath. "I want to be certain my lungs will fill up and empty at my command."

Celeste bent over the curled figure of Etienne and contented herself with breathing in unison with him, hoping that would somehow help him. "I'm so sorry," she whispered between breaths.

By and by, Etienne recovered enough to sit up and then stand. He helped Celeste to her feet, and mustering a smile, he said, "These have certainly been the strangest ten minutes I have ever lived through."

Celeste laughed shakily at this remark, catching Nahia's eye.

The faery clearly mouthed the word sorry.

Celeste, Etienne, and Nahia took their seats again, looking somewhat tousled. Ederne, in the meantime, had released her tongue and was back on her chair, trying to appear chastised and downcast, waiting for Oihana.

"You know what we need from you," Oihana said calmly.

Celeste looked bewildered from Oihana to Nahia. "What do we need?" her eyes inquired desperately from Nahia, but Nahia's face plainly said, "Wait and listen."

"No, I do not," Ederne said dismissively. "But I'm certain you'll explain it to me."

"What of your intentions when you were caught?"

"Protection from the cold?" Ederne said offhandedly.

"You were weaving a blanket?" Nahia fired back.

Ederne cast a venomous look toward her, "An *impervious* one, if you must know."

"Do you speak the truth, Ederne?"

"I do. May I be dismissed now?"

"You are dismissed … so that you may ready yourself for the journey," Oihana said plainly.

"What journey?" Ederne asked, her eyes narrowing in challenge.

"The journey we must make to retrieve the thread, of course," Oihana said in a tone that precluded any and all negotiations.

"You cannot be serious," Ederne scoffed, looking away dismissively and hooking a lock of her red hair between two fingers. She brought it over her nose and took a relishing whiff of it before lazily letting it drop.

"Oh, I am perfectly serious, Ederne," Oihana said slowly. "You know very well, a weaver need only be within two or three feet of the stolen thread, and the rest will happen on its own. Glamour will seek out its source."

"Can any faery be within two feet from Arantxa to make …" Celeste began eagerly.

"No. It has to be the weaver," Nahia whispered back.

"The magic in that thread will want to mesh back with its source, and the source is you, Ederne. Your presence there is the easiest way to render the thread powerless," Oihana said, again with that unquestionable finality in her voice.

Ederne's countenance showed traces of anxiety for the first time. "But you cannot make me do it."

"Why would I have to make you do it? Do you not wish to make amends for your disobedience?" Oihana remarked.

Ederne laughed a mirthless laugh. "Make amends? You must be joking."

"Do you not agree that had you followed the law, Celeste's mother would not have —"

"Oh, Celeste's mother. *Celeste*," Ederne exploded. "I thought we had already established that they mean nothing to me. And I question your loyalties, Oihana, that you should care so much about humans who have persecuted us incessantly through the centuries, who, if they had it their way, would destroy us or entrap us just for their amusement."

"It is the same with every species, as you well know," said Oihana with a hint of annoyance in her voice. "There are good, and there are bad. But you must not judge them all on the example of one."

"One? *One*! Spare me your philosophies. If *that* were true, I might consider your request. But you are asking me to sacrifice my life for that of a human. You are asking me to," Ederne stopped short.

Oihana and Nahia had turned narrowed eyes on Ederne, and Celeste noted that, indeed, the lithe Ederne now had the fierce look of a cornered beast. Her eyes darted anxiously from one suspicious face to the other.

Ederne had said too much. Celeste looked from Oihana to Nahia, realizing something momentous had happened, but she was, as yet, ignorant of what it might be.

Oihana was deadly composed when she next spoke. "The time has come for you to speak the truth, Ederne."

The faery had said too much indeed. Of those present, Oihana and Nahia knew very well that retrieving a thread posed no real threat, for all a faery need do is bring herself in close proximity with the thief so as to draw the stolen glamour onto herself, and with the glamour strengthening her, she ran no risk of becoming visible. The thief would be dazed and bewildered over the unexplained loss while faery sped away, safe and undetected. Unless, of course, the thread had not been stolen to begin with.

Subjugated by their accusing glares and evidently out of recourses, Ederne sagged into her chair. She grudgingly told her story in the following words.

"I was, as you said, going through an episode after the death of my father. I wanted nothing more than to be left alone, to remember him, to mourn him, and to decide what was to become of me."

Oihana raised an eyebrow at this, which Ederne took note of directly, and she addressed it in heated tones. "Oh, I know all about your precious laws, Oihana. I know they say I must linger pointlessly in your wake, for I am a royal successor, that is, I must make myself available should something happen to you or Nahia, *may the stars forbid it*," she added without a trace of sincerity in her voice. "But I am an individual unto myself, Oihana, and I believe I have a choice. I believe I can go out into the world and be who I am rather than wilt and fade in your shadow."

"So your intention, then, was to leave and never return?"

"Precisely."

"Pray tell, where did your plan go awry?" Nahia interjected, her question thick with derision.

Ederne eyed her cousin maliciously, but she continued in a moderate tone. "I had descended into the valley, aiming to reach the coast, and I followed the river for a while, taking refuge in abandoned burrows or hollow tree trunks along the way. A crippled, hideous woman happened upon me. *Yes*, that would be the very clever Arantxa," Ederne said sneeringly when Celeste made to interrupt and then went right along. "I was in a weakened state, for I'd been weaving the last two days, and even though I must have been flickering between visible and invisible, the clever Arantxa would never have been able to spot me had she not had that dratted self-bored stone. She trapped me under a net made of horsetail hair, and she demanded I give her my work thus far.

"I knew the power residing in my work could be dangerous in the hands of such a creature, so with the last bit of strength I had, I made my weaving unravel and burn. At this, the old woman ripped away the net and clasped me in her hand, almost squeezing the life out of me, while with the other she pulled a dagger from the folds of her cloak and cut off the slack thread before it was consumed in flames. I must have lost consciousness, for I knew not exactly what happened next. I awoke in a darkened chamber, which turned out to be a trunk in a musty stone prison. She caged me for an entire day, through which I drifted in and out of consciousness until, at last, the meager light coming from the keyhole of the trunk told me it was close to dusk. It was then that she entered the chamber again. She said to drink from the cup she offered me, and I obeyed, for I hadn't had food or drink for almost two days. She watched me gulp it down, and when she was certain I had finished, she began to laugh a horrible, cackling laugh. I had drunk it so greedily that I had failed to catch a scent or flavor until it was too late.

"'Now you listen to me, faery, and you listen good,' she said. 'What you just drank is a potion that secures my intention, and it secures it with no less than your *life*. You have provided me with a most precious ingredient, faery, so you can appreciate that I won't take any chances. I simply cannot have you return to me with regrets. Yet I must have you live until I am certain of my success.'"

"What are you saying? What does that mean?" Celeste asked bewildered.

"Ignorant *human*," Ederne spat. "The potion she gave me will act as a poison should I venture anywhere near my thread, the thread, I gather, she used for the transformation she so effectively achieved. The power of my thread resides in her now, and I'm sure even *you*, with your limited human wit, can discern that my proximity to her would result in my immediate death."

"But how did you manage to escape? Clemente tells us you were caged," Nahia put in irritably.

Celeste and Etienne leaned forward expectantly.

"I was not as weak as I had made out," Ederne said slyly. "And the respite granted me while the trunk remained open revived me somewhat. It was nothing to will the mechanism of the lock to spring open for me, and I've known how to disperse weight for a great many years now, so the lid of the trunk was no challenge."

Silence reigned in the tablinum while all present assimilated this new portion of their circumstances. At last, Oihana spoke.

"You'll remain confined until such time as I can decide how to proceed," Oihana said calmly.

"You cannot do this," Ederne raged.

"I can, and I will," Oihana said firmly. Then, to the guards who had been summoned unbeknownst to any of them, she said, "Take her away."

"You'll regret turning your back on me, Oihana."

Then the only sound to be heard was a jumbled disarray of guttural moans and grunts, for a wrathful discharge of force in the shape of red spears had issued from Ederne with incalculable swiftness. The two guards, whom the flashing spears had been aimed at, were directly plastered against the painted wall, and they slumped to the ground unconscious.

Ederne took to the air, a blur of burgundy sheer and red hair that darted over the crumpled guards and into the passageway with such speed as to astonish even Oihana.

"As for you, Celeste. All will be taken from you as it has been taken from me." Ederne was gone before her echoing threats had died down.

CHAPTER 17:

FAERY GLAMOUR AND HUMAN

SKILL

"What are we to do now, Oihana?" Celeste pleaded. "Ederne won't be coming back anytime soon."

"No, she will not, but it is just as well," said Oihana. Then, to Bakar who had been wordlessly summoned again, she said, "Please make sure these men recover and then be so good as to bring us refreshments. Passiflora if you would."

Gray-haired Bakar bowed and proceeded to where the guards were leaning against the wall. They were already rubbing the backs of their necks and gingerly feeling for knots in their heads.

Oihana turned her attention back to Celeste and the question she had asked. "For many years now, Ederne has endeavored to disappoint my expectations of her and has made a habit of defying the laws of this court. But tonight, I confess, myself astounded, that her attack on you, Etienne, although it was meant for Celeste, was made with the intent to take life. *That* I would never have expected of her," said the queen.

Celeste squeezed Etienne's hand and eyed him nervously. The sight of him convulsing on the ground, gasping for air after Ederne had hit him, was still quite vivid in her mind.

"Please don't concern yourselves over me anymore. I'm perfectly fine now, see?" he said, taking yet another deep, reassuring breath and looking awkward at finding himself the object of their fretful glances.

"That *was* a very narrow escape," Nahia said, still shaken by the recollection.

"That she channeled such force and so quickly amid the confusion of all three of you pouncing on her," Oihana remarked, shaking her head lightly. "Reprehensibly remarkable."

Bakar arrived with a tray on which four delicate glasses shaped like harvest cones hovered. The glittering burgundy liquid in them swished slightly as he went from chair to chair, offering the drinks to them. He retreated as soon as the tray was empty.

"This will calm *all* of us," said Oihana, drinking the rich liquid in her cup and motioning for them to follow her example.

"The dried passiflora flower makes an excellent sedative," Celeste whispered in Etienne's ear. "Oihana turns it into a fine powder and then dissolves it in red wine."

Etienne, who held the glass pinched between two fingers, tilted it into his mouth. It only afforded two gulps, but he appeared to have enjoyed its rich, woody flavor. "Ah," he said, smiling at Celeste who collected his empty glass. "Excellent."

Celeste watched him keenly, and within the few seconds it took her to place their empty glasses on the table, she had to smile herself. The tingly effects of the passiflora spread warmly from her midsection up to her scalp and down to her toes, even to the tips of her fingers. "Excellent," she whispered back to him.

Within five minutes, they were perfectly relaxed in their chairs, all bearing contented smiles. The chaos preceding Ederne's exit seemed a distant dream to all of them, and Celeste and Etienne were once again opposite Oihana and Nahia.

Oihana's amethyst eyes paused on each of the other three, ascertaining the success of their passiflora-induced composure, and seemingly satisfied that all was in order, she addressed them with an admission.

"What I said earlier about the way to recover a stolen thread was not entirely accurate. You see, I wanted to give Ederne the opportunity to do the right thing, so I hinted that only through her presence could the thread be retrieved. But she refused the opportunity, and instead, we can now be certain that she harbors no regrets over having parted with it, that what she did may have even been voluntary." Oihana shook her head apologetically. "Fortunately, however, the faery who loses the thread is not the only one who can retrieve it. By all means, it is the easiest way but not the only way."

"If only she hadn't been so quick. We could've put her in a cage and dangled her within a foot of the old witch," Nahia said wryly. Celeste couldn't hide an approving smirk.

"I suppose your heart is in the right place," Oihana said soberly. "But I cannot condone sacrificing a life, even the life of a conspirator such as Ederne."

Nahia shrugged, glancing toward Celeste as if to say, "I could."

"What other way is there?" Etienne asked.

Oihana seemed to consider this for a moment, then she replied as casually as she could manage. "Knowing the intention with which the thread had been spun and woven would enable me to extract it without much difficulty. You see, glamour is live magic, as unique to each faery as are their intentions. Raw glamour, at the point it issues from the faery but before it flows with a purpose into the object it is destined for, is a most unruly thing. The intent of the faery in producing it is the one thing that tames that raw power and forces the glamour to enter and remain inside an object or person. So you see, the intent with which this magic flows out of a faery is what makes it unique, makes it her own."

Nahia fretted in contrast to Celeste and Etienne who listened raptly as Oihana continued to explain.

"Now, for glamour to be retrieved, to be drawn back into a faery other than the originator, it is imperative that it be summoned with the same aim, the same intent as it went out."

"But, Mother, you have told me yourself it is likely the faery attempting such a thing could die. Especially since we don't even know if Ederne told the truth. Good grief. Do we actually believe she was making a blanket?"

"That is why I would have to be the one to do it," Oihana replied patiently. "Either she told us the truth and she was in the process of weaving a mantle to keep dry, or she lied and she actually volunteered the thread to Arantxa, in which case the thread only had its raw power. I trust myself above anyone to identify the intention saturating that glamour. I know the signs I need to look for, and I know I can probe successfully without lingering too long."

"Without lingering too long?" Celeste wondered out loud.

"Yes. You see, I must exert my power, extend the energy within me; like tentacles if you will, until I locate the glamour residing in Arantxa. And I must emulate the intent with which it was given to her before I can draw it back into me, or the thread will fail to recognize me as a source of magic and it will drain me of my strength instead."

"I thought you said you didn't condone sacrifices?" Nahia said anxiously.

"I made a promise to Paloma, Nahia. I told her that if it was ever in my power to help Celeste, I would not hesitate to do it."

"I can't let you take that risk, Oihana," Celeste objected at once.

"And I can't allow anyone to take that risk. No. I will need to establish contact, and I will need to summon the power of that thread to me."

"Contact? Do you mean visual contact or close proximity?" Celeste asked tentatively.

"Actual, physical contact, as in *touching* and gradually weakening," Nahia interjected dramatically.

"Let's not exaggerate, Nahia," Oihana said calmly. "I won't have to physically touch her, but I will have to be very close, no more than a foot, I should think. You see, the closer I am to her, the stronger my pull can be. It has been years since the potion containing the thread was ingested, and I am certain Arantxa would have laced it with every binding ingredient she could think of. No. I simply cannot trust anyone else to attempt this. If we are to draw the thread out of her, then I am the only one qualified enough to manage it."

Celeste gasped. "And how are we going to manage that? Especially since you'll be weakening once you begin drawing the thread. And that means—"

"That if I heard you correctly, Your Majesty, you'll be in danger of becoming visible," Etienne finished for Celeste.

Celeste made a mournful sniffing sound next to him. That Oihana should put herself in such danger on her behalf made Celeste feel miserable, and the possibility of losing Oihana to Arantxa was excruciating.

Oihana nodded. "As I progress in my effort, I *will* become increasingly visible."

"Allowing Arantxa the ability to fight back," Celeste sniffed and blinked away her tears. "I can't let you do this, Oihana."

"Mother, it will be so dangerous," Nahia protested with palpable concern.

"True enough," answered Oihana stoically. "But I've lived for over eight hundred years now, and you must grant that I've learned a few tricks in the interim. Arantxa is indeed a powerful sorceress to have succeeded at what she set out to do, but I am certain her trickery will succumb to my experience and power. I assure you, I will do this thing unharmed," she said, her eyes sparkling with appreciation for her daughter's worry.

Thoroughly unconvinced by Oihana's assurances, Celeste's fingers worked tensely at the base of her own throat, as if trying to coax her fear to stay low rather than erupt out of her. "This cannot be the only way, can it? What if we just …What if we just kill Arantxa?"

Nahia clearly approved of this idea as she sat expectantly at the edge of her chair, ready to pursue this possibility.

"She cannot just be killed," Etienne said reasonably. "Her true identity must be established, otherwise she'll die a queen, leaving a princess behind, whom *I'll* have to marry."

Celeste groaned in frustration.

Oihana nodded. "If we are to expose and defeat Arantxa, it is imperative that we consider all possible angles of this situation. Let us not waste another minute on the one thing that cannot be changed."

And so, over the next two hours, good and bad ideas were tossed about the tablinum. Objections surfaced, and solutions presented themselves. Obstacles rose before them, and one or another would think up a way to overcome them. Celeste had paced on the pebbled floor and on the sand. Bakar had fed them fried cheese with fruit jelly and tarts. He had also cleared the emptied serving dishes and left them with cups of steaming crimson tea. Nahia had switched chairs at least six times and often floated about, circling behind the mound representing the island of Santa Clara or skimming lazily over the sea-green water. The detailed maps Etienne had drawn on the white canvas, brought in special once the idea of staging the attack in Santillán had taken shape, were covered in marks depicting such things as pulpit, main entrance, altar, and central aisle. Oihana alone appeared unperturbed and in control. Furthermore, she seemed to have recorded in her disciplined mind every word and gesture issued by them throughout the evening, for she could quote and remind them of anything and everything without the slightest effort.

A balmy breeze picked up, renewing the air they breathed, and Celeste let out an exhausted moan. It was well past midnight outside, despite the perpetual midday in the tablinum.

With a tired groan of her own, Nahia agreed with Celeste and sagged into her chair for the hundredth time. "I can't think straight anymore."

"So why don't we summarize what we have already decided upon?" suggested Etienne, and all eyes fell expectantly on Oihana.

"Very well," she said. "The object is to expose Arantxa's true identity. Etienne tells us she is a sap for appearances, so we will use that to our advantage and carry out our plan during the course of the wedding ceremony. There she is more likely to check her reactions and restrain herself before her subjects giving me more time to do what I must. Also, during the ceremony we can count on the largest number of witnesses. Celeste and I will arrive, concealed in transparency shrouds, which will be completed within the next two days." At this, Oihana cast a significant glance toward Celeste, which Celeste acknowledged with a fervent or perhaps uncertain nod.

"What? Why are you rolling your eyes?" Celeste cried, affronted by Nahia's half doubtful, half amused expression over Oihana's assertion.

The faery replied casually, "Well, there's no denying you have a knack for weaving."

"A knack? *Knack*! Just a knack?" Celeste called out incredulously.

Oihana's eyes shifted warily from Nahia to Celeste and back again. "Ladies," said she with a cautionary tone in her voice. "It is late and we are all tired." But the girls did not hear and plowed on heatedly.

"Fine then. You're a *good* weaver. Is that better?"

"Oh, by all means, that is *loads* better. Thank you so much, Nahia the *begrudger*," said Celeste, her words curling nastily at the end.

"The *begrudger* is it? How can you have the gall to say such a thing to me when you know perfectly well I've never been one to withhold praise where praise is due," Nahia declared loftily.

"Except where it concerns me." Celeste declared reproachfully.

"What do you mean? I always acknowledge you when you've done well."

Etienne looked from one to the other, as if watching a lawn-tennis match.

"Let's forget for a moment that everyone else has a high opinion of my skill," Celeste retorted. "What you are saying now is that my weaving is not worthy of praise, that it is only a *knack*, so you won't be bestowing any praise upon it. But this is, at *long* last, fine and good with me, because I see now what you are doing. You insist on looking at my efforts as one rung lower than the model, *just* so you can excuse yourself and withhold your admiration. Think back a little, Nahia, and you'll see this has been your pattern. And if I'm lying, tell me, when was the last time you acknowledged me for a job well done?"

"Ladies," Oihana interjected in an attempt to moderate their escalating discussion, but in spite of her superb diplomatic ability, the queen of the faeries was again unsuccessful. She glanced at the empty cups of crimson tea with a blaming eye.

"I know exactly when that was. But that's not relevant now."

"Ha! It's not relevant because you can't remember, and you can't remember because it hasn't happened—ever."

"Ladies."

"Be serious! You *always* choose to forget the nice things I say to you, and what can I do about that? Nothing, that's what. The reality is that I'll *never* be able to acknowledge you enough. You're *never* satisfied with a compliment. You *always* want more."

"I thought your mother told you not to keep saying *always* and *never*. And I am not the attention-seeking fiend you paint me as. I think you're actually describing *yourself* for a change," Celeste added nastily.

"Ladies."

173

Etienne continued to follow the match, though the increasing heat of the argument made him shift uncomfortably in his chair.

As if she had suddenly remembered something, Celeste lightly tapped her forehead with the palm of her own hand. "Good grief. You know what I just realized?"

"*Girls.*"

"You're jealous, because you know perfectly well I don't have just a *knack* for weaving," Celeste said, wagging her head. "I am a *brilliant* weaver. And because of that, I am included in this undertaking and you're not. And you can't stand that. Ha ha!"

"You have lost your mind, *human*. You can't ev—"

"Girls!" Oihana actually raised her voice, which in itself was enough to silence them, but, perhaps as an added precaution or simply as a perk, Oihana cast an invisible gag upon them.

"For the stars in the sky, you will *never* stop, will you?" Oihana exclaimed.

Celeste and Nahia both raised a tattling finger to Oihana when she said "never," and for the first time in their lives, they witnessed Oihana lose her temper. It came at them in the shape of a forceful angry gust.

When the shock of toppling backwards (chair and all) had ebbed away, Celeste noted that not only were they still gagged, but she and Nahia had been invisibly bound, so tightly she could hardly breathe.

Etienne leaned back on his chair to get a better look at Celeste (she was still in the sitting position, except the back of the chair was against the floor, as was Nahia's). He gave Celeste a tight-lipped smile, obviously siding with Oihana, but also with a suspicious raised brow that seemed to say, "Temper, temper," which only added to Celeste's distress.

Well, he might as well know how things work between Nahia and me. After all, she's going to be in his life too, and may the stars bless him! He needs to get used to her, she thought, still bristling in her gag and bindings.

"How can we accomplish anything if you won't stay focused?" Oihana chastised Celeste. "And you!" She turned to Nahia. "You will leave at once unless you can hold your tongue! Or I will leave you all to fend for yourselves!"

Unable to speak through her gag, Celeste blinked twice to show she submitted. Nahia hung her head to one side in what looked like a feeble nod.

With a quick spell, Oihana released them from their restraints.

In very subdued tones and after having worked her jaw side to side several times, Celeste said, "I'm so sorry, Oihana, Etienne … *Nahia.*"

"Now, to set things right before we proceed," Oihana said firmly. "Celeste is a magnificent weaver. I might say her skill is outdone by Usoa alone."

Celeste shifted in her chair, wishing Oihana's validation would have come without the nasty spat preceding it. "Thank you," she said meekly, still discomfited about having made Oihana lose her temper.

Etienne, who seemed to have gotten past whatever discomfort the juvenile argument might have caused him, stroked Celeste's hand warmly.

Nahia, with an obvious show of effort and to add to her mother's most recent statement, murmured penitently, "And by this winter, Celeste is likely to outstrip Usoa."

Celeste's head jerked up at this, and Nahia fixed her round aquamarines on her birth sister. It was a silent, but very meaningful, exchange. Etienne, who happened to glance at Celeste at the very moment she mouthed off the words, "I love you," to Nahia, turned to Oihana shaking his head in utter confusion over their hasty change of emotion.

"It has been so since they learned to speak," Oihana remarked flatly, to which Etienne uttered an enlightened "Ah," while Celeste and Nahia grinned sheepishly.

"Celeste has indeed come a long way since she began weaving. But there is more to it than that. She and I have been working together these past months on something quite unique, something we discovered by accident really, but which gave us a start."

Nahia looked on the verge of interrupting with questions, but Celeste anticipated her with an answer. "Remember that head scarf I made, how I wanted it to be all brown, but Usoa said that with my coloring I should be making it in red or yellow?"

"Yes, vaguely."

"Well, on one of those days in her workshop," Celeste said excitedly, "I think I was half way through it by then, Usoa stood and watched over my shoulder for over an hour, unraveling spools for me and telling me how tight and even my weave was. But all the time, she must have been thinking that she wanted it to be *red, red, red*, because the next thing I knew, my beautiful russet scarf, gradually became a dirty rust color and soon went through every shade in between until, in the end, it was a brilliant scarlet."

"So that's what happened to it. And you still wear that red head scarf. I remember wondering why you had changed your mind about the color," Nahia said musingly.

"So you see, Usoa showed us that it was possible for glamour to work through Celeste to combine her marvelous weaving skill with the purpose-giving force the faery can provide. I admit that at first, I didn't know what higher meaning this would serve, but now I imagine it is clear to us all that

Celeste's ability will enable us to produce the two shrouds we will need: the shrouds that will make Celeste invisible, and me as well, should the moment arrive that I am weak to the point of being visible."

Celeste and Etienne were nodding their approval, but Nahia looked uneasy.

"May I ask now the question I didn't get to ask earlier?" Nahia said, pausing to glance nervously from Oihana to Celeste. When Oihana gave her the go ahead, she said, "What I wanted to ask was this, how will Celeste be able to weave these two shrouds before the wedding when, as far as I can remember, it took her over a week to do the single head scarf we just talked about?"

Celeste didn't have time to even react to this, for Oihana responded quickly. "You are quite right, Nahia. Celeste is very swift, and she cannot weave any faster than she already does. She is already quicker than any faery in Handi Park. But I *have* thought of that, and I am certain we will manage."

The lack of detail as to *how* they would manage didn't do much to ease Celeste's mind on an issue she too had been fretting over. And it certainly didn't seem to appease Nahia to know that Celeste and Oihana would be exploring new and exciting practices that she would not be a part of.

"But let us resume our summary," Oihana said quickly when it appeared that Nahia might quiz her some more. "On the wedding day, Celeste and I will be at the chapel, and her duty will be to explain to those present what is happening and why and to keep Arantxa distracted to give me the time I will need to affect the recovery of the thread."

"I'll be there as well and at your command. I'll do whatever you ask," Etienne assured the faery queen.

"Indeed, young Etienne, we must keep in mind that once the thread begins to dislodge, the transformation will begin right away, naturally disrupting the ceremony and shocking the wedding guests—to put it mildly. So it will be very good of you to do your utmost to avert a mass panic."

Nahia, who seemed to be picturing it all quite vividly, inched to the edge of her seat and said, "Have you ever seen it happen, Mother?"

Oihana shook her head. "It will be a first for me."

Celeste shook the foot at the end of her crossed leg, feeling a mounting anxiety for the many things that might go wrong. What if she couldn't finish the weaving in time? What if it took longer than Oihana estimated to recover the thread? What if the shrouds didn't work against self-bored stones? The more she thought about it, the more the likelihood of being discovered before they even had a chance to start anything increased in her mind. All at once, the thought of Arantxa frightened Celeste, that the woman commanded such dark powers, that she had no scruples—after all, had she not killed already without hesitation? Fear began to sink its teeth into her heart.

Disconnected images of her, Celeste, standing beside Oihana, slipped into her mind with prophetic persuasiveness. They were these two invisible, miniscule creatures hiding beneath their shrouds, hoping not to get trampled inside the crowded church while humans, *strangers*, carried on loud conversations that meant nothing to Celeste, and they laughed frivolously at things she knew nothing of, showing their nostrils and the roofs of their mouths as they threw their heads back in cold hilarity. A woman's voice high above Celeste said, "There is the queen! Here she comes!" Celeste fought her way through the sea of skirts and trousered legs that blocked her from the aisle on which Arantxa advanced. She pushed aside a silky, chocolaty skirt and stumbled onto Arantxa's path. Celeste looked into those vacant eyes, the same eyes she had seen seven years before when she foolishly dragged her sleeping mother to the border of the realm and that had visited her in nightmares ever since. Celeste wanted to call for Oihana, but that horrible Arantxa looked right at her—through the ineffective shroud—and said, "I hope you brought something more than just a *blanket*." Arantxa laughed an inhuman laugh that set Celeste to shivering, and before she could even wonder where Oihana might be, Arantxa raised her arms to the heavens and called upon lightning itself to strike them down. The first bolt struck at Celeste's feet. The vision was so real to her that she actually yanked her feet off the ground and up onto the chair.

The images melted away, and she was back in the bright tablinum, hugging her own knees dispiritedly. Etienne gave her a quizzical look, rubbing the side of her arm, and when she continued to look at him wide-eyed and anxious, he winked at her. Celeste smiled before she knew it, her body relaxing, and then responded with a playful wink of her own. *We're coming at her with more than just* blankets, she thought. *And I won't give her the upper hand. Not even in bad dreams.*

Etienne turned his smiling face back to Oihana and so did Celeste, and although she had not completely done away with her doubts, she had made up her mind not to even conceive of failing. So the next time a sentence starting with "what if" popped into her head, she promptly recited to herself, *Arantxa does not have the upper hand, and I won't give it to her!*

"Once the transformation begins," Oihana was saying, "I will return Celeste to human height, and she will be visible. This would be a good time for you, Etienne, to step in and beg everyone to pay attention to her." Etienne nodded. "She will tell the congregation how Arantxa plotted the death of Bautista and transformed herself into Paloma in order to take over the kingdom, how Arantxa took it upon herself to exile the pregnant Paloma, condemning her to Arantxa's own decaying body in a blatant, though fortunately unsuccessful, murder attempt. 'The real Paloma died only a few days ago, and I am her daughter,' she'll say."

"'The woman you see before you is nothing but an apparition, and I can prove it,'" Celeste added, raising her arm as if she were brandishing a sword.

Oihana wrapped up the succession of events. "And at that moment, having succeeded in gathering the glamour unto myself, and to a chorus of terrified screams from the wedding guests, Arantxa will appear in her true body, leaving no doubts as to the truths spoken by Celeste."

Nodding several times and trying not to sound sulky, Nahia said, "Yes, I think it will work."

The other three nodded pensively.

"And so, the wedding is in four days," Etienne reminded them.

"And we will be ready," said Celeste.

It was close to three o'clock in the morning, and Nahia looked as bleary eyed as Celeste felt. Etienne, however, appeared blissfully impervious to exhaustion, surely because of the jelly Oihana had inoculated him with.

"Indeed," said Oihana, rising from her chair and beginning to pace from the pebbled floor to the sand and back again. "So I'm bringing this conference to a close with a handful of directions. You will stay the night," she said to Etienne who had courteously stood up when she did and now bowed his assent. "Bakar will show you to one of our guest quarters. And Celeste, if you promise to actually sleep, for a long day awaits us tomorrow, you may stay with Nahia. Otherwise, you are to return to the grotto."

Celeste and Nahia exchanged happy smirks, and Celeste quickly said, "I'll stay with Nahia."

"And we'll sleep," Nahia promised.

"In the morning, young Etienne, I imagine you will be returning to your mother?"

"Yes, Your Majesty."

"Very well then. I should like to have breakfast with you before you depart."

"It would be my pleasure."

Bakar arrived to escort Etienne.

Oihana wished them all a good night, and the other three followed suit. Etienne bowed politely to the two faeries. Celeste watched him, longing to kiss him or at least embrace him, but she felt too self-conscious to do so in front of Oihana and Nahia. Etienne, however, seemed to find it perfectly fitting to kiss her hand.

Bakar lead the way out into the atrium, and Etienne followed him through the passageway marked with an amber lantern. Celeste trailed after

Nahia and Oihana through the royal passageway, fancying she could still feel the delicious tingle of Etienne's lips on her skin.

CHAPTER 18:

ARANTXA'S GAMBIT

Arantxa rose from her red high-back chair in the library. She could still hear Etienne's steps, following the valet out of the vestibule on his way to Clemente's cottage. She paused at the threshold of the library, and when she was certain they were gone, she proceeded to her chamber upstairs. Closing the door behind her, Arantxa walked over to the fireplace, which, at present, only smoldered, and she looked at herself on the ornately framed mirror above it. The suspicion Etienne's visit had roused was now evident on her countenance. Her smooth forehead bore a crease between her perfectly arched brows, which did nothing to enhance her green, unsparkling eyes (it had been years now that she thought of the stolen attributes as hers and no longer as Paloma's). Sparing a resentful thought for Etienne as the one responsible for her current misgivings, Arantxa tore herself from the riveting effect the sight of her reflection continued to have on her, and she slid her fingers along the top of the polished wooden mantelpiece and its underside. Having found what she sought, she exerted the necessary pressure on the latch that released the springs. The mantelpiece opened like a long lid, and the hidden compartment was revealed.

Arantxa rummaged through its contents: some two-dozen vials filled with liquids in various colors and degrees of viscosity. The air in the chamber momentarily filled with the sound of clinking glass until, at last, she pulled out a vessel containing a sort of murky, runny substance. She held it up to the light of the floor-to-ceiling windows opposite the fireplace. It was a dirty shade of green, but nevertheless, she was pleased with the degree of transparency it exhibited. Shaking the vial to emulsify its content, Arantxa walked over to the round breakfast table near the windows, on which stood a large vase filled with colorful, long-stemmed chrysanthemums and a silver tray with a pitcher of water and two glasses. With her free hand, and while still holding the vial appreciatively at arm's length, Arantxa filled a glass with clean water. She uncorked the vial, and with a very steady hand, she poured two single drops of the dirty green liquid into the water. She stirred it promptly with the stem of a chrysanthemum she pulled out of the vase. Arantxa corked the vial and returned it to its hiding place. She snapped shut the mantelpiece and rang the bell for her chambermaid.

A nervous, gangly girl of about seventeen came in directly. She had barely finished curtseying and straightening the crisp cotton cap covering her hair when Arantxa barked at her, forcing the glass of water on her. "Taste this."

Visibly distraught that perhaps she had failed to refill the pitcher with fresh water that morning, the maid reached for the glass being thrust upon her and drank down half of it. The girl smacked her lips, searching for the possible cause of Arantxa's displeasure. Finding none, she gave Arantxa an inquiring glance and murmured, "Begging your pardon, Your Majesty, I cannot detect a bad taste or smell. Is Her M—"

"Drink all of it," Arantxa said impatiently.

The maid did Arantxa's bidding and placed the empty glass on the tray. She then looked expectantly at the queen.

Arantxa watched her keenly. Before long, the maid, who had been squirming uncomfortably under the queen's silent glare, felt compelled to shake her head and blink repeatedly. A sneer curled Arantxa's lips. The girl wiped her forehead with the back of her hand, looking as if she would soon be sick, and Arantxa, far from concerned, nodded appreciatively. Arantxa's eyes narrowed in anticipation until the last indicator came upon the chambermaid. The girl's eyes had glazed over and now displayed a pearly, vacant gleam.

"Sit down," Arantxa said, and the lanky girl, whose cap sat cockeyed on the top of her head again, turned impassively toward the nearest chair. She sat very straight and very still. Her unfocused, gleaming eyes followed Arantxa but looked eerily through her. "You will wear this," said Arantxa, placing a brown hooded cloak on the maids lap. It was the standard garb of any sheepherder. "You will keep your head down, and you will talk to no one except me, do you understand me?" The maid nodded dreamily. "You will get to Clemente's cabin, but you will not go in. You will not allow yourself to be seen, but you will listen to what Clemente and his visitor say to each other. At the end of thirty minutes, you will return to me, and you will repeat to me what you have heard. Do you understand?" The maid nodded absently again.

The girl's head seemed to disappear within the ample brown hood, and not an inch of her was visible under the cloak. Arantxa was well pleased with the disguise. Closing the door after her, Arantxa remained alone, with nothing to do but wait.

As the potion would only work for one hour, Arantxa had taken no chances. The maid needed to be back in the residence and repeat whatever she had heard before the effects of the potion wore out, or she would become aware of what she was saying, which would no doubt cause a great deal of confusion and gossip. "If there is anything amiss with this impetuous visit of the young prince, I'm sure it will be revealed within the first half hour," she reassured herself.

A long forty minutes elapsed, and at last, Arantxa heard the sound of her chamber door creaking open. She closed her eyes and smiled, then turned her back on the window to see the cloaked girl standing mutely between the door and the fireplace.

"Close the door, and remove the cloak," Arantxa said silkily. The girl obeyed. "Now, sit down, and repeat me what you heard."

Apparently, the maid had arrived at her post once the conversation between Clemente and Etienne was underway, for in a very flat tone she recited the following: "'That because of you, being the dear tutor that you were to Paloma, she would have chosen to name her daughter Celeste. To honor you.' 'Hold your tongue, young man. What do you think you're playing at, saying such things!'"

Such first words coming out of the girl's mouth had the effect of a blow to the stomach on Arantxa. A searing, rancorous shock passed through her. Torn between strangling the maid and listening to all she would repeat, Arantxa rose from her chair by the window and paced angrily. She tried to piece together who might have said what from such fragments parroted by the girl as, "'The labor pains were quite advanced … The darkness of a cave … soon she had me vanished … A faery's weaving thread.'"

Every new sentence uttered by the maid was a fresh upset to Arantxa who, in her silent rage, had begun muttering and striking at intervals at her own chest and stomach with her fists to release her anger. She was startled when the maid abruptly stopped talking. Arantxa turned to her in a fury and recognized the signs of the girl's return from the effects of the potion. Arantxa deliberately turned her back in a final attempt to compose herself. Meanwhile, the wretched girl sprung from the chair, clearly horrified to find herself sitting on the queen's furniture and in her *presence*. In a most apologetic tone, she whimpered, "Mi-lady, may I replace the pitcher of water that so displeased you? I shall fetch it myself from the well."

Arantxa turned slowly and glared at her, again battling the urge to strike her. "Leave. This instant. Do you hear me? And tell everyone that I am *not* to be disturbed."

The chambermaid shook where she stood but did not wait to be told twice. The door slammed accidentally behind her, and for a moment, Arantxa thought of making her come back, just to give herself the satisfaction of at least slapping the girl over the slammed door, but there was simply too much she needed to think about. Instead, Arantxa punched her own stomach again and let out a rumbling outraged growl.

In spite of her instructions to the chambermaid, Arantxa was interrupted twice: once because Berezi demanded to see her and again because the servants wondered if she would take her meals in her chamber. Berezi was told by the servants her mother would not see her until Wednesday night. And regarding Arantxa's meals: "If my door is knocked upon or opened one more time while I am still within, I'll have you all flogged!" she roared in a fury. The chambermaid barely had time to close the door before the vase full of flowers and water crashed and shattered against it.

Seated at her table overlooking the garden, Arantxa's fingers made a steeple over her mouth as she tallied the broken facts she had learned, which were no less than daunting when she considered that a key event in the fulfillment of her scheme was to take place in only five days' time. The key event, the wedding that would unite both kingdoms under her, was in grave jeopardy. "Paloma has survived," Arantxa hissed, still shaking her head in disbelief. "She even managed to give birth to that child of hers. And Clemente—that old fool—has deceived me all these years. And that duplicitous *peasant* prince has met this ... this ... *Celeste*! Ah, and the faery thread has been mentioned. It must have been the old fool who knew about it. And now that traitor peasant lover will be sure to tell Paloma about it."

The light in the garden changed from bright midday to glowing dusk, and Arantxa still sat at her table, although her thoughts had simmered down considerably. "It is not hopeless. Not by any means. What can Paloma possibly do in four days' time? Nothing! The only real risk I am facing is that a faery should appear, and what are the chances of *that* happening. Just the same, I know what to do about it. And whatever Paloma and her daughter may concoct, I can undo," she reassured herself.

When evening fell, Arantxa allowed her ladies in waiting to groom her and requested that dinner be brought to her rooms, and *no*, she would not speak to Berezi this night. "Let the princess know, as I've already said, that I will speak with her tomorrow, but during the noon meal."

Through the entire night, and despite her own repeated reassurances, Arantxa could not help dwelling feverishly on her speculations. No sooner had she reasoned herself out of one predicament, that another would arise with the searing shock that made her want to strike herself. "That two-faced peasant, that betrayer. He will surely tell them about the thread. Oh, spirits of the dark, how have you kept me blind to this! Have you abandoned me? They are now plotting my destruction. But no! Paloma is not a threat to me.

No human is. Oh, that I knew if another faery can draw the magic from a thread. But what does it matter? Only the possibility of a faery matters. Yet what if Paloma has managed to change herself back?"

By sunup, tangled between rumpled sheets, her hair a matted mess owing to the restless night, Arantxa continued to brood. A single shaft of sunlight broke through the heavy draperies and into the darkened room. A myriad of dust specks swirled in it. That Etienne behaved as if the wedding was still taking place made it certain a scheme to break up the ceremony was underway. Perhaps Paloma and her daughter intended to arrive unannounced and uninvited. Maybe they could give themselves an audience by causing enough confusion. But Arantxa felt secure in the powers at her disposal, and that she had this intelligence in advance made her certain the advantage was hers. "Guards will be doubled, and no one will enter without an invitation," she said feverishly, preparing herself for the assault that was sure to come from Paloma and Celeste, for the drugged maid had not caught the part of the tale in which Paloma's death had been revealed or the fact that, for all these years, they had resided in the Realm of Faery.

"I know you are coming. I will be waiting for you," Arantxa said confidently, but she inevitably went back to, "But what about the faery. That treacherous faery. What if she had found Paloma and struck a deal with her as she did with me? Or what if another faery can draw the glamour from my thread? I must take precautions, because guards won't be able to see a faery, much less *stop* one. But what am I saying? What are the odds a faery would have found Paloma?"

"Still, if the transformation doesn't take place, Paloma and that brat of hers, *Celeste*, will have nothing. Paloma will be no more than a lunatic, the dangerous *Arantxa* returned. I can sentence her to death, and yes, imagine Prince Etienne's outrage when he wakes from the trance I'll put him under and finds himself happily married to my Berezi and already on his wedding night. Not only that, but he'll be informed by his admiring new bride that on his command, the conspirator's life has been ended. The sly Celeste is no more."

I will be waiting for them. Arantxa smiled to herself, anxious to begin her preparations. She got out of bed and rang for her attendants. Standing in front of the fireplace, she marveled at the beauty of her features reflected in the mirror, despite her tousled hair and craggy nightgown. Eyeing herself haughtily whilst lightly turning her face this way and that, she spoke in an intimate, honeyed voice, "As for Clemente ... my only loose end ... I must punish him for his deceitfulness. He shall pay with his life. What a grave loss it will be." She smiled seductively into the mirror, feeling increasingly confident. "I'll be waiting for you, Paloma. You were no match for me eighteen years ago, and you can be no match for me now. Of course, this time, I don't need you to survive for any length of time as before. So I won't just leave it to nature to do the killing for me. I'll make sure you and your daughter *are* dead, by my own hand." Her tapered fingers caressed the polished mantelpiece. "Now ... Where is my precious stone?" She opened the secret compartment, and the clinking of glass objects being moved filled the air in the room again. "There you are." Arantxa smiled fondly at the smooth rock. It was a perfect oval with a perfect oval-shaped hole right through its middle. She held it up to her eye and looked through it. "No faeries here," she laughed, closing her fist around it and shutting the secret lid. "You can't take me by surprise, faery. I will spot you if you should venture anywhere near me, and I will make sure you're good and dead this time."

There was a subtle knock at the door, and Arantxa admitted the two women who came to groom and dress her. She allowed them to do their work without so much as a nod or a shake of the head when they presented her with choices. *Without the transformation, Paloma will have no proof.*

The attendants left Arantxa dressed and ready to start the day. They promised her a breakfast tray within the next few minutes, and once it had been placed on the table by the window, Arantxa dismissed the attendant and server to once again open the compartment above the fireplace.

"Let's see, my dear Prince Etienne. All you need is a debilitating little potion. A vapor perhaps, clinging to a flower that I, myself, will pin to your breast." Arantxa crooned silkily as she pulled vials and jars from her store inside the mantelpiece. "With its sweet perfume, it will keep you—shall we say—relaxed and compliant." She laughed in the quiet of her chamber, mixing the ingredients that would render Etienne out of commission during the ceremony. When she finished, she held the small tin box in which she had deposited the crystallized blend, and she hid it in the compartment until the time came to put it to use.

Having put away all evidence of her work, Arantxa sat at the table and picked distractedly at the food on the tray. Her elbow rested on the tabletop, and her chin rested on her hand. Her fingers drummed broodingly over her cheek. "Now, what to do about Clemente," she said. "Something very special. No, not a potion for *him*. He needs to regret having lied to me, he needs to know I have found him out, and he needs to feel my anger and displeasure." Having hit on *just* the thing, Arantxa sat up straight, and her face split into a most deformed sneer, one that disgraced the countenance of one such person as Paloma. "But I must wait until at least the night before the wedding so that he will not be missed. That I shall kill him with my bare hands, there can be no doubt."

Chapter 19:

Of One Mind

All the preparations discussed during their late night conference were already underway when Celeste and Nahia came out near eight in the morning, puffy eyed and in a haze, because instead of sleeping, as they had promised to do, they stayed up discussing such things as Nahia's opinion of Etienne (which was favorable), their respective takes on upcoming events (which were hopeful), and whether or not Celeste would manage to weave two faery-sized shrouds in three days (which was daunting). The giggling and quiet chatting of those irksome early rising faeries on their way to the communal dining hall at five in the morning had taken them by surprise. With a pang of guilt over their disobedience and with not another word, Celeste and Nahia dropped onto their pillows and snored contentedly until Oihana's insistent summons a mere hour later finally penetrated Nahia's heavy slumber. She, in turn, woke Celeste.

It was the twenty-sixth of June.

Celeste and Nahia wound through the labyrinth of passages that eventually led them into the atrium and, from there, to the tablinum, where Oihana waited for them.

"Good morning," the girls yawned in unison.

"I see you are properly rested," Oihana remarked dryly.

The girls shuffled their feet on the pebbled floor, rubbing their eyes and looking sheepish.

"Well, sit down and have something to eat. I recommend you sprinkle bee pollen generously on your drink or you'll be useless today."

"Where is Etienne," Celeste asked, pouring a cup of steaming tea for herself and obediently adding a spoonful of the bright yellow powder she knew would keep her alert.   Stirring her tea, she sat on one of the chairs around the table, eyeing the plates with fruit and pastries, which were sliced and arranged so artistically that Celeste felt sorry to have to eat them.

"He wanted to check on his horse," replied Oihana, "which he said he had left tied by the pond. And then he and Amets are to go to the grotto and bring back Paloma's loom. I thought it best not to reduce it with glamour, although that would simplify its transportation immensely, but I don't want to take any chances with its calibration."

Celeste put two jam-filled puff pastries in her mouth and washed them down with gulps of hot tea. "Nahia, let's go have a quick bath."

Nahia only nodded, absorbed as she was in topping her shortcrust wedges with bits of cheese and berries, which she then drizzled with honey.

"Please do," Oihana remarked. "But make it speedy, because we need all the help we can get in spinning silk and picking cotton. I'm afraid we can't use what we have in our stores, as it might be tainted with partial intentions."

Once Nahia finished her breakfast, the girls raced to the pond, one on foot the other whizzing through the air in her characteristic zigzag pattern. They bathed briskly and were already dressed by the time Etienne and Amets came by. They had Al-Qadir with them. With the aid of a harness, the horse easily hauled the large vertical loom that Paloma had designed.

Celeste raced over to Etienne, experiencing a relieved excitement at the sight of him. "I thought you might leave without saying goodbye," she whispered.

"Hmmm, I might without saying *goodbye*, as those words will inevitably precede our parting," he said smiling. "But *never* without saying *good morning*."

Nahia and Amets, who had averted their eyes to allow the lovers the privacy their whispering and embracing required, now turned back to them, and the four of them made their way to the petrified tree as Oihana had instructed. Through the hollow trunk of the tree, they were to lower the loom into the celestial observatory where Sendoa and another male faery would be waiting to receive it.

When they arrived, Etienne undid the harness, and Nahia proceeded to disperse the weight of the loom by skimming her hands over it. This she did with a showy trembling of the hands and wiggling of the fingers that Celeste felt sure were an exaggeration, to impress Etienne. In the meantime, Amets weighted down one end of the rope (previously a harness) and swung it over a thick branch directly above the petrified tree, which rose some fifteen feet up in the air. When Nahia finished her strenuous work, with Etienne being none the wiser, they tied the other end of the rope to the loom's crossbar, and Etienne began hoisting it up while Celeste and Amets guided it cautiously so it didn't jar or knock against anything.

Oihana's plan for completing the two faery-sized shrouds in three days was as brutal as it was brilliant. Celeste would be made to weave in a human-sized loom with human-sized threads in full human size herself, inside Handi Park (to comply with the rules of the court). To be exact, Celeste would weave in the celestial observatory, as it was the only place in Handi Park that the loom could be brought into without having to reduce it. All the tools and hands required to spin the six hundred spools they needed to complete the shrouds were in Handi Park. Each shroud would be crafted in three separate panels. Each panel would require seven human-sized spools of silk for the crosswise threads and seven human-sized spools of cotton for the lengthwise threads. These spools had to be untouched by glamour, which meant the faeries had to gather it, treat it, and spin it by hand. It was no minor undertaking, but Oihana had commanded it, and the troop had risen to the challenge as one.

"I don't envy you this task," Nahia murmured to Celeste while they watched the loom descend out of sight within the dark trunk and into the waiting hands of Sendoa in the observatory.

Etienne, who had heard Nahia's comment and knew the particulars of what was coming up for Celeste, stole a worried look at her before resuming his efforts to deliver Paloma's loom without incidents.

Sendoa and another male faery got hold of it and guided it gingerly away from the water well, which was directly below the hollowed trunk. The boys deposited the loom safely on the glossy sapphire floor of the observatory and signaled their success to Nahia whose head had poked over the rim of the petrified trunk.

Amets, who, after a job well-done, had assumed the compact size most comfortable to him, excused himself and left.

Nahia, catching the furtive glance Celeste and Etienne had exchanged, briskly said to him, "I suppose I'll be seeing you again when this madness is all over."

"You most certainly will," said Etienne amiably as he finished reeling the rope and dropped it to the ground in a thick coil.

"And you," Nahia called back to Celeste as an afterthought. "Hurry up, because we have a lot of work to do."

Celeste and Etienne watched the faery flit away, gracefully dodging branches on her way to the mound.

Turning to Etienne and feeling that she already missed him, Celeste said, "I *do* have a lot of work to do."

He circled Celeste's waist with his arms and gathered her to him. "I wish I didn't have to leave you. Will you be alright in there?" he asked, motioning to where they had just deposited the loom.

"I'll be fine," Celeste replied, trying to squelch the emotion roused in her by his concern. "But will you miss me?" she asked, trying to sound playful.

"Oh, you can count on my missing you every minute. *Even* when I'm sleeping."

"I won't promise to do the same," she laughed. "Or I will end up counteracting what Oihana will be trying to do, and the shrouds will be nothing but twin portraits of you."

Etienne laughed even though his eyes insisted he would rather stay.

"Ride carefully down that ridge," Celeste said wistfully.

"And you be swift," he replied. "I don't like the thought—"

"Shhh," she said, putting her fingers over his lips. "It has to be done, so it's no use fretting over it."

Etienne kissed the tips of her fingers before she lowered her hand. Much as she had told him of the beautiful sapphire glass pavers on the floor and the soothing ambiance of the observatory, he didn't look at all reconciled to the idea of Celeste being trapped in an underground vault for three days. "I can't stand the thought of you down there."

"Oihana will see to it that I'm fine. And I will be," Celeste said confidently.

For one self-conscious moment, Celeste looked into his eyes, wishing he would kiss her. Then it occurred to her that *she* could be the one to kiss *him*. So while he continued to worry about her impending seclusion, she pressed her lips to his and felt him relinquish his concerns, if only for an instant, as he responded to her.

Flushed and giddy, Celeste tousled Al-Qadir's forelock and held him by the bridle while Etienne mounted the horse. Again, there was that look in his eyes saying he would much rather remain, but Celeste told him resolutely. "Even if you stayed, we wouldn't be able to see each other. No, it is best you go to your mother and stop worrying her needlessly with your extended disappearances, or she'll find out what you have been up to and dislike me at once for being the cause."

Etienne smiled grudgingly, and Celeste stood aside that he might pass. She blew him a kiss and watched until he disappeared between the trees. With a heavy sigh, she made her way to the cottonwood grove, anxious to begin the next three days and be at the other side of them already.

***

Had it not been so fraught with tension, it would have been a perfectly wonderful day, but the faeries were so frantic to collect enough cotton to fulfill Oihana's requirement that—even though the day was sunny and mild, picnic-style food and beverages were plentiful, and such a workforce had never been raised for a single project—conversation, laughter, and singing, which were an intrinsic part of a typical faery work party, had been rigorously deferred this time. As dusk approached, Celeste was glad that the tall baskets were at last brimming with fluffy cotton. Each basket was almost as tall as a faery, and each faery had filled about three. Celeste piled her cotton on a large bed sheet, and since the faeries were able to carry only one basket, she had them empty the additional ones onto her pile. Celeste then gathered the corners and tied them in a knot before hefting it over her shoulder. She followed the faeries who were floating single file back to Handi Park with the baskets strapped like knapsacks to their backs. Only faerlings (under fifteen) were left behind to glean the grove with the strict instruction to bring any and all bits of cotton they gathered back to Handi Park to be spun into threads.

Outside the mound, Celeste dropped her bulky load to the ground and stretched her back while Nahia flitted out of the access shaft to meet her. "I have been spinning silk all day long. My fingers are numb," she said, wiggling them in front of Celeste. "But we have all the spools of silk you could ever need. I tell you, it's one thing to use glamour and have the threads just stretch and twist themselves into a spool, but a whole other proposition to do it by hand."

"I can sympathize with you," Celeste groaned, twisting her whole body from side to side. "I've been picking cotton all day with a hundred crabby faeries who couldn't use glamour either."

"Hmmm," Nahia said. "Do you know that, of all the cotton we had in our stores, my mother only found fifty-two spools she could call clean?"

"Oh no," cried Celeste. "Now I wonder if we'll have enough with what we brought in. I suppose it had better be. I don't think we left any fluff at all in that grove."

"Then it *will* be enough," Nahia remarked simply. "In any case, Usoa is preparing the loom with the cotton spools we *did* have, and that should get you started with the first panel. The math on this thing is stupefying. My mother lost me completely at around, 'We must twist seven faery threads to make one human-sized thread, which means that seven of our spools will be consumed to make one of yours,' or something like that. And then Usoa started in with, 'Each panel will require seven spools of cotton and seven spools of silk—human-sized spools, mind you.'"

"Enough, enough. I see what you mean."

The faeries who had disappeared into the access shaft with their loaded baskets would soon return to collect the rest. Wistfully eyeing the cotton that still needed to be brought in one basket a time, Celeste remarked, "Oh, that you could glamorize this and shrink it. We'd have it done in the blink of an eye."

"Yes, that would be good, but mother said no glamour is to touch that cotton, lest it interfere with what the two of you will be doing."

"I have an idea. Help me spread the cotton evenly on this sheet," Celeste said, undoing the knots and stretching the sheet until it was completely flat on the ground with a bulging mountain of cotton in the center. She began raking and separating the tufts of cotton with her fingers. Nahia alighted on the sheet and began dragging her feet over the fluffy mass. Soon they had turned the mountain of cotton into a thick, even layer over the sheet.

"Now what?"

"Now, we'll roll the whole thing, tight and even," Celeste replied, taking a corner of the sheet and folding it over itself. Nahia cottoned on, and when the corner Celeste had started became wide enough, she knelt next to Celeste and helped her keep the cotton tucked in while rolling the sheet into a tube. "And when we're done, we'll feed it like a long pipeline through the access shaft."

"Excellent," Nahia remarked, and when Celeste glanced at her archly, Nahia defended herself. "Your Etienne says that a lot, and it's catchy."

Celeste thought it over a few moments and then said with a quirky grin, "I like it too."

By the time the faeries came back to fill their baskets a second time, Celeste and Nahia directed them to stand at intervals along the passage instead, so they could support the weight of the pipe, pull it through, and guide it all the way to the bottom, where it would be conveyed to the washing room.

When the last of the pipe had been fed through the shaft, Nahia said, "It's close to five, and Mother wants you inside so you can get ready."

"I'll be back in twenty minutes," Celeste replied. "I want to tell Mamma what we are up to."

"Tell her I said hello," Nahia called after her.

Celeste grinned. "I will." And she darted off through the aspens as fast as her legs would carry her, relishing the strength of her limbs and taking deep breaths of the clean forest air, for she soon would be required to sit still and breath only the underground air in the observatory. When she arrived at Paloma's grave, she slumped against the mighty oak to catch her breath and wipe her brow. So many of her fondest memories were encapsulated within the trees surrounding this clearing, and now Paloma herself had become an everlasting part of it. More than ever, Celeste knew she could not leave the realm.

The water tumbled merrily over the sun-bleached boulders and into the pond. The long tendrils of the willow dragged on the grass and clover, and the hyacinths exhaled their sweet scent. Celeste looked up at the darkening blue sky visible through the lofty branches, and she heaved a sigh. "Mamma, so much has happened since the last time we talked. You should know that tonight I'm taking on a challenge," she said fretfully. "Oihana believes I can do this, but I'm not so sure." Then, remembering the promise she had made to herself the night before, to not allow Arantxa the upper hand, not even in thoughts, Celeste shook her head and adopted a different tone. "Oihana is right. I know I *will* succeed, Mamma, because even though you are gone and I miss you something terrible, I don't feel so alone anymore. You see, there is this *man*." Celeste paused, smiling at the quirks of fate attending her situation. "Remember how you said that I should fulfill my destiny, and that in doing so, I would find happiness? Well, as it turns out, I found happiness, and because of that, I must now fulfill my destiny."

The evocative hoot of the first owl, raring to hunt, interrupted Celeste's monologue, she narrowed her eyes and scanned the darkening branches above and around her, suddenly finding herself in more of a predatory frame of mind, the kind that—she thought—would be necessary to ensure her survival as well as Oihana's. "I love you, Mamma," she said, getting up to leave. "I'll be back when my weaving is done." A vengeful sort of spark had ignited within her, and it fueled her imagination as she trudged through the forest on her way back to the mound. She sniffed the air, she fancied she smelled victory, and her body was ready to spring. Arantxa didn't know they were coming and she, Celeste, and Oihana were going to destroy her before a chapel full of her subjects. No, a chapel full of *Celeste's* subjects.

But upon entering the aspen clearing, Oihana's enchantments to ward off intruders began to do their work on Celeste. And they did it in a way they never had before. There were no nightmarish sensations or glimpses of murky slithering things. There were no scurrying noises and no frigid drafts to make the tiny hairs on her arms stand on end. Instead, Celeste had to contend as best as she could with a force dead set on breeding doubt and confusion within her. She suddenly dreaded the possible failure of this undertaking, but in turn, she celebrated at the thought of her success. She shrank from the horror it would be to lose the battle but felt exultant when she thought of Arantxa denounced as a deceiver. Celeste could almost see the horrible woman sprawled at the bottom of a grave: deformed, defeated, *dead*. And this thrilled her momentarily, but a little voice whispered in her ear, "Surely Mamma wouldn't wish anyone dead."

"But I am not Mamma," she said irritably. "And surely that woman deserves to pay with her own life, for the lives of my mother and father, and Etienne's father."

"Are you ready?" Nahia startled her to attention.

Celeste barely had time to nod. Nahia struck at once, and all Celeste could do was to let out a strangled shriek of surprise followed by an involuntary giggle over the tingles in her belly. "You need to give me a little more warning," she said, straightening up and brushing off her lawn dress. Celeste was now of adequate size to enter the access shaft.

"No, it's far more entertaining this way."

"For whom?" cried Celeste in outrage.

"For both of us," said Nahia. But when Celeste crossed her arms over her chest in disagreement, the faery added, "Well, I can tell you that it is *definitely* a great deal of fun for me. And as my friend, I should think you'd take pleasure in the things that make me happy."

Celeste shook her head. "How do you think up these things?"

"They're just out there for the plucking," Nahia laughed.

Celeste spent an entire hour being prepared for the three days ahead. She was bathed and rubbed down with oils that gave her flesh a superficial heat that she found most interesting. It was explained to her that the oil would give her much needed insulation so she wouldn't be distracted with changes in her body temperature or in the observatory's temperature. Her hair was washed, detangled, slicked back, and pinned up securely. Eventually, she would be wearing a pliant dress made with an elastic weave so as to not be constrictive, but for the time being, they covered her in a white silk robe. Her feet were dipped into ankle-high stockings rather than sandals, and she was made to recline on a goose-down settee while a faery with flaming orange hair and equally blazing eyes began deftly applying a multicolored emulsion on her skin. The faery made small circles with her soft, almost imperceptible fingers over Celeste's temples then on either side of her neck and below her ears. "This will feel a bit odd at first," said the faery soothingly while slipping her warm hand under Celeste's robe to trace circles over each shoulder. All the while, she talked to Celeste in whispers that had the eerie quality of being disembodied, for at times, it seemed she spoke straight into Celeste's ears, and other times, Celeste felt sure the voice came from across the room.

"You'll awaken within two hours," the faery murmured and went on rubbing.

Through the thin membrane of her eyelids, Celeste could tell the light had been dimmed. "You have never slept like this. You will be so refreshed when you come back." And indeed, Celeste could already feel a delicious weight settling over her, spreading outward from every point of her body where the faery had rubbed. Somewhere deep, very deep in her mind, she wondered if she should test this weight, find out if perhaps she had been cocooned inside a very heavy blanket. She should try to raise her arm or her leg. But she was perfectly content to discover she couldn't even twitch her foot. The faery now rubbed her elbows in the same circling motion, and Celeste could feel herself smiling, but she couldn't be sure her lips had moved. The robe was folded up to above her knees, and the faery made circles there as well. She thought she felt the stockings being removed but was blissfully gone by the time the faery made circles on the rest of her joints, the palms of her hands, and the soles of her feet. Handi Park and her weighted-down body dropped beneath her as Celeste was borne on the wings of swans high above tree tops into the night sky and into a restorative sleep that would have the effect of ten hours of uninterrupted slumber.

Exactly two hours passed in that blissful state, then the dim notion of being strapped to the crossbars of a kite slipped into Celeste's mind, and the string pulling the kite back to earth was Oihana's voice.

"The time has come," the faery queen said. "The silk is ready. The loom awaits. The threads are strung. We are ready, and so are you."

Celeste opened her eyes to see Oihana leaning over her and smoothing the inquiring crease that had formed between her brows. "Oihana, I feel so … awake," she remarked, astounded that her loss of consciousness, which had been impossible to struggle against, much less overcome, could have lifted as quickly and as completely as it had in the time it took her to swing her legs over the edge of the settee and into a sitting position.

"As you should. That was a highly concentrated valerian root oil emulsion I prepared for you. I thought it safest for you to absorb it through your skin rather than drink it or breathe it."

"Did you say valerian?" cried Celeste, taking frantic whiffs of her shoulders and her wrists. She even drew one of her knees to her nose, remembering the faery had rubbed the emulsion there as well.

"Don't worry," Oihana assured her with a smile. "I took care of the smell. Would I be willing to work back to back with you for three days if I hadn't?"

Celeste grinned, somewhat relieved. But her nostrils continued to flare intermittently, certain she could detect the pungent scent of rancid cheese typical of valerian root.

Supper was a light, subdued affair, as Nahia was not present. By the end of it, Celeste had managed to ease up on the urge to sniff herself every five minutes.

At length, Oihana finished her tea and serenely said, "Shall we?"

The moment had arrived.

Celeste gave a jerky nod, and she started after Oihana to the celestial observatory. She followed stiffly, laboring to overcome the anxiety that again visited her now that the moment was at hand. Celeste barely noticed the cheery expanses intervening along the narrow passageways like bulky knots in a rope and in which clusters of faery dwellings had been terraced into the earth. Colorful balustrades overhung with bougainvillea overlooked the widened walkways. Here, each group of faeries showed their competitive nature by striving to grow the most luxuriant gardens. The effect was a shocking assault to the senses, for upon emerging from a darkened passage, one found themselves in a somewhat rounded courtyard amid tall flowering shrubs and large mounds of phlox in every dazzling color imaginable. A meandering pebbled footpath lined with lampposts connected the dozen or so households to be found in each cluster along the way. Without exception, each had its own well, and some even enjoyed the benefit of a creek. The mingled scents of gardenia and jasmine pervaded the mild air around them and rose to the balustrades, from which a handful of adult faeries watched them pass. To them, Oihana looked determined and unwavering. The human, Celeste, looked off color, as if someone had slipped her a larkspur tincture and would soon be sick.

Oihana entered the celestial observatory, as did Celeste three steps behind her. The light of two lanterns bathed the chamber in a soothing bluish light. The sapphire glass tiles on the floor and on the walls gleamed like moonlit water. At the center of the room stood the reflection well whose base had been crafted out of clear glass blocks. Celeste ran her fingers over its glistening rim, gazing at the tranquil water on whose surface Oihana had taught them to observe the sky above, visible through the shaft of the petrified tree, to study the position of the stars and the moon and learn the significance of it all. To one side of the well towered Paloma's loom, occupying more of the chamber than was necessary, or so Celeste thought. A large cushion had been placed before it. Celeste gave Oihana a fleeting panicked look as she pictured herself returned to human height in this room.

This expression did not escape Oihana who promptly said, "Everything will be fine. You will be able to endure it. I know you will."

Celeste gulped, worriedly looking at the loom again and wishing her concerns could be dislodged with a simple shake of the head. They could not.

"There are spools of silk there to get you started, and more will be brought in as we need them," Oihana said, pointing to the large basket beside the loom. "There is also a comfortable cushion for you to sit on."

"Thank you, Oihana," Celeste said in a strangled voice she wished she could modulate so Oihana would stop looking at her with such concern in her amethyst eyes.

"I will be here with you, unraveling silk and infusing it with the spell I am to chant until we are finished," the queen of the faeries said reassuringly.

Celeste gulped again, not trusting herself to speak.

"Are you ready?"

"Yes."

"Take your seat then."

And no sooner had Celeste settled on the cushion before the loom than Oihana returned her to her full human size of almost six feet.

Having walked in at that very moment, Nahia gasped, "Oh, dear. This is a bit *snug*, isn't it?"

Celeste's confidence was, Oihana seemed to think, as fragile as a painstakingly erected house of cards, so she rounded on her daughter with a significant look in her eyes, as if Nahia had blown it over on purpose.

Irked that she, Celeste, had given Oihana reason to underrate her; she resolved to put an end to her own misgivings once and for all. "It's not so bad," she said to Nahia, sitting on her cushion, thankful for the flexibility of her dress and the slits that allowed more liberty of movement to her long legs. Then, in an even more hopeful tone, she added, "Once I start working, I'll forget all about the size of the room."

"And so we should," Oihana said, her eyes darting briskly toward the door that Nahia might take the hint.

"Good luck, Celeste," said Nahia, clearly pitying her birth sister.

Nahia left the celestial observatory and Celeste turned toward the loom. The cotton threads were tied to a wooden cross bar and had been weighted down with solid glass cubes. The lengthwise threads had been separated at even intervals by two cross rods, and these Celeste would be able to easily lower as she progressed. "Usoa did this?"

"She did," Oihana replied, coming around beside Celeste and admiring the old weaver's handiwork. "This setup will save you a great deal of time."

"It most certainly will," agreed Celeste, running her fingers over the cross rods and trying not to look directly at Oihana, because somehow, it seemed disrespectful to look down on her. Even in a sitting position, Celeste was a discourteous foot and a half taller than the faery queen.

Oihana took the first silk spool from the basket and went around Celeste. She placed an exact replica of Celeste's cushion, although a much smaller one, on the sapphire floor behind Celeste so they would be back to back, and the faery queen took her seat.

Being in Handi Park in full human size was a first for Celeste. Looking through the weighted-down lengthwise threads, it seemed to Celeste the wall on the other side of them was entirely too close as was the wall to her right. She shifted tensely on her cushion, hoping to catch the roomier center of the chamber in her field of vision. She tried to reason that the hollow of the observatory was indeed large enough for her to sit in comfortably while she wove, and it was only when she stood up that she would feel compelled to stoop. But there was an unreasonable part of her that, try as she might, she couldn't silence. It taunted her with debilitating notions such as, *I'm entombed in here. I can't bear this confinement. What was I thinking when I agreed to this.* She closed her eyes and tried to fight back, hoping to put things into a happier perspective. She fidgeted.

"You need to stop, indeed," came Oihana's voice from behind Celeste, startling her badly. "You need to let go of your fear, Celeste, or I won't be able to work through you or with you."

"I'm so sorry, Oihana. I'm just … I just feel a little *crowded* … and my heart is … I'm trying to adjust."

"Can you feel the gusts of fresh air coming in through the hollowed trunk?" Oihana pointed out. "I find that a breeze can have a most soothing effect."

Celeste glanced upward, and when she indeed felt a light breeze kiss her face, she closed her eyes relieved. Breathing the cool air calmed her down considerably.

"Let's begin," said Oihana, handing Celeste the tip of the first silk thread they were to use. Celeste held it tight, and Oihana ran her fingers over it while she unraveled the spool until there was enough slack for Celeste to load the shuttle. When the shuttle was properly loaded, Oihana began unraveling more, always twisting it between her fingers or running it through her fisted hand before it passed to Celeste.

Celeste began working the shuttle in the repetitive crosswise motion that would continue over the next three days. To the right, the shuttle went under. Loop. To the left, the shuttle came back over. Loop. To the right, the shuttle went under. And they were off.

New spools replaced the empty ones without Celeste or Oihana's notice. Every inch of silk passed through Oihana's fingers on its way to Celeste, and she simply loaded the shuttle and continued her work without even looking.

At Oihana's command, faeries throughout Handi Park continued to spin silk as fast as they could until the three hundred faery-sized spools of silk and of cotton they required were complete.

Somewhere between using up the second or third silk spool, a remarkable thing happened that surprised even Oihana. At first, Celeste believed it to be her own imagination, but with mounting excitement, she became certain that she was indeed hearing Oihana's voice in her head. The faery queen was so focused and forceful in transmitting her glamour through Celeste that her voice had pushed through as well and entered Celeste's consciousness. Exhilarated by this discovery, Celeste began audibly echoing Oihana's words as a way of communicating to her what had happened.

"Invisible I'll be, every bit of me conceal. From prying eyes, protect me with this mesh of silk and will," Celeste murmured, and Oihana's reaction was as swift as was her understanding of the momentous occurrence.

The floodgates had been opened, or so it seemed to Celeste. At once, she saw herself enveloped in a golden orb, and for a fleeting moment, she treasured the thought that perhaps, at long last, she had become a faery. But no, there wasn't even hearsay about humans being turned into faeries. Celeste continued to repeat Oihana's chant, settling in her mind that perhaps a trapdoor (rather than floodgates) had been opened somewhere, enabling her to somehow see things through Oihana's eyes, because she had certainly never seen her own aura or shimmering glamour with her naked eye before. But far from discouraging her, this made Celeste feel on top of the world. Anything was possible now.

The sparkling royal lilac silk flowed through Oihana's fingers into Celeste's golden aura, and by the time it passed into the shuttle and crossed the lengthwise threads, it produced a pale rose-colored weave.

Celeste and Oihana's fingers worked swiftly. They chanted in unison the spell that would render them invisible, and when the first panel was completed, Oihana asked her to stop.

"Why?"

"We are making very good time, and even though we may have to do this one over again, I want to put it to the test," Oihana said, holding the first panel in her hands.

"What? We'll have to redo it? Why?" Celeste cried, eyeing the panel nervously and becoming frantic at the thought of having to discard it.

Oihana placed the panel over her own arm, and indeed, the faery queen's shoulder and arm, clear down to her fingers, disappeared from sight. "So far, so good," said she with a satisfied smile. "Now, I want to enlarge it with glamour."

"But I thought you said—"

"I know, but I think it will be wiser if once we reach Santillán you are at human height rather than faery size, wouldn't you agree?"

"Well, yes," Celeste hesitated, for the first time picturing herself in faery height among hordes of humans. At once realizing the folly of that part of the plan, she added pensively, "I could get trampled, couldn't I?"

"Exactly. So I want to test if the panel can resist the enlargement without losing its quality."

A swirling motion of Oihana's porcelain hand over the twelve-inch panel suddenly turned it into a six-foot piece of cloth. Celeste picked up the end of it with keen anticipation and pulled it over herself. Since one panel made up only half the shroud, it covered only her front. "Well? Can you see me?" she asked anxiously.

"Not a trace of you," said Oihana moderately.

But Celeste could hear the satisfaction in Oihana's voice, and she had to smile herself. She pulled off the unfinished shroud and folded it in half. Oihana promptly reduced it.

"Onward," she said.

They were cautious not to check their progress more than once every five or six hours, lest they became discouraged or too confident. Extremely light meals were brought to them three times daily at exactly the same time, enabling them to automatically break their trance. During these breaks, the basket of spools was refilled as well.

Invisible I'll be,
Every bit of me conceal.
From prying eyes protect me,
With this mesh of silk and will.

Celeste no longer needed to say the words; they were now an unconscious thought only she and Oihana could hear in each other's heads. Their voices had become a continuous string from their brains through their veins and into their hearts, from which the meaning of the words was pumped to the tips of their fingers. Celeste worked the shuttle with her eyes closed, not realizing she rocked back and forth, softly humming the lullaby Paloma used to sing to her when she was an infant. Nahia had been delivering hyacinth blossoms since the seclusion began, and their scent now clung to Celeste's hair and clothing and to every spool they used as well as every thread stretched on the loom.

With her back to Celeste, almost touching her, Oihana unraveled more silk, infusing it with the power of her will, which was now compounded through her connection with Celeste.

To the right, the shuttle went under. Loop. To the left, the shuttle came back over. Loop. To the right, the shuttle went under. Six hours passed in this manner, then twelve, then twenty-four. The next day was the same.

It was the third day, and the basket of spools had been refilled for the second time already since morning. They only had one panel left to do. "We'll be finished before nightfall, Oihana," Celeste declared, stuffing one last handful of blueberries in her mouth and turning back to the loom.

Oihana nodded, running her fingers over the slack between the shuttle and spool, as if to make sure no bit of glamour had dispersed while they ate.

No sooner had Celeste swallowed the berries than Oihana resumed her chant. Celeste picked it up right away, and the seamless flow of it through her and into their work continued undisturbed, leaving a part of Celeste's mind free to wander off into happy memories of nights spent under the stars or swimming naked in the pond, an activity that had caused at least three altercations with Amets who, after color-shifting her clothes so they blended with whatever surface they were on, would perch himself on a branch of the oak tree, refusing to leave until she came out of the water, naked. In her stubbornness, Celeste would soak until she looked like a prune, just to wait him out. The thought that the rest of her might look as bad as her deeply creased fingers was the only thing that could make Amets desist.

Oihana cleared her throat, and Celeste froze with her hand on the shuttle halfway to the loop on the left. At once she realized that Oihana must have been seeing her memories. In the bluish light of the observatory, Celeste's cheeks flushed pink. When Oihana made no further comment and resumed the chanting, the corners of Celeste's mouth quivered affectionately over a thousand such remembrances of her years within the faery realm.

Celeste and Oihana had entered the observatory on the evening of the twenty-sixth, and it was early afternoon on the twenty-ninth when Celeste tied the final knot.

Oihana broke their silent connection, causing Celeste to involuntarily sag on her cushion, as if she had been held upright by Oihana's power all along. Celeste straightened up with difficulty, and she squinted in the dimly lit observatory, which, up until then, had seemed perfectly adequate, but which now seemed to blind her. The golden aura she had grown accustomed to seeing was no longer there, neither was the shimmering quality of the silk. But what she mostly regretted losing were the two things she hadn't even linked to the connection with Oihana: that infinite confidence of hers and Oihana's perpetual sense of contentment.

Celeste felt suddenly dim, exhausted, and discouraged.

"It's not all gone," Oihana said soothingly, and Celeste gave her an inquiring glance. "I'm not reading your mind anymore," Oihana assured her. "I'm merely responding to what your body is saying."

Celeste tried not to sag again, but she had to avert her disappointed glance over the loss of the connection.

"All is still there," Oihana insisted. "Your aura, your confidence, your ability to be happy, those things didn't come from me, you see. I only opened the part of your mind with which you can see it all."

Celeste nodded, trying her best not to look glum. She told herself she would set out to discover that trapdoor, rip it off of its hinges, and leave it open for good, someday. But at the moment, she didn't have even an *ounce* of energy to spare.

Celeste watched Oihana as she thoroughly inspected every inch of the six panels she had crafted. Each one was tested over Celeste's hands, and by and by, Oihana pronounced them to be flawless.

Now that she knew that no reworking was necessary, Celeste wanted nothing more than to erupt out of the observatory through that petrified tree like molten lava from a crater. *It has been almost three days!*

Folding the panels carefully and laying them on the basket beside the loom for Usoa to join them, Oihana smiled knowingly at Celeste and at once reduced her to faery size with an outward fanning of her porcelain hands. Celeste experienced that sensation of being drained into herself, followed this time by the instant relief of no longer being crammed in a small place. She stretched her limbs, which suddenly felt sore, and rubbed her neck and shoulders, which were suddenly stiff. "Thank you," she sighed, pulling out the two pins that had secured her long hair in a knot.

"Well-done," Oihana praised her, running her fingers over the silky panels that would soon be turned into two hooded shrouds. But Usoa would see to that.

CHAPTER 20:

UNEXPECTED IN THE ASPEN

CLEARING

Nahia flitted breathlessly into the observatory. Her turquoise-streaked curls were pulled away from her face with a silver band, and she wore a very becoming periwinkle sundress, which made the faery look fresh and rested, while Celeste felt worn and dull. "Celeste, you won't believe who's out there."

"Etienne?" Celeste said hopefully, now stretching her arms as high as she could. Her spine made dim cracking noises that she followed up with pleasured sighs of relief.

"Him too," Nahia murmured grudgingly. With a wicked little grin, she added, "Although I can't imagine why. He *is* getting married tomorrow."

"So who else *is* with him, dear?" Oihana said, a hint of impatience straining her voice. "Celeste has exhausted herself—for almost three days, she has been without sleep—and her body will soon let her know it. We have a tremendous day ahead of us tomorrow, and I had rather hoped that tonight we could restore her energy somewhat."

Celeste glanced up at Oihana whose protective tone and demeanor had forcefully reminded her of Paloma. In her exhaustion, Celeste was overcome with a pitiful sense of having been abandoned and left to fend for herself, without a mother's guidance or protection. Her eyes filled with tears, and she deliberately bent down to touch her toes, more for the sake of hiding her breakdown from Nahia and Oihana than further stretching her stiff muscles.

"So pray tell, *who* is with him?" Oihana insisted, curtly brushing off the few pieces of thread that clung to her corn-silk-colored dress, which was of the same flexible fabric as Celeste's.

Nahia, who had stopped at the edge of the well in the observatory and had assumed a chastised posture while her mother spoke, gave a little jerk and abruptly completed her announcement. "It's the old man."

"What?" Celeste straightened up with a gasp, and even Oihana's porcelain face registered an arched look of surprise.

"Yes. The old man, Clemente," Nahia went on, thrilled to have their attention now. "He doesn't look too good though. He says it's a miracle he even arrived at this place, *alive*. I didn't want to shrink him, you know, in case he wasn't exaggerating and really wasn't up for a shape-shift, so I left him waiting in the clearing."

Celeste could not believe her ears. Etienne was just outside. And with him was the man who had watched Paloma grow from a little girl into a queen. He had been at her side when she married and later as well, when she became a widow, and he would have saved her from Arantxa, had his body permitted it. Just outside was the man Paloma had told Celeste to think of as a grandfather. And tonight, after having provided a crucial piece of information to their efforts, here he was in the flesh, not a mere disembodied name, Clemente.

"Well, let's go see them then," Celeste started.

"Allow us," Oihana said, offering her arm to Celeste and motioning for Nahia to do the same. Celeste hooked her arms to theirs, and between the two faeries, Celeste felt herself leave the sapphire-paved floor of the observatory. They navigated so fleetingly through the narrow passages that the quarter-mile journey to the atrium seemed no more than a blur of alternating vibrant color where the dwellings clustered and inky shadows through the tunnels connecting them.

They burst into the atrium and shot directly to the bridge at the top of the dome. They alighted on it and proceeded on foot to the exit shaft. Celeste's eyes had been so accustomed to the bluish radiance in the observatory that when she emerged, the blazing light of dusk blinded her momentarily. "Over here," Nahia said, again hooking her arm to Celeste's while Oihana took the other side. They glided across the clearing toward the two shapes Nahia had pointed out: one crumpled against the trunk of an aspen and the other stooped beside the first. Nahia and Oihana deposited Celeste daintily on the soft grass a few feet from Clemente. In the few seconds the two faeries and Celeste stood there unseen, she heard Etienne's arresting baritone coaxing the old man to finish the contents in the cup he offered. She felt a warm burst of all that was tender over his sincere attentiveness to Clemente.

"I prepared a reviving tonic for him," Nahia whispered helpfully in Celeste's ear right before Oihana (with an outward fanning of her porcelain fingers) restored her to human size. Naturally, the sudden and unannounced taking of space startled the old man and made Etienne turn abruptly.

Clemente recovered himself and soon his smile gave way to easy, joyous laughter at the sight of Celeste and the two faeries, who had also shifted to human height and stood on either side of her. Etienne straightened up and gallantly bowed to Oihana and Nahia. Then his attention turned to Celeste, and again his eyes burned with that heartbreaking longing that made Celeste feel responsible for his suffering. She despised herself for it.

Here were these two men who meant so much to her. One was old and broken; his face, wrinkled like old parchment, was framed by long white hair, which gave him a venerable, endearing appearance. She also noted that Clemente still wore his sleeping clothes beneath his cloak, and this added to the anxiety she already felt on his behalf. *What could possibly have happened to him to force his flight? For surely something dreadful has occurred. And if Nahia isn't exaggerating, how did he manage to survive the journey into the realm in his condition?* Celeste's eyes then rose to Etienne who stood on the other side of Clemente, still holding the empty cup in his hand. The rapid beating of Celeste's heart confirmed to her just how much she had missed him. That the sight of him surpassed the idealized version she had been clinging to for the past three days made her flush pink as in one swooping glance, she took in every detail of his rugged appearance: the warrior boots over the coarse breaches, the sword in its scabbard hanging at his side, the white shirt under the worn leather coat, the rough stubble on his tanned face, and the blue eyes that pierced her with such intensity as to make her look away.

A fleeting thought of what she might look like to *them* gave Celeste a moment's concern. She stole an uneasy peek at herself. The pliant dress she had worn for three days now, which turned out to be a mild sage green color, would have to do. If only the slits on either side of the dress weren't so pronounced. The intent had been to allow Celeste a comfortable sitting position on her cushion in the observatory, but now the slits seemed to serve no other purpose than to reveal the sides of her legs clear up to her thighs, which Etienne appeared to have noticed with evident partiality.

Remembering herself and the fact that Oihana and Nahia were flanking her, Celeste said to the old man, "Sir, I am told you are Clemente. May I present to you Oihana, queen of the realm, and her daughter Nahia." When Clemente had bowed as best as he could from his sitting position, and Nahia and Oihana had nodded their acknowledgement, Celeste added, "And I am Celeste, Paloma's daughter."

"Let me see your face, child," Clemente said at once holding a trembling hand out to her.

Celeste smiled warmly and knelt beside him, hugging the old man directly. Clemente patted the back of her head in a very grandfatherly fashion while repeating over and over how remarkable it was to see her.

Clemente now smoothed back Celeste's long hair and tucked it behind her ears as if she were a little girl, all the while talking to her, seemingly engrossed in every detail of her expressions. She stole another glance toward Etienne, thinking mournfully how awkward it would be to embrace him in front of so many witnesses. Unable to contrive an excuse to, at the very least, hold Etienne's hand, Celeste contented herself with casting a yearning look his way, so effectively, as it turned out, that he responded with an instinctive start toward her. Celeste's heart thumped in her chest, and she colored, but Etienne stopped short, seeming to consider the presence of an audience along the same lines she had. Celeste resignedly thought that, in any case, he was sharing in her misery.

"Your mother was like a daughter to me, you know," Clemente was saying. "But, oh, how you resemble Bautista. You have his distinguished stature. Yes, I most certainly see that. But I also see your mother's soul shining in your eyes."

"She loved you so, Clemente," Celeste stammered, moved by the tears welling in the old man's fierce eyes. And not wanting to start crying herself, she cleared her throat and asked earnestly, "But why are you here? How did you find us?"

"Ah, well, there's a story for you, *and* a warning," he said, raring to tell every detail of his ordeal.

"Let us make ourselves more comfortable before we begin," suggested Oihana. And to Celeste, Nahia, and Etienne, the immediate appearance of Bakar was not a surprise, for they knew that a mute summons had taken place. But Clemente watched Bakar's every move with great interest as the old faery, in his diminutive size and distinctive black garb, deftly produced five cushioned seats large enough for humans and arranged them in a ring around a squat table he then burdened with glasses and a decanter filled with red wine. There were also bowls filled with shortcrust wedges, sliced cheeses, and berries. After an approving glance at his arrangements, Bakar left the clearing and disappeared through the mound's access shaft.

Etienne helped Clemente to his feet, although the tonic seemed to have improved him somewhat already, for he insisted on walking unassisted to one of the chairs. The others followed and arranged themselves around the table.

"It was the unicorn who found me," Clemente told them. "He brought me to this clearing and watched over me until I succumbed to exhaustion. When I came to, he was still there," Clemente said, pointing to the foot of the tree where he had been slumped. "And judging by the light in the sky, no more than a couple of hours had gone by since my arrival. Feeling a little more like myself, immensely reassured by the presence of the unicorn, I studied my surroundings, and in no time at all, it seemed, I caught a glimpse of Her Royal Highness," he said, smiling broadly in Nahia's general direction. "She graciously agreed to keep me company, *only* because the unicorn left and *only* after I had explained who I was. Although I must say, I'm quite sure she knew who I was even *before* I told her my name," he added, and Nahia beamed, for otherwise, Oihana would have scolded her later for being careless in concealing herself from humans.

"I am sad to say, however, that she dabbed my eyes with something or other that prevents me from fawning over her and now you as well, Your Majesty. But let me assure you both, I came prepared, and indeed, I intend to dote over you even if you should soak my entire head in jelly."

Celeste and Nahia laughed outright, and even Oihana smiled warmly at his remark.

"The Lady Nahia told me what you were up to, dear Celeste, and as she expected you would be finished shortly, we decided it was best to wait a little longer to tell the story of how and why I got here. Then this young man arrived," Clemente said, turning to Etienne and clapping him paternally on the shoulder. "Evidently too anxious to see you again, my dear. And so the three of us waited until, by and by, Lady Nahia told us that her mother was summoning her, that it was done. And I knew that before long, I would at last be able to look upon you."

Celeste, who was seated next to Clemente, fondly held his hands in hers and gave them a squeeze. "I'm here now. Please tell us what has happened."

"And so I shall," he said most obligingly and again tucked a stubborn lock of her hair behind her ear. "While you, dear Celeste, were deep in a trance weaving away last night, Arantxa came to my cottage," he said gravely. Then seeing that Celeste's eyes had grown round with alarm, he added, "But you shouldn't fret, my dearest. I had prepared myself for that eventuality, you see. Since that fateful night when I bore witness to the crime committed against your mother, I have lived every day of my life with the certainty that the moment would come when Arantxa would want to do away with me."

"What did she do to you?" Nahia wanted to know. She had already inched to the edge of her chair, anxious for the gruesome details she felt sure would come.

"It must have been close to midnight that she slithered into the cottage. So silent was she that she reached the head of my bed without waking me, and I am a light sleeper." He clarified. "So it happened that she was upon me, and it wasn't until I felt her cold hands tightly gripping my neck that I came around. For a few terrible seconds, I saw her crazed face by the light of the reading candle I had forgotten to snuff out. Then, with unseemly timing, the wick drowned in the puddle of melted wax, and the light of the candle was no more. I was plunged into darkness, and the nightmarish vision of her disappeared from my sight, but the strength of those hands strangling the life out of me were real enough even in the inky blackness."

Celeste gasped. Oihana, remarkably composed, said nothing. Nahia hung on Clemente's every word. Etienne scowled and shifted uneasily in his chair (he had taken the chair on the other side of Celeste).

"The realization that this was no bad dream took all the traces of sleep from my brain. As terrified and as shocked as I was, I contrived to fake a spasm convincingly enough and forced myself to go limp. Her grip on my throat eased up with infuriating indolence, but I commanded myself to lay still. I dared not even breathe even though the desire to cough was nearly unbearable. Arantxa bent over me, poking my chest and lingering over my face as if trying to detect my breathing. I was struck with the ghastly notion that she might be able to smell death, that she could somehow sense it, and she would know I was faking, but I was relieved to be wrong. Arantxa backed away from me, yet I could still feel the weight of her stare." Clemente's fierce eyes paused on each of their faces, then, in a strident voice that made Celeste and Nahia jump involuntarily, he repeated the embittered words Arantxa had said to him. "'To think that all these years you were fooling me, you miserable *wretch*. I should have killed you on the very night I carried Paloma to her death.'"

Celeste's hand flew to her mouth to stifle a cry.

"I heard her walk toward the door, and I thanked the Lord in heaven for having been delivered, but there she stopped again, and I felt a horrible chill pass through me as she said, 'I should have waited until tomorrow night to do this rather than risk your being missed tomorrow *morning*.'"

"Oh, Clemente," Celeste exclaimed.

"'Just as well,'" Clemente continued in his strident imitation of Arantxa, which gave the narrative the hair-raising quality of it being told by one possessed rather than one impersonating. "'I owed myself the pleasure of finishing you with my own hands, you *deceiver*. I could not contain myself, you see. I've been so stressed as of late that an immediate release became essential to my well-being.'" Celeste was shaking her head in disbelief while Nahia listened slack jawed, her aquamarines as round as saucers. "'And what better release than to silence forever a deceitful swine.'"

Etienne let out a derisive grunt at the irony of Arantxa branding Clemente a liar.

"I heard the sound of her skirts brushing against the threshold. I had been stealing short puffs of air ever since she left my side, but I so desperately needed to cough and draw a normal breath. At last, she was out, and I heard her pull the door shut with such deliberate force as to cause the bar on the inside to fall onto its cradle, thus locking the door from the inside. I counted to sixty in my head before rolling over onto my pillow and clearing my throat, which had been torturing me the past five minutes."

Clemente smiled benignly at the anxious look of concern stamped in Celeste's face. He patted her head as if she were a child, and like a child, Celeste felt immensely soothed by his touch.

"I don't know how long I lay there, astounded that I had survived such an attack," Clemente sighed. "The night was still and quiet, probably close to two in the morning, I figured, but I stayed on my bed, as if dead, not taking any chances. Perhaps another hour passed, I'm not certain. By and by, the need to put the ideas I had conceived of into motion became more and more urgent. I got out of the bed in which I had nearly died, threw a cloak over myself, and packed this portrait to bring with me," he said, rummaging through the folds of his traveling cloak and at last producing a rolled-up canvas. "I had to remove it from its frame, you see, but I'm sure we can get a better one for it," he assured Celeste apologetically.

Celeste unrolled it, and the unexpected sight of Paloma, furtively smiling beside a handsome man she knew must have been her father, caused her to turn away. Overcome with emotion, she hid her face on Etienne's chest who at once put his arms protectively around her and kissed her hair and forehead.

Nahia stooped to pick up the canvas Celeste had let drop and held it open it for Oihana to also look at.

"She is half of each of them, it seems," Nahia remarked in a whisper to Oihana, wondering at the similarities she could observe right away. "She has her father's eyes, and look," Nahia added, pointing at the mark beneath Bautista's eye. But Celeste was somewhat composed by now, and she had withdrawn from Etienne's embrace to face them again. Nahia offered the portrait to Celeste, and she took it with a watery sniff.

Patting Celeste's knee consolingly, Clemente went on. "Making sure the door was latched behind me, as she had left it, I limped to the stable and mounted the first horse that didn't object to me. Not bothering to saddle him, I headed for the mountains determined to find you. Fortunately, the darkness lasted only while I traveled on trails I already knew. By the time I arrived at the waterfall and prepared to take on Wizard's Pass, the eastern sky already heralded the coming sun. The horse refused to descend to the ledge, and I was in no condition to force him, so I continued by myself. Dear Celeste, surely I should have died in that crossing, but fate, it seems, didn't intend for me to end my days there. I came through to the other side and sat there, thanking the Lord in heaven for my good fortune and weeping for my queen, for all the years I was of no help to her," Clemente cleared his throat. "It was there that the unicorn found me, surely responding to my feverish pleas during the hour it took me to traverse the pass. You see. I remembered Etienne telling me about the keeper of the forest, so while engulfed in the deafening roar of that wall of water and sidling with my back against the cold granite, I called for him. 'I beg thee, do for me what you did for Paloma,' I said over and over again. And so upon emerging on the other side, and after scaling the slippery ledge there, he made himself known to me. I felt infused with new life. I swear to you, for a moment, even my leg seemed to ease up on the hurt, and I was able to clamber up the gravelly ridge to where he waited for me and … and so, here we are," Clemente finished hoarsely, gazing around at them in thrilled disbelief that he was where he was.

While deep in their listening to Clemente's story, Bakar had conjured lanterns covered in colorful screens to diffuse the light and arranged them around where they all sat in conference. It wasn't until Bakar lit all the lanterns simultaneously that they realized evening was well upon them.

Celeste eyed Clemente fondly and again opened the canvas with the likeness of Bautista and Paloma impressed upon it. Her eyes lingered on the image of her father, this man who smiled pleasantly under his dashing short boxed beard, whose arm was locked with her mother's, and on whose broad shoulder Paloma's head rested lovingly. Tears smarted in Celeste's eyes again for the loss of that man, Bautista, the father she had never known. "Thank you, Clemente, for being here," she said, kissing him briskly on his crinkled cheek.

"Yes, but," Nahia began.

All eyes turned to her, but she addressed Clemente who straightened himself on his chair and assured her with every civility in his power that she had his undivided attention.

Immensely flattered, Nahia too sat up straighter, and with her shoulders readily shifting from side to side (a gesture that Celeste had often told her made her look like a hen settling on a batch of eggs), she put a question to Clemente. "If Arantxa wanted to kill you, wouldn't that mean she somehow knew about your conversation with Etienne?"

"Therein lies the warning," Clemente trailed off, visibly distraught.

"She *must* know," Celeste said fretfully.

Oihana, who until then had been listening in silence, seemed to decide *now* was a good time to interject. "There are two questions, Clemente. How much does she know, and is she aware that you have survived."

"I *know* she believes I am dead," Clemente answered vehemently. "Tomorrow being the day of the wedding, the bustling is bound to double, and she is counting on the fact that no one will find my body until well after the ceremony. Besides, in my condition, it is not unusual for me to remain indoors for three or four days at a time. She knows this, and she is counting on the commotion generated by the *happy* event to delay any concerns anyone might feel on my behalf."

"If only we could confirm," said Oihana still not persuaded.

"I'm happy to oblige, Your Majesty," Etienne offered gravely. "Clemente tells us he left Santillán this morning, well before dawn, but my mother and I arrived there midmorning today. You see, it takes several hours by carriage to get to Santillán, and with the wedding ceremony scheduled for noon tomorrow, we had no choice but to arrive a day before. I admit I delayed our journey as long as I could in order to avoid a forced encounter or invitation from Arantxa."

A smile flickered on Celeste's lips at this, and Etienne, who hadn't released her hand since he took the opportunity to comfort her when she first saw the painting of her parents, now gave her hand a squeeze before he proceeded with his report.

"At the gate of the stronghold, we were directed to a chalet happily retired from the royal hall. My mother found this to be dismissive, perhaps even a little insulting, but I congratulated myself on our good fortune. Once settled in, I walked down Santillán's market street and happened upon a merchant who was moodily packing his wares for the day. He despaired over not having carried out his expected volume of trade, and when pressed as to why he felt that way, he stated bluntly that the entire kingdom was in complete disarray over the wedding. The queen and her daughter were in a right state over the lack of a suitable group of musicians and about there not being enough flowers to suit the princess's liking. 'Why should that affect me?' asked the merchant, and when I couldn't come up with a response to that, he went on to tell me how on his way to Santillán three days before, he had indeed come across four disgruntled young men, all with broken instruments and spitting curses back in the direction of Santillán. They told him the princess wanted a piano quintet instead of just a string quartet, and when the four musicians failed to produce a piano player, the princess (in a complete rage) had proceeded to snap the necks of their instruments over her knee; although she did give up on the thick-necked cello after two tries and a tantrum."

This commentary was listened to by all with expressions of utter disgust on their faces, Celeste more so than the rest. She gulped anxiously, sickened by the thought of what would have become of Etienne had their paths not crossed or if Paloma had not died. But the implications and consequences of that were too much for Celeste to delve into and, at present, so immaterial that she shook her head dismissing it all and listening to Etienne as he continued.

"After talking to this merchant, I made my way to Clemente's cottage, but I found your door bolted, old man, so I looked through your windows and ascertained that the cottage was empty. I walked back to our chalet, all the while wondering where you could be. I still cringe to think that I might have asked someone where you could possibly have gone."

Celeste gasped audibly at this, and recognizing the hand of fate in his choice to not inquire about Clemente, she let out a hopeful sigh that things would turn out right in the end and squeezed his hand warmly.

"I suppose something told me to just keep it to myself. But it was no good, though. You see, I had been looking forward to talking things over with Clemente, because he is the only other person who knows, but when I didn't find him, well, it was a matter of minutes before I made up my mind to come see you. And, well, here we all are. And to your question, Your Majesty, I feel very comfortable in saying that Arantxa and her daughter are much too preoccupied at this time with last minute arrangements."

"I imagine they're listening to the preambles of every waltz ever composed," Clemente remarked sourly. "You see, there is music to be played while guests are arriving and during the feast and while people are settling into the chapel."

Etienne nodded, feigning concern for the dilemma. He turned to Celeste and added, "You really should drop in tomorrow. I understand it's going to be quite the event." He smiled agreeably, but Celeste pushed him away half-heartedly, not quite ready to joke about the day to come.

However, having caught Nahia's smirk, as if the *faery* had found Etienne's remarks humorous when she, Celeste, hadn't, she felt compelled to protest. "You shouldn't be so light-hearted about this," she scolded him. "And you had better not cross me, or I'll not show up at all. How would you like *that?* Being left at the mercy of Arantxa and that … that … what is her name?"

"Her name is Berezi, and *you* wouldn't do that to me," Etienne grinned broadly as he leaned warmly into her. "Would you?"

"I suppose we'll find out tomorrow, won't we?" Celeste threatened, pushing him away a second time. Nahia still smirked appreciatively, and it donned on Celeste that Nahia wasn't finding Etienne's remarks humorous; Nahia found Celeste's annoyed *reaction* humorous. *Oh, I need sleep*, Celeste thought, remembering Oihana's warning that her body might soon collapse from exhaustion.

"Celeste," Oihana called her to attention. "This is not the time for this young man to learn about your flighty temper or your wavering feelings."

"Thank you, Your Excellency," Etienne bowed to Oihana. Then, from Celeste, he inquired apprehensively, "When she says *wavering* and *flighty*, does she mean that in a good way?"

No one answered him, but Nahia giggled, which didn't ease Etienne's concerns in the least.

Clemente, who had been listening attentively, delighting in every expression uttered by those around him, and memorizing all the details attending the situation he happily found himself in, suggested, "Shall we rest then? For as Her Majesty Queen Oihana, has said, 'Tomorrow is a big day for everyone, and we must be ready,' but before we part, may I propose a toast?"

Everyone agreed. Nahia quickly rose from her chair to pour the wine, and Celeste made sure they each had a glass in their hand before she took her own.

Clemente's eyes lingered significantly on each of the four people he had been conferring with for the better part of two hours, and in a voice hoarse with emotion, he said, "Life in this world is fleeting, but the memory of our loved ones is everlasting through those who survive us. Let us drink tonight to the memory of Edmond, Bautista, and Paloma, beloved parents of these children, who tomorrow will wield the power of their love to bring justice and restore truth to those who have been living in a lie."

They raised their glasses and repeated, "To Edmond, Bautista, and Paloma!"

They all drank, but Celeste had a hard time swallowing through the knot that had formed at the top of her throat. The thought of *tomorrow* suddenly loomed over her like a guillotine. Clemente's poignant words had conveyed such finality to the day—tomorrow—that it had struck a chord of fear in her, fear that she might fail, that Oihana might die in the process, that Etienne could be lost to her forever. She became so absorbed in her reckless imaginings that she gave an involuntary jolt when Etienne lifted her hand to his lips. Celeste looked around and, in a haze, cottoned on that Oihana had already made arrangements for Clemente. She would walk him to the grotto where he would spend the night, and along the way, he was to describe to Oihana exactly where everything stood within the citadel. Nahia had convinced Etienne that he should be spirited to at least below the waterfall rather than riding the full five or six hours in a moonless night, and Celeste gave her a grateful smile for this.

"Of course, I've never glamorized a horse before," Nahia added archly, but her face split into broad grin as soon as she saw the fearful look she had hoped for on Etienne's face. "I'll be back for you and Al-Qadir when you're through with your goodbyes," said the faery, alluding to Celeste, and she shifted to the compact size most comfortable to her before disappearing through the access shaft into Handi Park.

Bakar, meanwhile, stood to one side, waiting patiently to clear the chairs and table.

Clemente clapped Etienne on the shoulder. "Remain steadfast tomorrow, young man."

"I will," promised Etienne.

Clemente offered his arm to Oihana. She took it, and soon they disappeared between the tall aspens, headed toward the grotto.

Celeste's heart skipped a beat, and she felt herself flush crimson the instant she and Etienne were left alone. The thought of how much she had been wanting to kiss him quickly returned to her, and she was instantly thankful for the faintness of Bakar's lanterns. *Oh, it's just not dignified to be in this state,* she thought. Since Etienne was thinking along the same lines, she had little time to torture herself with how unbecoming her behavior might be. He circled her waist with his arms, and all her worries vanished. All she could think of was how extraordinary it felt to be in his arms again. "I want to stay like this forever," she whispered in his ear.

Etienne squeezed her tighter. "We will," he whispered and grazed her cheek with his lips, not daring to do more in the presence of Bakar.

Celeste, however, seemed to consider Bakar a non-witness compared to their previous audience, and with her signature singleness of mind, she satisfied the longing to kiss his mouth that she had been keeping in check for the past three hours.

When they surfaced from their kiss, Bakar had already cleared the table and chairs. Only the lanterns remained.

"Promise to come save me tomorrow," he said, holding her tight in his brawny arms.

"I'll be there to save you," she promised, pressing her lips to his one last time before Oihana arrived.

The faery queen alighted beside them, and with no other evidence of the shape-shift but a swirl of dry leaves at her feet, she was suddenly at human height.

Coming from the direction of the forest, Celeste heard voices she thought she recognized, and all three of them turned to see Amets, Sendoa, and two other raucous boys batting branches out of their way as they darted through the aspens and into the clearing. Nahia was with them.

"And this is the entourage you have assembled for Prince Etienne?" Oihana said to her daughter, eyeing the boys with concern as they kept elbowing and shoving each other.

"We can keep them under control," Sendoa assured her with a dashing grin.

"Amets?" Oihana said, unconvinced.

"You have my word," Amets replied, casting a punishing glare at the two boys who instantly stood at attention. "Sendoa and the boys will guide the horse, and I will guide the prince," he explained. "We're prepared to descend to the waterfall as Nahia has suggested."

Turning to Oihana and removing his hand from the small of Celeste's back where he had let it linger, Etienne said, "And tomorrow, I should expect to see you both at half past noon, approximately?"

"Indeed," Oihana smiled.

"Then I suppose this is good night," he said, turning to Celeste in the hopes to steal one last kiss from her, even with all the witnesses, but Nahia had other plans.

Celeste saw Nahia pulling her sleeves in preparation, but the flourished, double flick of Nahia's hand came much too quickly, and Celeste, who had hoped to at least warn Etienne, saw nothing more than his eyes, round with shock, and then he was gone, that is, shrunk, to where she had to kneel and bend down in order to be at eye level. "Please forgive her. She loves surprising her victims. She does it to me as well," Celeste said apologetically.

Al-Qadir arched his neck nervously, pulling at the reins Etienne had secured to a tree trunk. Leaving Etienne flanked by Amets and Sendoa, Celeste walked over to the horse and stroked his forelock soothingly. "It'll feel a little strange, but you will be fine," she promised while she undid the reins. "I've got him," she called to Nahia, and the faery at once condensed the proud Al-Qadir to a version of himself, proportionate to Etienne's new height of little over a foot.

With the boys guffawing through the trees, Etienne and Al-Qadir were spirited away far below the waterfall, following Nahia's lead.

In the morning, Nahia would tell Celeste how frightening and comical it had been that once they had flown over the ridges outlining the realm, the benefits humans enjoyed through the power of the unicorn had lifted, and the faery entourage became invisible to Etienne. He had let out a roar that nearly gave them all a heart attack, causing Amets to nearly drop him. But thanks to her quick wit and level headedness in the midst of a crisis, Nahia had realized what was happening and granted Etienne the gift of faery sight. "I figured he had already seen us, seen where we live and all. It was a pity that he should lose faery sight outside the realm."

To make up for the scare, Nahia had prompted everyone even farther than intended and deposited Etienne and Al-Qadir beside a creek, a mere hour from the citadel. There she returned the rider and his horse to their normal size, and they parted ways with knowing smiles and well-wishes.

The clearing fell silent after their departure, and Oihana grazed Celeste's cheek with her fingers, as if to rouse her from her thoughts. "Clemente was very happy to be in Paloma's last home," she remarked. "His eyes swept greedily over all he saw there. He became fast absorbed in his thoughts, so I thought it best to leave him to it."

Celeste nodded, and Oihana reached across to rub Celeste's bare arms, which had been cooled by the night air. "But what will *you* do?"

Celeste embraced Oihana and said, "I will spend the night by my mother's grave."

Oihana nodded, and they too parted ways.

Celeste walked out of the clearing and into the aspen forest, feeling that she could no longer ignore the growing emptiness that had been maturing in her chest. A whole portion of her life would be over tomorrow, giving way to something completely new and unknown to her. She felt a compelling need to spend the night out of doors, to soak in every bit of nature and every particle of its freshness for fear of possibly losing it all tomorrow. Because tomorrow, she would be forever changed.

Celeste began to realize this was good-bye, but then, purposely trying to lessen the unexpected depth of her feelings, she told herself, *maybe it isn't goodbye at all. Maybe all it is is that I've been underground for three days.* Whatever the case, it seemed to her the only way to ease her heavy heart would be to really breathe in the fragrant alpine air and touch the green of the forest with her own hands. She wanted to feel the rough and fissured tree trunks warm against her arms and chest when she hugged them. The forest was in her blood, and through the night, she thought she might draw from it the strength and courage she needed to face the morning when it came.

These reflections brought her over three miles of meandering trails to the edge of the woods. There were the grassy slopes, there was the white sand, and there was Moon Dancer Lake. The three-day old dress she had pulled off her body and flung up in the air fell heavily on the cool grass behind her. Feeling immensely free, Celeste stood naked under the stars. Moon Dancer Lake gleamed like a dark gem before her, cool and inviting. The corners of her mouth quivered with a smile, and she took on the lake at a full run. Her long legs soon had her splashing into the water where the heat of the day still lingered. Down Celeste fell into the embrace of that magical place and all its power, and as she went under, she let it flood her mouth, her nose, and her ears. For a moment, all was blissful silence. Then, longing for oxygen, Celeste erupted out of the water, taking mouthfuls of air into her lungs, her heart soaring up to the million stars twinkling in the sky. Floating on her back, she thought of Etienne while she smoothed her long hair away from her face, letting it spread in a cloudy mass beneath and around her head. "We will win the day, and then we'll be together forever." She said to the winking heavens overhead.

From the shore, a tall figure watched—a man. His eyes bore into the floating silhouette as if calling to her, and when Celeste finally looked his way and started at the sight of an intruder, he deliberately picked up the dress she had dropped and held it to his nose and mouth lustfully.

CHAPTER 21:

UNEXPECTED BY THE LAKE

A violent tremor shook Celeste from head to foot, rooting her to the sandy lake bottom. The water lapped at her waist. The intruder started toward her, and something in his tentative steps let her know at once that it was not Etienne. Celeste could not make out if she felt disappointed or relieved. Of course, the more pressing question, who *is* he, demanded an immediate answer. For a few seconds, she scrambled her brain, searching for likely possibilities. She dismissed Clemente at once, for the old man certainly didn't have the stature of the man standing on the shore, and he most definitely wouldn't have been able to walk so quickly from the grotto to Moon Dancer Lake with his bad leg, which left only the possibility of a faery. The breeze kissed her skin, reminding her that she was naked, and along with the goose bumps, it came to her. *Amets! But why has he shifted to human size?*

Amets stopped abruptly as if he had felt himself being identified. His irises glowed like fireflies, and now that he was closer, Celeste could detect the distinctive, though dim, amber haze enveloping his bare torso. The breeze played with his shoulder-length hair and made his loose-fitting trousers flap against his legs. He intentionally let her dress drop at his side, and his glowing eyes seemed to say, "Look … it's right here. Come and get it."

"I will not be made to sleep in the water," Celeste shouted at him, suddenly angry that he should impose on her solitude and ruin her idyllic last night as a living part of the realm.

Amets kicked the sand with his toes, goading her to play their old game.

"Amets, I mean it," she yelled, her anger mounting. *If he thinks I'm going to sit here until I shrivel.*

The Via Lactea streaked the vault of heaven with its milky sprawl of stars, illuminating the scene below in a silvery light. Waist deep in water, Celeste fumed, already irritable from exhaustion and now seeing her plans for solitude and reflection truncated, she glowered at Amets, who continued to inch closer to the water's edge. She could tell he was smiling. *Why you little. But I don't care. I'll walk back to the pond naked if I have to.* Celeste straightened her shoulders defiantly and walked out of the water, closing the distance between them in five angry strides, daring him to look anywhere else but into her dagger-throwing eyes. She stood before him, and it became Amets's turn to freeze up. Here at last was his chance to get an eyeful of Celeste in her naked splendor, a sight he had privately longed for, the culmination to the little game, which her stubbornness had always thwarted. But her challenging stance and the brash stare she fixed him with prevented his eyes from wandering even an inch from her face. "It's too dark anyway, you fool," she said contemptuously. "By tomorrow, you won't remember what you saw, if anything." She snatched her dress and stalked toward the woods, shoving him as she passed and leaving him smirking under the stars.

"I have eighteen years of you in my mind, Celeste," he called after her.

Celeste stopped.

"And over the centuries to come, I will not forget you," he said huskily.

Celeste turned and was shocked to find that he had followed and was only inches from her. He was no longer smirking. In fact, he appeared positively on the verge of tears.

"I am yours," he said, reaching for her fist and prying the dress from her fingers. "Do with me as you wish," he told her resignedly. His eyes were respectfully fixed upon her face while he motioned for her to raise her arms.

She obeyed. He slipped the dress over her head and pulled it down to cover her naked body. Celeste raised her eyes to him and felt the traces of that familiar pain the sight of him had invariably produced in her. He was so heartbreakingly beautiful. "Do with me as you wish," he had said.

What she would have given to hear him say those very words just months before. Amets had been many things in her life: a big brother, a friend, even an accomplice. And during a particularly turbulent period, he had been her and Nahia's romantic obsession.

He said nothing. He was simply waiting for a response from her.

Years of memories weighed heavily, yet ever so sweetly, on Celeste as she gazed at his beautiful face. She stole a glance at her surroundings, and it seemed to her every inch of the basin could be tied to something Amets had said or done. She could not help tallying up the various roles Amets had played in her life, and in spite of her brazen, unsuccessful efforts to involve him romantically years before, his presence in her life now added up to a single, and in view of their respective situations, very sad word: friendship. *Do with me as you wish.* Celeste repeated his words in her head, wishing she had misunderstood Amets' meaning, but she had not, and it was a tragedy indeed. Amets was confessing that he had lost a battle, a battle Celeste never really knew he had been fighting, for all along, he had categorically treated her as her superior in age and experience, never giving her any real hope that he might return her fleeting affections.

"I know your heart is full to the brim with someone else," he said despairingly when she failed to respond. The light in his eyes seemed to flicker as he said this, enough for Celeste to realize that Amets had been hiding his feelings from her from the start. He had rejected her long ago to save himself from the very thing he was now willing to have her do. *Do with me as you wish* meant Amets had given up and confessed himself prepared to live a life without love if Celeste should still want him on this night.

"Amets ..."

A sad smile crossed his face like a shadow. "I know, *human*. I just wanted to see you one last time, that is, before you leave us." His fingers grazed her cool cheek.

"Amets ... I don't know what to say."

"There is nothing *to* say," he shrugged. "Well, there *is* good-bye."

"But I will see you again. I know I will," Celeste pleaded.

"But not like this, not like yesterday, and certainly not like we've seen each other your whole life," he said. "Tomorrow you'll be someone else."

Celeste's eyes filled with tears. "Amets, I ..."

"Say good-bye."

"What?"

"I told you, there is nothing to say except good-bye," he insisted, lifting her chin up with the tips of his fingers.

"Good-bye then," she stammered.

"Now go," he pressed. "I'm sure you have a bizarre sort of ritual planned for tonight." An unconcerned laugh issued from him, so transparent in what it tried to hide that Celeste despised herself for being the cause of such despair in someone she treasured.

"You are more a part of this ritual than you think," she offered, realizing that his presence, at that moment, gave a voice to the entire Realm of Faery. And what a beautiful voice it was. If she had to say farewell to the world of faery, what better way to do so than through Amets.

"Beg your pardon?"

"You call me *human*, Amets, but the truth is, one can't help but become a faery in eighteen years of living and breathing with you. And I mean *you* as in Oihana, Nahia, and this place, everything around me. I feel I am a faery at heart, and I will always be, although tomorrow, I must begin learning how to be a human," she said fervently.

Amets gave her a curious smile, the kind an adult might give an exuberant child pleading her case. "For him?"

"What?"

"You will learn to be a human for *him?*"

"As much as for the memory of my mother, I suppose," Celeste said, including that second fact so as to spare Amets's feelings from further injury. "Although I do believe he would learn to be a faery if I asked him to," she added with a smile.

Amets laughed out loud at the thought of that, and Celeste joined him. When they sobered up, however, he pursued in his questioning. "*How* do you love him?"

"What?"

"Tell me *how* you love him."

Celeste tensed up. How could she answer such a question without wounding him? Yet she could not encourage him either, so she plowed on truthfully. "I love him enough to save him from a horrible fate tomorrow. Enough to follow him wherever he should lead," she said, shrinking a little with each word, as if such confessions had a physical weight she hadn't accepted until Amets, with the immense regret in his eyes, made her feel it as he felt it. "And enough to let him do with me as he wishes," she added, looking at him slantwise for his reaction over the use of his own words, with which she had hoped to convey the similarity of their feelings. However, if Amets understood, he didn't show it.

He laughed that heartbreakingly transparent laugh and said, "*You?* Let someone do with *you* as they please?"

"It was bound to happen sometime," she said guiltily. Then, elbowing him lightly and with a playful smile on her lips, she added, "The trick is to not let him know that's how I feel."

"Ah," he sighed. "Perhaps you *are* a faery at heart."

They laughed and walked through the darkened woods for the better part of an hour, reminiscing about the passing of the years, about their experiences together, and wondering about the years to come. By the time they had reached the pond, the three sleepless days had taken their toll on Celeste. She could barely remain standing. She retrieved a sheet and a blanket from the hall of glamour, and Amets helped her stretch them at the foot of the mighty oak, beside Paloma's grave. Celeste crept under the blanket and closed her eyes. Her exhaustion was such that she could have sworn her spirit rose out of the tired flesh and bone exterior to merrily slumber without aches or pains among the clouds. She fell to dreaming of Etienne at once.

Amets kept watch over her, listening to her breathing and smiling when he detected a drowsy smile on her face.

***

A pale blue light began to fill the misty forest. Before long, the sun would rise.

Amets, who had not slept a wink the entire night, glanced at the sleeping figure of Celeste for the hundredth time. She rolled over on her back and rested her head on her hand, still fast asleep. The pained expression on Amets's fine-looking countenance took on a resolved air. He bent over her and pressed his lips to hers. In her dream, Celeste responded, thinking him Etienne.

CHAPTER 22:

DEPARTURE

Morning took everyone by surprise at their various sleeping quarters. Oihana and Nahia rose bleary eyed after seemingly endless hours of fruitless attempts at slumber. Clemente, who had wandered out of the grotto to stretch his legs as soon as the first traces of dawn were visible through the jasmine doorway, rested momentarily on a fallen moss-covered tree trunk, and from there, he watched the sun rise in earnest, gradually illuminating the misty forest to the riotous song of the larks. Under the mighty oak, Celeste opened her eyes to see the buds of the morning glory begin to open and the haze lingering over the pond already thinning. Patches of deep azure sky peeked through the treetops above, and Celeste smiled placidly at the waking magnificence around her, dewy and fresh, poised to begin a new day. *A new day*. Her expression sobered by degrees of awareness: first at finding herself beside Paloma's grave, then that she must avenge her mother and free her love, Etienne, and finally that the dreaded and anticipated *tomorrow* had arrived at last. *It's all going to happen today*. Her stomach lurched uneasily at the thought.

Outside Handi Park in the clearing and sitting around the same squat table Bakar had conjured up for them the night before, Celeste found Oihana, whose tense and rigid body contrasted sharply with the resolve blazing in her amethyst eyes. Nahia sat on her chair, pouting lethargically and showing every sign of a deficient night's sleep. Clemente, however, appeared remarkably sanguine amid the two impassive faeries.

Through a superfluous yawn, Nahia pointed toward the edge of the grove from where Celeste had emerged. "Here she comes."

Clemente rose at once and prompted her to take the empty chair next to him. This Celeste did after planting a nervous kiss on his crinkled cheek. She greeted Oihana and Nahia with a reserved good morning of her own. Feeling not at all courageous, she mechanically helped herself to a cup of hot tea and buttered bread, convinced she ought to put something in her stomach to sustain her through the events to come. But try as she might, she could not savor it, and in fact, her mouth was so dry she soon had to pour herself a second cup of tea to properly wash down the solids.

By and by, the sun announced that it was close to nine in the morning, and the looming wedding ceremony in Santillán, with all it represented, was upon them at last. "If we are to avoid crowds and get a good look at the battleground, we must leave at once," Oihana remarked curtly.

Celeste nodded. Surely the prickly anxiety plaguing her would ease its hold once they left the ground, once they took action. Clemente's optimistic smile told her thus, but Oihana's tension gave Celeste an ominous feeling despite the faery queen's resolve. The four of them said their goodbyes succinctly. The faery court that had gathered in the ten minutes it had taken Celeste to swallow her breakfast expressed their most fervent wishes for the complete success of the mission. With one last glance toward Clemente and Nahia, Celeste took Oihana's hand.

"You have the painting, my child?"

"I do, Clemente," Celeste said, patting the bundle secured around her waist with a band and in which the portrait and her shroud had been neatly folded and stowed. A quick sideways glance toward Oihana confirmed that the faery queen had her shroud as well. They were both dressed in very fitted clothes to avoid excess material flapping and tearing in the wind.

Clemente kissed Celeste's forehead and blessed her.

Nahia looked sullenly at them, utterly displeased to have been ordered to stay. "You must understand, Nahia, and accept the reality of it. I cannot have you running rampant out there. There is simply too much at stake," Oihana had said sternly, and no amount of whining or begging on Nahia's part had persuaded the queen to allow otherwise. The lack of confidence shown by her own mother had visibly upset the faery princess, and Celeste couldn't help reading Nahia's displeasure in her unusually short goodbye. But there was nothing to be done.

Without further delay, Oihana reduced Celeste to faery size, and they took to the air straight away.

The faery court dispersed. The majority of them returned to Handi Park through the access shaft, while others drifted into the aspen grove on their way to Oihana's vast arboretum where plant life needed daily looking after. Nahia, who had shifted to the compact size most comfortable to her, perched herself resentfully on a branch of the nearest aspen. There she continued to brood over not being an active part of this big adventure, and she gave free rein to her jealousy over the newly strengthened bond between Oihana and Celeste. Inwardly, she felt thoroughly disappointed in herself. Nahia knew

Celeste and Oihana had good reason not to trust her with this task. The faery princess had, for too long, taken pride in her clever, ingenious schemes to repeatedly dodge responsibility. She had even wondered why those around her reacted to her efforts with annoyance rather than praise. Now at last she seemed to understand, but alas, all her cleverness of old had come back to punish her. "I have ingeniously worked myself out of this one, haven't I," she muttered angrily.

"What's that, my dear?"

Nahia's bleary aquamarines fell on the old man who had been pacing below, clearly at a loss for what to do next. She cocked her head to one side, and her eyes narrowed musingly. The faery's swift mind quickly honed in on something that could *indeed* be done. The idea rooted itself in her lovely head of turquoise-streaked curls, and she smiled shrewdly at the thought that her only challenge would be to persuade Clemente. The briskly conceived notion became fact with haste comparable only to that of Celeste when an idea wedged itself between her brows, demanding to be acted upon. Never mind that Nahia had often found this speed of conviction reprehensible in Celeste. This was her opportunity to prove to Oihana, once and for all, that even though she would always be Nahia, there were qualities in her to be prized, qualities that made her a worthy holder of her mother's legacy.

She floated down to a lower branch, one that would permit her to be at eye level with the old man, and she laid out her plan before him. Clemente listened intently to Nahia's scheme, and just as she had suspected, the old man saw no harm in going to Santillán to witness the ceremony.

"I think it is a well-thought-out plan," Clemente praised her. "Not only will we be there to assist your mother and Celeste, should they need us, but it gives us the opportunity to witness Arantxa's defeat firsthand."

"Precisely," Nahia beamed. "Much as they mulled this thing over, I'm most certain they've missed something, and you know they don't have a second plan to fall back on."

"Yes. It is most definitely a sensible idea," Clemente agreed, his eyes sparkling with anticipation. "Will Your Highness be conveying me to our destination?" he asked, the slight tremor in his voice betraying his excitement at the imminent prospect of being reduced to faery size for the journey.

Nahia nodded. Her lips pursed mischievously.

"Are we ready then, little one?" he said eagerly.

"Soon you'll also be a little one," Nahia laughed, and with one swift, outward flourish of her delicate hands, she glamorized Clemente into a foot-tall version of himself.

Holding Clemente's hand, Nahia took to the air at once, and she smiled into the wind when she heard him laugh out loud.

"Southbound, my faery princess," cried Clemente delightedly. His body tingled with Nahia's glamour, and although the sudden upward thrust made his heart jump to his throat, he felt exhilarated.

They were a mere half hour behind Oihana and Celeste.

Chapter 23:

The Battleground

Oihana took to the air with Celeste's hand firmly gripped in hers. Over treetops and across the sky they flew—so fast, it seemed to Celeste that within mere seconds the aspen grove was gone, as was the wide arboretum and the pine forest at the south end of Moon Dancer Lake. In the space of a single breath, Oihana had whisked her over the mighty cliffs Etienne had named Vulcan's Palings, and now there was nothing below that Celeste recognized, giving her, for the first time, a true measure of how small her world had been. Her mind filled with a great many thoughts, so divergent as to be disconcerting. The debilitating fear that she might fail attacked the electrifying euphoria to be experienced should she win the day. The thorny guilt that blamed her curiosity over the unknown *today* tried to stomp out her loving devotion to all she had known up until *yesterday*. Back and forth her outlook rocked, with no definite attitude being resolved upon.

This was the longest flight Celeste had ever embarked on, guided by the queen of the faeries, no less. Yet the exhilaration of flight she had counted upon to embolden her lingered just out of her reach.

Celeste gave an involuntary shudder, and Oihana's head jerked toward her. "Are you alright?"

A hesitant smile and a clipped, "All is good," was all Celeste could muster.

Celeste had a vague sense of a change in temperature, but glancing over her shoulder, the spray and mist surrounding the waterfall explained it all. She spared a disconnected thought for the passage that had conveyed Etienne and Clemente into the realm, which she knew should be somewhere behind that brutal rush of water, but she could not detect any evidence of it.

With the torrential waterfall behind them, the air turned balmy again. By noon, the summer heat would be sweltering. Oihana turned her attention to the rolling landscape below, but not without giving Celeste's hand a meaningful squeeze that made her wonder if those amethyst eyes could see how humbled and chastised Celeste felt at the sight of the new world sprawling before them. If only Celeste could make out her feelings. Was it fear or excitement that she felt, or was it both?

The realm had seemed enormous to her, used as she was to covering it on foot or, at times, holding Nahia's hand while darting between branches or skimming over treetops. How they had puffed themselves up, boasting that they knew the territory better than the unicorn himself. And the faery court, who, for the most part, preferred to remain underground, would listen good naturedly to their outrageous tales and smile at them, some impressed, others condescendingly, for they guessed the truth, which was that Celeste and Nahia only had a half dozen secret places, some more remote than others, but always within the boundaries of the unicorn's territory, and they would journey to those places, not once deviating from their original tried and true path, regardless of their exorbitant preparations and in spite of all the hinting to their mothers that harm was sure to come to them. As fearless and reckless as they wanted to be thought of, Celeste and Nahia would arrive at their destinations, and once there, they did the same things they had always done. At one location, they gathered the roots or herbs native to it and which they needed for Nahia's remedies and experiments. At another, they would bathe in steaming springs until they were pruned beyond recognition. While yet another would provide endless hours of fun and terror in a labyrinth of inky caverns plagued with bats, but which would ultimately lead them to their most prized discovery: an underground waterfall surrounded by a myriad of stalactites and stalagmites, that guarded the place like eerie sentinels, frozen in time for their amusement. *This is no weekend excursion with Nahia*, Celeste thought grimly, pushing away the happier memories of uncomplicated days gone by.

They were fast approaching the majestic citadel of Santillán, and upon seeing it for the first time, Celeste felt overwhelmed with thoughts of Paloma, the rightful queen of all she beheld.

White wedding banners hung down the entire length of the towers that marked the four corners of the stronghold, at the center of which stood the royal hall with its own turrets crowned with crisp white flags. The sight of the citadel in its festive splendor surpassed Celeste's expectations of its size and beauty. It took her breath away, and she understood in one eyeful what Paloma had tried to describe on countless occasions. The towers, the banners, the royal hall, all of it conveyed a sense of wealth and prosperity, but it also spoke of domination and power. Celeste thought of the grotto, carved inside a living mountain, and of Handi Park, completely underground, and it struck her that humans built up and over, while in the realm, they endeavored to incorporate themselves thoroughly to the landscape, to not disturb it.

As Etienne and Clemente had reported, the ceremony would take place in the elegant chapel just in front of the royal hall. So they passed over the main gate, and from there, the chapel was hard to miss, as it too had white panels draped on either side of the main entrance and down the length of the belfry, each bearing a chalice embroidered in gold.

"What do you suppose the cups mean?" Celeste wondered.

"It is quite distasteful really," Oihana remarked. "A chalice is one of four tools employed by humans who practice magic, you see, and it represents femininity along with the traits attending it, such as the ability to be a nurturing mother, to be receptive to the needs of others, and to direct ourselves and guide others through wisdom. But as with every symbol, there is always an opposing meaning to it, and knowing what we know of Arantxa, these chalices undoubtedly celebrate her cruelty, her selfishness, and her desire to conquer through destruction."

Celeste felt something chilly flip inside her belly, and she tightened her grip on Oihana's hand. "What is it that we have come to fight?"

"No more than a mortal," Oihana replied reassuringly as they soared high above the thronging market street. "Albeit a clever one, but a mere mortal nonetheless."

Eyeing the hordes of people below with increasing trepidation, Celeste issued a tremulous inward plea to Paloma. *Oh, give me strength, Mamma.* And then audibly to Oihana, she said, "Let it be that no one looks up. I should have worn blue, the better to blend with the sky."

"Try your best to look like a bird," Oihana recommended flatly, and Celeste again detected some anxiety in the faery queen's voice, which considerably added to her own.

But the humans below were much too preoccupied with what was right before them to even bother looking up. Celeste and Oihana landed airily on the carefully manicured lawn at one side of the chapel where a planter filled with tall tulips provided excellent cover for them. Momentarily enthralled, Celeste watched the comings and goings of the people of Santillán: harried people delivering linens and flowers into the chapel, children intent on knocking marbles out of a circle marked on a sandy walk, ladies strolling leisurely under flimsy parasols to keep their faces from getting too much sun, and elegant men donning hats and walking sticks loitering around the fountain in courteous conversation with others. Oihana tapped her lightly on the shoulder, and Celeste jumped. "Sorry. Yes, I'm ready." She quickly withdrew her shroud from the bundle on her back and quickly covered herself with it. Oihana was invisible to all humans, as they were quite beyond the realm.

"I can see your chin," Oihana whispered, pulling the hood lower over Celeste's face.

"I can see *all* of you," Celeste grinned under the shroud.

"I'll wear my shroud once we separate in the chapel," said Oihana, the slight furrowed brow betraying her disquiet. "Are you ready?"

"Yes."

"Wait, where are you? Maybe you should let me see your toes so I know where I should aim and how much space I should give you," said Oihana nervously. Then, more to herself than to Celeste, she added, "We should have tested all three panels, not just one."

Celeste had slightly raised the hem of the shroud, and she wiggled her toes for Oihana who backed away a couple feet to give Celeste sufficient space. Only a couple of trampled tulips followed the instant shift in size. The cloak shimmered briefly, becoming invisible straightaway with Celeste safely concealed in its folds. The weave remained as tight as it had been in its original size.

"It worked," Oihana whispered, unable to hide her relief. "I must confess I had serious concerns for this portion of the plan. Last night I must have drunk at least three pots of Nahia's chamomile infusion," said Oihana with uncharacteristic agitation, and Celeste couldn't help but be thankful she had been blissfully unaware of Oihana's concern; otherwise she would have been strained to the point of physical pain. "Now, how will I know where you are?" said Oihana, eyeing the depressions made by Celeste's sandaled feet on the soft dirt between the tulips.

Celeste moved onto the gravel walkway. "I think it's best if I carry you now. Here," Celeste raised the hood slightly to show her face, and Oihana propelled herself to Celeste's shoulder. With the ample hood now covering both of them, Celeste proceeded to the front of the chapel, doing her best to avoid accidental contact with the people crowding the walkways.

"Oihana?"

"Yes?"

"Me too," Celeste whispered.

"You too, what?"

"What you said a little while ago. I wasn't sure about this either. I mean, last night, I thought maybe … I didn't want to do it, that maybe it wasn't going to work, you know? But now I know it's going to be fine. I'm glad I'm doing it, and I am *ecstatic* that you're here with me."

"Everything *will* turn out fine. You will see," Oihana whispered back, patting Celeste's shoulder.

Celeste stood to one side of the main door of the chapel, waiting for an opportunity to slip inside without stumbling over the numerous flower-

and ribbon-bearing attendants still bustling about. "You'd think by now they would be through fixing things up," Celeste muttered. Oihana merely exerted the slightest pressure of acknowledgement on her shoulder. At last they spotted an opening and darted in. A quick glance resolved Celeste to head for the altar where the activity seemed to be minimal at the time. The central aisle was the busiest, so she scurried to the aisle opposite the entrance and moved toward the altar as quickly as she could without knocking down flower arrangements or ribbons. Up the three marble steps she went, and although invisible, she crouched behind the altar, hiding while she caught her breath. Her heart was beating too fast, and she felt light-headed.

"Shall we take a look at the layout?" Oihana whispered after a few moments.

Celeste rose to her feet and turned to face the structure Oihana had called the battleground. She placed her hands on the altar to steady herself.

"Don't forget to breathe," Oihana advised, seeming to guess Celeste's disquiet.

"Why is nothing ever as you imagine it?" she muttered, feeling suddenly irritated. "Or why can't I imagine things as they are so that I can save myself the trouble of being so ill surprised."

"Now, now," whispered Oihana soothingly. "There is really nothing to be shocked about. Everything has gone remarkably well thus far. The only thing I expect bothers you is your own reaction to the sight of so many humans."

Celeste let out a disgruntled sigh. "Of course, you are right. And I'm just a fool who—"

"You are no fool, Celeste," Oihana objected at once. "And neither are you a procrastinator, so let us not delay anymore and do what we came here to do. Shall we?"

Although stung by Oihana's rebuttal, Celeste could not fail to see her justification. They had not spent three days entombed with a loom, and they certainly hadn't come all this way just for Celeste to vent her childish inadequacies and be patted indulgently on the back out of pity for her predicament. No. They had come to accomplish a great deal in one morning, and dawdling over uncertainties was a sure way to achieve nothing. Celeste took a deep breath as Oihana had advised, and like the faery queen on her shoulder, she scanned every inch of the battleground.

They were inside a rectangular structure with white plaster walls. There were three aisles extending the length of the nave—a central one with ornate wooden benches on either side of it and two narrower ones outside the rows of pews—to allow people to sidle into their seats without setting foot on the central aisle, which Celeste noted was covered with an impeccably white runner. Twelve very tall stained-glass windows (six on each side) broke up the walls of the nave at even intervals, filtering the light of the sun into colorful patches on the benches and on the crisp white runner. An enormous wooden cross dominated the wall behind Celeste, and the altar upon which she leaned was a solid block of marble covered in white linens. On either side of the altar, but standing at the bottom of the marble steps leading up to it, two full-size statues with outstretched hands faced each other, dressed in pale robes pinned at one shoulder.

Celeste observed that, besides the main door they had entered through, there was also a small door to their right. She imagined that had to be the everyday door used by the cleric. She also noted two small iron gates at the opposite end of the chapel and concluded that they must be additional exits.

"I think I should stay behind this altar," Celeste whispered. "I can see everything from here, and Arantxa is bound to be close by."

"I agree. As for me, surely the mother of the bride will be in the front row, but I'll have to wait and see which side she takes. In any case, either of the two statues there will get me close enough to her," said Oihana, and Celeste agreed that the statues were close enough to the first bench on either side of the aisle.

While they were thus occupied, a stealthy shadow moved high up in the choir box above the chapel's main entrance. It scanned the interior of the chapel through a monocle, with meticulous consideration for every inch of the nave. Seemingly pleased to find everything in proper order, the shadowy figure slithered down a narrow staircase and disappeared through the small iron-gate closest to the main chapel door.

The ceremony would soon begin, and Celeste felt shaky, as people of varying noble rank began to file in. Oihana, having put on her own shroud, left Celeste's shoulder, meaning to take her post on the outstretched hand of the statue to the right of the altar. Celeste could no longer hear or see Oihana. She was alone. *Where are you, Etienne? What wouldn't I give for a sip of passiflora tea right now.*

The chapel soon filled to bursting with whispering guests.

Safely hidden beneath her cloak, Celeste paced behind the altar, trying not to bash into anything while admiring the enormous white bouquets of orchids and rose buds. She took deep breaths of their sweet fragrance as she noted the perfectly coordinated arrangement throughout. She let out a derisive snort whilst observing the painstaking precision of the flower bouquets, all positioned so as to not block the bride from anyone's view as she glided down the aisle. Celeste imagined Berezi's grand entrance, and she felt an instant pang of jealousy. *She will look beautiful surrounded by all these flowers. I wonder if Etienne is going to change his mind when he sees her. Oh, don't even think it. Still, I should've thought about wearing one of my nicer dresses.* That her clothes were less than adequate suddenly obsessed her, and she toyed momentarily with the idea of revealing only her head to the congregation when the time came. *That would certainly get their attention*, she mused.

The cleric's door to her right opened, allowing a sudden shaft of bright sunlight to streak across the floor, and in came Etienne. His entire frame denoted a rigid tension, although his face expressed none of it. He looked around deliberately and, at last, proceeded to his place before the altar.

Celeste, whose heart had stopped beating when she realized it was him, took in the sight of Etienne in his wedding finery and felt torn between admiration for his looks and insane jealousy that he should be thus attired to marry another woman. *He won't be marrying anyone today*, she reminded herself forcefully. She resumed gaping at the deep blue (only two shades darker than his eyes) double-breasted coat he wore over a crisp white linen shirt and the wide cravat tied in a loose bow at his neck, which enhanced his chiseled features with a stately air. His dark blond hair had been tied with a black ribbon, except for a stubborn strand he kept tucking behind his ear. His father's sword hung in its scabbard at his side, and his gray breaches were tucked into black boots. The buttons on his coat sparkled, his freshly polished boots shone, the jewels encrusted on the scabbard and hilt of the sword gleamed, and Etienne was unbearably handsome. Celeste cleared the short distance between them and brushed his cheek with her lips, wishing she could lift the shroud to feel his skin directly against hers, but she settled for the feel of him through the tight weave. A slow grin spread through his handsome face as he whispered to his invisible assailant, "So, you *did* come to save me."

"It couldn't be helped." Celeste whispered, her voice filled with wicked humor. "But I can't believe you got so dressed up to marry that ... what did you say her name was?"

"If I marry today, it will be to Princess Celeste," he started, but stopped short when he realized Arantxa had arrived and was walking toward them.

Arantxa, dressed in a high-waist rose-colored gown and elbow gloves of white satin, looked beautiful in the guise of Paloma. She smiled cordially at Etienne as she approached him, and in her outstretched hand, she held a white rose.

Celeste underwent a vast range of sensations at the sight of her. It took all her will to not reach out and embrace the impostor. *Mamma!* her mind screamed to the rhythm of her pounding heart. She shut her eyes beneath the shroud, endeavoring to stifle the cry aching to come out of her. She tried to sort out her thoughts with some degree of reason. *I knew perfectly well she would look like my mother, but, my stars, how can I not have foreseen my own reaction.* Her eyes welled with tears. In direct conflict with her mind, every muscle in her body ached to be rid of the shroud and to hug and kiss the woman before her. The painful void Paloma's death had left was ever so raw, and how she longed to feel her mother's touch again. Through the haze of her confusion, Celeste imagined Oihana standing on the outstretched hand of the statue. Was her porcelain face as altered with the shock of Arantxa's arrival? *Oh, that we were in Handi Park or at least within the realm. Then I could hope to at least hear Oihana inside my mind,* Celeste thought desperately, aching for the calming effect Oihana's words might produce in her.

Horror of horrors! Arantxa began to speak, and the beloved voice coming out of her further shook Celeste's unsteady frame. *This is not Mamma. I was there when my mother breathed her last. This is not Mamma.*

"You look very dashing today," Arantxa crooned. Her eyes swept over Etienne with a hint of disbelief. "Only one thing missing," she said, deftly pinning the white rosebud to the lapel of Etienne's blue coat. "There now. You are the picture of elegance. Berezi will be so pleased." Etienne made a curt bow.

Take your seat already, Celeste pleaded mutely, transfixed by the sight of this woman fussing over Etienne. What a pleasure it would have been to know that the real Paloma approved of Etienne, that she, and not Arantxa, should be standing before him, telling him how happy she was to soon have him for a son.

Arantxa went on to dust Etienne's shoulders with her gloved hands, a maternal gesture that made Celeste cringe under her shroud. "We should be ready to begin momentarily. Ah, I see your mother has come in," Arantxa exclaimed, and this at least had the ability to wrench Celeste from the recent shock of seeing, first hand, Paloma's features inhabited by such murdering, darkness of spirit.

Waving airily and with condescending smiles for the nobility already seated nearest to the front, Arantxa sashayed over to the elegant lady who had herself arrived at the front of the chapel and had taken a seat on the front pew to Celeste's left. Something in Celeste at once warmed up to this regal woman, dressed in a simple lilac tunic gathered below the breast with a silver ribbon. Her elbow-length gloves were silver, to match the ribbon, and her hair was gathered away from her fair face in cascading curls. She nodded agreeably, though shortly, to whatever Arantxa said to her. Celeste was happy to see that this conciseness on Elise's part prompted Arantxa to take her seat on the pew opposite her and straight across from Oihana.

Celeste let a barely audible sigh of relief escape her. *Good.*

In the meantime, Etienne turned to face the altar. He looked through Celeste, as was to be expected, but even though she knew he couldn't see her, something in his expression troubled her. It was as if he had forgotten their very recent interlude. He didn't appear to be looking for signs of her, in fact, the tension she had noted in him when he arrived seemed to have left him completely. *It's like he forgot I'm here.* The chords struck by the musicians startled her out of her reflections and conjectures. Soon Berezi would march down the aisle. *I hope she is a toothless, hairless hag,* she hoped angrily. With fiendish delight, she noted there was no piano after all.

A choir began singing the Ave Maria, and Celeste raised her eyes toward the ceiling at the opposite end of the chapel. There was a loft where a choir entirely made up of children sang stirringly, but Celeste was nevertheless distraught by it. The thought that she hadn't noticed the loft before unsettled her immensely. They hadn't inspected it. There had to be some significance to that. *And Etienne with that blank stare. What is wrong with him?*

In spite of Celeste's evil wishes for her instant destruction, Berezi entered the chapel through the main door, unharmed. She proceeded to the center aisle where she paused, gazing haughtily at all the people gathered there to honor her. Satisfied that she had been admired enough thus far, she started swaggering, with paused steps, down the white runner, looking down her nose at her subjects as she went. Celeste's eyes bore venomously into her. Her hopes to find Berezi toothless, gaunt, deformed, or anything remotely opposite to what she turned out to be were utterly dashed. Berezi wore a golden gown, reminiscent of the chalices embroidered on the banners outside. It was fitted over her shape, and it had a scoop neck and long sleeves. A long hem like a cloak, made of the same fabric as the dress and cleverly fastened to its back collar line, trailed heavily behind her. Around her neck were coils upon coils of gold cords, and her black hair had been elegantly slicked into a single knot at the base of her neck.

Celeste continued to glare at the approaching bride, feeling at every moment more self-conscious of her own—not in the least glamorous—white dress and her wild hair, which, at the moment, seemed to be sticking to her perspiring neck and forehead.

Berezi arrived at Etienne's side, and it dawned on Celeste that Berezi had not once looked at him. During her dragged-out march to the altar, her head had swiveled on her neck only to look at the people filling the seats, not once toward her future husband. *He is* not *her future husband,* Celeste thought mutinously. *One good thing about Etienne's blank expression, at least, is that he has offered no rapturous reaction at the sight of her.*

Arm in arm now, Etienne and Berezi faced the clergyman who was happily unaware that Celeste stood trembling behind him.

To the right of the couple, Elise watched her son through misty eyes. On the other side of her, Arantxa enjoyed her moment of triumph, nodding at her guests and repeatedly inspecting the décor of the chapel through a fancy monocle, which, when not in use, dangled from a thin silver cord around her neck.

To Celeste, Arantxa appeared to be in complete ignorance of what was about to happen. The crowd stood up as instructed by the clergyman's raised arms, and in the midst of this, Celeste caught a very strenuous glance Arantxa had aimed at a young attendant Celeste hadn't even noticed before. He was leaning placidly against the wall by the side door. *What is that look for?* She followed Arantxa's intent gaze to where the attendant stood at attention and watched with mounting trepidation as the boy caught the drift of Arantxa's intent and advanced to the foot of the beautifully chiseled statue, on whose outstretched hand Oihana stood.

"We are gathered here today," boomed the clergyman, but Celeste neither heard nor understood what followed.

Etienne stood like a stick in the mud, and having a sudden sense of imminent disaster, Celeste looked from him to the place where Oihana should be. The young attendant pulled something out of the breast pocket of his uniform, and before she could put two and two together, he threw it over the statue's hand. Celeste now saw that it was a fine silk net, which the boy proceeded to tie in a tight knot. The faery queen was trapped. Celeste wanted to scream.

In that most excruciating moment, a strangled cry seeped into Celeste's head. *The shroud didn't work!* It was Oihana, although her cry of surprise had been lost in the loud murmuring of the crowd praying for the couple, it had not been lost to Celeste. Through their common desperation, the trapdoor inside Celeste's mind had been unbolted after all, just as it had in Handi Park.

Arantxa again reached for the monocle dangling from her neck on the thick silver cord, and as she brought it to her eye and looked through it, Arantxa smiled knowingly at the attendant and motioned for him to leave. This the boy did, and Arantxa quickly turned her attention back to the clergyman.

A wave of heat incensed Celeste as she recognized the clever adaptation of a self-bored stone, and she fought the urge to cry out. *The shroud didn't work, but the self-bored stone did.* It had all taken place in the blink of an eye, it seemed, and there Celeste stood, invisible, helpless. The queen of the faeries was trapped, and their plan was ruined. *Nothing to do but watch the ceremony*, Celeste thought ironically and went from livid to wanting to claw out Arantxa's heart.

I can't just stand here, I won't! Sheer desperation overtook her. Blinded by rage and confusion and without further thought or consideration, Celeste shoved the clergyman out of her way. She would tear that silk sack with her teeth if she had to. The man fell to the floor, more shocked than hurt, by the invisible force that brought him down. Etienne tried to go to his aid, and as Celeste went past, she saw no outward traces that he even suspected what had caused it. "What is wrong with him?" muttered Celeste under her breath, glaring at Etienne as she made her way to free Oihana. But the attendant, obviously following Arantxa's precautionary orders after the unexpected tumble of the cleric, returned to his post by the statue.

Celeste would have to show herself.

Berezi clung to Etienne's arm, hindering his efforts to assist the clergyman and began to whine loudly. "My ceremony is ruined! Mother! Do something … do something *now*," she screeched unpleasantly.

Chapter 24:

Celeste Revealed

Having climbed the marble steps back to the altar, Celeste paced back and forth like a caged beast. The eyes of the congregation were, at the moment, fixed on the fallen cleric and on the bleating bride, but she knew that once she pulled the shroud off, they would all turn to her, Celeste.

Stars in heaven! Celeste's breath came in rapid bursts.

"You imbecile, what are you about," Berezi hissed at the wobbly cleric who rounded on her in confusion and mortification.

"Your Highness ... I ..." the poor man stammered, tangled in his long robes and not knowing how to account for what had happened.

Arantxa rose from her seat, clearly intending to intervene, and the sight of her counterfeit, condescending sneer, so out of place on Paloma's face, twisted Celeste's insides with revulsion. "Celeste ... My strength is leaving me ..." Oihana's voice seemed so faint in Celeste's head. Her face contorted with wrath and frustration beneath the shroud. *Your stolen time us up!* Her anger seared away all trepidation, and she walked around to the front of the altar where, only a couple feet in front of her, the cleric continued to spurt apologies to the nearly hysterical Berezi who kept a frantic hold on Etienne's arm. With one last exasperated glance at Etienne's impassive countenance, Celeste lifted the hood of the shroud over her head and let the whole thing drop behind her. She was momentarily enveloped in a cloud of sparkling dust, which had an impressive impact on the crowd, and it afforded her a few seconds in which to arrange the expression on her face into what she thought was a forbiddingly composed resolve. Her jaw was set, the golden flecks in her eyes were ablaze, and her wild mane gave her the distinct air of contained havoc to be wreaked upon anyone who dared cross her.

Celeste was pleased to see the intense shock in Arantxa's face. She could smell it in the air. *So you didn't know I was here, you old hag. Can't see invisible humans with your little rock?* And before anyone had a chance to assimilate what had just happened, Celeste's voice rang within the chapel walls.

"My name is Celeste," she proclaimed, scanning the room fiercely and not failing to note, with increasing discomfort, that every eye was on her. *Oihana is trapped,* she thought frantically. *I have no back up for what I am about to say.*

Celeste steadied herself with a short intake of air, wishing the tremor in her legs would leave her, but she went on nevertheless, irrationally deriving strength from her own rage over the helplessness of her predicament.

"I am here to reveal the truth about the woman who calls herself Paloma," she seethed, pointing her finger at Arantxa and hoping no one would notice her trembling hand.

The crowd protested loudly, and she noticed that Berezi had begun to hyperventilate. Etienne was all concern for his bride, fanning her with his hand and expressing shock at the sight of Celeste, as did the rest of the people in the chapel. *He doesn't recognize me!* She felt the white plaster walls were closing in on her, that the seconds would never tick away into a different moment.

Arantxa, having regained her fleetingly disturbed composure, looked at Celeste with rancor barely disguised as astonishment.

"Who do you think you are, barging in here with such trickery?" Arantxa demanded confidently.

"I am Celeste," she repeated, her anger seeming to steel every fiber of her being. The words issuing from her mouth were utter fury as she addressed Arantxa. "I am the daughter of the true Paloma. Your *true* queen," she said rousing a wave of objections from the crowd before her. But Celeste's voice rose even clearer and louder when she continued to address Arantxa. "*You* sentenced her to death eighteen years ago by exiling her from her own home. She, whose body you have stolen, is the true queen! But you imprisoned her in your own rotting flesh. She was with child, you beast," cried Celeste, not daring to take her eyes off Arantxa, though she desperately wanted a sign of recognition from Etienne. *What did you do to him, you snake?*

As Celeste spoke, Oihana worked feverishly to unravel the mesh that held her captive on the statue's hand, but her limbs were increasingly sluggish. "I can't tear it," Oihana said faintly to Celeste, and Celeste realized with crippling dismay that the mesh had to have been doused with a debilitating enchantment. "She was expecting us," Oihana echoed Celeste's own conclusion.

Arantxa laughed Paloma's beautiful laugh, which was echoed by the supportive smiles on the faces of those assembled. "I must say, I had feared you were a dangerous criminal, but now I realize you are just a mad woman, raised by wolves perhaps?" she said, eyeing Celeste's wild mane and crazed look. The congregation murmured appreciatively. Arantxa glanced through her bejeweled monocle once again, and the malevolent sneer said all was well with the entrapped faery.

Celeste wavered where Arantxa, who had seen the faery weakening, exuded confidence in her success.

"You have disturbed my daughter's wedding. You have embarrassed me in front of *my* subjects and *my* guests with your unfounded insinuations, and you will pay for that," Arantxa said loudly, though quite in control of her voice. "But I will show you mercy, child, and rather than taking your life, which is the rightful punishment for your infraction, you will be taken to the west tower until I can devise a sentence for you, that is, once the celebrations are concluded," she said to Celeste with a twitchy smirk that, try as she may, she could not make look sincere or benevolent. "It's too happy an occasion to be darkened with such grim nonsense. Wouldn't you agree?" Arantxa suggested to the room at large, in her most ingratiating tone, while bringing the monocle to her eye, yet again, and this time, she couldn't suppress an outright smile.

Celeste feared for Oihana's life now. To measure the faery queen's fading life force through Arantxa's increasing satisfaction was beyond endurance. Celeste hated the impostor's voice and the words that came out of her mouth, but most of all, she hated the fact that Arantxa stood there, living, breathing, and laughing her stolen laugh while Paloma was dead and buried, while Oihana struggled and might soon expire. Fury burned inside Celeste, and for an instant, she could make no answer to all that Arantxa had said. She again tried to make her way toward Oihana, but Arantxa was not about to allow that.

"Guards," Arantxa motioned imperiously to the men standing at attention by the entrance. "Remove her from our sight and place her in th—"

So many feelings and reactions were queued up inside Celeste. They pressed at her throat to get out. She felt her entire head would soon come off, and all would explode out of her. The guards, with their hands over the hilts of their swords, started toward Celeste, and the finality of their attitude gave way to a sort of resignation deep within her, a resignation fraught with a blind urge to shut down her mind, to stop thinking and just relinquish her reason, to give way to her body, to let her mouth do what it would, let her limbs do what they must. After all, did her body not falter only because of her wavering conviction? Celeste rounded on the approaching guards, commanding them to stop with one hand, while with the other she pointed at Arantxa and declared icily, "It was you, *Arantxa*, who murdered my father, Bautista."

The guards stopped, not so much because of Celeste's halting gesture, but because, although she had not realized it, it had been the first time in many years that the evil name had been spoken in front of those present. The congregation gasped at the sound of that long-forgotten name.

"It was you, Arantxa, who attempted to murder queen Elise, but you killed her husband instead."

At this, Etienne stopped fanning his bride, who was engrossed in blinking spastically and revealing the whites of her eyes as she reclined dramatically across two of the three steps leading up to the altar.

"It was *you* who exiled my mother, believing she would die in the mountains, and *you* took on her appearance by means of your dark sorcery!" *Etienne, what is wrong with you,* Celeste thought, but that was all she could spare. Her mind hovered somewhere above her head while her body appeared perfectly poised and in control.

Elise, who had been anxiously gripping the armrest of her kneeler, rose from her seat and strode regally toward Celeste, visibly distraught by the girl's words. Elise demanded, "Explain yourself, child!"

"Your Majesty, what I say is the truth! As it was told to me by my mother and—"

Arantxa quickly interrupted, "This is utter nonsense. I cannot allow this to go on."

"I can prove it," Celeste pleaded with Elise, who had suddenly become her only ally.

"Let her speak," Elise said with a halting gesture to Arantxa. The long-ignored question of what exactly had happened to Arantxa burned with new fury in her, and perhaps the girl had an answer. "What is this proof you speak of?"

"This portrait of my father, Bautista." Celeste held out the canvas for Elise to see. "I bear the same mark. You see?" she said, brushing her cheek with her fingers.

"This is no proof," Arantxa laughed. "It is a good likeness of my dead husband, but you could have made that same mark upon your face to resemble him. What is it you truly want, child, because your story is crumbling fast."

Celeste's tenacity forbade her to admit defeat. She raised her chin defiantly and eyed Arantxa with as much disdain as she could muster, refusing to look in Elise's eyes, which would surely say she had no choice but to agree with Arantxa. *This battle will not end here, not like this,* Celeste thought with that detached resignation that seemed to strengthen her resolve, even though a favorable outcome was not within sight. Her mouth started again of its own accord, buying her time, though she did not know for what.

"If you don't believe me, you can ask Clemente, whom you, Arantxa, tried to murder just two nights ago!" Again, the congregation gasped, but this time, the outrage she detected in their murmuring wasn't all directed at her.

"You think you were clever to vanquish the faery that could break your evil spell, but you were not clever enough! And everyone here will bear witness to the transformation; the return to your true form." Celeste bluffed.

"I would not come up against you unprepared, Arantxa, and I tell you, today will be your last day of living the horrid lie you created eighteen years ago." *Stars in the heavens! How will I ever back this up? Please help me, someone please.* Celeste begged silently. *If only Clemente were here.* She wanted to close her eyes and have it all disappear—perhaps if she climbed under the shroud again and went away as she came in—but the thought of giving up revolted her. She deliberately took a breath of air deep into her lungs. Her eyes fixed on Arantxa once again, but she also caught a miraculous glimmer of distinctive turquoise streaked curls cautiously approaching over the white-carpeted aisle right behind Arantxa. Relief spread through Celeste's tensed limbs like a soothing balm. *Nahia!*

Celeste's mind fused with her body at once. The sense of detachment quickly left her, and she was body and soul in the situation. She almost laughed when Nahia clearly mouthed the words, "Thank me afterward." *And that is no laughing matter,* thought Celeste. *Oh, how I'll have to thank her!* But it was certainly not the time to laugh or make light of anything, so Celeste glowered at Arantxa, reveling in the certainty that Arantxa was dead where she stood.

Etienne held tight to the convulsing Berezi who had taken to moaning loudly at even intervals. Her moment in the sun had been clouded with distasteful events beyond her control or understanding. She did not care about the horrid accusations made against her mother, and she did not care about the outcome of the events taking place. All Berezi cared about was the fact that no one was looking at her. That the admiring gasps of only a few moments ago had turned into curious whispers about the strange girl who had appeared out of nowhere, stealing the adoring stares that should be hers. Beyond that, nothing could hope to penetrate her thick disappointment.

In contrast to Berezi's state of mind, the assembly present had become remarkably contained, intrigued by Celeste. Several times during Celeste's brave proclamations, Arantxa's eyes had flickered over the nobility in attendance. Upon perceiving one person after the next clearly wavering on the subservience owed to her, Arantxa's breast had swelled furiously with every outraged breath she took. None of this had escaped Celeste's notice, and with no dim satisfaction, she understood the congregation no longer seemed concerned or affronted by her as they had in the beginning. They were presently curious and doubtful, and Celeste knew that Arantxa had seen it in their eyes. Her subjects were daring to question, they were remembering obscure details, and they were silently giving free reign to their conjectures.

"You cannot harm me, child," cried Arantxa, shaken by the fading support from her subjects. She looked through the bejeweled monocle again and became further confounded on confirming that the faery was still trapped.

Celeste gave her a deliberate, knowing smile and watched Arantxa shudder involuntarily. *You have just realized I have another plan, have you not?*

"Your insane notions will be your doom. I'll have you jailed and sentenced to death for your insolence," Arantxa shrieked, startling the crowd with her unexpected outburst and setting them to murmuring among themselves. Arantxa rounded on them, and noting the distasteful frowns on the faces of her subjects, Arantxa lost her decorum once and for all. She now appeared mad herself and on the verge of striking Celeste with her own hands.

"It's over, Arantxa! It is you who will be jailed and sentenced," Celeste pressed on in full control of herself now.

Arantxa exploded into peals of mirthless laughter at this affirmation. "You are mad, child."

Nahia hovered ever closer to Arantxa.

"I am here to see justice done," Celeste clamored, silencing Arantxa. "And today, all your lying and scheming will come to an end. You will be seen as you truly are: a murderer!"

Nahia was in position a mere foot behind Arantxa who still confronted Celeste. At the faery's nod, Celeste lunged at Arantxa, pinning her to the floor. She tore the monocle from its chain and threw it to Elise who caught it and made a protective fist around it, even though she didn't know what she had caught. Berezi screeched shrilly, trying to free herself from Etienne, but he gallantly held her back, fearing the wild stranger might try to hurt her. Berezi lashed out at him, the picture of a rabid beast, and in doing so, she dislodged the white rosebud pinned to his breast.

Etienne looked disoriented momentarily, but it did not take long for him to understand how things had progressed. Celeste was straddling Arantxa, Oihana was nowhere to be seen, but Nahia floated behind Arantxa, and if he was not mistaken, something really strange was about to happen. He continued to hold tight to the flailing Berezi, but this time, he meant to keep her from harming his beloved Celeste.

"Let go of me, you imbecile," spat Arantxa, writhing in frustration under the weight of Celeste's body.

"Your hour has come," Celeste snarled. *"and you will feel every minute of it."*

Celeste caught a peripheral glimpse of Nahia and would have become enthralled by what she saw had Arantxa not been thrashing so violently under her. The faery had descended to ground level and stood only inches from Arantxa's head. Her crystalline aquamarines had closed in concentration, her arms were bent at the elbows, and her head swayed from side to side, enveloped in a glittering haze that pulsated with the rhythm of a heartbeat, Nahia's heartbeat. What took place next, though gradual, horrified those who beheld it.

"Guards," Arantxa croaked, but no one moved, transfixed as they were by the sudden change in her voice.

The comb securing Arantxa's hair had come loose with her thrashing, and her hair was a tangled mess over the white runner. She wailed in pain, yet no one came to her aid. Her features became distorted, as if something were bubbling just under the skin, and it was soon evident to those nearest her that she was aging rapidly. The supple skin fractured into deep wrinkles over the suddenly elongated cheeks and the celebrated green eyes swiveled dizzyingly in their sockets, all the while taking on an unhealthy opacity. The renowned red locks became stringy and were steadily turning a dull gray.

"Can't you see I am being murdered?" Arantxa raged, her voice rattling hoarsely as it came out of her.

But the guards would not move. The terrified ladies looked on with their hands over their mouths. The gentlemen stole furtive glances at Celeste when they could tear their eyes off the horrific mutation taking place at their feet.

Berezi buried her teeth in Etienne's forearm, and he was forced to let her go. She raced to her mother and looked down in horror and disgust at the sack of bones writhing on the floor, fiercely held down by that girl with the gnarled hair. It was impossible to tell if Berezi was horrified to realize who her mother had really been or if she just couldn't conceive that her mother would ruin her very special day with her antics. Covering her face with her hands, Berezi ran out of the chapel wailing. No one bothered to stop her or follow her.

Not even Etienne, Celeste noted when she stole a strained glance toward him. His eyes pierced her with that fire that warmed her from the inside out, reassuring her that she was everything to him. With her heart racing, Celeste turned to Nahia and saw with dismay that the faery was wearing down swiftly. Unable to remain on her feet, Nahia had stretched on the floor with her arms extended toward Arantxa in an obstinate effort to complete her mission.

To Etienne, Celeste said, motioning to the statue with her chin, "Oihana! Over there!" And to Nahia, over Arantxa's wailing, which seemed to be the only noise filling the entire chapel, she said, "Don't be wilting on me now, you hear me? We're finishing this! And I'm here to protect you!"

The nobility in attendance had abandoned all pretenses and were now standing in the aisles and between pews, hoping to have a look at was happening at the foot of the altar. In her weakened state, Nahia had become visible to those directly around her, and the news that there was a faery among them soon reached every corner of the chapel. At this, people shamelessly climbed on the pews to get a better look, or they raced up the narrow stairs to the choir loft, hoping for a bird's-eye view.

Clemente, who had been biding his time, made his way from the main door of the chapel to the center of the commotion where Celeste struggled with Arantxa and watched over Nahia. "It is not over child," he said hoarsely.

Celeste could see the worry on the old man's face. It spoke of his fear that Nahia might be giving up her life in this endeavor. "What do you mean?"

"The thread must be physically extricated," he said.

With a convulsing jerk of her body, Arantxa went silent yet she pushed forward suddenly and with such force as to almost knock Celeste over. She managed to dislodge her bony arm from Celeste's grip, and the skeletal hand at once clamped over the decaying mouth, grappling for the bit of squirming, shimmering thread attempting to escape from within. In a horrific flash, Celeste realized what was happening. This was Arantxa's last stand. She would not let go of the thread, and Nahia's inexperience might cost her her life; the faery was so weakened already. Yet the thread needed to physically leave Arantxa's body, that much Celeste understood, and return to a source of glamour before that source ceased to be.

Celeste heaved her whole body over Arantxa again. "No, you don't," she cried, seizing the gaunt wrist in her hand and feeling, with revulsion, some of the many bones there snap under her own forceful grip.

Etienne arrived at Nahia's side with Oihana cradled in his hands. The faery queen was so weakened by her entrapment within the toxic silk sack that she too had become visible.

"*Two* faeries! *Two* faeries!" the nobility clamored in awe, realizing where she had been all along. The news filtered through the congregation, mouth to ear, faster than Etienne could cautiously deposit Oihana beside her daughter. Celeste could hear Oihana whispering to Nahia, "It's raw power, my love. There was no intent."

Celeste had succeeded in pinning Arantxa's arms with her knees. To keep Arantxa's mouth pried open was more than a struggle, but having hooked her finger on the lower jaw, Celeste bore it down, almost to where Arantxa's chin cut into her own heaving, rattling chest. With a grimace, Celeste proceeded to ferret in Arantxa's mouth with her fingers, determined to catch the shimmering thread, which the lolling tongue kept trying to push back near the throat, that Arantxa might swallow it again. The thread contracted and elongated itself like an undernourished caterpillar, yet it was clear to Celeste that it was trying to eradicate itself from its current home and reunite with the glamour summoning it.

Arantxa thrashed with inexplicable strength beneath Celeste. Clemente knelt down to hold Arantxa's shoulders, and at last, Celeste managed to grip the tip of the squirming thread. She yanked on it, quickly looping it twice around her index finger. Some ten inches of it had emerged from the depths of Arantxa's throat, causing her to gag, and fearful that she might retch on her, Celeste crawled backward with the whole thread safely in her hand.

Even though Arantxa had stopped writhing altogether as soon as the thread left her body, Clemente continued to hold her down firmly. He gazed into the bulging eyes of the woman who had killed his queen, and at once, he saw what he had hoped to see. The evil darkness that dwelled in Arantxa's eyes had been conquered at last by fear and defeat. She had been found out, her lies had been exposed, and nothing she did or said could save her now.

Celeste came around to Nahia's side. "You can stop now, my sister," she said to the faery, laying the shimmering thread over Nahia's trembling body. There the thread seemed to melt through Nahia's clothing and into the dwindling light she was emitting. Oihana nodded weakly. Her amethyst eyes watched the place where the thread had disappeared, wanting to make sure it was completely gone, all the while whispering unintelligible words to strengthen and guide her daughter to the end.

Celeste sat protectively between Nahia's faery-sized body and the still figure of Arantxa. Etienne crouched opposite her on the other side of Oihana and shielded her from the jostling curiosity of those around them.

Releasing Arantxa's shoulders, Clemente rose to his feet, supporting himself on the back of the ornate bench nearest him. Fixing his eyes on the now quivering sack of bones that was Arantxa, he declared, "You have done evil to innocent people. The pain and loss you've caused has known no limits and neither has your greed. See how it has brought you to your death?"

"But I killed you, old man," she stammered in a strangled croak that caused renewed gasping from those assembled, shocked that the mangled thing could yet speak. "I should not have left you for dead as I did Paloma! Greed has not been the end of me! *Inefficiency* has," she cackled, her lips peeling away to reveal a pair of sickly, purplish gums from where several yellowing teeth dangled perilously. "But I'll not make that mistake again," she cried, and with one swift surge of unexpected strength, she lunged at Celeste and clamped her bony hands around her neck, literally lifting her off the ground. Celeste instinctively raised her hands to her throat, yet conscious of the two faeries lying on the floor, Celeste heaved herself away from them, dragging Arantxa with her. The surprising speed of the attack took Celeste's breath away, and the uncanny strength of those leathery hands squeezing the life out of her, even with a broken wrist, made her panic. People were screaming around her. She could smell Arantxa's stale breath on her face, and she began to feel faint. Her sight became blurry at the edges, and her field of vision was shrinking fast. Soon all would be blackness.

This is where I die, Mamma. We'll all have died by her hand.

Although for Celeste it seemed an eternity, it was only a matter of seconds. Her temples pulsed with the blood trapped in her head by the leathery hands clamped on her throat, and just when it occurred to Celeste that her neck might snap, Arantxa arched her back with a rattling shriek that pierced Celeste's ears. Arantxa's eyes were fixed on Celeste, unbelieving. The deadly grip loosened, and Arantxa toppled over, crumpling at Celeste's feet, her eyes agape.

Looking up from the carcass, Celeste saw Etienne towering fiercely a few feet behind it. He moved slowly toward the corpse and removed the dagger that had flown swiftly from his hand into Arantxa's back. He wiped the blood off the blade on Arantxa's very gown and sheathed it before offering his hand to Celeste. He helped her up, and she embraced him tightly. "You saved my life," she whispered in his ear.

"And you saved mine," he whispered back.

Celeste and Etienne turned to Nahia who, now cradled in Oihana's arms, seemed to be recovering somewhat. Nevertheless, Celeste's eyes filled with tears as she knelt beside them. "Thank you, faery. Thank you, my sister," she sobbed.

"You did very well, my Nahia. Very well indeed. And I am so very proud of you," Oihana whispered hoarsely.

Nahia's crystalline aquamarines flooded with tears momentarily. "I love you too, Mother" was all she managed to say before burying her face in her mother's neck.

Having recovered enough of her strength to do so, Oihana carried Nahia onto the altar where they could rest a bit longer without fear of being trampled. From there, they saw Clemente offering his hand to Celeste. She took it and allowed him to guide her up the steps so they stood beside the altar near the two faeries that Celeste might at least rest her fingers over Nahia's hand. They faced the assembly who appeared duly rattled by the swift turn of events. After all, the certainty had not quite seeped into their minds that the person they thought was their queen had been an impostor and a murderer all along, although Arantxa's disfigured body continued to shrivel on the floor, clamoring to be acknowledged as evidence.

Those standing closest to Celeste now murmured amongst themselves, and remarks soon reached her ears regarding the "statuesque figure of the young lady," "such regal stature. So much like her father." "And her eyes," said another. "I can see Queen Paloma in them."

These comments and opinions soon percolated to the back of the chapel and came back to Celeste with even more professions of agreement from these people who seemed to be gradually counting themselves as her subjects.

But there was also the presence of two faeries among them to contend with. Those who were farther back objected to the reports coming from the front that faeries could not be seen unless one were granted faery sight, but those objections were rebuked with new intelligence that a faery in a weakened state became, in fact, visible to the naked eye. Reports from the choir loft claimed that Arantxa had had a self-bored stone, which, as everyone seemed to know, was the only other way, besides the gift of faery sight, that could enable a human to spot a faery. On hearing this and the subsequent description of a self-bored stone, a pudgy jeweler who had been in Santillán for the past two weeks, at Berezi's request, elbowed his way to the front and claimed to have adapted one such stone to resemble a monocle only *yesterday* at the queen's request.

Elise opened her fist and gazed curiously at what Celeste had thrown to her and smiled.

Indeed, the events had been enough to rattle any mortal out of their wits. However composed, the assembly couldn't help crowding the front portion of the nave, hoping for a good view of the faeries on the altar and to better hear what was being said.

"I present to you," Clemente's voice boomed in the buzzing chapel, "Celeste, your *true* queen! The daughter of Bautista and the *true* Paloma. She is the rightful heiress to the throne of Santillán."

The echo of Clemente's voice did not have a chance to die down when the thunderous cheering and applause of Celeste's subjects filled the chapel, engulfing the loud beating of her heart in their warm approval.

Etienne, smiling broadly, bounded over to Celeste's side and caught her in his arms just as her knees seemed to give way under her. She was trembling head to foot in spite of the overwhelming acclamations reverberating around her. She gazed into his eyes, drawing strength from the incandescent joy lighting his features. "My bride," he whispered so close to her face that she stole a fleeting kiss. Her eyes sparkled with tears of happiness and thorough relief that all was done, that the nightmare had ended and they were still standing, able to hold each other. Etienne held her tighter, but seemingly not content with just that, he lifted her off the ground and whirled with her in his arms. She threw her head back and laughed to the thunderous applause of the people of Santillán.

With resplendent smiles on their faces, Celeste and Etienne turned to face the assembly once more. Celeste's eyes fell on Elise who nodded her liking of the turn of events, much to Celeste's satisfaction.

Epil⊕gue:

A Dream Fulfilled

Berezi fled the kingdom, despairing over the notion that she would never be queen and that she had never, in fact, been a princess. The thought that everything would be taken from her, even her title, drove her out of her mind, and in desperation, she mounted her mother's black horse and galloped away, still in her golden wedding gown.

Berezi and the black horse she rode found their deaths at the bottom of a cliff. The jewels she had hastily stolen from the jeweler's chamber surrounded her body and the carcass of the horse, as if in a protective circle. Such were the reports from the shepherds who found her two days after her flight.

Clemente told the details of Arantxa's deceit to the people of the kingdom, and Queen Elise confirmed a great deal of the story so that, in the end, there were no doubts as to Celeste's true identity.

Celeste and Etienne prepared a lavish outdoor wedding, so as to accommodate the faery court. And on a beautiful spring day the next year, Clemente walked Celeste down the grassy aisle to where her adoring husband-to-be stood, most elegantly attired. Celeste wore a gown she had fashioned herself, and her heart swelled with satisfaction when she saw the sincere admiration in the eyes of everyone present.

Celeste smiled beneath the thin veil covering her face, certain that Etienne could see her, and he smiled back. His dazzling blue eyes twinkled, as if daring her. She wanted to let go of Clemente's arm and run to him, but she kept pace with the old man until they arrived at Etienne's side.

Clemente lifted her veil and kissed her forehead. "I love you, and I am as proud of you as Bautista and Paloma would have been on this very day, my dear child. Blessings to you," he whispered.

Celeste smiled and allowed the old man to kiss her forehead a second time. Then, much to everyone's consternation, the bride turned to the groom and kissed him square on the lips before the ceremony had even begun.

Laughter erupted from the faery court assembled, and it soon radiated warmly to everyone gathered. Eventually, the ceremony *did* take place, and Celeste and Etienne were married at last.

Nahia and Oihana's enjoyment of their newfound appreciation for one another was positively contagious. And true to their bond with the Realm of Faery, Celeste and Etienne never disclosed from whence the faeries had come, but Santillán and St. Michel thronged with reports of faery sightings, which Celeste felt certain were a testament to Nahia's vanity and her desire to be known and acknowledged above and beyond Celeste, wherever she might be.

Clemente lived a few more years, in which he thoroughly enjoyed getting to know the daughter of his beloved Queen Paloma, and he thrived on the time spent with his new friends at the faery court. He died peacefully one autumn afternoon after walking through the woods with Nahia.

When Nahia told of it, she said Clemente had sat under a tree to enjoy its cool shade, to close his eyes and rest before he headed back home. He never woke up.

Celeste and Etienne never left each other's side. They had three children, Exteban, Xiomara, and Bastien, and theirs was a life filled with happiness, not to mention glamour. At the end of many years, Celeste passed away, and Etienne followed a few short months later.

Amets, who, until then, had come to believe that the curse of the first kiss (exchanged with someone outside his own kind) had been, after all, a myth, found that no sooner had Celeste exhaled her last than he was burdened with the full effects of it. She had been the holder of his heart whilst she lived, and she had taken it with her into the light, leaving his breast a brittle, empty husk. Amets withdrew from the society of other faeries, and much to Nahia and Oihana's dismay, one day he left Handi Park altogether, never to be seen again.

The End

CPSIA information can be obtained
at www.ICGtesting.com
Printed in the USA
FSHW020506070819
60800FS

9 780999 434673